A NET FOR SMALL FISHES

A NET FOR
SMALL FISHES

LUCY JAGO

FLATIRON
BOOKS

A NET FOR SMALL FISHES. Copyright © 2021 by Lucy Jago. All rights reserved. Printed in the United States of America. For information, address Flatiron Books, 120 Broadway, New York, NY 10271.

www.flatironbooks.com

Library of Congress Cataloging-in-Publication Data

Names: Jago, Lucy, author.
Title: A net for small fishes / Lucy Jago.
Description: First U.S. edition. | New York, NY : Flatiron Books, 2021.
Identifiers: LCCN 2021028644 | ISBN 9781250261953 (hardcover) | ISBN 9781250261977 (ebook)
Subjects: LCSH: Somerset, Frances Howard Carr, Countess of, 1593–1632—Fiction. | Turner, Anne, 1576–1615—Fiction. | Great Britain—History—James I, 1603–1625—Fiction. | LCGFT: Historical fiction.
Classification: LCC PR6110.A375 N48 2021 | DDC 823/.92—dc23
LC record available at https://lccn.loc.gov/2021028644

Our books may be purchased in bulk for promotional, educational, or business use. Please contact your local bookseller or the Macmillan Corporate and Premium Sales Department at 1-800-221-7945, extension 5442, or by email at MacmillanSpecialMarkets@macmillan.com.

Originally published in the United Kingdom in 2021 by Bloomsbury Publishing

First U.S. Edition: 2021

10 9 8 7 6 5 4 3 2 1

To George Szirtes,
with love and gratitude

The Principal Actors, 1609

Anne Turner, holder of patent for yellow starch, mother of six, wife of Dr. George Turner

Frances Howard, Countess of Essex, ill-treated wife of Robert Devereux, Earl of Essex. Daughter of the Earl and Countess of Suffolk

Robert Devereux, Earl of Essex, husband of Frances Howard, father beheaded 1601

George Turner, Treasurer to the College of Physicians and medical doctor at the Court of James VI & I

Katherine, Countess of Suffolk, mother of fourteen children, ten still living, including daughters Elizabeth, Frances and Catherine, and seven sons including Theophilus, Robert and Harry

Thomas Howard, Earl of Suffolk, Lord Chamberlain, one of the King's Trinity of Knaves with his uncle, Henry Howard (Lord Northampton), and Robert Cecil, Earl of Salisbury

Henry Howard, Earl of Northampton, Lord Privy Seal, great-uncle to Frances Howard

Robert Cecil, Earl of Salisbury, Lord High Treasurer and Secretary of State

King James VI of Scotland & I of England and Ireland, son of Mary Queen of Scots and Henry Stuart, Lord Darnley

Queen Anna, Queen Consort of Scotland, England and Ireland, second daughter of King Frederick II of Denmark

Prince Henry, heir to the thrones of England, Scotland and Ireland

Sir Robert Carr (formerly Kerr), gentleman of the bedchamber and the King's favorite since 1607

Sir Thomas Overbury, best friend and adviser to Sir Robert Carr, knighted in 1608

Richard Weston, bailiff to Dr. George Turner

Old Maggie, Anne Turner's maid

Eustace Norton, Anne Turner's brother

Mary Hinde, Anne Turner's sister

Lucy Russell, Countess of Bedford, favorite lady-in-waiting to Queen Anna. Member of the Essex crew

Sir Arthur Waring, close friend to Anne Turner

Simon Forman, necromancer and physician

James Franklin, corrupt apothecary

James Palmer, Purchaser of Paintings to Prince Henry

Sir Edward Coke, Chief Justice of the Common Pleas, later Lord Chief Justice of the King's Bench

Dr. Edward Whiting, minister of the Church, confessor employed by the King's Bench

Mary Woods, cunning woman

Sir Gervase Elwes, Lieutenant of the Tower of London

What griefs lie groaning on the nuptial bed?
What dull satiety? In what sheets of lead
Tumble and toss the restless married pair,
Each oft offended with the other's air?

. . .

And to their wives men give such narrow scopes,
As if they mean to make them walk on ropes:
No tumblers bide more peril of their necks
In all their tricks than wives in husbands' checks.

—Ben Jonson's prophetic *Masque of Hymen*, 1606,
written to celebrate the wedding of the young
Earl and Countess of Essex

A NET FOR SMALL FISHES

PART ONE
January 1609

The servant led the way as if into battle, his torch throwing monstrous shadows of my form against the walls. Fog muffled the light and dewed the stone. Although midmorning, the place felt to be just waking.

As we threaded our way through a maze of passages, the cries of a woman disturbed the torpid peace. The servant sped up. It troubled me that we charged toward the sounds of anguish.

I confess, so that you hold no illusion of me, I have never learned to govern most of my faults, nor even tried very hard, especially those of ambition, curiosity and pride. A godly woman would have run from that place as from the maw of hell; everyone knows that the jeweled façades of courtiers thinly veil their greedy, scurrilous, vain, lascivious souls.

Me? I rushed in.

Crossing an inner courtyard, we passed a fountain on which figures in pale marble wrestled, their naked limbs frosted by the English winter. The water at their feet was stopped and a stench rose from the puddle in its scalloped bowl, yellow with the piss of noblemen and their dogs; even the places these people relieved themselves were not ordinary.

We arrived on the third floor of a building against the Thames and entered a large apartment. Here the crying was loud enough to be described as wailing without risk of exaggeration, although the people standing in the entrance hall ignored it. I twisted my head about like a pigeon; every surface glowed with polish, tapestry or gilt, the air itself perfumed with such exotic scents that my nose was as greedy as my eyes for the extravagance with which I was enveloped. A tall gentleman tried to attract the servant's attention. He accompanied a man clutching a drawing board, a painter, I assumed, but the servant ignored them and I was chivvied through a series of magnificent rooms glinting even in the dull January light. Too soon we reached a door upon which he knocked, gave me a look that said, "God's blessings, you'll need them," and fled.

The door was unlatched and an old eye looked at me blankly through the crack.

"I am Mistress Anne Turner, wife of Dr. Turner," I announced over the noise from within. "I have been summoned."

The servant opened the door on a scene fit for the Globe. A hundred candles illuminated the tableau of a woman, a girl really, on her knees and sobbing. Long chestnut hair swung about her blotchy face, giving the appearance of a lunatic, an impression heightened by the undershirt slipping off her shoulders, kept up by nothing but a black armband. In one hand she clutched a string of pearls, while the other was buried in the silken pelt of a small white dog that whined each time she howled. The chamber appeared to have been ransacked. The contents of a sewing box were strewn upon the floor among shoes, undershirts, bird droppings and a little pile of dry dog turds. From the bed canopy swung a green parrot and circling like distressed mayflies were three maids, the ancient one who had opened the door and two very young ones, holding lace-edged handkerchiefs, hairbrushes and wine.

As another of my faults is not to know my place as well as I should, I stepped forward. "My lady," I said with a deep curtsy, for this unhappy creature was the Countess of Essex, Frances Howard. She was wife to an earl, daughter to an earl, great-niece to an earl and lady-in-waiting (second rank) to the Queen. The Howards were as close to the King as his own family; oftentimes they appeared more favored. I had not seen Frances in the three years since her wedding nor had I ever known her intimately, but we were acquainted, both our families being Catholic and living within a short distance of each other in the country, near Saffron Walden. "My husband is Dr. Turner, your husband's physician."

She gave no indication of having heard me. Slowly, however,

after much hiccupping and sniffing, her crying subsided. The silence that ensued was not of the peaceful kind. No one moved, the fire did not spit, all eyes were on the bowed figure, even her dog gazed into her face with concern. As her stillness became unbearable, she extended an arm. Without hesitation, the maid with the cup stepped forward and placed it in the girl's outstretched fingers. She drained it and sat back on her heels. With eyes closed, she pushed the hair back from her damp face. Only then did she look at me.

Although her cheeks were mottled with crying, still I received a little shock from her beauty. Her hair and eyes were a lustrous brown and her skin, as if laid on cream not flesh, was that which comes only from dining on the food of princes. Life was coiled tight within her and it sparked in me a moment of envy, for I had borne six children and sometimes endured days in which I yawned more than I spoke.

There seemed no point in asking how she did, so I repeated my name and explained that I had received a note that morning from her mother. She scowled and opened her mouth to comment but at that very moment the lady of whom we spoke, the Countess of Suffolk, sailed into the room like a ship fully rigged in court dress, every inch swinging with pearls and gold chains. Behind her came her other two daughters, one older, one younger than Frances, sumptuously apparelled but plain by comparison to their sister. They came to a halt, skirts swaying on willow hoops as wide as their arm spans, a priceless armada. The little dog shot under Frances's undershirt.

"Do I look like a kennel, Brutus?" Frances said.

"A sty," exclaimed her mother. In the fingers of one hand she was rolling what looked like an owl pellet. "Why are you not ready? What is this, hmm?" She gazed around her daughter's chamber as if a stranger to it. Under Queen Elizabeth, when she was not yet a countess, she had not the nerve to develop strange tics. But the fortunes of her family had soared with the arrival of King James and she adorned her new status with a variety of affectations, the most annoying of which was a rising "hmm" at the end of her pronouncements. Perhaps she thought it fashionably French. Or was it to disguise her guile as intellect? The achievement of her vaulting ambition had been entirely due to a generous dowry, uncommon comeliness and the fortunate quality of having no scruples. I have known her all my life, for my mother was in her acquaintance and remained so even after she sacrificed her position to marry my father; so lean is society in the countryside that the Countess would have had no company at all if she had been too strictly observant of rank.

"I cannot hear you."

"I crave your blessing," muttered her daughter.

"Why is Larkin out there? He is meant to be taking your likeness," said her mother, rather foolishly, I thought; no portrait I had seen took distress as its subject. "Your father is furious. When you feel sorry for yourself, remember that he was already widowed by your age as was I. Think of your family, even if you cannot please yourself with your match. 'We must marry our daughters before they marry themselves,' he always says, and he is right, especially in your case," said the Countess, slapping the back of her hand against the girl's forehead, peering at her as one might at an animal with a leg missing.

"You are not feverish. Stand up. Turn around."

Her daughter rose, flinching as if wasps stung her, and swiveled on unsteady feet. As she turned, her back was revealed through a rip in her undershirt from collar to coccyx. The skin was slit all over with bleeding welts. I could feel the burning pain in those lashes and the hair on my forearms pricked up in shock and pity for this girl. How furious her mother would be at the damage inflicted on her beautiful child.

Yet there was no cry of horror, not even a gasp. To protect one's child is the first compulsion of any parent; to determine cause and fault follows later. Not, it seemed, with Frances's mother. Her sisters also stood mute. "Why are you still not dressed, hmm?" said the Countess, her face glistening, hard as a sugar sculpture. She turned to me. Every time we met she affected barely to know me unless we were alone. "I have heard you are talented with apparel," she said. I curtsied but said nothing, unsure what the statement insinuated. "You have come to help my daughter dress."

It was not a question.

"I cannot dress," mumbled Frances.

Her mother stepped forward, I thought to hold her, but instead she put ringed fingers under her daughter's chin and forced the girl to look at her. Was she envious? The Earl of Suffolk was known to favor Frances above his other children—perhaps above his wife too? Did he whisper in the girl's ear that she understood him best? I have seen daughters thus favored become unhappy wives when they cannot bewitch their spouses as they did their fathers.

"If you do not attend today, your husband will send you to his estate at Chartley, hmm?" she said, as if to a half-wit. "It is far away and comfortless. He will keep you there, whipping you without cease if he wishes, until you submit to your marriage as your sisters have done to theirs."

I sensed the distance between myself and Frances Howard contract and wanted to take her in my arms. It is a hard fate to have a cruel husband. He was barely seventeen and already pitiless.

"You will feel better when you look better," said the older sister, Elizabeth, not kindly.

"Do you?" asked Frances.

The sister flushed. "Your self-interest reflects badly upon us all. You have not even the hardest of it." Frances only shrugged. Her mother put the white object she had been pinching into Frances's hand and tugged her daughter's shift into place as if it were a presentable thing not ripped and bloodied by her son-in-law.

"Please see that she is dressed by midday," she said, neither looking at me nor making clear how she intended to make my intervention worthwhile. She left, trailed by her more tractable daughters.

Frances sent out her maids, then glared at me.

"My mother pays you to make me obedient?"

"Indeed, no. I had no idea why she called me here and will leave at once if you permit it."

The girl narrowed her eyes at me and took a long drink straight from the bottle in the manner of an apprentice on his day off. "I remember who you are now. You are the wife of the fashionable doctor."

"My husband was physician to our late Queen, God rest her

7

soul. We are hardly the latest thing," I said, dissembling. I considered myself ahead of the latest thing.

"And you concoct medicines and colored starch like an apothecary and dress boldly. And word is that you have a lover in the Prince's household. Put off your cloak." The gossip was relayed with a hint of admiration and was true. Even so, I did not like to be spoken to in so familiar a tone by a girl of eighteen years at most.

I could have marched out, as her mother had done, and no one would have blamed me. I was not a servant to be ordered about. My mother was Margaret St. Lowe, sole heir of Sir William St. Lowe. My father, Thomas Norton, was a Cambridgeshire yeoman whose family bore arms with eleven quarterings and had the head of a greyhound in a golden collar as his crest. My two elder brothers had good houses in or near Hinxton, the village where I was born, on the road between Cambridge and Saffron Walden. My youngest brother, Eustace, was falconer to the royal family and my only sister, Mary, had married Sir Edward Hinde, recently knighted, inheriting the family farm after my father's death. My own husband, George, had no title but was a member of the College of Physicians and on good terms with Sir William Paddy, its President. The late Queen herself instructed her Chancellor to recommend his election when the College hesitated due to his Catholicism. It was just as George had said that morning: "The Howards always take more than they give."

Throughout our nineteen-year marriage I had nagged him to take me to Court, to find clients for my fashioning, but he had always refused.

"The place is a cesspit. All depravity is there, bed-hopping and syphilitic, trussed up in velvet. Who could know that better than their doctor? Do we not have enough? We are happy, aren't we?"

"Very happy, husband," I had said, kissing the back of his soft, baggy hand. We shared love for our children and pride in our fine household in Fetter Lane. Of each other we were fond and trusting. Only the Court did he deny me.

"Do not go."

There was a firmness in this command that I rarely heard from him. It so surprised me that I laughed.

"You would stop me?"

"That place ruins people."

I meant no insult to him, but it is a foolish woman who puts her whole trust in a husband. My own father drank and gambled away my mother's inheritance and together they died in want; grief for her lodged in my ribs and has not waned. It is a hurt without remedy. One cannot act as if these things never happened. George neither drank nor gambled, but to move in Court circles, even as a doctor, incurred enormous expense. Debt hung around our necks and a short run of bad luck would have bankrupted us. If there was something I could do to make our lives less precarious, and to recover the honor forfeit by my mother for marrying beneath her, I would do it.

I took off my cloak and put it on the bed. The miserable young Countess looked at me for so long I thought I should charge. What did she find? I took great pains to preserve the remnants of my youth so the years between us were less marked than they might have been. We could pass for sisters, just. Compared to her rich potency, my looks are muted. Blue eyes brighten an oval face framed with pale gold curls. I have been called beautiful, but I am not vain. For my blessings I thank God and my angel keeper, who embraces me with unfelt hands and guards me from harm even though I spend little time at confession.

"You dress like a man," she finally pronounced.

She was beguiling and noble, but exceedingly rude.

"Moll Cutpurse dresses like a man. I dress as if I am not afraid," I countered.

She paused a moment to consider that. "My mother does not like to be outshone. Why would she ask you to dress me? Does she think that if I look like a harlot, as you do, my husband will bed me more often?"

How was I to reply to that? "Does he need encouragement?" I said.

She was angry with him, perhaps with everyone. With a combative lift to her chin she weighed up what was safe to tell. I tried to feel indifferent to her judgment but something of her defiant spirit had already captured me. "Better a sheep than a shrew," the saying goes, but not to my mind. My courage would appeal to her, and my greater age and lower rank would save us from rivalry, but my taste would be too outlandish.

"I can trust no one," she said, "not even my family and servants."

I shrugged slightly, making clear it made no difference whether she confided in me or not. She lifted her chin higher, yet never took her eyes from mine. Suddenly her face softened. She took a great breath and a step closer, as if spies listened at the door.

"My husband beats me because he has been home from his travels for two months and I am still a virgin."

That net of words and meanings, cast with little self-pity and great faith in my discretion, ensnared me. I was fascinated that the most appealing young wife at Court remained a virgin; nosiness is another of my failings. Frances kicked at the clothes forming soft piles on the floor, like molehills. She was a most disheveled creature, but not defeated.

"Has he not suffered from the pox since his return?" George had told me this.

"He is not too ill to whip me. I am of the new way of thinking about marriage, in which man and wife are friends, the wife is not slave to the husband," said Frances.

"Of course," I replied, "but husbands rarely are." I looked at the clock on the mantel, an elaborate confection of golden mermaids who rode their dolphins valiantly but could not steer back time. There was less than an hour 'til midday.

"I advise you to dress. It seems you will be unhappier if you refuse."

"I will kill myself," she said, pausing for a response, but I felt only embarrassment at her irreligion. I busied myself with picking up clothes and laying them on the bed. Her mother dressed her in fungal hues, perhaps to dampen her allure.

"If you take your life you will go to hell, which is worse than marriage," I said.

"It will be hot, otherwise the differences will be few."

"A woman should not decide her future."

"I am deciding against a future."

"That is the same. If you obey your husband, he might be kinder,"

10

I said, knowing that she would already have been told that a hundred times. Indeed, she snorted.

"He only cares for horses and dogs. Even those he thrashes. He says women are parasites, like ticks." She sat abruptly on the edge of the bed, head bowed. "I am very unhappy," she whispered, and slipped her hand into mine.

A powerful memory rose to the surface. I had taken my older children to see a baby elephant in the Tower. The dejected creature was so thin its skin hung off its bones and it kept its eyes to the ground as though ashamed. Yet, even in dejection, the animal placed its trunk in the hand of its keeper, as if its trust were not broken. The keeper, long hardened to the prolonged deaths of his charges, had no clue what to do with it. We left that place quickly, our hearts sore. The fantastical nature of the beast had not brought us the pleasure we had anticipated. I felt the same that moment with Frances Howard. The wealth and distance in rank of this young woman were not sufficient to shield me from her anguish, and I could not remain unmoved by the soft weight of her hand in mine.

In that moment, I recognized Frances Howard to be the dream I had long held and suffered from, because it had appeared unattainable. She was a young thoroughbred, stamping about in her dark stall. If she allowed me, if I dared, we could take off her halter and together race the course in our own fashion. With Frankie, I could have the life I had always wanted and regain the honor I sought for myself and my family, and with me she could forge something more satisfying from her own.

She looked at me over the bottle as she took another drink. Had she an inkling of what I imagined for us both? I had no plan, no scheme, just a basket of desires. I sensed that deep-lying in us both was a longing for something to happen; we scanned the horizon daily, expectant. She lowered the bottle to the floor and stood, she in bare feet and I in heels, so that our faces were level. Her eyes flickered minutely as she tried to see both of mine. She held out her hand, like a man. It was a strange gesture but exactly what was required. I shook it.

That was it.

My entry to her world.

From this stemmed everything that followed.

"You have a weapon," I said, picking at her clothes for items not offensive to my tastes. "Your beauty. You must harness it to better serve you."

"It is a curse. Essex chose me over my younger sister because of it. You would think she would be nicer to me. My husband is already blind to it."

"I doubt it, and others won't be; they might protect you."

On Frances's palm sat the white oval, like a large, fluffy pearl. It quivered unnervingly, as if some manner of insect lived within, but it was only the trembling of her hand.

"What is that?"

"Nothing of value if my mother gave it to me," she said, tossing it to her little dog. I unpinned her hair and brushed until it was bright from crown to knee.

"Will your husband give me something more potent than wine to numb my misery?" she asked.

"I myself brew a hypericum tincture that lifts the spirits. Have you silk?" Frances pointed to a chest and I pulled out a fine piece from which I cut a strip, coated it with a balsam to cover and heal the seeping welts, and pressed it to her back. I asked about her black armband as I untied it. It was a few moments before she answered, in a voice that had lost all its bravado.

"My little sister Margaret fell ill this autumn and gave me her pearls to look after until she got better," she said, rubbing her thumb over them. "I was nearly ten when she was born and was allowed to care for her like she was my own. God took her three weeks ago. She was nine." I was pained by that news. It explained perhaps her mother's hard face and the depth of Frances's despair. My keeping angel had spared me that grief but, like all mothers, I lived in fear of any hurt to my children and I made the sign of the cross.

"You think that will protect you?" she asked.

"It costs nothing." In truth, I had stopped attending mass four years previously. Catholic fanaticks had attempted to blow up the royal family and their ministers in the Powder Plot. I could not align myself with such people. Its discovery made the lives of all Catholics in these isles harder, with renewed fines and greater abuse. Even George stopped attending confession. I did not know if Frankie went and had not the familiarity to ask her, yet I knew she and her family were Catholic and that made me feel safer than I would have done in the great Protestant houses.

"All my love and prayers did not save Margaret. Her loss has turned earth to water beneath my feet. I feel her in my arms, her weight on my lap. Her death is as if I saw it on a stage and nothing convinces me that she will not skip into the room at any moment and demand kisses as she always did."

I worked gently and in silence, hoping that she could feel my care. Words cannot dam sorrow, nor should they. They can make a soul feel less alone, but I did that with my work better than my talk.

"Everyone is angry with me," she said, after a long moment of companionable quiet. "My mother thinks it my fault that my husband hates me and my eldest sister believes that I have made a much smaller sacrifice than her own."

"You and your sisters have married well," I said, cutting the ruined undershirt from her perfect body and dropping a clean one over her head.

"We have married high," she corrected, "Elizabeth to a man older than our grandfather would have been had he not been executed. None of us has produced an heir."

"Why did you deserve a whipping?"

"For a sigh when again he could not penetrate me. He says I must not talk unless it is in answer to a question. Nor laugh."

"Perhaps he is ashamed," I said, fitting a stiff bodice like armor, flattening and broadening her chest. She eyed it, the horse resentful of its tight girth, but said nothing. "Shame can make a person cruel. He has returned from Europe to find his bride a woman while he is still a boy."

"He is aggrieved that my brothers and cousins are given positions at Court while he is ignored. His father's treason taints him still."

I caged her hips in a farthingale wide as a cart. Over it I tied a carmine skirt, pinning up the hem to reveal her ankles. My hands darted like a bird pecking seed, working needles and pins, laces and points, circling Frances like a whole flock of maids though I was but one woman. My deftness pleased me, as if the pins and laces grew from my own body as silk comes from the spider. I enjoyed the feel of the sharp metal broaching cloth made on looms in foreign lands, by hands as quick and sure as my own. It pleased me to sculpt fine materials into the shapes in my mind's eye. To the bodice I tied sleeves, pulling them into sharp peaks above her shoulders. From the shambles of this whipped child rose a castle, every swag and buttress a testament to her worth.

"He has been restored to his titles and lands, he should be content with that or try harder to be liked by my family, who might help him," said Frankie. It was not for me to discuss the savagery of her husband's whipping, so I concentrated instead on what I was there to do. I rolled her hair over fat pads and stuck them with jeweled pins. The parrot attempted to steal the jewels but we batted it away and it came to rest among the rose-dyed ostrich feathers atop Frances's bed, as if among the foliage of its homeland. I took three of the longest feathers and pinned them to her hair, to give her another foot or more of height.

"My great-uncle Northampton sent me that popinjay this morning as a New Year's present. With it was a note that green is the color of hope and physical love. He has a nose for trouble like no other," said Frances.

The Lord Northampton was so high a person that to talk casually of him would be like gossiping about God. That her father and great-uncle were, alongside Lord Salisbury, the King's three closest advisers, his "Trinity of Knaves" as he called them, made me feel again the distance between us.

"He claims it can say 'Hail Mary,' but for me it only shrieks and whistles. Comfit?" she asked.

I declined but watched in admiration as she tossed the sweetmeat high in the air and caught it in her mouth. "My brother Harry taught me," she said with a laugh. "His eyes will pop when he sees me tricked out like this."

"Your husband's too. And all the women in your acquaintance. Now I will paint you."

"My husband says that the woman who paints puts up a sign, like a tavern, that she is open to visitors. 'Jezebel-finery for strumpets and followers of false prophets,'" she said, mimicking her husband's glum tone.

"Indeed? It will excite him all the more then. No smiling until you wash it off tonight."

"I am not allowed to smile."

I painted egg white onto her naked skin and into it drew blue veins. As it dried to a perfectly smooth sheen, I darkened her eyelashes and brows and reddened her lips, cheeks and nails. Finally, from the linen sack I had brought with me, I took out a ruff dyed with my own patent starch recipe. You would have thought it was a severed head, so repulsed was her expression. I wondered if she had been in the crowd when her father-in-law was executed. Many of her relatives had gone to the block. It made my fingers fly to think that I was in the presence of people talked about in taverns.

"Yellow? That is too bold. Only drabs wear yellow," Frances said.

"Drabs and Irish peasants," I agreed, tying the ruff round her neck. "They use urine but, if you can afford it, saffron gives a deeper color without the stink. It is somewhat outrageous but that can prove arousing." She looked unconvinced but allowed me to pin it in place.

I pushed up her skirt to roll on stockings. She had the slim, taut legs of a girl. Her feet, young enough that the bones did not show, were as pretty as ducklings. I felt, for an uncomfortable moment, as if I were arming a child. Still, her husband had no qualms in attacking her, so I must have none in fortifying her.

The bells of Westminster chimed midday. I rolled on the stockings, elaborately embroidered at the ankle, and tied the laces of green silk shoes with high heels. From strong boxes came bracelets, rings, necklaces and earrings with which I finished her armature, tying the most valuable to her body with black thread to keep them safe. I helped her to stand by pulling on her lower arms so as not to smudge her painted hands. She towered a good two feet above me.

As she stared at herself in the long glass, I was suddenly nervous. The dreary little mushroom was magicked into a goddess, barely human although wrought of human artifice, a statue brought to life by enchantment, highly sexual yet not approachable. Could she carry so brave a façade?

She turned to me. Although her face was stiff under the ceruse, her eyes shone with delight.

"You may call me Frankie, but not in public," she said, swaying to the door. "Ready?"

"For what?"

"To join me."

"I am not dressed!"

"No matter. We are only going to see the King's worms."

2

Frankie and I shuddered in her carriage along the frozen road inside the wall of St. James's Park. She sat still and upright to keep her hair from harm, asking every few moments if her skirt was not too short, her cuffs too yellow, her lips too red? I kept up a patter of encouragement as I looked through the window at that to which only the Court was allowed entry. Part-hidden by the frozen fog, workmen were digging the canal of Prince Henry's design, about which I had read in the broadsheets. Beyond it, like a jumble of jewel cases, was the King's menagerie. Men in red coats strolled around.

"Who are they?"

"The keepers," said Frances. "They are treated like princes."

The cages were empty, their exotic prisoners sheltering inside small huts except for a dark-skinned man wrapped in a blanket. His eyes followed the progress of our coach.

"That's an Indian, and there are pelicans from Muscovy, antelopes from the Great Mogul, Virginia squirrels that can fly and Cassuare birds that cannot, although they swallow hot coals without harm, and the courtiers' favorite, two crocodiles." Frankie loved to laugh. I checked her face for cracks.

At the western end of the park we came to an orchard of saplings wrapped in straw to protect them from frost. At the center squatted three long sheds, little taller than a man, steaming in the pale January light. To one side were coaches, horses and servants, all emblazoned with the crests of noble families.

"So many," I said. Frankie barely glanced at what impressed me.

"You will get used to it. The King is never unattended."

"The King?"

17

She looked at me curiously, as if I were a foreigner with different understanding. "This is the King's new silk factory. We are here to admire it."

I had known Frances but a few hours and already, in her company, I was to be admitted to the King's presence. Frankie noticed my agitation and took my hand.

"I will keep you safe from the monsters," she said as the footman helped her down; he helped me too, but with less deference. I was ashamed of my sweating palms.

Inside it was so dark that at first I thought we were alone. The place was hot and wet and reeked like a turgid pond. Frankie held her perfumed gloves to her nose to mask the stench. There was a strange noise, like rain drumming on canvas, so loud that I looked about for its source but could find none in the gloom. As my eyes adjusted, I saw that the low building was crammed with courtiers, fantastically silhouetted against the slatted shutters, many of whom were members of Frankie's family. They all gazed toward a short, rather scruffy man. The moment Frankie spotted him she lowered her gloves.

There could be no other reason for her sudden movement than that this was the King. He held a shiny leaf on which feasted a caterpillar, as fat as a carpenter's thumb, heedless of its monarch. Awe possessed me like a devil, making me stare when I should have looked down. Although his clothes were a poor fit, his cap was magnificently jeweled and adorned with feathers tall enough to brush the ceiling. His countenance was unlovely, with drooping eyes and jowls, and his body encased in a doublet so thickly padded it resembled a turnip, but it mattered not for the King is appointed by God and stands as high as Him. His courtiers were more richly dressed, a host proclaiming the glory of their Lord, and I felt touched by divinity in my nearness to him; it is one of God's mysterious workings that he should raise this small man above us even while all about are men of greater strength and beauty.

"Have we entered hell, after all?" Frankie whispered just as I was thinking myself in heaven.

"The noise we hear is their eating," I whispered back, nodding toward trestles that stood between us and the King. These were piled with glossy leaves that the caterpillars were noisily devouring. Frankie's face was a picture of revulsion.

"Lady Frances, this will interest ye!" said the King, ensuring all became aware of our late arrival. He spoke in a Scotch accent so strong that at first I thought it was a different language. "The clothes on yer back are spun by these wurrums. They pissed on yer ruff too, p'raps?"

At this, fifty pairs of eyes turned to Frankie. Women opened fans behind which they whispered; men grinned. The Countess of Suffolk stood very still, her rigid lips alone betraying distress at the great alteration in her daughter.

The King examined Frankie as one would a horse before laying bets. I did not breathe. George had told me that our monarch loved to create mischief in his Court, to keep his nobles on their toes. Ridicule is harder to survive than scandal. My jaw ached with fear. He began to clap. Slowly at first, then in a childish burst in which those around him were obliged to join. Frankie curtsied with such great dignity that the King nodded along with the applause.

As a hundred jeweled hands finally came to rest the King called out, "My commendations to yer tailor, Lady Frances. We like our Court to shine." Frankie inclined her head but mine fair burst with pride. That morning I had never been to Court; by dinnertime the King himself was commending my work.

Frankie found my hand and squeezed it.

The King grew bored of us then and turned his attention to the young man beside him, who was as fresh and lovely as Frankie herself. He possessed male and female beauty equally. I guessed him to be about twenty or twenty-two summers, half his sovereign's age, beardless and smooth-skinned as a girl, yet broad in the shoulder. His fair hair was elaborately frizzed around his face and from one ear dangled a sapphire of a size that could only have come from a King. Not yet masked for Court life, his face revealed the heart below and I found in it the melancholy of a man needing love. He gently took the worm from his monarch's hand while the King fussed over him like any besotted man would his wife. He patted his cheek and smoothed a fold in the young man's collar, picking off a loose thread. But when the youth glanced up it was not at the King but at Frankie. She immediately looked away and I wondered who he was, and for how long he had been flirting with her.

"Go on, Stallenge," the King commanded.

A man standing at the end of the tables began to talk of mulberry trees, white and red, their leaves the diet of the worms. After a very short time the Court grew restless and the guide ushered his audience toward the adjoining shed. The King kept the young man as close as the miniature greyhound that shivered at his heels. The dog was so thin that every bone was visible through its pelt, the tail an osseous crescent no thicker than a pencil line. In that moment I understood that our monarch felt as vulnerable as his elfin hound. From this sprang his need for strong wine and padded doublets.

I was not so self-assured as to push my way among nobles and was last to enter the second shed. It was lighter and cooler than the one we had left, festooned with thick cobwebs in which lodged a multitude of small, opaque orbs.

"That was what my mother gave me," Frankie whispered, making space for me by her side. She was treating me as an equal and a friend, although I was neither. Several courtiers looked me up and down, then turned away without so much as a nod.

"In here cocoons are harvested," Master Stallenge continued. "We will soon outstrip France in the production and finishing of silk." The King clapped and all followed suit.

"Every county will buy ten thousand mulberry trees at a shilling a hundredweight," the King announced, "and I expect you courtiers to do the same. Sir Robert will be the first." The youth at his side bowed and the clapping grew strained; this was applause with hatred its rhythm. I gadded very often to the theater, it was my greatest pleasure after fashioning, but here was a performance finer than any I had seen, and it thrilled me to have a walk-on part.

"That is the King's new favorite. Sir Robert Carr. Everyone hates him," whispered Frankie.

I remembered George's response when I had quizzed him about rumors that pursued the King. "Sodomy is punishable with death, even to mention it is a crime. The King has written at length to condemn it in the strongest terms," he had said, as if from a pulpit.

"Of course. But what have you observed?"

My husband paused for a long time. He and I were ever honest with each other.

"He has decried drinking and swearing with equal fervor yet indulges prodigiously in both."

"That Sir Robert might have ample space in which to plant his mulberries," the King continued, "it pleases us to grant upon him royal lands abutting his estate of Sherbourne."

Sir Robert Carr looked abashed, as if the King's gifts were heaped upon him whether he sought them or not. At his side, however, was a man who appeared vexed.

"Who is the cockerel?" I asked quietly.

Frankie smothered a smile to save her paint. "Sir Thomas Overbury, Carr's bosom friend," she whispered. "He is hated even more."

His head was unusually narrow with deeply indented temples, the divine fingers that pulled him out so thin from his original clay having left their mark. On top was a cockscomb of red hair and his beard was clipped to a sharp point. The avian impression was completed by a very thin nose and small, darting eyes that missed nothing and disdained all. He seemed like a fighting cock on his post, surveying his territory for intruders. I wondered at the King's favorite wanting the protection of this strutting companion.

We moved into the final room and came to a halt before simmering vats. Thousands of cocoons danced on the surface.

"When boiled sufficiently," explained Stallenge, "the end of a cocoon comes free, is caught and threaded on to a wheel, unravelling in a single filament as long as St. James's Park." The sight of dead caterpillars floating on the heaving water appeared to disturb Frankie but I did not share her dismay. I thought the beauty of silk worth the lives of a few grubs.

"Is there a use for the dead worms?" asked one.

"They could grace your table!"

"Would you like that better than beef?"

"The poor could eat them!"

"A feast for orphans!"

Eventually Master Stallenge made himself heard above the braying courtiers.

"They can be used as bait. Fish appreciate them very much."

Over the sniggering came a serious, female voice. It was Frankie's. My skin prickled at her bravery.

"If the babies are boiled, how do butterflies emerge to make more?"

"A good question, my lady," said Master Stallenge, a man keen to prove himself modern by not taking fright at a woman speaking in public. "Some of the cocoons are allowed to hatch into butterflies. The eggs they produce become the next batch of silkworms. And so it continues," he said with a flourish.

At that moment a corpse arrived.

A tall, skeletal man of extreme pallor pushed his way to the front of the group. He seemed fit for the grave. His face was painted with a thick layer of lead that did not quite disguise the livid spots disfiguring his complexion. A straggly black beard showed very dark against his pallid cheeks. Frankie stepped backward, crushing my foot.

"Declare yourself, man!" said the King, rattled. He had too often been subject to kidnap and assassination plots to take such an appearance calmly. The figure bowed to him stiffly.

"Sire, I am Robert Devereux, Earl of Essex."

This! This was Frankie's husband?

I was astonished. I had last seen him at his wedding, exactly three years before, and had been surprised that the son of a handsome hero could have no notable features other than the thinness of his legs and the bitterness of his expression. He was but fourteen then, and I had expected time and travel in Europe to improve him. It had not. George had told me that the Earl's nickname at Court was "Grumbling Essex," which I found too mild a jibe for this pitted lad who whipped his wife. It was well known that his father had not written to him on the eve of his execution, an exceptional disregard that had left his ten-year-old son with the conviction that everyone around him was more fortunate than he. It seemed to me that the growth of his heart had been stunted at that moment, by the implacable hatred he felt toward those responsible for his father's execution, namely Lord Salisbury and his allies, the Howards.

"Ye're back then," said the King, eyeing the Earl's spots with alarm. "Ye've been ill?"

"I have, Sire, but I am recovered."

The King looked doubtful. "Come to claim yer bonnie lassie?"

The Earl of Essex followed the King's gaze. He looked blankly at Frankie until a start of recognition made him flush. His eyes traveled with increasing alarm over her high heels and exposed ankles, yellow ruffs and cuffs, the armature of clothing, her painted face, up to the pink feathers that made her much taller than him. Where was the bleeding, sniveling girl he had chastised that morning? He forgot, or refused, to bow to her. Frankie's face was as blank as a new-plastered wall.

"With such a wife, ye might need to visit a tailor yerself, man!" laughed the King, and the whole Court joined in, though I sensed with reluctance. Essex was dressed in plain English wool to plain English design; those who could afford velvet but did not wear it, did so to denounce fashion, luxury and everything else originating in Catholic lands. No Spanish leather in glove or boot, no Venetian velvet or embroidery, enlivened his appearance. The young Earl had even refused to visit Catholic countries during his tour of Europe. I wondered then, not for the first time that day, who had considered it a sensible notion to marry him into a Catholic family for whom luxury and display were more important than air?

Humiliating her husband was not Frankie's plan and she curtsied deeply to him. He ignored her and Robert Carr smiled; it would be a kindness for him to flirt with a beautiful woman whose husband appeared only to scowl.

"Come, lad, give the lass yer arm!" said the King, whose love of peace was as controversial as his love for men. Essex had no choice but to allow Frankie to put her hand on his forearm.

The King draped his own arm across the shoulders of his favorite and shuffled out, his dog close behind. Essex followed with Frankie, who winked at me as she passed.

After the King and Robert Carr had left, Frankie's husband and parents climbed into her father's coach. As Frankie joined them, she offered me her own carriage to take me home. Her mother and husband looked aggrieved. Did the Countess of Suffolk regret her order to me? Had I done too good a job?

"Go on, Anne," said Frankie, laughing, the paint cracking outward from her lips like an eruption, "then my coachman will know where to find you."

The nobles departed in order of rank, with much shouting and jostling to enforce precedence.

"Fetter Lane," I said to Frankie's driver when only our vehicle remained. I climbed up, for all the world like Elijah into his chariot, and sat forward on the upholstered bench so as to be seen. We traveled familiar streets made strange and important by the golden frame through which I viewed them. By the time we left Westminster and joined the Strand I was accustomed to the stares (how quickly we adjust to admiration) and settled back in comfort. I thought of Frankie and the Earl of Essex, children of opposite sides of the divided Court, married to heal wounds . . . or rather, to bring Essex to heel. The plan to muzzle him and his supporters through marriage to Frankie was optimistic, some might say unpardonable. I grasped at that moment, with equal dread and pride, what her mother had understood at the sight of Frankie's wounded back; the marriage, vital to Howard interests, would rupture unless a remedy could be found, and the person best placed to provide it was me.

3

I waited to hear from Frankie as if from a new lover. Toward the end of January, I gave her up as a beautiful dream.

It was a mild but wet winter and I was content to keep indoors with my family, away from skidding carts and starving dogs. Poor harvests and high taxes were creating discontent in the markets and drinking shops. Not a day passed when I did not thank the Lord, my keeping angel and husband George for our smart new house on Fetter Lane. Its brick walls, glazed windows, large garden and views across the fields of Holborn, provided a spacious sanctuary for us and our six children. Nonetheless filth and pestilence were ever at the door in this City of Babel. I requested our cook to make a daily batch of bread to hand out to the beggars outside St. Andrew's and under the gibbet at the junction with Fleet Street, but it assuaged my conscience more than their hunger.

"Paddy goes everywhere with an armed guard now, Kennedy has twice tried to kill him," George said, chuckling as he watched me attire a cloth poppet, a French Baby, with a new design for Lady Kennedy's approval. She had requested something daring in which to attend the Queen's Masque, having grown too thin for her heavy Scotch gowns. As I stitched, I pictured her running bare-legged through the streets at night in nothing but her nightgown, chased by her husband, who had discovered her in bed with Sir William, George's friend and President of the College of Physicians.

George was sitting almost in the fire, his round form wrapped in a blanket, books all about him and his great white cat on his knee. We had no monkeys or finches on account of this cat, despite the children begging for them, and I loved the animal more because of it. The room was littered with the flotsam of children's play, every surface covered in bottles of George's medicine, penny broadsides, small trinkets precious to one or other child, all coated with cat hair and ash from the fire that was continuously burning to keep out the damp. The shutters muffled sound from the street. I felt safe in this patch of warmth and light; several times I had thought to tidy but had not found the inspiration to do so, it being dark and cold beyond this room.

"Mama," said Katherine, our youngest daughter, barging into the room. She was swathed in so thick a shawl only the top half of her face could be seen. My neighbors laughed at the care I took of my children, jibing that I was a "fuss-a-lot," but when their own fell ill they ran to me, shamefaced, for remedies. Katherine's eyes were huge with wonder and she held before her a painted doll I had not seen before. "There's a princess at the door," she announced. Maggie, my aged maid, trudged past carrying a cloak with great dignity, for all the world like she was properly trained. I rose quickly, cheeks burning at the state of the room.

Frankie appeared in the doorway.

"Your ladyship!" I could not call her Frankie, so glorious did she appear among the detritus of family life. George pushed the cat from his knee as he stood and Katherine slipped her free hand into Frankie's. How trusting are the young and greedy.

"Forgive my intrusion," she said, making way for Mary, who elbowed past Frankie's skirts to stare at her sister's doll. "I would have come sooner but have been daily required to rehearse the Queen's Masque. I am to play a warrior queen who leads the wives of my kingdom to slaughter their husbands!" Her laughter was strained and her eyes darted around but rested on nothing. I ushered her in.

"May I present Dr. Turner?"

"My husband speaks very highly of your care."

"Gratified," George said, bowing again but not smiling. He gestured to Frankie to take his chair and made to leave the room.

"Do stay if you will, Dr. Turner," she said. Frankie wanted something from us, something more than I had already promised. I, who knew George's face much better than my own, saw the dislike in it. It was not for Frankie herself, but for the Howards. He shuffled awkwardly through the clutter to perch on my low stool. At that point, three more of our children jostled their way in and stared at Frankie most rudely.

"Please introduce us," she said. Neither George nor I really wanted her to meet them, I sensed it in us both. We had assiduously protected them all these years from every source of danger, humoral, accidental or divine, with tonics and medicines, watchful care, prayers and amulets of wolf's tooth and coral. My children, though released from my belly, still fill me completely with love, for all the cares they bring with them. Nothing is more important to me than their safety, health and affection. Frankie's arrival was like that of the Trojan horse; we did not yet know what she carried within her magnificent carapace.

"Your ladyship," I said, as the last child crammed into the room, "may I present our eldest son, Thomas, fifteen summers old and with a head for business." I did not add that I wished he were our second son and not our heir, for he is a surly, argumentative slugabed. Our latest battle with him was over a sword. Even a simple rapier costs the same as a good horse. He wanted it so that he might run with other roaring boys, get into brawls and be called "gentleman." As Thomas is clumsy, slow in wit but fast in temper, we were resisting his furious begging, but it was wearing. "Our second son, John, is fourteen and hopes to enter Oxford," which words did no justice to this serious soul who made up for his brother's unbalanced humors with consideration beyond his years. He worried too much about our good opinion of him and sometimes I hoped he would do something naughty. "Barbara is sixteen and exceeding excellent at stitching and tinctures." Frankie looked at her keenly. They were but two years apart, yet Frankie had been married for three already. "She is not yet betrothed," I said, in some vague hope that a connection with a noblewoman would bring about a better match. "Mary here is just five, Katherine is four and Henry will soon be three." The little ones, with reddish-brown hair where the elder were fair, had careful manners when not taken by surprise and all of them curtsied, even Henry. His sisters nudged him and he switched to a bow, his face steaming.

"You bow graciously, Henry, your parents must be very proud of you," said Frankie. "I see you are also strong in limb. There is a sack outside the door, oblige me by fetching it."

With an air of great importance, Henry pushed his way through his siblings and struggled back with the sack. She reached down and pulled from it a smaller bag, which she gave to him. Henry tipped this up and out fell a red leather ball and nine wooden pins with carved faces. He looked at Frankie and then away, then threw himself at her and wrapped his arms around her neck, saying, "Fankye, fankye." She held him close for as long as he would permit. He kissed her repeatedly on the cheek until all but Thomas laughed, then jumped down and set to arranging the ninepins in fighting formation.

There were finest Italian marbles for Thomas, made not of clay but of colored glass with what seemed to be cat's eyes within. He looked intrigued until Frankie explained that they were an artifice and not real eyes. For Barbara, a bottle of curious shape filled with perfume. For John, Camden's book of histories and proverbs. For Mary, a doll like her sister's, only with different hair and clothes. She blushed and reached for it gingerly, as if Frankie might be a spirit. Mary is a polite and tender child; she only forgot to thank Frankie because she was overwhelmed by the gift. I did not remind her, as I would with the others, for her intentions are always of the best. She has a weak chest, is much prone to coughing, and I cared for her with minute attention.

Frankie had listened keenly to all I had told her of my offspring; her gifts to them were perfectly chosen and I felt flattered yet heavy with the burden of them. What need had she to bribe me through gifts to my children? I glanced at George and knew he was thinking the same.

"Will you drink something?" I asked, sending out the children and the cat.

"Brandy," she said. As George unlocked the cupboard and poured them both a tot, Frankie pulled a final gift from her sack. She handed me a flat, wooden box, inside which lay a pair of perfumed silk gloves with long fingers and embroidered cuffs. I had never owned anything so fine in my life. They were worth two years' wages for my maid, at least. I stammered thanks but she waved these away, downed the brandy and handed the glass back to George. We all sat, he and I uncertain whether we were permitted to start a conversation with so high a personage. Frankie was looking at her fingers, listening to the children, who had gone upstairs to play.

"Dr. Turner, is my husband quite well?" she finally inquired. I felt him relax beside me and wondered what he had expected her to say.

"There is no danger; the smallpox is receding."

"But he is still lacking in . . . appetite."

"Do you find it so?" Thank you, George, I thought, for concealing my indiscretion. I had informed him of the Earl's failure to consummate his marriage, along with every other detail of my visit to the palace and the silk factory. George, in turn, had told me that the Earl had not admitted this insufficiency to him.

"Sometimes he thinks he is hungry, but when it comes to . . . it . . . his appetite deserts him. I worry he will not regain his vigor or else that he will seek food from other tables that better accommodate his tastes." There were rumors of prostitutes. "I believe that he will accept assistance only from you, Dr. Turner, and only if you have no other patients at Court, he is so afeared of talk. My proposal is that you both come to live in our household. It has taken all this time since I saw you, Anne, for him to agree to my coming to ask this of you, even though I could not broach the reason why I wished it."

I knew that George would not agree to the Earl's stipulations, and nor would I, but I felt a strange desperation not to lose her.

"That is a generous proposal," I said. "We could not leave our children but can offer help in other ways." I looked to my husband, but he said nothing.

"You would see them often," said Frankie.

"We are too tenderhearted toward them to do what others do."

"My wife is right," said George. "I cannot abandon my children or my patients. Your husband must trust to my discretion, as did the Queen of England, God rest her soul."

"It is not a lack of trust, only shame. He will not speak of what ails him. He becomes enraged if I so much as hint at it."

"That is not to be surprised at," George said, gently. "He is but seventeen. A wife must not question her husband any more than I may question a King; especially a young husband, in need of the support and obedience of his spouse as he brings to bear his authority over his household. When all is in its proper place, then he will rule with kindness and mercy. I have observed that too lusty a wife can dishearten a husband. Until he sees fit to speak of it to me, I can do nothing to encourage him. However, you are wan. I suspect you are suffering from greensickness, for which I can treat you until such time as it is cured by your husband's seed."

Frankie's face and neck flushed, her pallor momentarily banished. She was unused to refusals and resented George's assertion that she was to blame for her husband's lack of desire. She did not know that this was a grievous subject for us also, and that she was the recipient of ire provoked by his own impotence. She looked away from George and we sat in awkward silence awhile. Each laugh from above made her shrink further into herself.

George stood and bowed, but Frankie did not acknowledge him as he left the room. I was angry that he had made no effort to please a woman whose friendship I sought. I expected her to rise and ask for her cloak but she sat silently; it was not awkward between us, even then.

"Have you more brandy?" she said eventually.

The cupboard was locked and only George had a key. I found one of my hypericum brews, distilled in brandy.

"Small sips whenever you are enervated. I will give you more to take with you," I said, allowing her a gracious exit with that cue. There seemed little point in discussing George's homily; obedience to God's will is a challenge for all, especially for women like us. She stood, but instead of leaving said, "Will you show me round your house?"

There could be no other reason to look into my life but that we were to be friends and my heart jigged about like a child at the fair. The house would be a mess but I made no apologies. Frankie wanted to know me; best she knew the truth. Taking a candle, I handed her another.

"Is there a kitchen?"

"You want to see the kitchen?"

"I want to see everything."

It dawned on me that Frankie had never been in a middling sort of home. She had probably never entered a kitchen, never stoked a fire or opened a shutter, certainly never boiled water in which to wash or cook a pottage. There can be contentment in these simple things, especially when they are done for children, and she wanted to experience it. And so I let her taste my life, hoping it would not turn bitter in her mouth as she returned to the opulent prison of her own, bereft of her little sister Margaret and maltreated by a husband infuriated by his inadequacies.

Old Maggie, the cook and the kitchen maid were affronted by our invasion of their realm but could not object to my showing Frankie our modern range with built-in bread oven and spit. Sitting by its warmth, feeding titbits to the cat, was Richard Weston, George's bailiff. In his sixtieth year or more, he was tall and strong. Although from Essex, near Hinxton where I was born, he had been apprenticed to a London tailor as a young man and had taught me much about men's clothing. That aside, he was little educated and quick with his fists. He rose, hoping for an introduction, but as he is of no rank I only nodded. I left George undisturbed in the smaller parlor but took Frankie into the distillery that we had built onto the back of our house, where he and I brewed medicines, elixirs and tonics, and formulated new recipes, such as that for my yellow starch, which we had also patented. Of course, many women distil cures for their families and neighbors, there is nothing unusual in it, but I knew no other goodwife whose recipes received a patent.

"You are allowed?" asked Frankie, repeatedly. Although I was envious of the honor in which she was held, I understood that day what it cost her.

I led her back into the house and upstairs; she ran her fingers along both walls, perhaps never having trod stairs so narrow. She spent a long time in the girls' chamber, asking them questions, letting the little ones play with her clothes, discussing recipes for face washes with Barbara. She made my younger daughters hoot like little owls, her affection for them unfeigned. How could I have thought her a Trojan horse? At one point, as she ruffled their curly heads, she looked at me inquiringly. I had been waiting for that look since she saw my children gathered in the parlor. The eldest three, fair and blue-eyed like George and me, so different from the little red-brown squirrels.

My husband understood that, being twenty years my senior and impotent for the past few years, my frustration would lead to greensickness. He liked and approved of my lover, Sir Arthur Waring, and knew I was no bedswerver. Arthur visited regularly and took the youngest three for rides in his carriage but was never openly referred to as their father. Knighted the year we met, he was carver to Prince Henry and steward to Baron Ellesmere, but earlier that month he had turned up at our door, elated.

"Francis Woolley has died!"

"Is that cause for celebration?" I asked him.

"I inherit."

I was not pleased. More young women needing husbands would be thrust beneath his nose. I loved him. I loved George too. And I loved my children more than my own life. Neither in its giving nor receiving did I lack for love, yet still I sought honor. Reputation. The safety and respect that accompany title and wealth.

Arthur's increased eligibility and the never-ending business of running my household meant that I, like the children, became fractious as dark fell early and dragged on long that month. There was an itch in me that I had caught from my first encounter with Frankie, of which I could not be rid.

None of this did I tell her then. Our friendship was as yet a tight bud, I did not know what variety of flower would emerge.

"I hope I have not given offense," said Frankie, having taken her leave of the children and followed me downstairs. It was true that she had treated us as if we were Indians in a menagerie; but she was envious of what I had and had behaved with tact. I signaled that she should follow me into the parlor. Throughout the visit,

I had thought how to give her what she had come for. I shut the door behind us.

"Despite what George said, he understands a woman's grief at having no children. I know what he would prescribe to cure the Earl's difficulties," I said in a low voice so that he would not hear in the next room. "If you can promise me, on your life, that you will never tell your husband or mine, then I can provide what you need."

Our heads were almost touching.

"I promise," she whispered. "Is it a crime to give medicine to another without them knowing?" She seemed excited by the idea.

"It is not poison you are giving him!"

"But to give it to him secretly?"

"How else? His melancholy humors obstruct the path to happiness for you both. Your children will be proof enough of the rightness of your actions."

"We are so rarely together, he and I."

"Ask him to teach you something; husbands like to instruct their wives. French?"

"He never learned it well."

"Music?"

"He dislikes it."

"Not dance then."

"He studied military defenses during his travels."

"Could you pretend an interest in it?"

She shook her head. "He would not think it seemly."

"Is there nothing at all that you have in common? Theater?"

"I love plays. He hates them."

"Walking in the park?"

"He says it is for women and children as are coach rides, shopping at the Exchanges, fashion, card games, any form of gambling, bearbaiting, pleasure gardens, quoits . . . anything except preparing for, or fighting, a war."

"Then you must buy a puppy. Not a lapdog, a big dog. He will train you to train it."

As Frankie considered this idea, I searched quietly among the bottles clustered about the room.

33

"I must talk frankly. This is chafing ointment: in it there is mustard, pepper, cinnamon and ginger. Rub it on his part to make the sap rise but remember to wipe it away before he uses it, or your insides will sting. It is something any wife could make so there is no need for secrecy. Pretend it is only to give him pleasure." Frankie nodded, as eager to learn as the good child at her psalter. "Have warm meats prepared for him: hens, capons, young doves, sparrows, mountain birds and lambs. Also, eggs, asparagus and quinces. He may object but encourage the eating of parsnips and turnips, they provoke lust and nourish good seed. Also, any white foods like milk puddings, artichokes and shellfish. Of course, the stones of male animals are very potent, be they of bulls, bucks or boars, and sparrows' skulls and bones, crushed and ground with their meat, are all good; these foods stimulate an appetite for venery and fill the body with seed. This," I said, handing Frankie another pot, "is to rub on his privy member at any time he will allow it and especially just before the act; use it after the chafing ointment. Rub it on your own privitie too, for it provokes lust and improves fruitfulness."

Frankie pulled out the cork and sniffed. "It smells strong."

"Lust smells strong. Be not too clean if you wish to stir him up."

"What is it?"

"Crushed and powdered brain of crane mixed with goose fat and the grease of a fox's stones together with dried hare's womb. Your husband has an excess of the cold humors, it is very marked in him. He needs to be warmed up. All that I have given you, of advice and ointment, is easily found. This," I said, holding up a small bottle from the highest shelf, "is brewed nowhere else but here and is very secret." I looked at her before handing it over, to be sure she had understood to tell no one. She nodded. "Put three drops in his food or drink. It will force his yard erect and make it more likely that you will conceive a boy, especially if you lie on your right side after he has put his seed in you. Give him too much and it will blister and burn his body, cause him to pass blood, then bring delirium and death."

Frankie held it with the very tips of her fingers. "I *am* giving him poison."

"It is medicine in the correct dose."

Very carefully, she placed the pots in her hanging pocket. The tiny vial she wrapped first in her handkerchief before gingerly placing it in the pocket and tying the drawstring very tight.

"Thank you," she said, rather formally.

I held out my arms and she gladly let me embrace her. "God bless your efforts, Frankie, go forth and multiply." She laughed, a wonderful, deep chuckle that set me off too. There was some madness in our cackling, no doubt about it; we were wild with our own defiance.

I called for her cloak and showed her to the door. As she stepped up into her coach she asked, "Do you know a good place to buy a dog?"

4

"This?" asked Frankie a month later, holding up a sleeve of beige silk.

"It is worth nothing without its pair," I said.

Frankie stood barefoot, as if in rising water, surrounded by the disarray of her chamber. It was clear that this was her first attempt to bring order to her belongings, or even to know what she had. She leaped, as if at an escaping pet, and dragged a sleeve from the pile of clothes half under the bed. Her little white dog barked and dashed about, enjoying the game, while the new puppy shivered in the corner where it had been put after chewing the heel off a shoe.

"A guinea?" she asked, dangling the matching sleeve.

"At least," I said, laughing. Only with Frankie could sorting clothes be so entertaining. I thought how much my younger children and Barbara would have enjoyed playing among these riches, many items more valuable than all our vestments combined. Frankie had asked me to bring them, as often I did, but that day they were with my sister, Mary, who was staying with us while her husband was away on business.

Frankie's mother had summoned me again to Whitehall when it became clear that her daughter intended to befriend me; she suggested, or rather ordered, a more modest style for her daughter, an entirely hypocritical campaign as she herself was the brashest woman at Court. I listened politely and ignored her; Frankie must be above the ordinary, only in that way could she inspire respect until such time as she had male children. The more she was noticed and admired, in particular by the King, the less freedom Essex would enjoy to abuse her. Frankie's mother pretended not to notice our defiance, then told Essex to give her daughter less money, which was why Frankie and I were sorting through her clothes and trinkets, so as to pawn those she did not like.

As we were propping the pile against the bedstead, Frankie's husband entered. In his hand was a whip and what looked like a long leash. Frankie's shoulders hunched over. He looked first at his wife's bare feet, then at me, then at the disorder in the room. He neither greeted us nor bowed, but nor was he scowling. He whistled at the puppy, who pattered obediently after him and we followed, Brutus yapping at our heels.

"Here," said the Earl, pointing at the floor. Frankie hesitated, unsure whether he meant her or the dog. He clicked his fingers in her direction.

"Why are your feet bare?"

"To run after the puppy," Frankie lied, standing on the spot he had indicated. They were bare because she disliked the restriction of shoes.

"We do not run after dogs. They obey us," he said. "Mistress Turner, take Purkoy to the far end of the room." I started. He had never used my name before and, I think, allowed my visits only because Frankie had been making greater efforts to please him since my arrival. Not only had she asked him to choose a puppy from the litter she had found, but also to name it. Essex had decided on the same name that Frankie's kinswoman, Anne Boleyn, had given her dog. French for "why," the Earl claimed it was because the puppy was inquisitive, an unfortunate trait in dog or wife; I suspected it was to remind Frankie of the consequences of displeasing a husband.

I carried the puppy to the far end of the long chamber.

"Call your dog," he instructed Frankie. "Once, firmly."

"Purkoy!" she called.

The puppy lolloped forward promisingly but lost interest halfway and sniffed at the floor. Brutus, however, rushed with all enthusiasm at his mistress and jumped as high as her waist. She deftly caught him, laughing.

"Down!" roared the Earl, grabbing the tiny dog by its scruff and slamming it onto the floor, pressing on the neck of the whimpering creature. Frankie's hand flew to her mouth. Once the dog was silent, the Earl released his grip and pointed toward the open door of Frankie's chamber. "Go!" The little dog sloped off, his tail pressed between his back legs, looking at Frankie reproachfully from the corner of his eyes.

"You must show a dog who is master," said the Earl. "Now, call the pup."

"Purkoy," said Frankie, all enjoyment gone from her voice. Purkoy ignored her and Essex marched up to the dog, tied the long leash to its collar and carried him back to me. As he pushed the dog's tail down to make him sit, he spoke quietly.

"I hear from Dr. Turner that there are tonics to improve the balance of my wife's humors. I would have you give them to her." I was, as rarely happens, lost for words. I thought it contemptible that he should whisper to me while Frankie was in the room. That he and George had talked about her also annoyed me, although I know that was unfair as I had spent many hours discussing Essex with Frankie. "And dress her with greater modesty," he continued, which remark restored my tongue to life.

"I humbly suggest, my lord, that outward bravery will encourage inner sanguinity. This, in turn, may produce a general amelioration in health, which will allow her menses to flow more completely, unblocking those passages that . . ." He quickly held up a hand to stop me; I find that young men with no genuine interest in women dislike any mention of the practicalities of their fertility. Embarrassed by the turn the discussion had taken, he instructed me to keep hold of the dog's collar and walked back to his wife, paying out the leash as he went. I was slightly ashamed, he was only just eighteen, but the feeling soon left me.

"Call the dog," he ordered. Frankie obeyed. The puppy bounded forward as before but this time, when it grew distracted, the Earl jerked the leash. With a yelp, the dog stumbled and looked around, baffled. Frankie took a breath to call the puppy, but Essex again held up his hand for silence. When still the dog did not come, he jerked the leash harder. Whimpering, ears down, the puppy was dragged to Essex's feet. Frankie bent to stroke the soft head but Essex stopped her.

"No praise until it does exactly as you command."

The fripperers arrived at that moment, the wife and daughter of the pawn merchant whose services I had used since moving to Fetter Lane. They were both stout, well-dressed women, and I wondered who had surrendered the clothes they wore as we pointed them toward Frankie's chamber. The Earl eyed them with obvious disdain.

"People listen more to their tailors these days than their soulmakers," he said, loudly enough for the fripperers to glance back at him. "To gild and ornament yourself is an insult to Him who first fashioned you." He glared at us in turn. "The Devil sews vanity and reaps discontent. Bare breasts and painted faces might please the Court, but you insult Our Lord." The ardor of his speech was more alluring than his usual whining, yet his passion for obedience and prudery would not excite Frankie. He drew breath to sermonize further but was interrupted by a most unexpected visitor. Frankie looked at me with raised eyebrows when her steward announced his name.

Sir Thomas Overbury entered while still being announced and bowed to Lord Essex, more briefly than was proper. Frankie and me he entirely ignored. Overbury wore deepest black and Essex the plainest brown; there could be no less joy in their attire had they donned sacks and ashes.

"You are not expected," stated Essex with his usual bluntness, although it seemed to me that Overbury's arrival unnerved him. While greatly inferior in rank, Overbury was his senior by ten years and his reputation for combative arrogance preceded him. Frankie swayed in her skirts to force Overbury's acknowledgment of her, but it was as if she were not present. Her husband, far from enforcing respect for his wife, indicated that Overbury could speak.

Frankie beckoned me over and I dragged a reluctant Purkoy with me. She turned her back on the visitor as if to speak to me, but her attention was fixed on their conversation. Overbury was offering some manner of aid, though I could not fathom how a recently made knight could assist an earl of ancient lineage. The conversation was punctuated at frequent intervals by Overbury wiping his nose on a plain handkerchief. Many nobles were spoken of and Robert Carr's name passed Overbury's lips like a prayer; each mention clearly annoyed the Earl, but Overbury was oblivious or unconcerned. Members of Frankie's family were also discussed. It was wondrous to me that neither the Earl, nor Overbury, felt it necessary to move away; they treated Frankie and me like children whose wits were too few to understand what they heard.

At the close of the conversation, the visitor gave the shallowest of bows and left before he was given permission. Perhaps irritated by Overbury's presumption, or maybe his own failure to correct it, Essex was short-tempered on resuming Purkoy's training. He snapped instructions at the three of us until we were exhausted. When finally he left, we trooped gladly back into the bed chamber. The fripperers were nearly finished sorting clothes into separate piles. Frankie lay on the bed with Purkoy in her arms, feeding him small biscuits.

"If you spoil him, he will feel his training all the harder," I said.

She looked at me. "You don't mean that."

I sat beside Frankie and stroked the puppy's fine coat, enjoying the smile on his face. When Brutus emerged from under the bed, I lifted him up to join us.

The women offered a price, about what I expected, and I was minded to accept on Frankie's behalf when she sat up and refused the sum. She proved a fierce and unashamed negotiator, bolder than I, and I am not shy. The women, resentful of being bettered, arranged to collect the clothes on the morrow and left.

The moment the door closed behind them Frankie turned to me. "What thought you of Overbury's diplomacy?"

I was amazed anew by her ability to hide her feelings in front of others.

"Very rude."

"Rude? Did you follow his meaning?"

"I heard ill," I lied, unwilling to admit my ignorance of Court affairs.

"He called my family 'ungodly.' He was offering the services of Robert Carr to voice to the King the discontent of our enemies: those who hate Catholic countries and Catholics in this country, those who blame us for Raleigh's fall, old, armored families for whom we are overly fashioned milksop upstarts. All this in front of me!"

"He thinks women and servants have no ears. Did you see how often he wiped his nose?"

"And never a sneeze."

"George calls his sort 'hypochondriak'. It is a form of melancholy."

"My brothers will make him sorrier still for his speeches against us."

Overbury's lack of courtesy toward Frankie was unusual, but his assumption of her impotence was not. When first we met, her sleeves were so tight she could not bend her arms and the long fingers of her gloves rendered her hands useless. Attire speaks for us; what says incarceration? It is an unpleasant truth that a wife of high rank must sacrifice speech and independence of thought to her husband, and permit servants to perform every task, bar the procreation of heirs.

"Tomorrow we will shop at the New Exchange," said Frankie with a huge sigh, flopping back on the bed beside her puppy. "There must be some compensations."

Two months later, in early summer, Frankie took me on an extraordinary mission. Rain dripped from the velvet window curtains onto the floor of her carriage as we turned sharply under a gatehouse into a bustling courtyard. I had passed the Queen's palace on the Strand countless times, but never before been allowed entry.

Approaching the inner court, we were forced to a standstill by a vehicle coming in the opposite direction. The drivers argued as to who had precedence. Minutes passed and a queue built up behind us. Frankie ordered her footman to talk to the passenger in the other coach. After the briefest of exchanges, he ran back, trying to keep his wig dry in the downpour.

"The coach belongs to Sir Robert Carr," he said.

"Is the King in there?" Frankie asked, perplexed. As a countess, she had unarguable precedence over a knight, even a favorite knight.

"No. Nor Sir Robert. It is Sir Thomas Overbury inside."

"Does he know whose way he blocks?" asked Frankie, amazed.

"He did not ask."

"Tell him to make way," she ordered, sitting back in her chair. "That man's insolence is beyond crediting!"

It took some time for Carr's coach to back up and there was a riot of shouting and cursing by the time it was accomplished. Frankie opened the curtains fully as we passed through the gate. She waved graciously to Sir Thomas but he was reading papers and took no notice of us. We looked at each other, astounded by his incivility, then burst into laughter that I hope he heard. Why we found it so funny is hard to explain; nerves were surely part of it (I had hopes of the occasion and had hired expensive apparel to wear for it), and watching a cock strut around his little kingdom is comical to those who can put him in the pot whenever they choose. Frankie had told her father and brothers about Overbury's meeting with Essex and they had assured her that he would be taught to show her respect. It seemed the lessons had not yet started.

We drove across the inner courtyard to a gracious sweep of stone steps up which we ran to get out of the rain, the footman hurrying behind with the large linen bag I had brought with me. At the top, just inside the doors, our way was again blocked, this time by Sir Robert Carr, rubbing his arms against the cold. He bowed.

"Silk is a brave choice for so foul a day," teased Frankie, ignoring the need for an introduction. I loved how carelessly she broke the rules of engagement.

"Overbury took my cloak," he said, "and my coach too. I'm sorry he tried to barge through, he's always in a hurry." At least I think that is what he said. He seemed to be making great efforts at clarity, yet his accent remained somewhat unfathomable to me. England's Court had to learn a new language to understand their King and his Scottish nobles. "Sir Robert Carr, your servant," he said. Perhaps in Scotland you are allowed to introduce yourself to others? I prefer the English way. It is occasionally frustrating but deters strangers who would pester you for favors.

Frankie swept past him and Robert Carr followed us up the

stairs, his presence somehow welcome; perhaps it was his unguarded enthusiasm that made him appealing. He was also exceedingly handsome. He tugged the bag from my hand as we climbed, hoisting it over his shoulder like produce. It was said that the King had started to involve Carr in affairs of state, but I found it hard to see that he would contribute much; the man had no cunning. Perhaps that was why he kept company with Sir Thomas Overbury, who had wiles enough for them both.

At the top of the stairs was a very large chamber with long windows looking down onto a formal garden that stretched all the way to the Thames. The walls were hung with tapestries and the floor covered with woven rush, I could smell the meadowsweet in them, but still the place was noisy. There were at least a hundred people gathered, all of them hoping to gain something for themselves. It was thanks to Frankie that I was among them.

Several weeks previously, I had mentioned to her my financial woes. It took courage; I feared she would think I befriended her solely for advantage. As a daughter of the King's Chancellor, I thought she would have little notion of the consequences of debt. Her kind are immune from arrest for it; George and I risked imprisonment if we could not improve our situation. Our embarrassments had arisen, in the main, through our friendship with Frankie. The slight amelioration in her marriage and the transformation of her appearance resulted in other courtiers hoping I could work the same effects on them. As spring opened into summer, I found myself advising ladies how to make their own façades as impressive as their titles and grand houses. On occasion, I was also asked to accompany George. He would let blood and examine the stool; I would offer cordials and suggest a change of wardrobe. In this manner we saw to inner health and outer beauty, and demand for our services outstripped the time we had available. Rather than this vexing our clients, we became ever more sought after. How strange is life at Court.

However, our growing acclaim raised us to more elevated circles, requiring greater outlay to maintain appearances. Our eventual expectation was a knighthood for George and a Court position with a generous stipend, but our coffers were draining in the meantime, what with buying or renting suitable clothes and hiring a carriage in which to travel, to keep our finery clean as we moved between London and the Court at Westminster. The coachman and groom were not in livery, of course, but still they had to be paid. Our other major outlay was gambling. I hated it and so did George, but anyone seeking preferment must indulge. With no wars to occupy our noblemen, they defend their honor with duels and high-stakes wagers. We did not play at their tables but when invited to join a smaller game it was an insult to refuse. A courtier needs a thousand a year at the very least, an earl five thousand, and that is if he has no official position; much more if he has. Hospitality and entertainment, a well-appointed town house, clothes, traveling coach and town carriage with grooms, drivers, footmen, horses, livery and stabling, and gambling; these are the barest requirements for a nobleman and do not include the hangings, furniture, glassware, plate, cabinets, spices and other luxuries that come from around the world to London's docks and bring additional honor to the homes of those who can afford them.

The income from my patented starch recipes covered the wages of our servants, which were generous at twelve pounds a year, and the clocks and crystal I received in return for my skills I sold to pay our most vociferous creditors; but our combined earnings were about a quarter of what we needed. Having witnessed my parents' rapid decline, I did not consider it a sin to want better for my family, so I had finally asked Frankie for advice. She had appeared to take little interest, but later I realized that this was from tact, for some weeks later she extended to me the most extraordinary invitation of my life.

"Will the Queen notice us in this crowd?" I asked.

Frankie tried to hide her smile but failed. "This is where supplicants wait," she explained, leading me toward a pair of guarded doors. Was I not a supplicant?

"Sir Thomas Overbury didn't wait to see the Queen," interjected Carr. "There's no love lost between them."

"He is bold to let that be known," said Frankie. "She is kind to her supporters but terrible to her enemies."

"I'm only telling you."

"You and the Queen, however, are great friends?" she said, eyebrows raised, and Carr let out a great bark of laughter.

"I've been sent to make it so."

"I wish you luck," said Frankie.

"Aye, Sir Thomas said it was a fool's errand."

There was not a hand's breadth between their heads. He was flirting shamelessly but at the same time appeared lost; he had no friends at the Queen's Court and was hiding behind our skirts.

We were only halfway across the room when the doors opened and the Queen was announced. Conversation ceased; the air filled with the sigh of silk as we sank low. I was not alone in peering through my lashes at the tall woman who walked into the chamber. She had a nose like a sail. Her face was too long to be pretty, the chin too bulbous, but it was the noblest countenance ever I beheld. Her fashioning was a mistake to my mind, all girlish bows and ruffles, when her countenance was that of a prince, but I approved the white ruff, wired up to cradle her head like a shell, magnificent jewels pinned to it. These jewels appeared in all the woodblock prints I had seen of her; the C in emeralds was for her brother, King Christian of Denmark, and the S in sapphires for her mother, Queen Sophie. She liked it to be known that she was the daughter, sister and mother of kings, and, as such, held a better pedigree than her husband.

She nodded greetings or exchanged brief words with petitioners. I felt hotter and hotter as she neared, my guts bubbling with elation as she reached our little group. I stared at her shoes, each adorned with a pink silk rose larger than my hand.

"Lady Frances, rise. How is your mother?" said Queen Anna, in an accent from the Continent, laced with Scots. Frankie's mother was Keeper of the Queen's Jewels but not among the first tier of ladies-in-waiting, who were all from the Essex camp. The Court of Queen Anna welcomed those who found no favor with the King.

"In good health, ma'am, thank you," said Frankie, at ease in a situation that was making me sweat.

"And this is Mistress Turner?"

I was so shocked to be mentioned by name that I might have

toppled sideways had Robert Carr not put a steadying hand to my elbow.

"It is, ma'am."

"Rise, Mistress Turner."

I did, shamed as I heard my knees crack. The Queen ignored it; we are of an age. "Your yellow starch has become quite the fashion."

I bobbed a curtsy like a dumb kitchen wench. I could find no words. Frankie rescued me.

"Mistress Turner is as modest as she is talented, ma'am."

"Come," the Queen said to us, as if Carr were not there. He remained doubled over in a deep bow as I took the bag from his grasp. I passed the obeisant throng, pretending it was me to whom they paid homage. I enjoyed every moment, who would not? When again would I have a great crowd of people at my feet?

We followed the Queen into her privy apartments. That she had noticed my designs was even more wonderful to me than the King's attentions, for she is admired and copied, whereas the King is prone to eccentric dressing and would never take advice from a woman.

The room into which we were led also faced the river and was filled with light and reflection, even on this wet day. Ladies-in-waiting of different ranks were gathered. Some I knew, for I had fashioned them or George had purged them, but most I did not. Their eyes, guarded and expressionless, watched us as we entered.

"Let me try on something yellow," Queen Anna said, as if it were forbidden, like tobacco, although I knew she was not timorous. Frankie had spent hours telling me of the wondrous masques the Queen commissioned every year, with women appearing on stage, moving scenery and outlandish, often military, costumes. The King railed against women adopting men's dress but the Queen clearly enjoyed being armed and victorious.

I took from my bag the finest ruff I had ever fashioned. Her ladies came to unpin her own and replaced it with mine. They tucked the matching cuffs into her sleeves and a long mirror was brought. Only one kept her distance. I knew her to be Lucy Russell, Countess of Bedford, the Queen's favorite and influential in all matters; her parents, staunch Protestants, were the guardians of Prince Henry and brought him up in their household. Frankie was afraid of her, for she was clever in everything from poetry to politics, and an open adversary of the Howards and their allies. Although possessing taste, she was restrained in fashion and stood aloof from our experiment with yellow.

The Queen looked at herself a long while, without expression. If she disliked my yellow starch the news would ripple through the Court and out to the far edges of the country in days; George and I might not survive it. He had stressed this to me when Frankie first suggested the meeting; "Nothing ventured . . ." I had replied, but was now regretting my lack of caution. Never had a face said so little as the Queen's at that moment. Beyond the doors I could hear chatting and laughter; how I wished to be back out there.

"They are brave," she said, finally, "but I am not so brave."

I felt heavy in every part. To agree was insolence; to contradict, also. Frankie was very still beside me. The Queen turned from the mirror and looked at us. Was I meant to apologize? Doubt froze me.

"And so I will require more from you than your starch." She smiled. It was as if a shutter had been thrown open to flood the room with sunlight. Frankie let out her breath. The ladies-in-waiting began talking at once, especially those already in yellow. I was still cold from dread and thought it would take me a week to recover.

The Queen led me to a mound of lumpy sacks in one corner. She spoke quietly, so that only I could hear. "I would welcome your talents, Mistress Turner, to turn these clothes belonging to the late Queen into something more of the moment. I know you do not sew yourself," she added, even in her majesty not wishing to cause offense, "but a change is needed. I am always in a crowd," she said, her voice intimate, "and I must stand out."

Although not long immersed in Court intrigue, I understood her words. For the first time in her long marriage, the King was raising a favorite above her. She needed to recapture his love or, at least, his respect. She faced the same difficulty as Frankie: engaging the attention of a husband who was not interested in her.

I pulled the clothes from their sacks like a necromancer summoning corpses from the grave. Still perfumed with the dead Queen's scent, some were encrusted with jewels and gold thread and stood up, as if their late owner still occupied them. I was not alone in feeling her ghost among us, for the Queen offered thanks to God for her predecessor's long life. The Protestants looked uncomfortable, as if we did some sort of magic, but Frankie and I were at home with such prayers; in gathering darkness, flanked by glittering husks of power that the current consort sought to inhabit herself, I found credit with the Queen and her ladies as if I were, indeed, a magician.

"They stand about like guards," said the Queen, eyeing the stiff garments.

"I am a great believer in armor, Your Majesty," I said, forgetting myself in my relief. She looked at me with a wry expression and suddenly laughed, very loud and long, so that we all stared in wonder for a moment before joining in.

There was dignity and courage in the Queen that I admired deeply, beyond the fact of her crown; that she wanted me to display these qualities on her body I took as the greatest compliment. She called for her seamstresses, her French musicians, and for wine and biscuits to be served.

Once I had chosen the best pieces, she told her ladies to try on whatever they wished from the remainder. Queen Anna, her maids and I retired behind a tiring screen. As I stripped her of all girlishness, she spoke of her mother, still living, whom she described as a wise and affectionate parent and the most learned woman in Europe. The latter she mentioned without embarrassment; I have noticed before that foreigners prize learning, even in women, whereas in this country we hide it, as if the pursuit of knowledge is not godly. The Queen's message was clear: her mother had withstood forces in Denmark that sought to fetter her. Queen Anna would do the same. She would not allow her authority to be diminished by her husband's love for Robert Carr. I wondered if he was still waiting outside and if he had any idea of how much the Queen hated him.

Lady Bedford came to the Queen and asked permission to leave, which the Queen gave. Beyond the screen, I could hear the other ladies calling their maids to pin a ruff, fold a partlet, raise a skirt, tie a shoe. The more that was drunk, the louder they became. It amazes me how much the rich drink. At one point, Frances meandered by, hunting for something to wear on her head.

"Is your husband's health improved?" the Queen called out.

"Yes, thank you, ma'am," Frankie said, coming near.

"I find our husbands very alike," Queen Anna said, having herself drunk enough to untie the tongue. "Both suffered greatly in early childhood, both lost their fathers, both have mothers who were unable to care for them. It makes them hard to love but you must persist; there is no joy greater than is to be found in children, and only your husband can give them to you." Frankie smiled and curtsied deeply, if a little unsteadily, and the Queen waved her away.

Studying her reflection gravely, the Queen assessed my tactics. I endeavored to read her face as I replaced the woman with the warrior, setting out to meet her husband, monarch to monarch. I exposed her chest to the nipple, leaving an expanse of white skin above, smooth as metal, interrupted only by the ruff that haloed her noble head.

I expected her to lose courage, to demand I reverse my work. She would not be a rare wife who did that; for all those who sought my aid, there were a hundred afraid of it. I finished by pinning her great, jeweled letters to the golden ruff. When I stood back to admire her, I could not read her expression. As we emerged from behind the screens the room fell still, despite the drunkenness of most of its occupants.

There was a long pause during which the ladies, all tricked up and slightly askew, took in the new Queen before them. Her Majesty looked so serious. After what felt like an hour, but was probably moments, she laughed. Oh, lovely sound!

Her ladies clapped, long and hard. The Queen walked over and kissed me on both cheeks. She called her musicians to play and instructed her grooms to fetch any gentlemen still waiting outside. About twenty trooped in, among them Robert Carr and my own Arthur. I chuckled like a rook as he stared at me, quite unable to fathom how I could be in the monarch's presence. He looked around the room and then took my hand and kissed it with such fervor I was afeared the Queen would notice. She put up with a great deal without taking a lover and I did not want to earn her disapproval having just won her trust.

"If we could always be thus," he said, enjoying the novelty of our being together in his world rather than mine. How proud I was of his love. He was a handsome man, a coming man, and many sought to betroth their daughters to him; but he was faithful to me.

Robert Carr strolled past and I could not resist calling out to him.

"What a time you have waited!" I admired his courage in entering a Court where he was loathed, to win over the Queen and her supporters. His use of fashion I also approved. Where I drew on the power of male attire to embolden ladies, he understood that womanish beauty invited possession. Carr's surfaces were all silk and velvet, spangled and brightly colored, irresistible to the magpie King whose dull plumage was brightened by the sheen of those he kept close. Carr's shoulders touched mine, although he was looking at Frankie.

"It was worth the wait," I think he said.

Arthur seemed dumbstruck that in a single afternoon I was better connected than he was after six years. He took my hand again, proud of my advance.

"You have won her over," said Frankie, coming up to us, quite drunk. I'm not sure she even noticed that I was standing between Arthur and Robert Carr. "I would not be surprised if she asked the King to knight George," she said. "'Lady Turner,' how does that sound to you?"

The dance ended at that moment and my cheeks blazed for shame the Queen had overheard Frankie's presumption. The room was full of chatter and laughter and yet she turned toward us. What must she have seen? I flinch to think of it. Frankie and I, flushed with dancing and our paint smudged; on one side stood my lover, holding my hand, on the other the man Queen Anna most hated at Court. Without the slightest change in her expression, she turned back to her musicians and signaled for another dance. I could not quite enjoy it as before.

"Will you dance, my lady?" asked Robert Carr of Frankie. She lowered her eyes and did not reply. It amused me that although very drunk she would not stoop to dance with knights, even charming ones. "Will you?" he asked me. I was honored to be his second choice and danced two in a row. Carr had the knack of making people feel that nobody else interested him. His humor was warm and not too clever, which suited him very well, for otherwise his extreme handsomeness would have kept him apart.

"Can you persuade her to dance with me?" he asked as he led me back to Arthur and Frankie. I wanted for her the pleasure of dancing with him; but she was implacable in matters of honor. He looked so wistful that Frankie laughed. Then he did too, knowing himself ridiculous. He gave her a deep bow and walked away to find another partner.

"Frankie?" I was nervous to introduce her to Arthur; she understood his place in my life, although I had never been explicit. She turned to study him, taking note perhaps of his age, somewhere between mine and her own, his handsome face and apparel, but I sensed she saw him very differently from the way I did. He executed an extravagant bow but Frankie struggled to find something to say. Perhaps she was thinking too hard of what she must avoid discussing, such as children and spouses.

"I understand that you are a keen falconer?" she finally managed. Arthur did his best to be witty, but there was no sympathy between them. Even so, she allowed me happiness where I found it; we were generous to each other in this respect as many are not. Frankie knew as well as I that everything conspires against happiness. Chance, time, the rules of civilized life, grief, pain, an imbalance of humors, all make it extraordinary that any of us are ever happy. When we are, it is fleeting.

It struck me that Frankie and Arthur could be jealous of each other, wishing themselves sole beneficiary of my love, but I immediately dismissed the thought as extreme hubris for which God would punish me. I prayed to my angel to keep me from too great pride and vanity, for all that I depend on those sins in others. I had reached a place beyond my most preposterous dreams that day, thanks to Frankie; I was not ready to fall.

It was three in the morning when the Queen withdrew and the

party ended. Several of the ladies-in-waiting were asleep on cushions, gentlemen lolling in window seats. Precious pieces of the old Queen's clothing were scattered about like furniture broken in a fight.

"Shall I accompany you to Whitehall?" asked Robert Carr of Frankie, as her coach was brought to the door. The puddles had frozen and he was shaking in his silk, slightly damp from exertion. She ignored him and gave me great kisses on both cheeks before climbing in. "We're both going the same way," he persisted, smiling at her hauteur. "Your maid is with you, there'll be no talk."

As the driver reached his seat, her hand appeared through the unglazed window, holding a fur rug for him to put over his shoulders on the walk home. He took it and blew her a kiss. She sat back so that he could no longer see her and Robert Carr set off walking, throwing the rug over his head and shoulders, like any bog-dweller, laughing.

Arthur was low in precedence in this august group and it was a long time before his coach was summoned. We fell asleep against each other on the journey and were too tired, once we reached his apartment in St. James's Palace, to take advantage of a rare night alone.

From that day, for almost a year, I was entirely happy.

F ive days after Christmas, I sat with Barbara beside a good fire, Mary asleep on my lap. She had woken with a fit of coughing and come downstairs. Her little sister Katherine did not want to sleep alone, so she was curled on Barbara's lap. Henry, finding himself the sole occupant of the bed, had also come down and was sprawled on a floor cushion with the cat. I knew I should get them back to bed but we were too comfortable to leave the warm parlor. Around us were remnants and half-made poppets. Henry had cobbled together some cloth soldiers, veterans of fearful campaigns, so disheveled and misshapen were they. Katherine's dolls were slightly less gruesome and Mary had arranged hers, elegantly sewn although she was but six, on George's chair, little dishes of sweetmeats in front of each. The sweetmeats were a gift from Frankie and the children had spent much time sucking the gold crests from them, laughing at their glinting teeth. I had not seen Frankie for a few weeks. George and I avoided Court over the Christmas season, for the King and his nobles gambled and drank so much that a single evening there would ruin us.

A coach rattled into our street but I did not stir; George was dining at the College of Physicians and would not be home until midnight at the earliest, somewhat merry, accompanied by Sir William Paddy and his armed guards. It was a bad time of year to be out beyond the curfew. London was swollen with visitors, all bored of country mud and Christmas guests. The rich toured the royal tombs at Westminster, the Tower lions, the camel on London Bridge and the playhouses. The poor begged alms. Those not satisfied with meager charity cut the purses, and sometimes the throats, of bewildered tourists and drunken locals.

Barbara and I chatted quietly. She was soon to remove to the household of Baron Ellesmere whose second wife, Arthur's aunt, had offered her an advantageous position. The household was on the Strand, a short walk away. Barbara could meet a good sort of husband there. I had been much preoccupied with finding one without such obvious defects as would accept her with so small a dowry.

The coach stopped at our door and immediately I was alert. The knocker was dropped and Barbara and I listened as old Maggie answered. I stood, Mary's sleeping form still in my arms, and opened the parlor door. The cold in the passage was thick as mist.

To my astonishment, Frankie's brother stood in our hall.

"Good evening, Mistress Turner," said Harry Howard, with a low bow. Although long-married and many times a mother, I still felt like a young girl before these peacocks of the Court; their clever quips, polish and perfume, snared one. Harry was two years younger than Frankie and the glow of his skin made me want to stroke him. I did my best to curtsy.

"None of that!" he cried, pulling me up and kissing my cheeks and Mary's head. "My sister is outside." Barbara came to the parlor door and Harry gazed at her. I would not introduce them, for he was not to be trusted with pretty girls.

"Does Frankie require me?" I said, shifting Mary's weight in my arms.

"*Require* you, no, she thought you might be as bored as are we. Though that cannot be the case in such company." He lunged for Barbara's hand, caught and kissed it. "Bring your cloak and pattens," he said, as if to her, "nothing else is needed."

"Barbara," I said, "Richard Weston is in the kitchen and your father will be home around midnight. Sleep in my place and give Mary one spoonful of the syrup if she wakes with coughing. No more than three spoons before morning. Lay her against the warming pan, she must not get cold."

Barbara nodded, took Mary from me and climbed the stairs without looking back at Harry. I was proud of her dignity.

I called old Maggie to bring my best cloak and overshoes and to take the other two children to bed. After several weeks of careful domesticity, I was ready to breathe some different air. Harry handed me into the carriage, although two footmen stood ready to do so. Frankie was asleep in one corner while two of her elder brothers, Theophilus and Thomas, dozed opposite.

"We've had a long afternoon at the tables," explained Harry, talkative for a young man of seventeen or eighteen, "but we won more than we lost, which I believe is a first for us all. We are celebrating."

Frankie roused, saw me beside her and opened her arms. "Dearest Anne, I wake and you are here like magic."

We embraced and I settled beside her as the coach jolted into motion. At times, our friendship had the ease of loving siblings.

"Where are you taking me?" I said.

"Ah . . ." she said, holding a finger to her lips. "My brothers think I need to learn new tricks to win over my husband." She put her head on my shoulder and fell asleep immediately, the smell of wine strong on her breath.

"The King held a game yesterday," continued Harry as if there had been no interruption, "that only those with three hundred pounds on their persons could attend. Lord Salisbury lost five hundred at least. You can buy a decent house with that! He must wish the King had not made it a fashion to lose money to him at Christmas."

I tried to look impressed but tales such as these made me feel very far from Court life.

When we reached Temple Stairs, I roused Frankie and we huddled in our cloaks as we crossed the Thames in hired wherries.

"I hope my husband appreciates the discomfort I suffer for his sake," she grumbled. I thought he might. The seduction of Lord Essex was a project in which Frankie's brothers had recently involved themselves, mainly for sport, but also because the discontent of the Essex faction, further stoked by Overbury's machinations, was increasingly plain. If Frankie could produce an heir, a child in whom mingled the blood of enemies, they thought the Essex crew would need to complain less, or at least more quietly, at being overlooked for Court positions.

"He did not wish to accompany you tonight?" I asked.

"He abhors Christmas. He is forced to spend time with people and occasionally to dance. He is in very choleric humor."

As we neared Paris Garden stairs, Frankie handed me a full-face mask.

"Wait," Theophilus said as he uncorked a silver flask, took a long swallow and handed it round. I went last, not cheered by the grimaces of the others as they drank. The liquid tasted so strong my mouth puckered, as if filled with vinegar, but almost immediately a sense of hot vitality flooded my body from crown to toe. All tiredness vanished and my eyes felt larger and able to see in the dark.

"What is this?" I asked, thinking to take it after sleepless nights with Mary.

Theophilus winked and grinned. "You are not the only potion-maker, Mistress Turner. Come, the Queane of Holland awaits!" He climbed the stairs as he tied on his mask, then walked off, arm-in-arm with his brothers. I followed, mystified, until I stopped so suddenly that Frankie barged into me.

"I have heard such scandal of the place I did not believe it existed!"

"The most wicked in all the world," agreed Frankie, the glee in her voice not muted by mask and hood. She linked her arm in mine and pulled me along, not wanting to lag too far behind her brothers. I felt as I had done when Harry related his tales of gambling: out of my depth off an alien coast. Holland's Leaguer was the most infamous brothel in all these Isles and, possibly, beyond.

The gate into Paris Gardens was busy but all made way for us, for there was no mistaking a party of courtiers, masked or not. To the western end of the vast enclosed field, somewhat obscured by greasy smoke from cookshops, I could make out baiting pits, skittle alleys and taverns. We walked away from their stench and noise along a bricked path. Almost immediately we left the throng and the air cleared. Bushes of rosemary and laurel lined the way and in the distance I could see a fortified manor of great age whose gatehouse was topped with spikes, as at London Bridge, although here there were no heads impaled upon them.

At the gatehouse, Theo handed a token to the keeper, who examined it carefully before tossing it in a bowl and waving us through a wicket door set into the huge, studded gate. The manor was built to withstand a siege. We crossed a drawbridge over the moat, guarded at each end by halberdiers in black and orange, as if the Royal Mint lay within and not a bawdy house.

We followed Theo, Thomas and Harry through a formal garden, neatly kept even in those days of winter. As we neared the door, it was opened by a man so large that he blocked out the candlelight within. He stood aside to let us pass and, once inside, I saw that his complexion, hair and eyes were all white and pink. He wore a black waistcoat above ballooning orange hose that reached his ankles, all his garments of silk. The enormous muscles of his bare arms twitched, as if kicking their way out of his skin. Servants, also in black and orange livery, removed our outer clothes. They took the brothers' swords and daggers.

Theo then stretched one arm theatrically toward the giant. "Ladies, this is Hartmann the Dutch. Do not be fooled. His name means that he is full of strength, not of heart. He is Queane Donna's personal guard and my friend. Now he is yours too." The great white giant nodded and twitched again the muscles of his arms. Frankie squeezed my hand, not from awe, I suspected, but a desire to laugh.

When the servants had gone, Hartmann pulled aside a thick curtain to his left, allowing noise and light to pour out. He indicated that we should enter. Frankie's brothers, clapping each other on the back as if they had achieved something, stepped into the room. I checked that our masks were still in place and followed.

Immediately we were in a different world. Here as elsewhere were shadows and human misery no doubt, but that evening they were banished by a display of glistering wealth and all that opens to it.

The great hall was lit with so many candelabra it was as if the sun's rays had been caught and released inside. What first drew my eye was a stage at the far end of the chamber, on which was a golden throne. On it sat a woman, unmasked, her large white breasts entirely naked. From a distance, it appeared that her nipples were gilded. The rest of her body was encased in purple silk, shot with orange, her plump arms visible through the orange gauze of her sleeves. Short skirts revealed pretty ankles in gold stockings above high-heeled shoes. On her head was a jeweled crown and her face, round and attractive for her age, which I guessed was similar to my own, was carefully painted. Behind her throne stood three young women and two girls. The three were dressed in similar fashion to the Queane, although in different colors and with less ornament. All had naked breasts, with nipples unnaturally red. By contrast, the two girls wore ordinary country clothes. Their hair was loose and long, but their heads were covered with plain coifs. They looked like they were being brave.

"Come, let us pay our respects," said Theo, leading us through the thronged room. Although masked, I dropped my head for fear of being recognized. Frankie did not. It took us some minutes to push our way, through clouds of smoke and perfume, past noble bodies trussed and swagged in every hue and stripe. My eyes, behind the mask, missed nothing.

"May I present Queane Donna Britannica Hollandea," said Theo, gazing at the throne's occupant. Close to, I saw that she was, in fact, old enough to be his mother, but that did not seem to bother him. She nodded at the Howard brothers, who executed the sort of bow one gave a real monarch. I was shocked at this treachery but around us people laughed and even clapped.

"Queane Donna rules here at Holland's Leaguer," he explained, indicating the walls. I only noticed then that they were covered in portraits, each with a gilded board beneath bearing a name: Rose Alba, Donatella, Laura, Phoebe, Daphne . . . It took me a few moments to grasp that these portraits were of the queanes on the stage and those moving between guests, pouring wine. Also prominently displayed was a sign: "King James Stuart slept here."

Harry laughed when he saw me staring at it. "He likes Bess," he said, nodding at a full-length portrait. The figure was seemingly that of a woman, but the gauzy cloth around her hips did not obscure the masculine nature of what lay beneath. Under the mask I could gawp as much as I chose, and I did.

"I thought this place was naughty. So far it is much like the Court," Frankie said into my ear, sounding bored.

Our party was handed cups of wine by a young drab. "I need a little courage," I said to Frankie. She clinked her cup against mine and we lifted the masks to down the contents. Little dishes of stewed prunes were also passed around. "Don't bother with those," she said. "They cure syphilis but that, thank God, is one predicament we do not face." Another queane was handing out small linen bags with fat, brown pellets inside that smelt strongly of nutmeg and vinegar.

"Stick it up your whibwob before he gets started," the young drab explained, "to stop a baby coming."

"The smell alone would be sufficient deterrent," said Frankie.

The noise soared with the general drunkenness and, I confess, Frankie and I also grew merry with wine. Many looked repeatedly at the stage. Something more extraordinary was to happen than the tableau thereon. Harry suddenly shouted, "Rabbie! Over he'e, Rabbie!"

Harry's Scots accent was delivered with such precision and seriousness that it took me a few moments to realize that he was hailing Sir Robert Carr, who grinned beneath a mask that hid only his eyes. Beside him, also narrowly masked, was Sir Thomas Overbury, pursing his lips at Harry's mimicry of the King.

As Carr made his way toward us, all eyes turning to watch his progress as sunflowers follow the sun, I had a sudden picture of Queen Anna before my eyes. She had not made me her chief dresser but often asked me to design clothes for public occasions. In them, she was strong and powerful; out of them, she was still ignored, for her husband was entirely besotted with this young man eagerly approaching us. Upon him were heaped estates, titles, responsibilities of government, and kisses, such that the hatred of other courtiers, both Scottish and English, kept pace with his vertiginous rise.

Carr slapped the Howard brothers on the shoulders with a forwardness they suffered only for the sake of further sport with him. Carr glanced at Frankie. She did not acknowledge him. Thomas nodded and walked off toward another group.

"First time?" asked Harry of Carr.

"For Sir Thomas," he replied, as Overbury reached them.

Harry and Theo ignored him.

"Which one's yours?" asked Harry, waving at the portraits. Carr looked at Frankie, again.

"I just come to drink," he said, avoiding the question rather well, I thought. "Have you met Sir Thomas Overbury?" he said, before Frankie's brothers could divert him. They were forced to acknowledge him. Overbury should have replied with a low bow but gave the briefest of bobs. I had never seen so public a snub; instantly the air around us thickened. Frankie pulled me to her. Carr laughed very loud and slapped Overbury on the back, as if to remind him to bow, but Overbury ignored his friend and did not break eye contact with the Howard brothers.

"You are server to the King? How do you find it?" asked Theo, stepping closer to Overbury and removing his mask; he was a head taller. It was widely known that the King did not like Overbury and Theo's smile conveyed this perfectly.

"An honor," said Overbury.

Harry moved to stand beside his brother and also removed his mask. He was shorter but broad-shouldered and together they made a formidable pair. They would have been trained since childhood in the use of arms while Overbury was at his books.

"Does the King like his meat cut thin or thick?" Harry asked. Overbury flushed with anger and did not reply.

"He likes it red and plentiful, like his wine!" said Carr, laughing. Theo and Harry kept their eyes fixed on Overbury. I could not imagine what had persuaded the man into this place, which held everything he most despised. Was it simply to keep Carr company? There were, of course, whisperings about the manner of the friendship between them. Overbury behaved toward Carr with the presumption of a man toward his wife, acting and speaking in his name. The King, although above earthly law, also loved Carr in public beyond what any other man would have dared. Such gossip greatly augmented the loathing directed at this pair.

Overbury attempted to move his friend away but Carr was eager to remain in our group, which promised him conversation with Frankie.

"We have excellent hunting at Audley," said Theo, putting his arm over Carr's shoulders and separating him from Overbury. "You must visit. Are you acquainted with my sister, the Countess of Essex?" Frankie's eyes widened behind her mask but she had no choice but to acknowledge Carr. He bowed very low and she gave him her hand, which he kissed devoutly. Neither of them mentioned the previous occasion on which they had met.

At that moment music came from the stage. Without us noticing, the queanes had departed and smoke was now drifting across the dais. Men dressed as hags and witches had occupied it, playing instruments and dancing.

Overbury, a handkerchief to his nose, pushed his way back to Carr's side. "You said we would leave before the performance . . ."

"No stomach for the ladies, Sir Thomas?" said Theo.

"Not this sort," Overbury replied, his gaze raking Frankie and me. I felt my skin crackle with the fury this insult provoked. Frankie and her brothers moved as one against him, unseen by those around us who were mesmerized by the dancers on stage.

"Of course, you meant no disrespect," Theo said, over the music and drunken catcalls, leaning in very close to Overbury.

"Women who venture here defame themselves without my help," Overbury replied, openly sneering at him and his sister.

A flash in the candlelight told me that Theo had smuggled in a weapon. It was too dark to see clearly but he was pressing something, probably a small dagger, into the soft place below Overbury's ribs. Harry moved behind Overbury, making escape impossible. I thought Carr would dither, afraid to offend his new acquaintances, but he stepped forward with no fear of the blade.

"You're not helping me make friends."

"If you want to make friends with harlots . . ." Carr slapped his hand over Overbury's mouth.

"Teach your tongue manners or someone will cut it out," he snapped.

"And how then will you lick your friend's boots?" asked Theo.

At that moment the Queane's guard arrived.

"He has a blade," blurted Overbury to Hartmann, the moment Carr removed his hand.

"You have been troubling of them?" the Dutchman inquired of Overbury.

"He is armed!" Overbury repeated.

"You wanted to leave," said Carr, nodding toward the outer hall.

Hartmann took Overbury's arm but he whipped it free and walked out before he could be ejected. Carr immediately turned to Frankie and me. With a slight blush, he said, "I'm sorry for his rudeness. My friend's always offending somebody."

He bowed and made to follow Overbury. Theo and Harry looked at each other, trying to think of some way of keeping him with them, but it was Frankie who stepped forward.

"Stay, Sir Robert. Your friend can get home on his own two feet."

I could not tell whether she was growing to like this surprisingly diplomatic eye-catcher, who clearly admired her, or whether she had simply seen a way to show her brothers the power she wielded despite her sex. Theo put his arm around Carr's shoulders and led him and Harry off to a cupboard for wine, saying over his shoulder to his sister, "You've got studying to do."

Slowly, we turned toward the stage. On it, I saw such things as I never thought to see in my life. Frankie and I stood very still, too astonished to feel shame. We did not speak, nor drink.

When finally it was over Queane Donna, naked, stood at the front of the stage watching the audience intently. Her handmaidens walked the two country girls, who had cowered at the back throughout the performance, to stand either side of her.

"What is she doing?" I whispered.

"Taking bids," said Frankie. Sure enough, around the room, tiny signs were made. The spell that bound us, broke. I saw Barbara in those two girls and thought I would be sick.

"I must go," I said to Frankie. I threaded my way through the crowd to the entrance hall and allowed the servants to put on my outer clothes. As I went to the door, a massive hand came down on my shoulder. It was the Dutchman. Each time I tried to leave he respectfully, but firmly, prevented me. Frankie pushed her way through the curtain.

"Sir Robert Carr has gone to fetch my brothers, we will leave together," she said.

"I am sorry," I said, half-ashamed not to share the tastes of the highest ranks, at the same time appalled by them.

"I am glad to be leaving," said Frankie, as she was helped into her cloak.

"They've gone," Carr said, when finally he returned. He looked embarrassed and it was clear that Frankie's brothers had gone off with queanes or, worse, had won the bidding.

I made to leave but again the giant prevented me. I felt panicked. I wanted to be home, watching the faces of my sleeping children, away from this depravity. It seemed that I could not leave without an escort and no one here would waste their time on a married, middle-aged, middling sort like me.

"Mistress Turner, if you would honor me with your trust, I will gladly escort you to your door. I have a guard of four and my own sword and can offer you my protection." This was all said without a glance at Frankie. Robert Carr was responding to the distress he saw in me and I was moved by that and was sure that Frankie would be too.

"With gratitude, sir, I accept your protection."

Slowly, Frankie removed her mask. Her cheeks were pink and she looked pure and vital compared to what we had just witnessed. Carr stared at her.

"I too, would be grateful for your protection," she said, bestowing on him a smile that was brief but warm. He bowed, I think unable to speak, and accompanied us both home, across the river, to our doors. The gaucheness I felt at my own outburst was soothed by his obvious pleasure in rendering us service, and I was grateful to him. Frankie leaned against me in the wherry, laying her head on my shoulder; she thanked me for taking her from that place.

"I cannot think how my brothers expect me to learn anything from Queane Donna," she whispered, "except how to stomach crudeness."

For months after that night, Frankie did no more than nod in acknowledgment of Sir Robert Carr, but feelings for him began to stir her heart. She had reached an age to choose for herself whom to love and she was falling for a man who eminently suited her. It worsened her distress in her own marriage, for now she had someone to compare to her husband, and in no area did Essex triumph. It worried me that Carr's attentions to Frankie appeared to be overseen by Overbury, who could have encouraged them only in hope of the disgrace it would bring on her family if she were discovered in adultery. Frankie told me to stop worrying, that she had no intention of encouraging Carr, his flirtation simply made her feel more loved than did her husband's scowling.

Friendship with Frankie was bringing me the benefits I had foreseen; foremost among them, love. Although I sensed a slight distance between us, as was perhaps inevitable in light of our differing ranks and ages, we were like a happily married couple, our talents complementary and our shortcomings thereby ameliorated. My beloved George was invited to the investiture of Prince Henry as the Prince of Wales; a knighthood was likely to follow. Barbara had settled well into the household of Baron Ellesmere, John was almost ready for Oxford and Thomas had his sword, a gift from Arthur, although it did nothing to alleviate the young man's hatred of my lover. Mary's cough did not go away but it did not worsen. Richard Weston redoubled his efforts to recover debts owed us and by that means we kept afloat.

My angel keeper saw me laughing with Frankie, loving my family, dancing with my lover. He must have seen me satisfied and content in every aspect of my life and looked away for a day or two. It was long enough.

6

G eorge fell ill. It was the end of February and snowing, a little over a year after Frankie and I first met. The winter was unusually severe; the Thames froze solid, the water wheel with it. My husband asked me to bring Arthur to him, which frightened me.

"Shall I fetch Dr. Mayerne?" said Arthur when he arrived, bashing snow from his hat and boots.

"He will kill George with his foul mercuries. Sir William Paddy has been. He says George has a stone in his bladder." Arthur stopped shaking out his cloak and looked at me. We both knew several men who had died of the stone and few who had recovered. I hung up his outer clothes and he followed me upstairs. George lay in bed, our two elder sons by his side. John nodded at Arthur but Thomas ignored us.

George opened his eyes and beckoned me over, whispering that I must call for the priest. I sobbed on his chest until Arthur gently prised me off.

"Thomas," I said when I had composed myself, "go to my brother, he knows where to find the priest."

"He doesn't need a priest. He's getting better," said Thomas.

The difficulties with our eldest son began as soon as he could talk, which he did at a later age than his brothers and sisters. Year upon year of misunderstandings had hardened into a decade of hurt, on both sides, that brooked no improvement. Always, somewhere in my mind, I was trying to find a way to help him believe he belonged to our family as much as did his siblings, for he never seemed convinced of it.

"I'll go," said John and left the room. I heard the outside door close quietly.

Arthur bent down and George began to whisper to him with an urgency that could mean only one thing. Arthur cried; his shameless tears were one reason I had fallen in love with him.

"... There is little coin but a property ..." said George, staring at Arthur to compensate for his weak voice.

"Do not trouble yourself," said Arthur, placing a hand on George's forehead.

"Do not trouble *yourself*!" shouted Thomas, stepping forward as if to strike the visitor.

Arthur flinched but George appeared not to hear him, although people passing in the street must have done. My husband took my hand and placed it in Arthur's, as if officiating at a wedding. Thomas wrenched them apart.

George was too weak to shout but he held up a hand to his son who, with vile looks, took a step back, cursing us both. Arthur wrapped his fingers firmly around mine and relief confused my heart. If George died, I would not be left alone with the care of six children and a large household because Arthur would protect us; but I did not want my husband to die. I rarely lauded his part in my happiness; he was unnoticed but essential, like the foundations of a house. Love for this man completely filled my heart and I lifted his hand and bent to kiss it while not letting go of Arthur with the other.

At that moment the notary entered, ushered in by Barbara. If he thought it strange that a dying man's wife was holding hands with another, he did not say so. Richard Weston also appeared and George beckoned to him.

"Look after them ..."

"I promise," said Weston, although I wondered how this lowborn, pugnacious man could serve us.

"Are the signatories present?" the notary asked. Arthur and I nodded.

"Why is *he* an executor? Why not me?" said Thomas.

George closed his eyes and I squeezed my hands together to stop them from slapping my son.

"'As shall please my executors, I give to my eldest son, Thomas Turner ...'" The notary read on for a while but I was too upset to comprehend the formal and complex language of the Will until Thomas shouted: "A *ring*? You give *him* money to buy a ring, so he can marry your wife?!"

"'. . . engraved, "May Fate Unite the Lovers,"'" the notary droned on.

"You want the world to know you are a cuckold?!" yelled Thomas.

George tried to speak but could not be heard.

"Leave, Thomas," I said, quietly, hiding from George the fury inside me. The notary, acting as if Thomas were not in the room, held out the Will for us to sign but Thomas pushed Arthur away.

"Who are you to sign *my* father's Will?"

I grabbed my son's arm but he shoved me against the wall and pressed his forearm against my neck. It was not the first time Thomas had attacked me, but it hurt my heart more than my body. It pained me that he could not love his family, nor anyone, it seemed. In an instant Richard Weston twisted Thomas's free arm behind his back and marched him from the room, Thomas screaming in pain and abusing Weston, Arthur and myself with foul curses that we heard until he reached the end of the long garden and was thrown into the fields beyond with the gate locked behind him. Even then, he pounded upon it for far longer than most people would have done before giving up.

Arthur signed the Will and kissed George. "God bless and keep you," he said.

"I will make you a caudle," I said to Arthur, but he shook his head and kept vigil beside George until the priest arrived, disguised as a porter.

The youngest children trooped into the room and stood around the bed, quiet with fright. I lifted them, so that they could put their small arms around George's barely moving chest and kiss his stubbly face. He did his best to kiss them back and rub their heads, but trembled with the effort.

"'May the Lord Jesus Christ protect you and lead you to eternal life . . .'" the priest recited. When he had given George the final sacraments he left, Arthur following to ensure he went unmolested. The young children were led out by old Maggie, weeping.

Barbara gave her father a final kiss. John held George's hand, looking white-faced and lost. He kissed his father and then left us alone. I lay down carefully beside my husband and whispered in his ear. George moved his head slightly so that my lips brushed his cheek.

"Do you remember the day you came to ask my father for my hand? At first I thought you were too old, but you talked to me of your travels through Europe, of your studies in Venice, of how the women there wore their hair, of the fine mirrors, paintings, waterways and doges." Gently I threaded my hand into the open neck of his nightshirt and laid it over his heart, which trembled like a baby bird tumbled from its nest. I willed it to regain strength.

"After we married, you would run your fingers over my skin and name the organs beneath. You told me the humors by which each was governed, the places where the soul is hidden. I delighted in your words." His cleverness had averted my attention from his freckled body, his rounded belly, his back as bristly as a hog's. The pause between each shallow breath was growing longer. I blew on his lips, to lend him my breath. "While I waited for a child to be upon me, you spoke of medicine and alchemy, prouder of my wits than I was myself. The agony of that wait! Do you remember? We formulated the yellow starch recipe together, though how far from your interests that must have been. You cared only to distract me from my fears. And when Thomas was born, his tiny face so like yours, I understood how very deeply I loved you. I have never stopped loving you. Look how fine a family we have built."

I spoke to him of my mother, whom he would soon meet. The Norton family shattered without her to hold us together, shards landing close and far away, never again to form a whole. I was close to my sister, Mary, and younger brother, but not to my two elder brothers, by reason of their own characters and that of their wives. But I did not say that. I asked him to tell her that our marriage had been contented and blessed with children. She had talked to my sister and me often about love, but what we felt most was shame that she had lost her family position and brought upon us the condescension of our relatives; I regret that she died before I felt proud of her. "Tell her I love her," I whispered. For my father I had no message. If George met him in heaven, he also would struggle to find a good word to say.

I heard the household go to bed. I listened to the "goodnights" and closing doors that brought silence to the street. At midnight, the watch ceased his pacing. The bells stilled, until only one tolled the passing hours. I did not sleep; I listened, remembered and loved.

Just after the bell at four, the rattle and wheeze of George's breath ceased and he went quietly into eternal stillness. The little bird had perished.

I lay as motionless as my husband, but the room seemed to fall away, pulling the light with it. My heart dropped in my chest and I was suddenly cold and increasingly distressed that my shivering did not stir George. I held him tightly, perhaps I cried, I recall only the aching desire for him to wake. I clung to him until noises in the street warned me that the city was coming to life. With a final kiss I said, "Goodbye."

I rose stiffly and opened the window so that the angels could collect his soul for heaven, then I left him and checked on the sleeping children who were unaware that their father had died. I went downstairs to feed his beloved cat, which had been forgotten in the strangeness of the previous day. I checked the fire in the parlor, even though my companion of almost twenty years would never sit beside it again, talking to me about his patients. It was incomprehensible to me that ordinary things should be done, and yet I did them. The foundations had crumbled. I felt the press of his body against me, but now I was alone.

As custom and my grief demanded, I stayed home for a fortnight and did not venture beyond the parish for three months. George was buried with all due pomp, his coffin escorted by the men of our family and fellow physicians. My brother Eustace told me how it passed off and I was glad that so many of his clients and friends had paid their respects. Many visited us at home, but only once. I spent much time stroking George's cat and staring into the flames of small fires. The dirt and cold of March gave way to spring, but I did not venture into it for fear of tainting beauty with sorrow. For the children I put on a smile and gave them enough love for George and me both, but I was shaken. It was not only grief for my husband, but for myself. Mistress Turner was dead, toppled into the grave as irrevocably as my husband's body. Only thirty-four years old and still so much to give, but I was become a shadow, a ghost in black and gray. Widow Turner. Widows on the whole are a sorry lot, poorer than the cats on the street.

In May, the King of France was fatally stabbed by a Catholic fanatic. In response, sentiment in the City of London against Papists grew as fierce as ever I had known it. Broadsheets were posted on every available surface, with woodcuts depicting the punishment meted out to the assassin. He was tied, by each limb, to four horses; the distressed animals were then walked away in different directions until the man was torn to pieces. I could not wipe this death from my thoughts and dreams. I could imagine the terror of those poor beasts, by instinct careful of life, how they must have been whipped and yanked to pull that man's limbs from their sockets. The blood, the screaming of man and horse, the baying of the crowd—the horror of it woke me many nights and made me feel less safe in a City that was Puritan by inclination. Visiting foreigners disguised themselves as Englishmen, whether they hailed from Catholic countries or not, to avoid Londoners' violent hatred of outsiders. Our King's doublets were reinforced with yet another layer of canvas.

It was unclear how my children and I would live until the mourning period was over and I could marry Arthur. George had seen death too often to want to face it himself, the consequence of such weakness being a rushed and inadequately considered Will. Arthur promised to execute it in a manner that would keep us respectable, but I had been left only the usual Widow's Third in addition to the use of several rooms in the house for my lifetime and bequests of furniture, items of jewelry and so forth. George had been as generous as he could because he knew that Thomas would not be, but there were many debts to discharge. My eldest son insisted that the younger children and I quit all rooms in the house except for those specified in the Will. We crammed ourselves into three

chambers while he filled the rest with paying lodgers. He banned
Arthur's visits and forbade me to work. Arthur went to court on
my behalf, and I did nothing to annoy Thomas while waiting for
the lawyers to pronounce my worth. I was not unduly worried;
the Will barred Thomas from marriage until the age of thirty
and what father would put this in writing unless he feared for his
son's state of mind? I had three young children to care for while
Thomas had none. What judge would put such a son in authority
over a good wife and mother?

Frankie paid her respects as soon as she heard of George's
passing and became a regular visitor to Fetter Lane. My children
were in love with her and her two dogs, although George's cat
made herself scarce. Even Thomas behaved when she was around.
I would lend her a loose house jacket and she would open shutters
and stoke fires and attend to all the tasks she was forbidden to do
in her own apartments. I encouraged her to use her hands and together we sewed French Babies. It seemed Frankie was new to the
pleasure of friendship between women, the comfort we bring each
other when sharing labor and confidences. Her mother and sisters
strictly upheld the rule of obedience to a husband, never complaining, never voicing their unhappiness. Other women at Court envied Frankie or were afraid of her boldness. In that strange time
of grief, shuttered up with her and my children, she and I became
as close as fish and the water in which they swim, no secret too
intimate for us to share. These domestic moments rooted the profound sense of recognition we had felt in each other's company
from the start. I spoke of my grief and she of her mounting fears
that the efforts to end her virginity had failed and that soon her
husband would start to whip her again.

"The two Roberts in my life could not be more different," she
said on one occasion.

I raised an eyebrow at the idea of Sir Robert Carr being "in
her life," but he was certainly in her dreams. "Your love is wasted
on both," I said. "The one does not value it, the other cannot
marry you for it." It was true, though perhaps bleak. She did not
take offense. I think she was glad I understood the depth of her

frustration; to be the most beautiful woman at Court and not to know love. I was a good enough friend to tell her things she did not want to hear.

"My mother has affairs, why should I not?"

"She has given your father fourteen children, ten of whom she has kept alive, and he is a very different man from your husband."

On later visits, I saw bruises on her arms.

It was a strange spring, one moment brilliant with sunshine and empty blue skies, the next battered by tempest, the streets running with water in which floated ordure and the stiff bodies of small animals. They were months pregnant with the possibility of great advance or total destitution. I could marry Arthur and be higher in rank and fortune than even my mother had been before her marriage. Or fall entirely, bullied by my eldest son, lost to all society. I pitied myself, but I pitied Frankie more. My marriage, though arranged, had been a match of mutual respect and contentment. Frankie's had been motivated by politics alone. She admitted that she would be delighted if her husband dropped dead. "Not delighted," she corrected herself, "but relief would soon triumph over grief."

As summer arrived, four months after George's death, the lawyers decided for Thomas. The house was two-thirds his and he could rule in it as he wished within the bounds of law. I could not suffer his injunctions, and Arthur would not marry me so soon after George's death, so I moved out. I am a proud woman, it is a trait Frankie and I share, and I would not beg from Thomas or Arthur. Anyway, begging never gets people what they want.

I found lodgers for the three rooms in Fetter Lane and used the income to rent a cheap dwelling within the City walls that my younger brother Eustace helped me to find. The plague was bad that summer, as it had been the year before, so I chose as clean a street as I could afford in a well-run parish with a water conduit nearby.

I could no longer entertain friends, go to the theater or the Exchanges, replace worn-out clothes, have a maid to dress my hair, hire a chair or coach, go to Court or, indeed, go into any society that required smartness; I presumed that it would mean the end of my friendship with Frankie. The differences between us yawned too vast. The rich can never truly be friends with the poor. Arthur would marry me as soon as permitted by custom, but by then someone else would be holding her hand. I experienced a second wave of grief and postponed telling her for fear it would make it impossible for me to be brave for my children. She would find out soon enough, when she called at my door and only Thomas was in.

A few days before the move, when I had sold or pawned everything I could and was standing in the parlor, bare of everything but George's chair, his cat, a small table and a box of French Babies, an anonymous note was brought by a servant from Whitehall. It requested my urgent attendance upon the Countess of Essex, but it was not written in Frankie's hand. I spent some of my little remaining money persuading a carter to take me there. All the way I pictured in my eye different scenes, but only one made sense. Frankie was ill or injured and close to death, for why else had she not written to me herself?

At Whitehall no servant awaited me. A runner was sent to Frankie's apartments and a maid soon arrived who would only shake her head at my questions such that I wanted to shake *her*. She let me into Frankie's chamber but did not enter and closed the door softly behind me. The room was dim and tidy. Very afraid by then, I opened the bed curtains. It was an effort not to cry out. Frankie was lying on her back, her eyes open but her face entirely blank, as if dead. Only the high color in her cheeks told me I was not looking at a corpse. I touched her forehead and she flinched. I looked under her shift, but her skin was unbroken. From the river came shouts. Someone drowning? Being drowned?

I put a few drops of willow-bark decoction in some small beer, but she would not lift her head. I went to open a shutter and when I turned she was upending the entire contents of the vial into her mouth.

"That amount will kill you!"

She swallowed and turned away.

I used every persuasion but she ignored my pleas for her to

vomit. After that, I could not help myself. Each and every anguish of the past six months struck me like the stones of a collapsing wall until I was sobbing, holding her close. To lose Frankie, by my own medicine, was more than my wits could contain. How long we stayed that way I do not know, but it cannot have been long. Suddenly, she rolled away from me and pushed her fingers down her throat until her stomach was empty. She lay back, her face damp.

"How are you here?" she said eventually, her voice thick from the acid in her throat.

"An unsigned note."

"Someone must care."

I did not ask questions. I simply held her. After some time she spoke, conjuring in my mind's eye the events that had brought her so low.

She was accompanying her husband to Richmond Palace to celebrate Prince Henry's investiture as Prince of Wales. All three Courts were on the river, that of the King, the Queen and the new Prince of Wales, and she was wishing me there to witness the splendor instead of her husband, for I was better company even in my grief. They were in her barge as her husband had none; he called them a tremendous vanity but used Frankie's when he needed it.

"What is that on your sleeve?" Essex asked, as if it were stained.

"A silk favor from the King's factory and my sister's pearls," she said.

The Earl snorted. Frankie was relieved that his disdain outstripped his curiosity, for the favor had been left outside her apartment that morning with a note reading: *"This was spat by royal worms only."* There was no signature but the hand was not elegant; it could be Carr's, the color was his, and among the folds were sprigs of purple heather, betokening admiration, beauty and luck. But the Court was brimming with Scots and she prayed that this was indeed from Carr and not some crusty old laird with a fancy for her. She felt like Brutus and Purkoy, straining at their leashes to find a mate. When she passed Robert Carr, she let out a sigh that he might walk through a cloud of her lust. He was a flirt, she knew it, but since the night at Holland's Leaguer she believed he had elevated her to his prime quarry.

"Why do you count?" said Essex. Frankie had been adding up the moments she had been near her admirer that week, counting on her fingers without realizing what she was doing. They amounted to no more than a quarter of an hour, a minuscule fraction of life upon which to dream of happiness.

"There are so many Howard vessels," she said calmly, "fifteen at least."

"A swarm."

"I meant nothing by it; an idle calculation."

"Idle? You are never idle but always running about the Court and hanging around in passageways for attention."

Frankie did not look at her husband. "I was told that not for a hundred years has there been an investiture of a Prince of Wales. Prince Henry has so long wanted his own Court." As she well knew, her husband had yet to be noticed by Prince Henry in any favorable way. Although they had been brought up together as children and both were strict Protestants, the Prince was elegant, agreeable, a seeker of beauty and adventure, and therefore had found no bond with the adult Essex.

Her husband grunted. "He's another one you've been accused of lying with when I was away. Did you think he'd make you his princess?"

"You know that gossip to be untrue."

"He's a nobler target at least than the lapdog Carr."

"Sir Robert Carr?" Frankie laughed, pleased to say his name aloud.

"What ambition, to compete with the King for love! In looks I give you better odds, but the King trumps even you in dominion. Tell me more of Carr," said Essex, knocking the toe of his boot against her knee. In another man, it might have been an affectionate gesture. "The King's dog will never be loved by us even if he has changed his name; he loses the esteem of his own countrymen in so doing."

"I know nothing of such things."

"He shows loyalty only to vanity; his collar and doublet are French, his narrow sleeve from Italy, breeches Dutch, his slops and boots Spanish. He is a traitor to his own land."

Frankie only shrugged and looked across the water.

"Still the King loves him best," continued Essex, knocking his boot a little harder against her knee, as if this were her fault. "The King even loves your mother better than his own true servants."

"Perhaps she serves him better."

"It's not him she serves, is it?" he said. Frankie did not know whether her husband was referring to her mother's long-standing affair with Lord Salisbury or her stipend from Spain, earned as an informal ambassador, passing information between the English and Spanish Courts. Both circumstances infuriated Essex, less for the ambiguous morality they displayed than for the fact a woman was acting outside of home and duty to her husband, to which narrow spheres she should confine herself.

"Why don't you join the winning pack, husband—then you will not need me to inform you of those close to the throne but will be one of them yourself."

"I will not frizz my hair for the King. He heaps wealth on his favorite like a boy gathering flowers for his sweetheart, not realizing that his coffers have hard floors. He risks the standing of us all."

"What you speak is treason, not to mention poisonous."

"Poison? Tell me of it, wife. The Court is alive with rumor that you wish to poison me."

"You will die of your own discontent soon enough."

He leaned forward. "I cannot desire a woman who speaks for herself, dresses without modesty, and is unchaste and disobedient. No man would, but for that you wish me dead."

"You should join a company of players, my lord, you have a talent for wild imaginings." She reached up and yanked shut the curtains of the awning under which they sat; anger had an effect on his member that tenderness had not. She fished a leather flask from her hanging pocket and took a small sip.

"What wife imbibes while her husband goes thirsty? Unnatural woman." Frankie handed the flask to him.

As she described the scene to me, I experienced a moment of fear. In that flask was the strong aphrodisiac I had given her. What was she going to tell me? Had it done him permanent harm? George had persuaded Essex to take a tiny dose, twice daily, but since his doctor's death, Essex had stopped.

Frankie described how she had bent forward to retie the ribbon on one shoe, her breasts near popping out of her lacings as she did so. She was careful to keep her head lowered; Essex's arousal was often halted if he caught sight of her face.

He drained the flask and closed the curtains nearest him. Frankie begged God, as she retied the second shoe, that this time her husband kept his member stiff enough that he could penetrate her and a baby result. Essex reached forward and gripped her arm. He steered her until she was kneeling on the hard floor with her back to him. She did not struggle, knowing he preferred her back view. He tussled with the willow hoops and fabric that encased Frankie's lower half and pressed her face onto the seat so that the velvet nap rubbed painfully. She could hear and feel him fumbling to get his yard free while keeping up her skirts.

He talked, as if to soothe her. "You are beautiful, like the perfume bottles on your dressing table." Frankie was encouraged. This was the first compliment her husband had ever paid her. "When I stamp on those, they shatter. I can break you too." She tried not to feel the impact of his words, to think only of the better love she could have once Essex had broken her, but fear rose in her; he did not usually talk at all. Frankie prayed continuously that this torture would bring a child and keep him from her for at least as long as she carried it. He slapped her buttocks and the back of her head, lightly at first, increasing in force as he pressed himself against her.

He hit her harder and suddenly she understood that he did not want her virginity, for that was something she also desired, but to break her spirit. She tried to twist around, to show him her face, but he pressed his hand so hard over her mouth that her neck bent back until she thought it would snap. Her throat was distended beyond screaming.

Then she felt a searing pain and for a moment thought he had stabbed her. He had entered her where no man should. She tried to scrabble away but he slammed a hand onto her back. He grunted as he shoved, his free hand yanking back her head to throttle her screams. Tears ran from her eyes but nothing else of her was at liberty to move. He held on tighter, grunted a few more times, then let out a thin, hissing sigh.

Gradually, as if wary she would bite him, he peeled his hand from her damp face. A fresh surge of agony accompanied his pulling out of her, but she could not cry out for he leaned his whole weight on her back, pressing her into the hard bench. In her ear he said, "Tomorrow you can have this again, and every day after, until you are obedient. Then I may give you a child." He sat back on his seat, pushing his now limp member under cover.

As I listened to Frankie, her voice strangely flat, I was mute with fury and disgust. I had provided the aphrodisiac, but it encourages only what is already in a person.

Frankie explained how afterward the pain was too intense for her to move, she could only cover her face with her arms. Essex began to nudge her backside with the toe of his boot as if she were a lazy dog. Each time the nudge was sharper but Frankie stayed prostrate.

"Get up," Essex snapped, but she was thinking only that she could no longer endure her marriage. As if dragging her sodden body from the river, she hauled herself onto the bench. The hatred she felt for her husband then could scarcely be contained; although she had not wanted him dead before, she did now. What other escape was there from this devil? This man who inflicted upon her his loathing of women and his fury toward those who sent his father to his death.

The rhythm of the oars changed as the barge neared the stairs at Richmond, each answering jolt of the vessel agony to her. As the boat slowed, Essex pulled back the curtains and jumped out. Milling along the bank was a noisy crowd of courtiers peering into arriving craft. With exaggerated gallantry, he held out a hand to his wife. Nearby, her mother and sisters were nodding at this unusual chivalry.

"Out," he said. Now that he had discovered a way to punish her, Frankie saw that her husband had grown taller. She ignored his hand and clung to the pole of the canopy as she gingerly stepped ashore, feeling as she did so warm liquid running down her thighs.

"Stand straight, cow, or tonight I will come to you again," said Essex. Frankie did not cry, not even with rage, for loathing had replaced self-pity.

"My lord . . ." she whispered, such that Essex was forced to lean in to hear ". . . if you visit me tonight, or any other night hence-forth, I will report you for sodomy to the Court of Arches." Essex heard her, for his eyes narrowed in loathing.

"Why would they believe a woman?"

"The evidence is writ upon my body."

Frankie turned away and walked carefully toward her mother, more of his seed escaping with each step.

"If you treat him with disdain you will not keep in his good grace," said her mother, noting the return of Essex's scowl. "His mood seemed briefly improved." Frankie, feeling cold and faint, vomited onto the grass. The crowd moved back, their pleasure in the day further heightened by the Countess's display and the sight of the Earl of Essex storming away toward the palace buildings.

"Are you with child?" asked her mother. Frankie wiped her mouth with her handkerchief and allowed the Countess, alight with self-importance at the thought of her first grandchild, to steer her toward the palace. Frankie's two sisters fell in behind with long faces.

Her father and great-uncle bowed as they passed. Behind them stood Sir Robert Carr, his cape lined in silk the same color as her favor, laughing with the Earl of Dunbar. She sensed him look at her but hid behind her fan, convinced that he would notice her humiliation.

For three days Frankie plastered the courtier's mask to her face as the nation celebrated its new Prince of Wales. She watched the great sea fight on the Thames and a river pageant with Ancient Britain as its theme. She painted herself blue from head to toe and performed in Queen Anna's masque, as the river that runs through the county of Essex. She danced at parties and, on the final night, gazed with the whole city at the fireworks that lit up the sky and the water around her, but she saw only false stars.

"God will judge him," I told her.

"I hope so," she replied, without conviction. She looked at me and hesitated; did she expect me to treat her differently? She was defiant, ready to assert her rank if I showed condescension; but since George's death I too had felt weak, humiliated by my sudden poverty and the behavior of my son as well as, on occasion, my lover. I was frightened that she would sense the loss of respect I had suffered, which sometimes left me dull and angry, and discard me. Her violation by Essex made me useful to her again, though what sort of sinful-hearted friend was I to think that way?

She was shivering with the effect of the willow-bark decoction.

"Go to the Court of Arches. Tell your family what has happened."

"Let the world know of my shame? Essex would grow strong on it."

"They might allow you to separate from bed and board."

"Then I will be put out to pasture somewhere distant."

"Could you bear that?"

"I would be away from everyone I know. It is hard to be always alone."

We lay together, two birds exhausted from long migration. To my thinking, Essex's savagery set Frankie free from any obligation to him. The anger I felt revived my spirits. Although in my middle years and widowed, I was not ready to vanish either. Where once I was proud to call myself wife of a good man, I was not content to be shackled to a dead one. I warmed Frankie with my own body and rubbed her back when her tremors became violent, conjuring the ways before us. More than anything, it was important not to feel trapped. As when dreaming up a new design for apparel, I strayed around my mind, following paths until I found one that led somewhere. The sun set, and twilight lent its grace to the air.

"Perhaps there is another way," I said. For the first time since

George's passing, I felt a spark of excitement. I sat up and hauled her upright beside me. "I know someone who might help us."

"An assassin?"

"No! But we must go to him in disguise."

"Is it unlawful?"

"It is a little desperate, and no one must ever know we are that."

7

W e do not know the significance of some events until they are long gone; others are heavy with import from the moment they begin. Our visit to Simon Forman was the latter. It started with a nightmare.

It was early autumn before he could see us. He requested we arrive after eight o'clock in the evening, it being too light for his work before then, and so I slept a little in the late afternoon. The weather was unseasonably warm and the window stood open in my chamber. The stench of mud and effluent rolled off the Thames at low tide. It forced its way into my dreams. I saw in them the weekly Mortality Bill with George's name on it, but also Mary's, dead from a cough, and then all my other children's with the cause listed against each name: worms, griping in the guts, plague. My own was missing but, bereft of my children, I longed for death. Someone was throttling me. I was choking . . . it was a tremendous relief to open my eyes and see only my elderly maid's wrinkled face. I was soaked in sweat.

Old Maggie opened the bed curtains, prattling on about the river's stink and that it was never like that in Fetter Lane. The move over the summer had been difficult for us all. The place in Paternoster Row was three hundred years old and near collapse, but cheap. Richard Weston had tried to persuade me to retire to the manor George had bought in Bedfordshire, but I might as well have climbed into the grave, for the place was damp and we would all have been dead before the end of winter. Nor would there be any profit from its sale, for it was mortgaged. There were not enough funds to send John to Oxford or provide a dowry for Barbara. I, four children, old Maggie and a kitchen maid, were living in a decrepit terrace that felt something akin to debtors' prison.

On the day of the move, Richard Weston had hired a large cart and loaded it for me. We had walked behind to guard the contents from thieves, all of us in tears, the children clinging to their few possessions that I had held back from the pawn merchant. It felt like a funeral. Henry, only four, suffered the loss of his father very badly and this further grief and turmoil sent him into a silence that lasted for weeks. I missed George so much that it weighed on my chest like a great stone in unexpected moments, such that I wept when I found a bag, neatly packed for a trip he had expected to take, or when a half-sucked sweet fell out of his document chest. Even so, I was angry that he had kept from me the level of our debt. I rose every morning for the children's sake, though the crumbling of their prospects doubled my grief. Arthur visited when he could, with hampers of food and good cheer, but he was required to follow Baron Ellesmere to his estates for some of the summer months, the city too fetid and plague-ridden for the wealthy to endure.

A letter had arrived from him as I slept and at the sight of it my sadness lifted a little. I put it in my pocket to read when I was alone and tidied the house before I went out, only able to bear the daily drama of widowhood on an ordered stage. My skin had erupted in red patches since George's death, making my grief visible for all to see. As I neatened our few remaining possessions in the parlor, Katherine and Mary entered, ready for bed.

"You may choose a Baby each but be quick," I told them.

I opened the cupboard to the left of the fireplace on the shelves of which sat more than a hundred French Babies dressed in clothes of my design. I had nearly thrown them out when we moved but could not; they were the relics of my married life and I might have need of them to earn our living.

On the top shelf were the earliest examples, shabby things made when I was a child, kept only because my mother helped me to sew them. When I married, the maquettes became smarter as I had money from George to pay for better fabrics. Only one shelf was labeled with a date, 1603, seven years before but a different life; it was the year that I fell in love with Arthur, the old Queen died, and the new King's arrival was delayed by so fierce a bout of plague that the city was filled with ghosts. Our neighbor, a lovely girl, collapsed outside our house on her way to be married and was dead by nightfall. Every family on the street suffered loss except us. The Devil was cheated then and has looked for any careless-ness on my part. Since George's death, he has been breathing down my neck. I placed two French Babies into the hands of my girls and kissed them many times.

I was sad but not miserable, for I am not someone with my head on backward; the house in Paternoster Row was not ideal, but it would be only a temporary home to us. Once I was married to Arthur, we would live in a house even finer than that in Fetter Lane and I would be admitted to Court through my own honor and not by clutching to Frankie's hem. Arthur and I loved each other, and his was the world to which I had always sought to belong. There was a chance for greater happiness than I had ever known.

Richard Weston arrived as the bells tolled seven.

"What news, Weston?" I said, using the commonplace greeting of people not, in fact, much interested in the person before them.

"Please," he replied immediately, as if he had rehearsed all day what he wanted to say and must unburden himself of it before he forgot his lines, "now that I am no longer your husband's bailiff but your friend and protector by dint of Dr. Turner's dying wishes, might you not call me Richard?"

I was too astonished to reply. Weston had been our servant for so many years that I balked at acknowledging him as a friend. Yet he was the only man upon whom I could call when I needed pro-tection; Thomas refused, John was often studying elsewhere, my brothers either lived too far away or were busy with their own lives. In the end I nodded but did not look him in the eye, for fear he would see the dishonesty in my own.

"How smart you are," I said, finally taking him in, noting that his hair and beard had been barber-trimmed and his leather jer-kin replaced with a cloth coat. "Are you hoping to impress the Countess?" He winced as if I had pinched him.

"You should not be throwing your lot in with the Countess,"

he said, too free with his opinions; he had never dared advise me when my husband was alive. "Dr. Turner did not want her to meet Dr. Forman."

"Things are different now."

"They will be if you take her there."

"Why?"

"Your husband saw danger in it."

"Nonsense. For whom?"

"For you." He looked at me in a way that made me see that it was not for the Countess he had dressed up. Embarrassment distracted me from his warning.

The evening was still bright and Weston's lantern unlit. The steps to the street were broken and I swore under my breath as I carefully picked my way down. Our shilling-a-week house stood, or rather leaned, halfway along the south side of Paternoster Row, the middle of seven identical buildings without workshops. Its single redeeming feature was the view from the back into St. Paul's churchyard. Paternoster Row runs along the north side of Paul's and its mercers, silkmen and lacemakers attract the better sort whose coaches entirely block the way every day but Sunday. These same stroll about the church to gather the latest news until a little after eleven of the clock when they repair to the Castle for their twelvepenny dinners, or to the threepenny ordinaries if they are saving, to listen to the poets and philosophers and to show off their latest purchases. When their bellies are stuffed with capon and wine they away to a play; but at night, when the shops close, the place is unruly. Not a day went by when I did not resent my eldest son for forcing us out of Fetter Lane or pray that Arthur would soon take us away.

My neighbor, a widow barely keeping herself from the gutter, was making the most of the fine evening, sitting on the top step in her open doorway sewing a needle-lace trim for a handkerchief. Three of her children played around her like strays. None had shoes. Nearby a huge man, helped by his young apprentice, knocked a thick post into the ground to protect the houses from being pushed over by the crowds that clogged the street.

I had first encountered my neighbor a few weeks before, on the day I had moved in. The nosy termagant had not bidden me welcome but instead barked, "The beadles are strict round here. Don't be entertaining gentlemen—and observe the curfew." That first exchange with Mistress Bowdlery, for so she is called, dragged me from the gentility of Fetter Lane into the Stygian world of Paternoster Row, as fast as the current in the Thames pulls a man below.

"Good evening to you," I said. She eyed Weston and did not reply.

"You want one?" shouted the workman, holding the pole like a giant phallus.

I pressed south along the street followed by my escort, trying to shield my ears and eyes from the relentless rattling of presses that worked later than the mercers and lacemakers, the noxious fumes of ink and glue throttling even at this hour. Above the workshops, families, apprentices and servants were crammed into the narrow buildings and jutting pentices, built so close they blocked the air and light that would have alleviated the stench and the gloom.

Frankie was late, as ever. To avoid talking to Weston while waiting at the river stairs, I broke the seal on Arthur's letter.

Dearest Anne,

I pray that you are settled in Paternoster Row without too much disruption? I have left Baron Ellesmere but am called to the Prince for a fortnight at least, after which you may expect a visit from me. I miss you and the children as if I have an ache in my side and pray that you are all well and suffer not too much in your grief.

I have received the ten pounds George left me and hope that it will go some way to defraying your expenses. I do not forget his request that I buy a ring engraved, "May Time Unite the Lovers," but shall spend my own money in its acquisition. What a soft heart was his! I pray, my sweetling, that you be as fortunate in me as you were in him. I will try hard to make it so.

Your servant ever,
Arthur

I read the words many times, finding comfort in them. George had, in fact, requested *May Fate Unite the Lovers* be inscribed on the ring, not *Time*, and the mistake made me uneasy; I was not sure why. Were not Time and Fate sisters? My feeling is that they both work against us, sometimes gently, sometimes harshly, with the briefest interruptions when the tide flows backward for a happy moment, mainly due to our own endeavors. Of course, they are both just other names for the workings of God. I had renewed my efforts to stay in favor with my angel keeper after George's death; I needed God, Time and Fate to work in my favor while awaiting the protection of marriage. Prince Henry was a stickler for the correct observance of mourning and Arthur had warned me that we would have to be more cautious now that I was widowed. We could not be seen in public together and our letters were to be sent only with a trusted servant. I wondered if Arthur would be so punctilious if it were he who was living in a hovel, but held my tongue. I folded the letter. Weston looked at me as I put it in my pocket.

"Sir Arthur did not attend Dr. Turner's funeral, nor send servants to help you move; strange carry-on for a man who promised to look after you. Does he know you've little money?"

"He's away with the Prince's household," I said, piqued that Weston felt it his place to comment on a knight and courtier to the Prince of Wales. He shrugged, which also annoyed me, because I agreed that Arthur's travels were no excuse for not helping me to move. There was a long pause, during which Weston made it plain he wanted to say something but awaited my invitation. I did not give it.

Moments later, Frankie arrived.

"You look worried," she said when finally we released each other.

"I thought your husband had forbidden you to leave," I lied. Most people fear poverty as they do sickness and I did not want to test whether Frankie was among them. I needed her invitation to Court so that I could continue to offer fashioning ideas to women who would bestow gifts on me in return, which I could pawn or sell. Her family were denying her funds until she settled in her marriage and returned to behaving as she should: silent and uncomplaining. Yet she had never known scarcity and would not understand my present position.

90

Frankie sent her maid back to Whitehall and we descended the river stair, Weston going ahead. The wherryman helped us into the boat and we rowed across a strong current.

"I am sorry to be late. My maid promised to wake me, but she conspires against me. All my servants do. They are either in the pay of my husband or my mother. I am the last person they have to obey." Despite her words, Frankie appeared surprisingly content. She was looking about as if the world had been made anew that evening for her. The skin of the Thames was alive with craft of all sizes; the bricks of Whitehall and Lambeth Palaces pulsed red in the setting sun. Smoke from hearths was snatched from chimneys before it could rise and on the far bank fishermen hauled their nets into pitching skiffs, watched by herons, their feathers sharp in the thundery light.

"Some say Dr. Forman is a charlatan," said Frankie.

"He sees a thousand patients a year. Would so many see a charlatan?"

"Yes."

"He caught and survived the plague of 'ninety-four—do you know any other physician who can claim that? He does not flee from it, like most doctors, and helps both rich and poor. For that alone, I trust him. He is a true magus but a dreadful gossip. Be discreet."

"You have kept me from him so long because you think I cannot hold my tongue?"

"You could have gone to your mother. Does she not dabble in alchemy?"

Frankie laughed. "With the wife of the Bishop of Bath! The Bishop wrote a book on alchemy and now she considers herself capable of turning toothache into gold. I don't have toothache, at least. My mother is almost tender to me. She thought the arrival of my monthly bleed meant that I had lost a child."

"Why did you not tell her what Lord Essex did?"

"For fear she would not mind. To her, it is unthinkable to take a husband to court, whatever illegal thing they have done." Then she pulled a note from her pocket and handed it to me.

O, nature too unkind,
That made no medicine for a love-sick mind.
Thus wishing you in all your desires remedy, I rest,
Your true servant.
The pamphlet carries a sole name. She only is the remedy for your love-sick mind.

"That means *me*," said Frankie, leaning forward to point at the last line. "*I* am the remedy for a love-sick mind."

I suddenly felt my age. I doubted a poem could work such magic upon me if Eros himself wrote it; there is no leisure for giddy obsession once children arrive.

"Who sent it?" I asked, already guessing. Sir Robert Carr was perhaps the most handsome man at Court but he was not the brightest; someone else must have written the poem for him.

"This morning, in the Privy Garden, Sir Robert bent to pick up a handkerchief as our paths crossed, though I had not dropped one. When he handed it to me, I felt the note hidden inside. My sisters were only two paces behind, but they suspected nothing."

"Was Sir Thomas Overbury with him? He has more of a reputation for poetry."

"Yes, but these will be Sir Robert's sentiments."

I handed the note back to her. "You are flattered that he is too busy to compose verses himself?"

"You are too harsh! He is probably shy of his talents as a writer," said Frankie, retying the scroll.

"Sir Thomas Overbury takes great pains to write his friend's love letters, despite his disdain for your family." For the first time I saw danger in what I had thought a benign distraction.

We were close to the south bank of the river by then. Fishermen at the edge of the marshes pulled their catches into boats, the gills of the thrashing fish catching more firmly in the nets as they struggled. At Lambeth Stairs, Weston pushed aside moored boats as Frankie and I put on our masks.

"Why do you hire a man so old?" she whispered.

"He is loyal and strong and distinguished in his own way. He was caught counterfeiting sixpences and would have hanged had any witnesses testified against him but none would, and not because he threatened them."

"I know nothing about my servants," said Frankie, clearly surprised at the length of my answer to her question. "There's no point, it is impossible to keep them."

We climbed the stairs and followed close behind Weston. Lambeth is not so scabrous a place as Bankside, but the street leading from the river stairs is lined with bawdy houses.

"Feel a real cock! Posh cocks don't suffice!" called a bawd standing in a doorway, and I smiled to think of her surprise if I told her how active were most Court cocks.

As we walked away from the river, cobbles petered into hard mud, rutted by carriage wheels and infested with clouds of biting flies. We grumbled, as if Weston should somehow have arranged matters differently, until we reached a long pale against Lambeth Marsh that led to a house of some importance. The windows, containing glass in all but the attics, burned red in the last rays of the sun.

Weston knocked and a young boy let us in and took our outer clothes, although we retained our masks. The entrance hall had a gallery, on which an unsmiling woman was handing a cloak and mask to another. Both of them stared down at us as Weston was directed to the back of the house and we to the parlor.

"Is the sour woman his wife?" asked Frankie, taking the only chair.

"He calls her Trunco, though her name is Anne. She is forty years his junior."

"How awful to lie with an old ruin," said Frankie, forgetting that George had been Forman's age. "That explains her churlish expression."

"He is a very active old ruin," I said, thinking his unquenchable appetite for his female patients a more likely cause of his wife's unhappiness. That, and having to look after his illegitimate children, such as the boy who had opened the door to us. I removed my mask and admired the well-set garden with its neat beds of herbs and plum, apple, quince, ward, apricot and pear trees.

"The other woman was Lady Coke. I did not expect to see her

here," said Frankie. "She ran away from her husband, the pompous, self-righteous, Catholic-hating Chief Justice. Have you met him? He is a despotic bully. Lady Coke is full of life and a quarter of a century younger than he. Fancy seeing her in the hallway of a necromancer!" she laughed—though her delight was immediately extinguished by the realization that, if I was right about Forman being a gossip, her own secrets might soon be as widely known as those of Lady Coke.

There was no chance for us to leave. Footsteps crashed downstairs and into the room flew the man we had come to visit.

"Ah!" he cried, as if seeing us made his joy complete. Forman's manner of dressing always made me blink. That evening he was tricked out in a doublet of crimson, covered by a gown of turquoise lined with yellow shag. Green hose and blue stockings adorned his thin legs, and on his left hand he wore an immense ring. His dark eyes, already large, were outlined like those of a black-and-white creature in the King's menagerie called a lemur. Forman's wrinkles were white in their depths against a complexion burned chestnut from his many hours of gardening; any shift in his expression was shouted out by the stripes on his face. He had the same twitchy curiosity as that creature, the same haughty rump.

"My dear Mistress Turner, I miss George. How he loved you," he sighed, as if his own conquests of women were attempts to reach the level of affection George and I had attained. "As you know, I am no stranger to the pain of a broken heart. There is help for those in grief." He patted my hand, unaware that I was there only to accompany Frankie. I handed him a French Baby I had sewn with a design for his wife, requested before George's death. He eyed it with dislike, as if remembering why he had to mollify her. He shoved the poppet inside his open doublet, then turned and bowed deeply to Frankie, his hair flopping forward as if it also wanted to please. I had not told him her name but as I had only one friend among the high nobility, he would know who she was. Frankie waved vaguely at the bright little conjuror that he might sit, but he walked to the door.

"Follow me!" he cried.

George had told me that Forman only invited women to his study with whom he wished to fornicate, but even he could not hope to tumble us together. He showed us into a large, dimly lit corner chamber, crammed with tables, stools, boxes, strange stuffed creatures and pale forms in glass jars. He sat and opened a ledger on his desk, waving Frankie toward the chair in front of him.

"Your name?" he asked, charging his quill with ink.

"You write?" she said, sitting. I was surprised too. I had never consulted a physician who wrote before he smelt the piss-pot and I had kept my motions back for the purpose. I was discomfited by his unprofessional behavior.

"Urine and stool tell me nothing of the mind or the heart," he explained. "For physick to work you must trust the physician. The unity of mind, heart and body renders the cure efficacious."

"I am not sick," said Frankie.

"But you seek remedies for problems of the heart," stated Forman. Frankie shifted in her chair, probably impressed by Forman's perspicacity, or that of the angels with whom he conversed, but I knew it was not those holy messengers that informed him of her concerns, but good intelligence. The entire Court knew of the unhappiness between Frankie and her husband, as did every laundress, maid and coach driver who worked there. Forman had probably slept with Frankie's chambermaid to collect the gossip he needed. Frankie removed her mask. Forman blinked his lemur eyes at her beauty. I had suggested she remain masked and unnamed; as ever, she listened to advice, then did as she pleased. Had she forgotten already that we had just seen Lady Coke in Forman's hall?

"Lady Frances Devereux, formerly Howard, Countess of Essex."

"Abode?"

"Whitehall Palace, Greenwich Palace, Windsor Palace, Audley End in Suffolk, Charlton Park in Wiltshire and the houses and estates of my husband, sisters and brothers in London, Westminster and the country." Forman wrote "various."

"Age?"

"Your questions are outlandish."

"Illnesses, including those of the heart, are frequently peculiar to certain ages."

"Twenty."

"Ask me your question," Forman said, consulting the clock on his table and noting the time.

"Will I ever be free from my marriage?"

"You have no children and suspect none to be upon you?" he asked, without hint of censure.

"My husband cannot get children upon me." Forman looked up but did not press for details. He moved his quill to the opposite page and wrote, "Mistress Anne Turner, widow, gentlewoman, Fetter Lane."

"I am only here to accompany my friend."

"There is nothing you wish to know? Let me help you, there will be no charge."

"I am now in Paternoster Row."

"Are you?" he said, not quite covering his surprise at the rapid deterioration in my circumstances. "Your age?"

"Thirty-four."

"My dear, the years are kind to you. Six times taken to childbed?" I nod. "Your question?" he asked, noting the time.

To my surprise, there was not one question I could voice. Forman had been George's friend for many years. It would sicken him to hear about Arthur.

"Come, Anne," he encouraged me. Frankie stood and moved away to sit in the window and I, with some reluctance, sat in the vacated chair.

"When will Sir Arthur Waring be able to marry me?" I said, the skin on my face burning as if an iron swept across it.

"Is he in a position to?" said Forman.

"You knew?"

"George sought remedies for impotence while you gave birth to three children. I did not know who fathered them."

We sat in silence until Forman looked again at the clock.

"Would he consider you as a wife?" Forman himself was the lover of many women he had no intention of marrying.

"Of course! It is not *whether* he will marry me, but *when*. Arthur has an estate in Shropshire worth fifteen hundred a year and is carver to Prince Henry and steward to Baron Ellesmere. He suffers only the usual financial difficulties of any man at Court. There is little difference in social standing between us," I said, fanning my face with my mask. Forman's raised eyebrow tugged every line and wrinkle in his face.

"Admit all that worries you, Anne, or how can I help you?"

After some hesitation, during which I realized I wanted his help as much for myself as for Frankie, I conceded: "He is younger than me by eight years, currently stands in better credit and, before I was widowed, I made him valuable clothes."

Forman rubbed the fantail of his red beard, producing a sound that made me flinch. How did his wife suffer him?

"Sir Arthur has little reason to marry you. You bring no title or wealth, you have six children to support, and you can no longer offer him costly gifts."

"He promised George!" I said, hearing how ridiculous the words sounded as they filled the space between us.

"Even so," said Forman, clearing his throat as though embarrassed by my naivete, "Pisces will be ascendant over Leo, feet over heart. His tendency will be to run from obligation."

"His tendency? His *duty* is to provide for his children and their mother!" I said, furious because I was afraid that Forman was right to question Arthur's honor.

"His reluctance is a common ailment among men of fortune and good looks in whom the humors are out of balance through various forms of dissipation," said Forman, smiling. "Do not be vexed. There are ways to encourage such men."

I was too cross and embarrassed to sit still and could not look at Frankie for fear of what she was thinking of me. She had certainly guessed that my youngest three children were Arthur's, but she had not known that I gave him gifts. I walked about, tinkering with strange items on tables, remembering the six occasions Forman had correctly predicted the sex of the child I was carrying. His accuracy now frightened me. Frankie sat in the window gazing out, her expression peaceful.

The room had grown dark. By the light of the candles on his desk Forman drew two astrological figures and consulted a volume as thick as three bricks before writing tiny symbols into the figures. He was still but for his left hand twitching across the figures, pecking them with ink. Eventually he sat back and stretched his arms above his head.

"I will prepare a philtrous powder for use when the moon is not full and the stars and planets are in correct alignment. I will write the dates down for you and you must keep to them strictly. Stir the powder into strong wine but only a small measure or his limbs will shake. It will render Sir Arthur desirous but you must not give yourself to him until he has proposed."

"When will we be married?"

"The charts rarely give specific answers; here I see only that you will not make forty." His tone was so jocular the comment passed me by with little impact as he followed it with, "Or you will live to be very, very old. But I see that you will be taken care of."

I suddenly had hundreds of questions, about the children, Mary's cough, Barbara's prospects, how I was to survive until Arthur proposed, but Forman turned to Frankie's chart. She took my place and I hers. The Palace of Whitehall and the great houses on the Strand were silhouetted darkly against the night sky, a few of their windows faintly glowing. There were many lanterns on the river but the moon and stars hid themselves behind cloud.

"Do you wish to escape your marriage because there is someone else you love?"

"There is one I *like*, but my family loathe him."

"Is it for him you turn your husband away?"

"Not at all. Are you acquainted with my husband?"

"I have not had the pleasure . . ."

"There would be no pleasure in it, I assure you. He has abused and violated me in every possible manner. His hatred for me stems from the fact that my family called for the execution of his father for treason. How can I overcome that?"

Forman put down his pen and looked directly at Frankie. "It seems the Devil has scoured the seeds of forgiveness from your husband's soul. Should he be exorcised?"

"He does not believe himself at fault."

"He thinks witchcraft holds down his member?"

"He does not consider fault at all, except that it be mine. He hates me."

"And you him?"

"Recently."

"Do you wish him dead?"

Frankie stood abruptly. "What are you saying?"

"Calm, sit, sit . . ." said Forman, pulling the great ring off his finger and walking around his desk to show it to Frankie. She stepped back.

"This is an Eagle Stone put in nests by those great birds to enable them to propagate. Within the gem is a smaller stone," he rattled it, "no one knows how it gets in there. These stones are exceedingly rare and protect a woman from miscarriage if tied to the right arm. I wear it to protect against bladder stones, such as killed poor George, God rest his soul, and from fevers and plague. I was given it by a wealthy woman I treated for her inability to have further children after her fourth baby. She had bought it from a Venetian. Four times it proved effective but thereafter she lost every child. Weakened by miscarriages and gravely ill, she pressed the ring on me but I did not want it, it had lost its power. Then she confessed that the dead babies were not by her husband, who would not sleep with her after discovering her shameful secret: lust for her own brother. The stone had caused the product of incest to fail; it knew what she had kept secret from everyone. For my interventions to work, only the truth between us will do," he said. "Do you wish your husband dead?"

She sat down, unsettled. "How else can I be free?" In the silence that followed I could hear the tiny creaks of the window-lead cooling in the darkness.

"The sacred bond of matrimony can be broken only by the death of one party and I am bound by the Hippocratic Oath," Forman stated clearly. "Angels are not. They must be called in this case."

"Will angels keep a husband from his wife's bed? Or speed his death? Is that God's work?"

"Ah! I have broken my brains in studying the Providences of God. They are beyond our comprehension. We can but ask and they will do as He wills."

"Can they keep the man I like faithful to me while they work?" she asked.

Forman's eyebrows shot up and he laughed, giggled really. "You are used to being obeyed, I see!" It was some moments before he gained control of himself. Wiping the tears from his cheeks, he said, "I need his name."

"My lady," I warned. Forman placed his hand over his heart and I raised my eyes to heaven.

"Sir Robert Carr," she said, ignoring me, again. She had only herself to blame if by her indiscretion her family came to know of her liking for him.

"The King's favorite? Does he not have a friend, that strutting Sir . . . Overbury? Is it he who admires you but hides behind Carr's cloak?"

Forman's giggling had lightened the air around us. Frankie and I caught eyes and laughed so hard we had to put our arms across our chests for fear our laces would snap. One after another, images came to mind of Overbury making eyes at Frankie, each more ridiculous than the previous. Forman appeared delighted by our mirth and circled his hands as if to stir up more. "Not Overbury," Frankie finally managed to say, "he hates women even more than he hates us Howards. His tenderness is all for Carr and it is returned. Carr has come to believe he cannot do without Overbury's wit, mainly because Overbury tells him so."

Forman's expression was instantly serious. "Then he will go to great lengths to keep Sir Robert Carr from you."

Frankie held Forman's gaze. "I am not afraid of Sir Thomas Overbury. He is low in rank and too widely disliked to do harm. It is my husband I fear. He has already done me great wrong."

Forman sat forward, clearly entranced by Frankie. "'Then surely He shall deliver thee from noisome pestilence, for He shall give His angels charge over thee!'" he cried, before becoming as businesslike as any tailor or jeweler, describing the processes of his trade. "As a magus, I follow in the steps of King Solomon. Once summoned, a spirit is named and thereby bound to a master, who can then call it at will. To use spirits against a person or their property is 'Magical Assault,' punishable by death according to laws introduced by our King as soon as he climbed upon England's throne. That is why I call only on angels. They cannot be made obedient to man and act only according to His will."

It was clear to me that he was aroused by desire to help two beautiful ladies, but he was also transformed by excitement at the prospect of communicating with God's messengers. What greater project could there be but to bring happiness to His flock? What nobler calling than to help work His mysteries? It was an act of faith, there was no sin in it. From every pulpit we were told to put our trust in angel helpers, to know that God's guardians looked over us and kept us safe. The Pope had created a Feast Day for guardian angels two years earlier. Even the strictest Puritan would not question our belief that help came from that source.

Having laid out his stall, Forman cried, "Let us call them!"

He looked at us to ascertain whether we possessed sufficient courage. What he did not know, but soon would, was that the problem with us was a surfeit of courage.

Forman locked and bolted the chamber door, closed the windows and shutters and pulled thick curtains over them. He cleared a space in the middle of the cluttered room and from a box took three metal sigils that he hung around our necks.

"These will keep us from harm if devils appear. Remember that angels are stronger and their love higher than the others' malice." I cannot say I found this comforting. That I might see devils terrified me and Frankie too, judging by the set of her mouth.

"Bugs, witches, fairies, ghosts, imps, puckrils, goblins . . . they will not bother us, even devils will be thwarted. We will tell the angels our hopes but they will only be realized if godly."

Forman pulled away a carpet, under which was drawn a circle and within it a star.

"Witch marks?" I said, close to calling the whole enterprise to a halt.

Forman tutted. "Witches use them perhaps," he conceded, "but they are ancient symbols used by great magi." In the middle he placed a great metal bowl and lit pebbles from which issued smoke and sweet smells. Our priests never risked burning incense in

London, there were too many Catholic-hating noses in proximity, but I knew what this substance must be. He took Frankie's hand and led her to one point of the star, within the circle, and half-dragged me to the opposite. Forman put on a black cloak that covered him except for his head and arms and blew out all but one candle.

"When spirits and angels come, they do not like to be clearly known. Do not step beyond the circle; it protects you," he said. My eyes watered in the smoke, its dryness caught my throat. Frankie coughed. Among the shadows, I thought I saw movement.

Then he threw something into the bowl, which hissed loudly, and the room around us filled with pungent vapors. Forman began to chant and call in a strange voice and it took all my strength not to run to Frankie in my fear. She resembled a phantom in the pale smoke. Her head was tilted back, I suppose to watch the angels descend, and her curiosity and stillness calmed me.

I began to feel the effects of Forman's magic. The walls of the room moved in and out, the ceiling rose and fell, like bread proofing. The creatures in the jars began to dance and sing, and then, on a cloud of smoke, I saw Forman fly into the air. With my own eyes I saw it. His arms outstretched, he talked in a foreign tongue, at times listening and nodding eagerly. I looked to Frankie, rising like a lark; and when she stared at me in wonder, I knew that I too was floating.

Then I saw them. All above me like a veil over my head but not touching it, angels. So many, they flew as if joined in one heavenly murmuration, but among them I saw faces, hands bearing golden trumpets, great wings and flying hair like ropes. They looked through me with dark eyes that beheld the whole Earth and all the rings of heavenly beings right up to the seat of God Himself. Their song engulfed me, frightening and uplifting; I knew the wonder of flight without fear of falling. I heard Frankie cry out in rapture and my voice joined hers.

Held in the arms of angels, Frankie and I flew over the whole world. We saw every living creature from the smallest mouse to the monsters that live in water at the Earth's corners. We saw kings and beggars. For each and every living being, tree and rock, we felt the compassion of God. George was there. Arthur too. My parents, and their parents, and six generations before them, and my grandchildren, and their children, and six generations to come, all dressed in bright garments. When I knew in my heart that all would be well, I felt the angels lay me down. They left as they had come. I heard movement in the room. The bowl was removed, shutters and windows opened, a breeze blew across us. Forman held burned feathers to our noses and we sat up, exhausted and changed.

"They will help," he said, his features radiant with joy and peace. "Be prepared, for your lives are soon to change."

8

Forman's intercession with the angels started well. Arthur returned from the Prince's hunting trip a week early and sent word that he would call that evening. The house and its occupants were scrubbed and sweetened in preparation; I did not want him to see how low I was brought.

He arrived at twilight, when the street falls quiet and the watchman is yet to begin his rounds, the godly are home supping, the unruly buying their first drink. Although late September, it was hot enough for me to smell the coat of his horse through the window. Old Maggie opened the front door and took Arthur's hat but immediately retreated, for she had been soft on George and thought my lover a greedy cuckoo.

I pinched my cheeks to hide my pallor, for black clothes are only flattering if one is not actually suffering the effects of grief. I had spent some time thinking where to hide the flask that Forman had given me but the parlor was almost bare of furniture. In the end, I hid it in the folds of my shawl on a stool.

As always, I was caught by Arthur's beauty. He pulled me to his chest, snatching the cap from my head and covering my hair with kisses. Then he stepped back to examine me.

"Poor sweetling, has it been hard?" he said. I smiled through a spurt of irritation, for it was unpleasant to be called "poor" now that I was, and for him to imply that it showed in my face.

"It is getting better," I lied.

"I have missed you," he said, kissing me on the mouth. The pressure of his body and his lips softened what had become hard and knotted but, before I was ready, he released me and went back into the hall to fetch a hamper. While he carried it in, I poured him wine with a dash of Forman's brew, then sat by the fire so that its glow would bring my complexion to life and add sparkle to my tired eyes. From the hamper he pulled pies, cheese, fruit and wine, speaking quickly and a great deal as he laid out the picnic, perhaps to cover nerves? It was true that our love felt different without George between us.

"Thank you," I said, although he had not bought the ring or returned the ten pounds. Perhaps he had spent it on pies.

"Are you cold?" he said, reaching for my shawl.

"Hot!" I replied. Arthur took any tincture I gave him to improve his appearance or his love-making, but I knew that he would be highly suspicious of a substance administered secretly. Who would not? And if he found out that the decoction was designed to inflame his need of me, would that not, in fact, produce the opposite response?

"Some wine?"

Arthur laughed. "You think I need courage?" I handed him the cup. "A toast to your beauty," he said, and drained it.

That moment sticks in my mind. I worried that he would taste the infusion or note a difference in my expression, but I felt no guilt. I believed that if we married our union would be legal and blessed by God, our children would have safety and prospects, and he could know them better. I saw only benefit—was that wrong? Was it at that moment I lost my way? It is hard to ask God's forgiveness for an act that I cannot, in my heart, perceive as wicked.

As we ate, I noticed that his cheeks grew redder. He sucked at a drumstick as if caressing my own thigh with his lips; he toyed with the breast as if his mouth were at my nipple. He licked his fingers, shiny with grease, as if they were dipped in honey; his eyes became unfocused and yet staring. He put an arm around my waist and kissed me. He tried to unpick my lacings, an impossible task with one hand, and quickly grew impatient. He stood and pulled me up with him.

"Where is your chamber?" he said into my neck. I ran my hand over his soft hair and murmured nonsense. His complexion was reddening alarmingly.

"My darling, I cannot get a child upon me while mourning the death of my husband," I said forlornly, the torture of declining him mutual. "There are six months to wait." He chewed my earlobes and near deafened me with his breathing. "As you said, we must be patient." His lips moved to where my breasts swelled above the line of my undershirt and I pulled gently away but he would not let me go. He kissed me with such intensity that my body replied without thought for the consequence; but my mind was not slave to it. Although light-headed with desire, I walked to the door, opened it and called old Maggie to bring Arthur's hat, which she quickly did. My heart was trilling in my chest. I had never refused him my bed before and I sensed how it exposed and tested the bond between us.

"I will come again soon," he said, confused, even slightly angry, and I nodded but did not trust myself to speak, suddenly afraid of the effect of Forman's draft. Would Arthur seek release with another woman? Then I reminded myself of the angels, of Forman's face after we had flown with them. I could trust in this remedy; it came from God.

I snuffed the candles in the parlor and went to bed, distracting myself from thoughts of Arthur by pondering ways to help my neighbor. A friendship had grown between us since a cart had knocked down her eldest son, badly injuring him. Far from feeling remorse, the carter was suing Mistress Bowdlery for damage to his vehicle. Her youngest was sick with a cough that turned her lips blue, and all of them were hungry, all the time. The harvest was poor; it was said that dogs were become a delicacy in some parts of the country, and badgers dead of unknown cause were eaten. It seemed that when giving out misfortune, the Devil had mistakenly heaped onto Mistress Bowdlery all of my share. I sought to keep her alive, for otherwise that misfortune would need somewhere else to go.

The evening was so warm that I left the window and bed-curtains open to catch any breeze. The night bell struck the hours as I lay sleepless. After midnight I heard a knock. Moths were fluttering around the watch light, I could faintly smell their singed bodies, and beneath it stood Arthur, his face patterned with their tiny, dancing shadows. He was peering through the downstairs window and I nearly let him in, aching to feel loved and secure beside his naked body; a woman not a widow. But Forman was right; I had given him everything and must give no more until the comfort of marriage was offered in return. I went back to bed, putting my whole trust in God, His angels and Simon Forman.

So it went throughout that autumn and winter until a year of mourning had passed and we gathered to remember George, on the tenth day of March, 1611. It is a Popish belief, much frowned upon by those not of our persuasion, and so we did it in darkness.

"We cannot wait longer or the Watch will have us," said Richard Weston, only his face and hands showing in the faint candlelight in the parlor, a "parlor" in name only, for I had moved my bed into that room, my two youngest girls sharing it with me, and let my bedchamber to a sign painter for threepence a week.

"Something must have delayed him," I said, moving toward the door and signaling the children to follow. I had wrapped them up against the cold of early March. Mary and Katherine had grown bickersome and pale since George's death, Henry was very quiet although he did speak sometimes. Thomas had refused to join us but Barbara and John had been given permission to leave Baron Ellesmere's house for the evening. I could not afford to send John to Oxford and he had gratefully accepted a position in the same household as his sister. There was a chance they would send him to study, if he proved himself useful and loyal to the Baron.

Mistress Bowdlery had asked to join our party, for her husband was in the same graveyard. Although not a Catholic, she was highly superstitious and had some notion that, if she begged near her husband's grave, he might more likely hear and come to her aid. On my last visit to her house, I noticed that she had placed little bottles near every door and window.

"Witch bottles," she had explained. "Urine and pins ... keeps them out." I hoped they would prove effective and stem the flow of misfortune she had suffered since her husband's death.

Weston took the lead and we set off in somber procession for the churchyard. We had gone but five paces when I heard my name being called. A servant was waving after me. I went back and took the packet and note he carried and he left immediately; no reply was sought. The note was from Arthur. In it he expressed his deepest regret that he could not join us at George's grave; the Prince had called for him without notice, but he did not want to delay giving me the enclosed. In the packet was a gold ring into which was pressed a small ruby. Engraved inside were the words, "*May Fate Unite the Lovers.*" He must have read George's Will again, for now Fate had replaced Time, and that made me uncomfortable anew, for was Fate not fickle where Time was relentless?

No matter. He had finally given me a ring and in the box were coins to the value of ten pounds. With these I would pay some debts, especially that to my old maidservant. The ring was too large and so I placed it in the box and handed it to Richard Weston to safeguard. By the time we set off again, the children were shivering in the icy wind.

"He proposes in writing?" said Weston quietly so the children would not hear, his scorn apparent.

"The Prince called for him."

"Does this Prince not go to plays? 'Defer no time, delays have dangerous ends,'" scoffed Weston. Sleet blew in our faces.

"Do not quote at me, Weston. It was not a proposal but an explanation. If it suffices for me, it should for you."

To my astonishment he reached for my hand, despite the witnesses behind us. The younger children stared, the others looked away and fiddled with shawls and hats to keep out the freezing rain. Weston's hand was warm despite the bitter weather. "I would not wait for others to tell me when I could ask for your hand. I would marry you tomorrow with all pride and pomp and tell the world you are my wife."

You will judge me, but I felt only anger. I had never sought nor encouraged Weston's affection, and his enthusiasm made Arthur's punctiliousness more painful to bear. Weston made it clear I should feel humiliated by my lover's careful observance of propriety, whereas I strove to view it as courtly necessity.

"You challenge Sir Arthur for my hand?" I said, not warmly.

"I would be proud to win it." He looked me in the eyes and would not budge from that windy spot until I acknowledged his gallantry.

"I am grateful for your concern," I finally said and walked on, not caring if I led the way, for it was too dark now for others to see. Weston seemed content to follow and took both Mary and Henry in his arms for they were chilled and sad. His care for us melted my heart, I do not deny it, but not in any way that I could repay with my naked body. I had married an old man once already; once was enough. From that night on, I broke into a coughing fit whenever Weston attempted a romantic phrase; in credit to him, he did not recoil from me.

My brother Eustace awaited us at George's grave and with him, disguised as his servant, the priest. We knelt on the bitter earth, picturing George sleeping beneath; we prayed to shorten his time in Purgatory, but I would have dug through the iron-hard ground with my teeth could I have brought him back to us. Weston knelt at our side to shield us from the frigid gusts, but nothing could.

Despite the philters and the angels, Arthur did not propose to me at the end of the first year of mourning. I remained in black, worked quietly for clients at Court, and sustained my family by pawning the gifts I received as payment, and with rent from lodgers and the modest stipend Arthur provided. I kept my exact circumstances from Frankie but took my children to see her whenever possible, that they might eat their fill and play with her dogs, the parrot and a new pet monkey, Caesar, so named because he did everything he could to torment Brutus. She would tell me the latest gossip and of Sir Robert Carr's rise in favor; at only twenty-five years old he was to be granted an English title, Viscount Rochester, and would therefore be the first Scot to sit in the House of Lords. Her observation of him was intense and unwavering, but at no time did it spill into indignity. She hid her feelings for him from everyone but me, confessing that his seeming devotion amused her, but nothing more. And I believed her.

She did not ask to visit me as she had when I lived in Fetter Lane; I suspect she understood that I could not welcome her as I would wish. I went often to Forman, always accompanied by Richard Weston, to devise new prayers for the angels and tinctures for Lord Essex and Arthur, to keep one away and the other keen. Frankie did not dare come with me; someone had written to her husband, warning that she sought to poison him. Was it Overbury, afraid that Robert Carr's attachment to her was eclipsing him? Essex crowed to receive "proof" of the suspicions he had long held about his wife, as if it was some form of victory.

Two months after our visit to George's grave, the angels gave me a message: they persuaded me to go to a bearbaiting. I loathe such entertainment and declined Frankie's invitation when it came, but Simon Forman sent me a bottle labeled, "Fortifies courage: large swig on rising. Avoid at full moon." Accompanying the bottle was a note, enthusiastically scribbled. "Throw off your widow's weeds! George would want you happy. The angels say go out! They will do the rest!" The imperatives made me anxious, but Forman could see the future and was telling me to find myself a new place in life, even as a widow. I did wonder if Frankie had asked him to persuade me.

On the morning of the event Frankie was half-dressed when I arrived. I handed her a parcel of biscuits made by the children. She opened it immediately and ate one.

"Margaret and I used to make biscuits in the shapes of beasts in the menageries: camelopards, a walrus, crocodiles of course, the white bear cubs, an ostrich," she said, her mouth full. She led me behind a screen where a tub steamed beside the fire. She had dismissed the servants and herself helped me remove my graying clothes. It was the first time that I had been naked before her. My body was thin compared to her fullness, but I saw only love in her eyes.

"I have put lavender in it and there is orange oil for afterward." She lined the tub with a sheet and helped me in. After the months of standing washes in my cold and drafty chamber, to fully submerge myself in hot water was better than any meal, or wine, or even money. The smell of lavender filled my nose with summer as I sat there like a queen. Frankie perched on a stool beside me, nibbling biscuits. She looked at the ring on a thin black cord around my neck.

"Arthur has proposed?"

"It is his intention. Prince Henry insists on two years' mourning, especially for Catholics, so we must wait another half year." I did not tell her that George had specified the giving of this ring in his Will and left the money for it.

"Prince Prude! He has a box at his Court into which to put money if you swear. If we had that at this Court, we'd all be bankrupt and the King's debt solved." I saw that Frankie was pleased I could not yet marry and she could keep me to herself, which flattered and annoyed me equally. My heart had been mightily sore when Arthur had explained the need for another year of mourning.

Once the water cooled, she helped me out and wrapped me in a warm sheet. It was shadowy and sweet-smelling behind the screen. She stood close, unembarrassed by my nakedness, pressing the linen to my skin. My heart began a crazy thumping; I understood completely what drew men to her. To be loved by Frankie was like the gift of power; rich with possibility and danger. Her husband was afraid of it; Robert Carr was not and nor did he want to rule her. I believe the nature and intimacy of our friendship had shown Frankie what she wanted. Our devotion to each other grew from mutual esteem. And attraction.

As if she shared my exact thoughts, Frankie leaned in and put her lips to mine. The shock of it slowed me and brought my every sense to its sharpest point. I felt the difference between the pressure at the center of our lips and the tender exposure at the corners; across them blew the slightest breeze; where her body was closest to mine, the air was thicker. It was a sincere acknowledgment of our love.

Before I could respond, she stepped back and wrapped the sheet around me. She led me out from behind the screen, dressed me in silk, and brought color to my face with paint.

"Arthur will not be able to wait," she said, steering me to the looking glass. The woman I saw was delicate and beautiful but also a confection; Arthur would struggle to recognize me. I had dressed boldly as George's wife, but always in fabrics suitable to our rank.

We left her apartment and walked to the river gate, her arm linked in mine, the swish of silk around my legs exhilarating. The beauty and wealth that seeps from silk through skin, Frankie was giving me. I was afraid to like it too much, as I could not afford it myself, but for that day I reveled in my borrowed cocoon.

Frankie prattled as we walked. "My sisters will be with us. Elizabeth is too thin, her old ruin of a husband suspects her of taking a lover." She talked too much and too fast when she was nervous, and it struck me that she had a secret. Her chattering was to keep me from questioning her.

"*Does* she have a lover?" I asked. Frankie looked at me sharply; I suppose it was a rather direct question.

"She does, but it's not how it seems. They were betrothed and in love and three weeks away from being married when Baron Knollys was widowed. His wife was about a hundred but if she could have held on for a few weeks, my sister would now be happy. Instead, my parents broke the betrothal and gave Elizabeth to the old Baron. She was eighteen and he was sixty."

"There are more and more speeches made against such matches," I said, shaking my head at the horror Elizabeth must have felt, forced to bed an old grandfather instead of the youth she loved. I had met the Baron. His nickname was "parti-beard" because his long, grizzled whiskers were yellow around the mouth, gray in the middle and white at the ends. He looked as old as God.

"Her lover is in prison for refusing to take the oath and she is growing as staunch a Catholic as he to revenge herself on our parents. Our mother is furious. She thinks religion is to ease our existence, not make it harder. She does not want any more of our family executed for it." For once, I agreed with her mother.

We sped downriver in Frankie's barge, her sisters giving me the briefest of nods as I settled beside her. What Frankie had said of Elizabeth was true: her hair was so pale as to look gray, the effect of premature aging completed by her thin cheeks and furious gaze. Catherine was as plump as Elizabeth was gaunt, her hair a polished auburn, but she had a watery sadness about her. In the two and a half years since her marriage, she had borne and baptized three baby boys; all had been taken to God in the first few weeks of life. The urgency to produce an heir meant she would be allowed no rest and would be pregnant again soon. She seemed as adrift in her grief as her elder sisters were furious with their own unhappiness. I wondered how the nobility had survived so long, given the exhaustion of those required to bear heirs and the discord in so many of their marriages.

The journey was fast and smooth compared to the wherries I was used to. At the Tower, the Court was crammed onto a new viewing platform of the King's devising over the lion pit. The Powder Plotters would have done better to save their gunpowder and saw through the supports of the stage instead, to have the royal family, the government and the highest nobility tumble into the mouths of lions below. I received approving looks and felt increasingly at home in my grandeur, sure it would bring me further commissions and encourage Arthur.

It was a gusty May afternoon and sunlight fell in hard shafts between gray clouds. A vermilion ostrich feather was plucked from a hat by the fingers of the breeze. Evading capture, a hundred pairs of eyes followed its nimble revolutions until the wind grew tired of its plaything and the plume sank to the floor of the pit.

"I have found you a new lace maker," I said.

"Is the old one not good?"

"Not as good as my neighbor."

"I trust your judgment in necromancers, so why not with lace makers?" she said in a low voice, examining the lace on her cuff. As she lifted it, I saw a fresh purple bruise on her wrist. "He keeps from my bed as if it were lined with nettles. Forman's magic is working in that respect at least. But the angels are taking a long time to free me from him. Can you see the pit?" asked Frankie.

"No. It is an argument for smaller hats," I said and Frankie snorted, causing those close by to look at us, including Lord Essex and her great-uncle, Lord Northampton.

"When will we be forbidden to breathe, do you think?" she said. Essex stared as if Frankie were a Billingsgate fishwife, and she stared back with a directness worthy of the epithet. He pushed his way to the corner of the platform farthest from us.

"If you did not challenge your husband, your life would be easier," I said.

"It would be over." She dabbed her mouth as if tasting vomit, looking over at her family. "Beneath those façades are some very hard hearts, the hardest lying within the breast of my great-uncle." I hoped we would never meet, having read much about him in broadsheets, none of it complimentary. Even to see him so close felt strange, like meeting Judas, someone known to all but seen by few. He was thin, nearing seventy, with gray hair cut close to the scalp; he was entirely dressed in black.

Although Frankie was the most exquisite, the Howards were always an extraordinary sight. It is no exaggeration to say that the value of a large estate was lavished on the clothes and adornment of each. They were ever encased in gold and silver constructions that took up four times the space of their naked bodies, sewn with so many jewels that they lit up the air around them, making them seem larger and, were it not a sin to say it, somewhat divine. At the very core of the family, however, was a man who did not radiate light but stole it.

"Is Lord Northampton married?"

"He prefers the company of educated young men. Follow me," she said. I grabbed her arm to stop her, preferring to stay near the back. She gave me one of her looks and pulled me toward her family. As we neared, I saw that the King was just behind them. We curtsied low, blood rushing in my ears and muffling the sounds around me, but the King paid us no attention; he was watching a keeper in the pit maddening the lions by passing in front of their cages with lumps of dripping offal. Queen Anna gave us a brief nod but Lord Salisbury was too busy trying to catch the attention of the young man next to him, Sir Robert Carr. Salisbury looked especially crook-backed, ancient and ill-favored beside Carr, who paid him no heed for his eyes were caught by Frankie's approach. He pressed his velvet cap to his heart and bowed deeply.

Dressed in bright blue, that made jewels of his eyes, I was stirred anew by his looks. His shadow, Sir Thomas Overbury, echoed Carr's gesture without sincerity, exaggerating his surprise to see us there at all. Having been officially introduced only in a brothel, and being of lower rank, Carr was still barred from addressing

Frankie in public. She, a married woman, was prohibited from paying him the slightest notice.

"How well you look, my lady," he said, her husband not twenty feet away. That Frankie did not rebuff Carr made me sweat. I pulled on her hand but she ignored me.

In a simple action that changed our world, she lowered her fan and lifted her eyes.

Until that moment, Carr had not known whether Frankie yearned for him or was indifferent. Now, she was flirting with the King's favorite in front of her family, husband, the Court, the Howard haters and her rivals-in-love, the King and Sir Thomas Overbury. This was her plan? To provoke her family to action before she brought disgrace upon them all? For the first time, I feared that she was oblivious to consequences. Overbury's fascination with their exchange confirmed my fears.

I was also aware of a deeper distress in myself that Frankie had not confided in me the depth of her feelings. I had thought Carr the subject of her pipe dreams, the man she would marry if Essex were killed while out hunting; but he had become more than that. She was putting him before herself, and before me.

"Viscount Rochester," she said, his new title still lower than her own, "how have the Lords welcomed a Scot into their midst?"

"They've not written me an anthem."

"And you are to be made a Garter knight, along with my cousin? At this rate, you will soon be an earl," she finished, with a little laugh that revealed her teeth and attracted the attention of the few who were not already listening to every word, lapping at their flirtation like dogs at the butcher's drain. The spectacle of the royal minion trifling with the unhappy wife of the Earl of Essex was more enjoyable than even the fiercest bearbaiting.

Sir Thomas Overbury turned to see whether the Earls of Northampton, Suffolk and Essex were as captivated by the performance as was he. They were. I saw in his narrow cockerel's face that he was enjoying the sight of Frankie compromised.

A bear was tugged into the enclosure and chained to a post in the center of the yard. Its open mouth was full of stumps for all its teeth had been broken by the keepers.

"It murdered a child," said Carr, noticing my distaste. His attention was touching; it was not difficult to understand why Frankie was caught by his charm. "The lion, King of Beasts, will kill it and restore justice," he said, with less solemnity than the King might have expected, for this show of justice was his monarch's idea.

"The child died through the negligence of its parents," said Frankie. "To punish the death of one innocent with that of another is not justice."

Carr looked at her with great seriousness. I believe I witnessed the very moment in which they fell in love. In that exchange of looks, they understood that no one else at Court was as well suited as they were to each other. This handsome foreigner, not brought up in the English Court, was less trammeled by its ornate hierarchies and stifling conventions. Although Overbury claimed him for the Essex camp, Carr belonged to no faction, only to the King. He did not need Frankie to access the power wielded by her relations. He could love her for herself. Frankie blushed and raised her fan.

I turned to the ring, despairing the lack of discretion in either party. A cage was opened to the side of the pit but no lion appeared, causing the King to mutter with frustration. Carr leaned in to his master, talking intimately, and the King ran his nail absent-mindedly up and down the lacing on the young man's chest. Then suddenly he bellowed into the yard, causing us all to jump.

"Enough waiting!"

The bear raised its great head and stared at the King. Shouting could be heard in the cages and an enormous lion bolted into the pit, followed by a keeper wielding a flaming torch, but it slunk away to the perimeter of the yard. The King swore long and loud.

"Bring the dogs!" he shouted.

The lion was shooed back into its cage and a man wearing leather arm protectors and a metal gorget was pulled into the yard by four mastiffs, strands of saliva swinging from their bulging jaws. Six men carrying long, leather-tipped staves followed. The bear retreated as far as its chain allowed.

The courtiers around me screamed. Even Frankie yelled at the bear to fight, but I only prayed for the quick deliverance of all the creatures in the pit. I had never found the suffering of others, even animals, entertaining. I would not watch hangings; I stopped up my ears to the calamities befalling others read out by news criers. There was enough over which to weep without going in search of more.

The first dog leaped at the bear's face but was batted away. The men sprinted to break its fall with their staves then laid it, bleeding, on the sand. The second dog sank its teeth into the bear's hind paw, putting it off its stroke and allowing the third dog to clamp itself to the beast's nose. The great creature let out a howl.

It shook its back leg, by chance striking the dog against the post. The animal fell to the ground, twitching, before lying still. There was a brief lull in the noise from the crowd until the final and largest of the dogs leaped at the bear's throat, the shock of impact toppling the bear onto its back. A terrible wheezing erupted from it. In a last attempt to free itself, the bear clasped its enemy to its chest, goring it until bones could be seen through the dog's flesh. Then it pried the injured cur away but in so doing hastened its own end by pulling out its windpipe, clamped in the dog's jaws. The bear collapsed with its killer across its chest.

"The King's justice to murderers!" shouted the audience. Only the first dog had survived and the keepers lifted it with their staves and carried it away to loud whooping. The King allowed the applause to continue, as if it were for himself, before standing. The Court fell silent, leaving only the sound of pennants whipping in the strong breeze.

"The font of justice flows from God to His creation, from the King to his people," he proclaimed, spittle leaping from his wet lips. And if the font was full of weeds and filth? Or shallow and yellowed with the piss of courtiers, what then? I looked around me. This.

The Court bowed low as the King left the platform and walked down into the lion pit. Carr followed, flanked by the other gentlemen of the bedchamber. I counted eight Scots to one Englishman and thought it no surprise there was ill will against the Scots, at Court as in the street.

The King bent and dipped his fingers in the blood of the great dog that lay across the bear, smearing it on the cheeks of his gentlemen. He held out his fingers to be cleansed and I felt a charge in the air. The bedchamber crew had not foreseen the need for warm, scented towels and the King would clean his hands no other way. There was a green-furred drinking trough in one corner and several Gentlemen looked at it as if it could be magicked into rose water. Carr, unruffled, took from his sleeve a lace-edged handkerchief of immense value, knelt and gently wiped the King's fingers.

"Do you hear the grinding of teeth?" Frankie whispered to me.

"Distinctly," I replied, glad to have her back with me again.

Once the royal hands were clean the King raised Carr and kissed his cheeks. Carr bowed, then held the bloodied linen to his lips before tucking it back into his sleeve. Queen Anna stood and Prince Henry, seeing his mother's stony face, bowed to his father and led the way off the platform. The Earl of Essex followed without Frankie, a snub that she ignored.

"What a beautiful creature," she said, watching Carr beside the King. Blood seeped from the bear, staining the sand as red as the feather that shifted in the breeze beside it.

The Earl of Northampton, moving rapidly for an old man, seized Frankie's upper arm and propelled her from the platform. Frankie protested but her great-uncle ignored her. Her plan was working. I was about to slink to the back of the queue when I saw Arthur. He was ahead, laughing with other gentlemen of the Prince's household, and I willed him to see me. He turned and looked appreciatively at the beautiful woman alone on the platform; then realized it was me. Would he acknowledge me and bring an end to our subterfuge? He stared so long that I was embarrassed.

When he walked toward me, his pace was slow, and I suspected he wished his friends to leave the platform before having to introduce us. He was not ashamed of me, only unsure of what to call me. If he had walked a little faster, or I had gone toward him and forced his hand, perhaps everything that happened after this moment would have taken a different course.

He gave me a formal bow but his words belied it. "How beautiful you look." He offered me his arm and led me out. I was the happiest I had been since George's death. In a few months' time I would be Lady Waring, wife to a coming man, safe with our children in his wealth and good prospects.

Frankie was standing beside a low wall above the stinking moat at the base of Lion Tower, looking out for me, while her great-uncle Northampton stood over her, talking. She waved us over, appraising the fact that Arthur had my arm.

". . . speaks to you in public, he may only do so following a formal introduction by your father or brothers," admonished Lord Northampton, unaware, of course, that Frankie's brother had introduced her to Carr in Queane Donna's brothel. Despite our presence, Northampton continued to berate his great-niece until he saw Sir Robert Carr and Sir Thomas Overbury returning from accompanying the King to his barge. They walked over to a red-eyed man and Lord Northampton again took Frankie's arm and steered her toward the little group, with Arthur and me following.

"My wife could not forbear to set eyes on that beast again," the man was saying. Carr handed him a heavy purse, which the man cradled, as if it held the remains of his child. I found it a pitiful sight but could not but think him and his wife fools to have left their child alone in the menagerie. The man bowed and walked away with his bag of coins.

"Lord Rochester," said Lord Northampton to Robert Carr, in his dry, high voice, "may I acquaint you with my great-niece?"

Sir Robert Carr bowed. The skin around Lord Northampton's nostrils wrinkled in what was, perhaps, a smile.

Before Carr could kiss Frankie's hand, a strange creature approached, somewhat like a lion but delicate and spotted, accompanied by a strong odor of decaying offal. As it drew near, it was clear that the stench emanated from its keeper and not the beast.

Taking advantage of this diversion, Robert Carr moved so that he stood close to Frankie. They did not speak, but the stillness of both revealed that they were aware only of the place at which their arms touched. Arthur, called by members of the Prince's household, whispered his love for me into my ear, then slipped away.

"Goodman," said Lord Northampton to the keeper, "tell us more of this beast." Carr took Frankie's hand, unobserved except by me, and entwined his fingers in hers. She kept her head still but glanced at him from the corner of her eye. He stroked her wrist and began to probe a finger under the lace of her cuff to feel the nakedness beneath. I looked around to see who would notice but none did, not even Sir Thomas, who was watching Lord Northampton. Seeing the gentleness in Carr's attentions to Frankie, I could no longer suspect that his plan was to ruin her, even if that was Overbury's aim.

The keeper, used to tourists and the coins they gave him, spoke immediately: "Noble gentlemen and ladies," he declaimed, as if addressing a multitude, "this wondrous Leo-pard from the Orient runs at such speed that the spots on its coat vanish. It is fifty years old but that is no great age as a Leo-pard can live to one hundred and fifty years or more. She was a gift to His Majesty from the King of France just before his murder, God rest his soul." I immediately pictured not the dead King, but the assassin, ripped apart by horses in the Place de Grève. The keeper encouraged us to stroke the nervous creature and observe the patterns in her shivering pelt. Whenever she growled, she was struck on the haunches with a stick. Frankie studied the delicate head of the animal and I wondered if she saw misery in the beast's golden eyes as I did.

"Do they remain loyal to *one* mate, like the swan?" asked Sir Thomas Overbury, looking directly at Frankie. She disentangled her fingers from Carr's. The pleasant mood among our party turned immediately tense. Robert Carr did not hush his friend but frowned deeply.

"They mate with whatever male is available when they are on heat," said the keeper. Sir Thomas Overbury smirked at this answer.

"Can they be trained to attack *unwanted* persons, like a guard dog?" asked Frankie, looking at Overbury. Robert Carr laughed and I confess I could not hide a smile; even Lord Northampton appeared delighted by Frankie's riposte.

"No, my lady, they do not seek engagement," replied the keeper.

"A pity," said Frankie, bending low to the animal. Carr followed her every gesture and Overbury watched him narrowly.

"When it is dead, I would like its skin," Overbury said. Frankie's face was still but I could guess her feelings.

"I had decided on the pelt myself," said Lord Northampton, smiling at no one in particular. Carr looked to Overbury, who did nothing to break the awkward silence.

"My Lord Northampton, of course you must have the pelt," said Carr. Overbury reddened but Lord Northampton smiled warmly at the young favorite. Robert Carr was the brightest star at Court and Lord Northampton a perceptive astronomer.

"They don't last long in confinement," said the keeper, clearly delighted at the profit he would make from the creature's demise.

9

About four months after the baiting I was shown into Frankie's parlor. Although a low, dark room, it was cooler here than outside, which was hot as a bread oven. Breezes from the river carried with them an eye-watering aroma of Thames mud. I had never known such heat and feared that fire would sweep the city and destroy the little I still had.

I had not seen Frankie since the bearbaiting for I had been unwell. Although I lived away from the pestilent courts and tenements near the Thames, where death stalks daily, we had such fevers and griping in the guts as I thought we had plague. My maid and Robert Weston nursed me until I was well enough to succor the children, who were afflicted each in turn. Simon Forman visited the very day I fell ill and every day thereafter until he was assured of our recovery. He brewed strong medicines for us and saved the lives of Mary and Henry, who would have been taken to God without his care. It therefore affected me very deeply that my old friend died suddenly during the period of our recuperation. I cried as if it were George dying again. I had lost a helpmeet whose love and care for me was that rare thing, disinterested.

There was, at least, no reason to leave the house that summer, no pretense to maintain. Frankie and Arthur were in the country. They sent medicinal herbs and food that helped us more than they can have realized. Arthur wanted to visit before he left but I forbade it, not wanting him among the miasmas that were rising from the evil-smelling streets and making us sick. My eldest, Thomas, did not call, nor offer us assistance. He had barged and screamed his way through childhood and altered little with the years.

I visited Frankie as soon as I and the children were sufficiently recovered. As usual, her apartments were busy. The summer progress was over for most, although Arthur was still away. I was shown into the receiving room, which Frankie had redecorated during my illness; the paneling had been ripped out and replaced with red leather, deeply tooled in repeating gold patterns, and matching gilded leather covered the seats of the chairs. In one corner, four men were hanging a large painting. I put my nose to the wall to inhale the scent of hides dyed in Cordova, stamped with gold in Granada, cities I would never see. There were fewer than five families in the land who could afford the luxury Frankie displayed in that room and yet, thanks to our friendship, I was admitted to that paradise. Even though she was a Howard, I did wonder how she had paid for it. Which tradesman would be fool enough to trust Frankie's promises of future payment? For a brief moment, I felt my heart grow cold, like a dying ember. Was I not doing the same as these credulous tradesmen? Investing my time and hopes in her?

"Whatever are you doing?" she said, approaching soundlessly across new woven rushes, accompanied by her little dog Brutus and Purkoy, now much grown and hardly a puppy. Around her neck was a long golden chain, set with enameled flowers and precious stones, that I had not seen before. Indeed, her every surface gleamed; I felt sympathy for those saps with their gilded-leather samples, they would have been lost the moment they saw her. "Have you found a fault?"

"No, I was . . ." I could not admit to sniffing walls.

Frankie embraced me and then stood back a pace, to study me. "Are you quite well again? You are grown thin."

"I will fatten up. I have to tell you, Frankie, Simon Forman is dead."

She stared at me, uncomprehending.

"How can he be?" she asked, and I understood her confusion. Forman was so close to the angels that it was a shock to think they had taken him.

"He predicted it," I said. "He told his wife at supper one evening that he would be dead within three days. She twit him in the teeth as he sat there full brimming with life, but he was right. He went out on the river to a warehouse in which he had an interest, suddenly stood up in the boat, then fell down dead."

"We will miss him."

"When I was with him, it felt as if George were still alive."

Frankie nodded and took my hands. She squeezed and rubbed life back into them, for they are always cold.

"I have his recipes," I continued quietly so as not to be overheard. "I will have our decoctions prepared by the apothecary who makes up my yellow starch. But the angels . . . I cannot persuade them to my bidding as he could. I went to his house this morning and made his wife give me everything from his study that pertained to us, especially your letters," I said. "But I'm sure she kept something back."

"She would not dare blackmail us, she is too timid."

"She is resentful."

"Much else has changed in your absence; the angels are already busy on our behalf. Come," said Frankie, leading me toward the men hanging the painting. One, taller than the rest, bowed low as we approached. I remembered him. He had accompanied the painter in Frankie's vestibule, the first morning I came to Court. He was perhaps Arthur's age and well favored, although his attire was unusual, as if he had lived a long time abroad and wanted people to know it.

"Mistress Turner, this is Mr. James Palmer, Prince Henry's purchaser of paintings, who is also finding wonderful things for the Viscount Rochester, for my great-uncle, and now for me." I curtsied and he bowed again, very correctly. "Mr. Palmer has not yet succeeded in persuading me to sit to Larkin for my portrait." Frankie's mother had long argued for it but Frankie refused to commemorate her marriage to Essex in any manner. "But he has found me this."

So shocking was the image before me that I was silenced. A young woman was severing a man's head from his large, strong body. Ribbons of blood flew out from the butchered neck as the man gazed beseechingly at his killer, from whose strength of purpose the artist had not shied away. Before this I had only ever seen portraits, the faces all much alike, on bodies stiff as corpses.

"Judith and Holofernes," said Mr. Palmer, "by an Italian. The artist has captured Judith's strength, has he not?"

"Indeed. These Italians are well formed," I said.

"It is thanks to the eye and talent of the artist as much as the beauty of the sitter, I believe. In this country, we seem rather more interested in displaying wealth than feeling."

"It is so like life, I expect the figures to move," I agreed.

"Mr. Palmer paints too," Frankie said in a soft voice, not sure if he would want this known. Painters are a low lot on the whole, on a par with actors, living among the rougher sort while not being quite of them. That Mr. Palmer should willingly associate with such people was most eccentric. He laughed.

"In this country it is freakish to paint for the love of it, and yet the noblest of men redecorate their houses and reorder their gardens," he said.

"They do not dig them," I said.

"They do, in secret, for there is much satisfaction to be had in it. Look closely at Lord Salisbury's hands and you will spy calluses. I have found you a *Susanna and the Elders*," he said, turning to Frankie and pointing to a large canvas propped against one wall. We gathered around and he turned the painting toward us. In silence we stared at the two old men hidden behind bushes, peering at a naked Susanna. So real was she I could feel the heaviness of her breasts, the slight swelling of blue veins under the skin.

"That is allowed?" I asked, in a display of prudery of which Prince Henry would have been proud.

"It is a Bible scene," said Palmer, his eyes full of amusement at my response. "Susanna refused their advances, hence the old men accused her of adultery; ever the recourse of frustrated men." Frankie and I glanced at each other in delight at our outspoken guide. "What think you of it?"

So rarely was my opinion sought by anyone other than Frankie that my tongue was slow. I enjoyed Mr. Palmer's attentions, yet felt exposed by them.

"The artist puts us among the Elders," I finally replied. Mr. Palmer let out another great bark of laughter.

"You have it exactly! The artist makes oglers of us all."

"Come and see my cabinet," said Frankie, her patience with the flirtations of others short-lived. I dropped a quick curtsy of farewell to Mr. Palmer and noticed, with pleasure, that he held my hand longer than necessary when he kissed it.

"It's beautiful, don't you think? Prospero likes it," said Frankie, nodding toward a black lacquer cabinet set between two windows atop which the parrot was perched. When Brutus spotted the bird he jumped up at it, clawing a surface shinier than anything I had seen before.

"Down! You will scratch it!" scolded Frankie, smacking the dog's nose. Purkoy was too well trained to do such a thing. "It is from China," she said, opening the doors of the tall cabinet whose black lustre was inlaid with flowers and insects in ivory and mother-of-pearl. I would not have been surprised had one of the insects begun a courtship dance. "There are smaller cupboards and drawers inside. It is a marvel that human fingers can coax out such beauty. I am making efforts to learn about painting and sculpture and such curious chests. Robin knows so much. He has been made a knight of the Garter now, with my cousin."

Robin? That silenced me. The last time I had been with Frankie it was "Sir Robert Carr" or sometimes "Viscount Rochester." With every new title the King gave him, it seemed the favorite grew closer to Frankie.

"Great-uncle Northampton has finished his new house at Charing Cross and he invited me to view his collections. Robin was there. He told me that my great-uncle reminds him of monks he met in Europe; they wear black and are profligate, just like my great-uncle, so Robin and Overbury call him 'The Dominican.' Clever, don't you think?"

"Robin" was every other word she spoke! He would not have thought of "The Dominican" himself; such archness would have been Overbury's.

"I told him that we call Sir Thomas Overbury 'The Cockerel,' which perhaps is not all that quick-witted as he resembles one so completely, we cannot have been the first to think it."

"You told him we speak ill of his best friend?" On her breath I smelt both wine and tobacco.

"He thinks it is funny. We are not alone in finding Sir Thomas arrogant; he's been banished from Court, have you heard?"

Much had occurred in my absence; illness had a high cost for me.

"Overbury and Robin were in the Privy Garden while the Queen was at her window. She claims that they laughed at her."

I am sure they did laugh; Carr innocently, Overbury because he considered himself above any woman. The Queen would not lightly suffer such an insult and I was glad she had protested.

"She says she will return to Denmark if the King does not punish them. Robin has apologized but Overbury has refused and been banished. Robin threatened to leave as well, if Overbury was sent away, but instead he has been very much with my great-uncle. We have met several times in the Long Gallery at Northampton House."

I could picture it exactly. Lord Northampton had provided Robert Carr and Frankie with a haven in which to become better acquainted, away from Whitehall, her husband and the gossips of Court. The political advantage to Northampton of a connection with the King's favorite was obvious, but would he gamble for it with the honor of his great-niece? It was a dangerous ploy, at least until her husband had known her fully. I wondered how intimate she had become with Robin Carr.

"My parents are trying to buy my obedience, so they paid for the new decorations. My great-uncle values the influence he enjoys with Robin through me, so he bought me the two paintings. Robin found the cabinet and I suppose he paid for it," Frankie continued, "or at least he has not presented me with a bill. All manner of people have come to admire it."

She laughed. I did not. I felt as if we were standing on a precipice that she refused to see.

"He uses all his ingenuity to meet and he wrote me another love poem," she said, pointing to a little scroll in a secret drawer. "We have kissed," she whispered, her face momentarily full of wonder and earnestness, as if she were the first person in the world to experience a kiss and unsure how to convey the thrill of it to me. I was appalled. "He sent this too," she said, lifting on her finger the new chain that I had noticed around her neck the moment I saw her.

"What does your husband say?" I asked.

"He thinks the gifts came from Lord Northampton."

"But will he not ask Lord Northampton about them?"

"It was my great-uncle who told me to say that."

My wits felt dulled, unable to keep up with the changes that had occurred in my brief absence. I could almost hear the thoughts in my head clanking and groaning like Inigo Jones's mechanical scenery, never quite setting one scene before the next was called for. It scared me to know that Frankie was meeting Carr; I feared he would replace me in her affections, or perhaps I did not want to be tainted by the scandal that would result if they began an affair and were discovered in it.

"Robin saw bruises on my wrists and complained to the King about them," she said. "My husband is with Lord Salisbury now, being reminded of his duties to a wife; he was Salisbury's ward, so it is not the first lecture he has received from that quarter."

Given that Frankie's own parents did not chastise Essex, it was hard to see what Lord Salisbury could do. "He must feel remorseful, having arranged the marriage."

Frankie clicked her tongue. "Never has love, nor charity, nor remorse interfered with his pursuit of self-interest."

"Do you hate him?" I asked. She had spoken no more of Lord Salisbury than she had of God. His was an all-powerful presence from which flowed both punishment and preferment.

"If he can make my husband stop hurting me, I shall be glad, but I bear no love for him. He is little, crooked, lacking good ancestry and ruthless, but I wager he is the greatest bedswerver among the King's nobles. He is rumored to be the lover of my mother-in-law as well as my mother. He will not understand my husband's reluctance."

"Are you not afraid Lord Salisbury will goad him to greater effort?"

"I will never have my husband in my bed again."

"That will limit other possibilities."

"Neither Lord Salisbury nor Lord Northampton know that I am still a maid," said Frankie, "nor do they know about the worst that Essex has done. But I will tell them if he attempts to enter my bed. As you told me once, things always change." I could not help feeling that I was being left out of a secret.

"Sir Thomas Overbury and the King will not wish you happiness if it is found with Robin, for they want him for themselves."

"Everyone wants him, but I have him," said Frankie. She opened her mouth as she laughed, took my hands and whirled me around. I was worried for her but felt relieved to be in her confidence again. She began to hum a tune, then sing, and we danced together on that soft carpet knotted by Turkish hands, steeped in the perfumes of Arabia and Spain, and I laughed at her boldness and joy. Frankie's energy was catching—I was glad to be alive, grateful that my children were well again, and I felt a little drunk without having tasted a drop. It was unfortunate that the Earl of Essex chose that moment to enter the room, although his humors were so bilious he would not have been appeased had we been at our prayers. He stopped short at the sight of us dancing and the sound of our womanish cackling.

"My lord," said Frankie, sinking into a deep curtsy and staying there while she composed herself. Lord Essex walked warily toward us, as if coming within reach of two hissing vipers, but was still clearly furious from Lord Salisbury's command to love, not beat, his wife. "Do inspect my new cabinet. It is of the finest workmanship imaginable," Frankie said on rising. "The marquetry is the most intricate to come to our shores." The Earl of Essex looked everywhere but at the cabinet and his wife. "It is in remarkably good condition for having traveled such a distance." She was trying to provoke some reaction in her husband to the beauty before him. She pulled open the tiny drawer inside which lay Carr's poem, but Essex ignored her. "I sense you do not care for the new cabinet, my lord," she finished, her arms dropping to her sides.

"I prefer English furniture," he said, speaking at last. "It is in keeping with our surroundings. One soon tires of exotic frivolities. I imagine it was very costly? It is important that those with means spend them on English craftsmanship so that our own people enjoy the benefit of the current profligacy." At this he shot a sideways look at the little group absorbed in hanging the painting.

"I believe there is no one in this country who could make such a cabinet."

"Because the cold and damp will soon warp it. An English craftsman would know that."

"I am sorry it does not please you."

"It does not. We leave for Chartley in two days. Alone," he said, looking at me with dislike although it was misplaced, for I shared his disappointment that all efforts to inspire love between him and his wife had failed.

"For how long?" Frankie cried.

"As long as it takes."

Essex would break her body and her spirit at Chartley, where there would be no one to stop him. I had thought him capable of killing Frankie since I first met him, but it seemed she only believed it then. Her provocative gamble had rebounded. She had thought her husband too spineless to fight back, most bullies cower when confronted, but she was wrong.

She yanked at the front of her dress as if to help her breathe, turned and walked to the door. I followed. Suddenly, there was an almighty crash. Spinning around, I saw the cabinet on the floor, pieces of splintered wood and shattered inlay all around it, the parrot flapping and screeching in alarm above the ruins. Essex was smiling.

"As I said, not sturdy."

10

So began a strange period in limbo, with Frankie gone but her predicament close. All we could arrange before Essex chased me from her room was that Richard Weston would act as messenger between us. She asked me to be her eyes and ears at Court; I was an unwilling spy, but could not sever the cord between us. She had become as near to me as my own heart. On All Souls' Day, Weston delivered a letter from Chartley. The night was clammy; thunder rolled over the city and a damp breeze rattled the candle flame as I read.

October 1611

Sweet Anne,
I crave your love and hope I have it and shall always deserve it. Please send me what Forman promised, for it remains as ever here. Send me some good fortune, for truly I have need of it.
My husband is merry and drinks with his men; he abuses me as doggedly as before and I begin to think I shall never be happy in this world. I beg, for God's sake, get me from this vile place.
Your affectionate, loving friend,
Frankie

The first fat drops pelted the window. I put the letter down and looked out. The rain quickly grew fierce, falling in sheets on the roofs and streaming noisily into the street below. I wondered if Frankie was also up late, staring out at the pitted surface of the deep moat that surrounded the manor. She had already told me of it, and I could picture her in the room that had once confined the

Scottish Queen Mary, using the same desk at which the Queen had written the letters that led to her execution. Through the night and the rain, was she gazing in despair at the sodden fields of Staffordshire? Frankie would have been alone as she wrote, her spying servants asleep, and the darkness or her distress had rendered her hand less elegant than usual. The words had a rushed air, like a note stuffed into a bottle and hurled quickly into the sea, the sooner that it may be recovered.

How could I get her from that "vile place?" If force were required, her brothers would be better placed to take her from Chartley to a Howard residence. All I could do was to send her Forman's tinctures. Before he died, he had made her a new one, brewed from galls caused by insects, fungus, parasites or injury, to temporarily weaken the force of the person who imbibed it, not unto death, only unto discouragement.

"She despairs because her youth is almost over," he had said to me during our last consultation. He had recently acquired a huge striped cat that he led about on a leash. "Fourteen to twenty-four are the years of youth. Twenty-five to forty-four are the years of middle age. Forty-five to fifty-five, one is aged. Fifty-six to death, one is old. I am fifty-eight and too old for anything but honesty. The astrological figure I drew for the Countess of Essex shows my future to be as full of contention and misapprehension as has been my past."

"Your future is in her chart?" I asked. Forman shut his eyes, as if the knowledge gave him a splitting headache.

"The connection destroys my reputation after my death."

"In truth?" I said.

Forman patted my hand.

"Calm yourself. The stars can exaggerate."

"Are you also in my chart?"

"Yours too."

"Why? What else is in it? What of Arthur?" But he held up his hand.

"My dear, to be happy in uncertainty is a skill that stands us all in good stead," he told me, unhelpfully.

Now I held Frankie's letter to the candle flame and let it burn to the tips of my fingers before throwing the curling ashes in the grate. The memory of my exchange with Forman frightened me, but I wrote Frankie a reply full of good cheer and gossip from Court. The following morning, I carried it downstairs with a vial of the new liquid and some buskins she had requested from her cordwainer that she might walk outside at Chartley where all was mud.

Richard Weston was in the kitchen and took the parcel. I had seen little of him since he had become the go-between for Frankie and myself. Sometimes Lord Northampton made use of him too and, I suspected, Robert Carr. I missed his company.

"You look tired. Will you have some broth?" I asked.

"Gladly," Weston replied. I handed him a bowlful. George's cat jumped onto my lap and turned around and around before settling down and rhythmically kneading her paws into my thigh. I stroked her velvet head.

"You are wearing the doublet of a man," he said bluntly.

"It was you who taught me how to make a doublet. Many women borrow the looks of men now that men are making full use of their womanish beauty."

"Some men," corrected Weston. "Not all of us grow our hair and pluck out our beards just as not all women wear a jaunty cap on their shorn heads. If my opinion is asked, it is unnatural, especially in a widow. If you married me, you could live a wholesome life again."

This lonely old man wanted company and someone to make his dinner; he loved me, but not enough to see that he could never be a good match for me.

"Thank you, Weston," I said, always forgetting to call him Richard, "but I am already promised to Sir Arthur, as you know."

He turned on his stool to look straight into my face. In his countenance was a remnant of the handsome man he had been. "It is my opinion that Sir Arthur will not marry you." The warmth I had been feeling toward him vanished. I had a momentary vision of my blood pouring into brass letting bowls all around me.

"He gave his word."

"He said he loved this family, which is not the same thing. I have lived many years and rubbed shoulders with the best and the worst of men. Sir Arthur will never come good."

"Sir Arthur knows what he promised," I said, sharply. Weston's words would pollute the air and make his dread vision more likely to occur.

"Why mention the ring in his Will if Dr. Turner wasn't forcing Sir Arthur's hand?" said Weston.

"Sir Arthur is merely waiting for the period of mourning to end. He loves me, and my friendship with the Countess of Essex will bring him advantage, even if I myself have no fortune."

Weston stood and put his empty bowl on the table. "Have you not already done enough for him? Other couples marry a few weeks after the death of a spouse, even Catholics. He is leading you a merry dance to which you are blind because he has a title."

I pushed the cat off my knee and rose too. "I wait because I love him. What would you have me do? Sit on my step like Mistress Bowdlery until I can afford that no more and sit instead in the gutter? The children with me? If Arthur does not marry me, that is what life holds in store."

"If you marry me, and even if you do not, you can take up your needle and become a woman of trade," said Weston, shrugging on a leather jerkin as scuffed and lined as his face.

"Go into trade? Should I send my children to be maids and water carriers? And when I am sick and cannot work, what then?"

Weston picked up the parcel for Frankie. "It is an honest existence."

"It is hardly an existence at all. You are a man of the last century, Weston."

"Court ladies have no loyalty to you. They let you attire them so that they can hear gossip about the Countess. She is a dangerous friend," he said, turning away and walking into the dark passage.

As he opened the front door, sunlight lanced the vestibule, alive with dust motes. He looked at me. "Renounce sham gentility and take up a reputable calling. You live above your station."

"The Countess holds us up by the chin," I retorted. "And you are happy to run her errands and fill your pockets with Robert Carr's money! You tell me to consort only with ladies of the middling sort and leave the fine ones alone while, thanks to my intercession, you spend your days trotting from one earl to the next?"

The sun lit Weston's hair into a wiry halo, an unlikely saint. "What is right for me is not right for you," he said. "You and the Countess would do better to save your strength for those realms in which you can hold sway."

"Hold sway?" I said, coughing out the words in my indignation. "And what realm is that? The realm of hungry, cold children? Can Frankie 'hold sway' while she is barren? You count yourself a practical man, but what you say is twaddle."

I shooed him out of the door and glared after him with arms crossed as he walked away. At the junction with Cheapside he turned and squinted into the sunlight. When he saw that I was still scowling after him, he raised his cap and bowed.

For five days in mid-November, the City was halted by snow. It felt to be an omen, but of what I could not say; the beauty and light of it augured well, but we were trapped, insignificant in the face of God's command of all things. When finally it melted, Mistress Bowdlery came out to make lace on her step. She now trimmed most of the Countess's cuffs and ruffs and Robert Carr's also, and had been as forthright in her thanks to me as she had been in her warnings about the beadles on the day we met. My growing fondness for her had prompted stories of her past; before widowhood, she had been a woman of substance.

"Is that for your daughter's wedding?" I said.

"Betrothal's off. Apparently we're too unlucky a family to marry into. What they mean is too poor."

I was wondering if there would ever be good news when Sir Arthur turned into the Row. He was looking pleased with life. As he came toward us, I thought how much better we had come to love each other during this year and a half without physical love. He made it clear that he wanted to be in my bed, but never insisted. He had become regular in his habits, visiting us every Thursday when he was in town and after church on Sundays. He was Catholic, like Frankie and me, but too ambitious to own it.

When he had secured the horse and removed his outer clothes, I saw that he was carrying a small package wrapped in green velvet. It was too early for a New Year's present and I wiped any hint of expectation from my face as I pictured Weston turning at the street corner and bowing. His warning had unnerved me; it would be exceedingly pleasurable, and a huge relief, to prove him wrong. Arthur was come to propose, five months before the end of mourning.

He followed me into the parlor and kissed me.

"Wine?" I asked. A glass was always ready, primed with Forman's brew.

"Are you sad?" he asked, as I handed him the drink. I was surprised that he noticed.

"The betrothal of my neighbor's daughter has been broken. Have you use for a maid?" I said, feigning indifference to the parcel in his hand.

"Is she in trouble?" he asked, drinking the wine and putting the glass back on the board. "I can't hire a whore." I hated to hear the word on his lips. "There's nothing to be done once they've slipped," he finished, sitting down.

The ignorance and carelessness of his response made me too furious to speak. His own daughters would be on the streets if I could not work and he halted his stipend, and that was little enough.

"What news?" I said, fussing with the wine to hide the redness on my neck that came unbidden when I was angry.

"The Prince has promoted me to Master of Arms," he said at once, unable to keep the news to himself a moment longer. Despite my ire, I was pleased. It put him in a better position to marry. "To celebrate," he said, handing me the parcel.

I pulled at the ribbon slowly, to conceal my eagerness. Pray God this was a wedding ring. The velvet wrapping came undone easily and revealed a wooden box slightly too large for my liking. I opened it. Coiled inside was a gold chain, like the one Carr had given Frankie, only shorter and with fewer flowers and stones. My disappointment was so great I could no more have kept it at bay than I could force the Thames back to its source. I could not meet Arthur's eye.

"Does it not please you?" he said, his lips pressed together in irritation. "Is it not as long or as bejeweled as the one the Countess sports?"

"You think I am ungracious and spoiled?"

Arthur looked surprised. I had never been rude or combative toward him before.

"What then?" he said.

"You need ask?"

I shut the box and placed it on the cupboard.

"You are angry I cannot take on every whore and waif?"

The temptation to slap Arthur's silly, handsome face was huge. "Am I a whore? Are your daughters? Is that why you do not 'take us on'?"

"Speak plainly," he said, running fingers through his hair, wounded that his moment of generosity had sparked not lust in me, but fury.

"I will speak plainly, Arthur. More than a year and a half has passed since George died. As you demanded, I have observed strict mourning and done nothing but work and worry. I have stuck to my word, but have you? If we are to wed in spring, why have you not proposed? We stood over George's bed and joined hands, witnessed by a notary. So why are we not married?" I put my shaking hands over my mouth.

"Do I not support you?" said Arthur. "I gave you a ring. We must behave in seemly fashion, I have explained that."

"Not such that I am convinced. You gave me a ring, yes, paid for by my dead husband and unaccompanied by any proposal of marriage. I am not your concubine, to be satisfied with trifles," I said, struggling to get the lace over my head on which the ring was strung. I must have looked ridiculous. Arthur helped me disentangle it from my hair. I thrust it toward him but he refused it.

"I will not take your baubles," I insisted, "for you are without honor."

Arthur recoiled. "You can say that to me?"

I turned away. I could hear him picking at the nails on George's chair and moving about the room, but he did not come to me. When I could wait no more, I marched to the door and opened it. I knew I should stop up my mouth but could not. "What proof have you shown me that you are a man who stands by his word?"

Very slowly, as if wading through water, Arthur passed through the open door. He took his cloak and hat from the peg and opened the front door. He did not so much as glance at me as he put on his hat and shut the door quietly behind him.

I went to the window and watched him untether his horse and walk down the Row toward Ludgate. I thought he would look back, was sure he would search for my face in the window, but he did not. I shook with rage and my heart thumped as if I were pursued by baiting dogs, but there was a strange lightness in my spirits too. As I watched Arthur turn the corner, I understood that it came from speaking honestly to him for the first time since George's death. Now he knew, without a doubt, my expectations and my disappointment, and there was some satisfaction in that.

I know it is often the case that an adulterous entanglement changes in nature when a spouse dies. Marriage provides the comfort that comes from long living together. Once that is gone, the adulterous affair founders in its own shallows. But I loved Arthur and believed that he loved me and adored our children. With the right encouragement he would still marry me. Couples often have a tiff before the reluctant partner agrees to marry.

Still, the heaviness in my gut told me that I had just taken the biggest gamble of my life. If Arthur was not goaded to action, and Frankie remained exiled at Chartley, then I would soon be on the doorstep with Mistress Bowdlery, my sons at work as rakers and jakes farmers, keeping the streets and cesspits clean for the feet and noses of the better sort, to whom we would never again belong and who would not notice as we starved, fell ill and died.

I turned from the window and was about to leave the room when I remembered the chain and wondered whether Barbara would like it; it was a long time since she had been given anything pretty. I went to retrieve it but Arthur had taken the box with him.

Lord Robert Cecil, Earl of Salisbury, the King's closest adviser, lover of both Frankie's mother and mother-in-law, died in May. Soon afterward, a message arrived from Frankie asking me to meet her at the sign of the Blue Lion on the upper floor of the New Exchange. Although we had written several times a week, it had been eight months since last we met, other than brief meetings at Christmas and New Year. Essex had declared that he would continue to drag her between the remote houses of his relations for the summer, so I was surprised that she was back.

"The world runs on wheels for many whose parents were glad to go on foot," grumbled Richard Weston as he forced passage for me through the carts and carriages backed up the Strand. It was exceedingly warm and a strong wind whipped a rhythm of brown cloak and crimson skirt at my heels. I had expected clear passage in my bold outfit, inherited from Frankie, but I was pushed about like any goodwife. I had not told Weston of my argument with Arthur, not able to forbear any "told you so" looks. Besides, I was still quietly confident that my lover would return, even though six months had passed since our argument and two since the second anniversary of George's passing. He still sent our stipend and I had seen him lurking in Paternoster Row on several occasions, looking toward the house. One of us would break, and it would not be me; it was not pride that stayed me, but desperation.

"You are dressed bravely today," said Weston, rocking along on bent legs, "expect a bit of shoving."

"For wearing red?"

He shrugged and looked down at his fingers, chafing patches

of flaky skin where they joined the palm. I did not remember him shrugging so often in conversation with my husband. "There are many who want women to look like women, even in these modern times. It is only at Court they go about in hats with feathers."

I could not stomach another sermon on that topic so held my tongue. We passed under an archway emblazoned with the coats of arms of the King and the recently deceased speculator who had developed the site, Lord Salisbury, whose arms were draped in black. Gulls gathered on the long roof, buffeted by strong gusts.

The gallery was, as always, a crush of traders, newsmongers, thieves and prostitutes, come to profit from the rich who, in turn, came to buy luxuries and compete with each other in looks, wit and rank or, failing those, in wealth. Lord Salisbury had tried to pass laws that would exclude the common and the criminal from his Pantheon of luxury, but had failed. I picked out those to avoid and those to greet as I passed along the colonnade, weaving through clouds of pipe smoke, catching snippets of conversation. I heard talk of the colonies in America and war on the Continent, of Catholic fanaticism and hopes of finding the Northwest Passage; of who would marry Prince Henry and Princess Elizabeth, and who invest in the East India Company.

I bought from the sweetmeat seller plump marchpane pigs with clove eyes for my youngest children. I could picture Katherine kissing the nose of her pig before nibbling delicately, hoping not to hurt its feelings. Henry would stuff his in his mouth at once and Mary would share hers with me. I handed the pigs to Weston, who smiled for the first time that day.

On the upper floor, occupying premises commodious enough for two or three to stand in, I entered the Blue Lion. The owner, an Ottoman of about my age, did not object as I ran my fingers over bolts of silks, damasks and velvets, imported from Italy, India and China. He brought me a stool and sweet wine in a glass of deep blue and green that nestled in my hand like a great jewel.

Frankie arrived late, accompanied by two attendants who remained outside as she squeezed her skirts into the shop. When finally we pulled apart from our long embrace, we searched each other for signs of change, hoping for none. Frankie looked a little tired and the skin on her face was closer to the bones beneath. She kissed me on the cheeks and kept hold of my hands.

"There is no way to express how happy I am to see you," she said. We sat close together and the merchant bowing, deep and low, as if enjoying stretching out the muscles in his back, brought Frankie a glass like mine.

"From Murano?" she asked him.

"Yes, my lady."

"I am learning, am I not?" said Frankie to me. "Not from my husband, of course. If it were up to him, we would eat and drink from clay and wear nothing but chain mail." I experienced a rare stab of jealousy. I envied her sophistication and was perhaps resentful of her efforts to impress Robert Carr, even as she suffered in the hostile palaces of Essex and his relations.

She pulled a parcel from her purse and gave it to me. Inside was an emerald set in gold. "My great-uncle sent the ring to me at Chartley. As he is doing nothing to rescue me from my marriage, I am delighted to give it to you. Your letters kept me alive and what little hope I had came from them. I was certain I would lose Robin to Overbury's spite or to a younger countess, but your letters told me he has remained loyal to me these long months."

And yet I wished Robert Carr had married one of the fresh arrivals at Court. Frankie needed to find someone less precarious upon whom to pour her love.

"How can I thank you?" I said.

"There are no bills of credit between us. You do more than enough for me." She was correct in that.

"I did not expect your return until autumn."

"And nor would I be back, but the King demanded we attend Lord Salisbury's funeral, at Robin's suggestion," she said. Frankie seemed agitated and glanced around as if expecting an unwanted guest. "If we sat here two days I could not tell you all that is occurring at Court," she continued, speaking quickly and picking at the lace on her handkerchief. "Lord Salisbury's death works like a holy sacrifice to raise the body of the Court from an obscure tomb. Men I have not clept eyes on my entire life stream from the shires to get a bite of the spoils, the hay still in their hair."

She drained the glass and released my hands. Standing, she moved between bolts of fabric, lifting the materials and observing the way they fell. I noted what she touched; translucent stuffs mainly. "The Scots are all there, snatching what they can," she continued. "The privy councillors squabble over Salisbury's monopolies, expecting to be granted what he had. The place is far more exciting than usual."

"Your family must be sad," I said, "to lose a great ally."

"God, no, all of us loathed him except my mother. He spied on us. My great-uncle was always plotting to be appointed Secretary of State in his place. Now he might succeed. My lady mother pushes Father forward and grumbles that Northampton is trying to profit at their expense. She cries a lot. She must have loved Salisbury in her way. The King wishes Robin to mediate between the Howard and the Essex camps, which he endeavors to do, but the task is impossible."

"No man has been as hardly treated in death as Salisbury. Have you seen the libels and broadsheets against him?" I asked, ill at ease before Frankie's nervousness.

"He cannot read them now. A cancer of the stomach. I believe he suffered greatly," she said, with no trace of sympathy.

"Have Forman's measures continued sufficient?"

"I leave my chamber only to dine, and that in order to give my husband the concoction. I have made resolutions during this exile, without Forman's help, or even yours," she said, running her fingers over the different textures of cloth. "Will you make me a dress? Only three people will see it but it has to be the most beautiful you ever fashioned." I made clothes only for masques, for my children and, in recent times, for myself. Frankie knew that this was a point of honor for me.

"You and I being two, and the third is not your husband?"

"No," agreed Frankie. "I think he will soon die of an excess of bile."

"Simon Forman would have warned you of it. Predictions of death were his speciality."

"A simple gown," said Frankie.

"What beneath?"

"Nothing. Closed with a single lace."

I must have raised an eyebrow.

"Reserve that look for your children," said Frankie, "I know what I am doing."

She unrolled a length of spangled silk. "He cannot stop writing of his love for me. It is his own hand, not Overbury's. There is talk again of whom Robin should wed and every pretty child is put under his nose."

I thought it unlikely that another woman would tempt Robert Carr, for he loved her strength more than her youth or even her beauty. None were like Frankie. No other had the same rigorous ambition for her own happiness coupled with the wit and courage to achieve it. No other was as bold and alive. I sensed a new flintiness in her. She moved to another trestle and examined the fabrics laid upon it.

"Will you let me meet Robin at your house?" she said, without looking up.

Surprise made me stupid. "The place is too shabby!" I cried.

"I doubt we will notice a lack of good hangings," she said, laughing. "You do not think I ask you to be my bawd?"

"You compare yourself to a whore?"

"What if there is a baby? I would want it too much to murder it in my womb."

For all this time I had been against Frankie becoming Carr's mistress; in every way it was to her disadvantage. Men of rank are as openly admired for the number of women they bed as for the number of deer they kill. A married noblewoman, who had produced children with her husband, was allowed a little love elsewhere as long as she was discreet and remained obedient to her family. Frankie, however, had yet to fulfill the first duty of a wife. Yet I saw that her mind was fixed and closed to argument. If I refused to help her, she would act alone.

"I can keep your menses timely," I said with a slight nod.

Frankie put her arms around me and we held each other close for a long time.

"If I wait longer I will be dead of greensickness, and I would rather die having loved Robin."

This resolve felt honest to me. "I will make you a dress, Frankie," I said, "and you will wear it at my house."

She kissed my cheeks repeatedly and the Ottoman brought us each another glass of wine.

"For this I have put concoctions in my husband's drink and offered prayers against my marriage," Frankie said, lifting her glass as if for a toast. "I defy the will of my entire family, except Lord Northampton perhaps, and imperil my standing at Court. I chance my soul by allowing Robin into my bed." We clinked glasses and gulped the wine. She was not terrified but elated. It was not a lack of religion, nor even that she believed Robin's love was worth her soul; she was convinced that God would know how pure was her love and would bless it.

Frankie soon left but I sat a while, cradling the empty glass. I watched the colors reflect on my skirt; little dark splotches that moved over the fabric as the moth shadows had over Arthur's face.

"It's late," said a harassed old Maggie when I arrived home. She took my outer clothes as the younger children rushed up, shouting "Mama!" Weston handed out their marchpane pigs and I picked up Mary, who was coughing. "Let me sit awhile," I said.

"There is no time," said old Maggie, "the Countess is here." She nodded toward the door to the parlor. How had Frankie come so quickly? Had she changed her mind? Was Robert Carr already with her? Above the sounds from the street I could hear high heels walking across the bare planks. Peeling plaster, cold ash, it would be worse than Frankie could ever have imagined. As if the visitor listened equally hard, the footsteps ceased.

As I entered the chamber, I faltered. It was not Frankie but her mother. She stood in the center of the room, as if keeping her distance from the four walls, for fear their shabbiness would infect her. Although she was in mourning, her hair was very high as were her heels.

I curtsied deeply.

"Rise, Mistress Turner. As you are close to my daughter, I

presume that you are aware of her contempt, her utter contempt, for her husband and for her family who chose him? She was happy enough to marry at the time, but has made no effort to gain his love since. And now word comes to my ears that she loves another, is this true?" Staggered by the directness of this address, although the same trait often surfaced in Frankie, I struggled for a politic reply.

"Your daughter is a woman of exceptional beauty and nobility. She is courted by many but she never forgets her marriage vows," I said. The Countess waved a hand as if batting away my words.

"Do not speak archly to me, Mistress Turner, for I am well versed in mealymouthed evasions. Is my daughter in love with Robert Carr?"

"Madam, do you wish your daughter such poor friends as would lay bare her soul?"

"I am her mother and the wife of the Lord Chancellor and you will answer me directly." Her eyelids were red. Perhaps, as Frankie had said, the Countess was grieving her lover Salisbury, whose death spelled change almost as great as if the King had died. To anger her would be folly; she was as spiteful as she was influential. I was amazed that Frankie had emerged from the womb of this woman. Their only common features were obstinacy and beauty.

"I believe that Robert Carr is enamored of your daughter, perhaps to please the King whose love for your family is well known, but your daughter behaves with propriety."

"Such propriety that the Court is alive with rumor," snapped Frankie's mother. She gazed about the room once more, a study in incredulity that her daughter should possess a friend in such a street, whose notion of friendship could surely be corrupted by her poverty. She had come to me, rather than summoning me to her, in order to see how I lived, to judge my motivation, and to better understand my weaknesses. "If your friendship is real, Mistress Turner, do all in your power to reconcile Frances to her husband. Such loyalty is pleasing to a mother."

Finally, she was offering me some reward for the responsibility she had handed over the first time she had summoned me to

Court. I was neither surprised nor offended by the proffered bribe; this was a woman known to demand payment for any contracts awarded by her husband or, previously, by Lord Salisbury. She assumed I was the same. "Nothing can come of any other union but disgrace and ruin," the Countess concluded. "Hmm?"

12

A crepuscular shadow hung in the air, pierced by rays of dusty light that dodged the towering buildings of Paternoster Row. All day, with the heat and rushing about preparing the house, I was "fidgety as a flea" as Mary put it, and not even sure they would come. And then it was night. Uncommonly hot, the malodor from the sewer outside seeped into the house.

I was ready for the knock, but still I jumped. Frankie entered my tiny vestibule with Weston, who said nothing and went directly to the kitchen. Frankie opened her mouth to remove her mask. She knew I disliked that style of mask for it was held in place by biting down on a bead that protruded from the back of the mask on a little stalk. It prevented the wearer from uttering a sound so perhaps she chose it to avoid having to converse with Weston or any watchmen they met on the way.

"I am broiling," she said, eyeing the difference in my circumstances as I removed her cloak. I wondered how long she and her kind would survive if all the servants in the world died or refused to leave their beds.

"You escaped without incident?"

"My younger sister is in my apartment to vouch she was with me all night," she said, handing me a jewelry case. I put it to one side and motioned her to the narrow staircase.

"Wine?" Frankie asked.

"In the chamber."

"Windows?"

"Closed and shuttered."

"The smell is bad."

"Not in there, I have strewn fresh herbs." Are men aware of the pains women take to catch them, or oblivious? Does it heighten or lessen the pleasure? Do they feel marched by an overbearing hand into the trap or are they flattered that such effort is expended to ensnare them?

Entering the chamber, Frankie went straight to the bed. The sheets were fine enough not to chafe but not so fine as she was used to.

"I am frightened," she said.

"It does not hurt much," I said, pouring wine and drinking a glass at once. Frankie did not join me.

"I am only afraid of what he may do afterward."

"He has waited a long time," I said, knowing that did not guarantee he would love her after he had taken her. I loosed and brushed Frankie's hair and began undressing her.

"What must I do?" she asked.

"He will guide you," I said, my face flushing.

"Of course, I forgot that I will not be his first."

"I am sure that you are the first he has loved. Do not be alarmed if this makes him fearful and he performs ill. Appear impressed, whatever happens."

Frankie nodded seriously.

"I fear he will find me repugnant undressed."

I laughed. "That is one thing you need not worry about."

We started at the knock.

"He's come," said Frankie, grabbing my hand, her eyes unblinking. I remembered the first time George and I had lain together. I was fifteen, and George just shy of my father's age. I had felt no eagerness, only worry that my repulsion would show. In fact, George had been gentle, wooing me with soft words and consideration. For Frankie though, I wished the sort of lust that Arthur provoked in me.

"I can turn him away."

Frankie shook her head.

I patted my hair as I hurried downstairs and opened the door. Lord Rochester's groom nodded but did not announce his master's arrival. I stood back to allow a cloaked, masked, and perfumed figure into the hall, a futile disguise, for the fancy shoe-roses gave him away immediately.

The groom followed his master into the hall and I shut and bolted the door. Robin Carr had removed his outer clothes and was attired in crimson embroidered with gold thread, the doublet and hose matching in fashionable and exquisite precision. Carr would have disappeared in Frankie's new parlor, so similar was his decoration. Especial attention had been given to his hair, which was brushed back from his high forehead and curled as it reached the nape of his neck. His cheek and chin were smooth, no hint of beard, his skin as plush as Frankie's, a very particular mark of prosperity, the want of which no amount of rich clothes can conceal. In one ear he wore rubies that matched his silken garments so perfectly that no small work must have been expended in choosing and mounting the stones. My thoughts sped to my neighbor, almost blind from such delicate work as adorned his cuffs. How suffered the man who had wrought the miracle of craftsmanship that dangled from the ear of this favorite?

Since Lord Salisbury's death, Robert Carr was acting as the King's Secretary of State, to the fury of all those who considered themselves better qualified for the role. I curtsied very low before beckoning him to follow. As harsh sunlight reveals every wrinkle on a face, the brilliance of Carr illuminated the poverty of my dwelling. I was acutely aware of the narrow staircase and the cracks in the plaster.

I knocked at my own chamber door and heard Frankie bid us enter. As Carr passed me, his strong, sweet perfume filled my nose and I had a wild urge to touch him. His nearness to King and throne was as a saint's to God. His glamour, the richness with which he was encased, the houses in which he lived, the beauty with which he himself gleamed, the deference with which he was treated—I wanted these. Although I felt nothing for him, I understood the love between him and Frankie; they were as perfectly matched as Carr's earring to his clothes. Even before I closed the door they had reached for each other, full of their own daring, so fully occupying each other's sight that the risks were nothing but little chittering creatures on the far horizon.

I showed Lord Rochester's groom to the kitchen where beer was waiting, but I myself sat in the parlor, on George's chair, which I had redeemed from the pawn merchant with a brooch of Frankie's, the cat upon my knee, a cup of wine at my elbow. The children were with Eustace, and the smell of the wild rose that grew on the back wall released its scent into the room and banished less pleasant odors coming from the street. I opened the jewelry case Frankie had brought. Inside was a gold chain that would keep my household afloat for three months at least, more if autumn was warm, and showed Arthur's thin offering to be the shameful shortcut that it was.

Some will judge me and say I was a pimp, a bawd. Others know that they would have done the same, faced with their children's hunger. Sometimes, as I am remembering, I cannot picture myself at all. I see Frankie and my children with clarity, but I am a cloud-person, ever-changing, seen not as I am but blown about by the force of others' judgment. How stupid we are, not just us women, but all people. We think we act with nobility when in truth we run in circles too low to the ground to see which path leads to heaven and which to hell.

13

"Ow," said Frankie, as I pressed the thin blade into her heel until blood flowed in a slow but steady stream into the letting bowl. She was settled in a great leather chair, Brutus in her lap, taking care not to move her foot from its position on the stool. All the windows of the apartment were open to catch the breeze.

"Where is Purkoy?"

"Essex has taken him to Chartley," said Frankie. Her husband's appetite for the education of his wife had been blunted by the months they had spent together away from Court; Purkoy, however, had become very obedient.

"Does he suspect anything?"

"He has always suspected everything since the day we married. Fortunately, he is not interested enough to notice any change in me. He has gone to Chartley simply because he prefers the country."

That summer, my home and a farm at Hammersmith, easily reached by boat, had become trysting places for Frankie and Carr. She was cured of greensickness but her menses were twice late. I gave her strong brews of boiled fern root, savin, mint and Cover Shame, to unblock the womb. When it failed, I let blood in the foot.

"I hate this," she said.

Indeed, it felt strange to be emptying her womb when she wanted a child above anything else.

"Until a child is quick there is no life nor soul in it," I said. I had not been sad when her menses flowed again but Frankie was quiet for a few days.

The ever-present need to keep Frankie without child had led me to strange quarters the previous few months. When I too often asked for herbs to avoid pregnancy, my usual apothecary in

Bucklersbury pretended to have none. I trawled instead those hidden in squalid courtyards, littered with the cages of filthy animals whose parts or blood were used in preparations. I was grateful for Weston's company. The badges of these "guild members" were counterfeit; they were frauds and thieves in the main. If they had the ingredients I sought, I oversaw the entire decoction, to their annoyance, so little trust had I in their talents. At these times I missed Simon Forman terribly. His fondness for George and me was an assurance that his angelic intercessions and brews would work to our mutual benefit and not solely for his profit. In the dark alleys and courts, I had no such privilege.

"I cannot stomach this for long," Frankie said. "We must find another who can work with angels. I have heard of a certain Dr. Savery and of a Mary Woods who do the work we need."

"To truck with them would be dangerous and futile. The first is a charlatan and extortionist, the second an ignorant cunning woman." It was from the likes of Savery and Woods that I sought to shield Frankie; there were many quacks about, some harmless, some villainous. I had encountered one particularly vile creature in a backstreet apothecary, lopsided from venereal disease that corrupted the marrow of his bones and dressed in clothes of the wrong size, in colors never normally seen together. He talked to me with unearnt familiarity until Weston hushed him; the creature's name was Franklin.

This unpleasant recollection was interrupted by Frankie's steward announcing Mr. Palmer. He entered, sweating in a felted and flowered cape that looked as if he might have made it himself, a rolled parchment in his hand. He gave us both an exquisite bow and kissed our hands, mine at some length. We had spent many hours with him over the summer. He thought women capable of wisdom to rival, or even outshine, that of men and for that alone I admired him.

"I hope nothing ails you?" he asked Frankie.

"Not at all, just a little rebalancing of the humors," she said.

"Forgive my tardiness, but I have moved home. I am now your near neighbor, my lady," he said, bowing again to Frankie. "The

Viscount Rochester has found me lodgings near the tennis court so that I might more closely oversee his growing collection."

This pleased me greatly; our meetings would be more frequent.

"He has asked that I find you a painting to celebrate your recent birthday and I have come to inquire whether it should be Dutch or Italian?" Mr. Palmer had been continuing Frankie's education in painting and statuary, begun in the Long Gallery of Northampton House. Robert Carr often joined the lessons, as did I. Mr. Palmer had a gentle curiosity that worked like sunlight on me; he asked questions and, beguilingly, listened to the answers. How rare is the man who does that. Perhaps it was a sign of my advancing years that I found such kindness attractive.

"Dutch. There is enough bare flesh in here now. Are you writing as well as painting?" said Frankie, pointing to the scroll in his hand.

"This is Sir Thomas Overbury's work," he replied, perhaps thinking to impress us with the acquaintance. Overbury never came to Frankie's apartments with Carr, so Mr. Palmer could not know how much we disliked him. "He writes rhyming sketches about milkmaids, lawyers and such, and this one has proved popular. Shall I read it to you?"

We both shook our heads and Mr. Palmer laughed so hard tears fell from the corners of his eyes. "I have yet to meet someone who likes the man," he said, once he had recovered himself. He tucked the scroll away and began to discuss Dutch artists when Frankie interrupted.

"Oh, Lord! It is too hot to think. Let's go on the river." She sent her coach to collect my three youngest children as I salved and bandaged her foot. By three o'clock, Mr. Palmer was handing us down into her barge. He could not spend the afternoon with us but, as he kissed my hand, he pressed the scroll into it.

"This is much discussed. It might be best to read it," he said quietly.

As we pushed off, we heard a shout. Robert Carr was running down the passage to the stairs. The craft was moving away from the bank. Frankie screamed at him not to risk falling in the water for he would be swept away. With a mighty yell, he leaped from the top stair and traveled through the air so fast that he nearly toppled out of the other side of the barge as he landed. Mary, Katherine and Henry shrieked and grabbed him. He fell into the bottom of the boat and pulled them down on top of him, rolling about like a hog and making them squeal. He picked up each child in turn and pretended to chuck them overboard, dangling them above the sparkling water so that the toes of their shoes were wetted as they kicked and screeched with delight.

"Shoes off!" he ordered. The children could not get them off fast enough, stockings too, and he sat them on the edge of the boat, holding them as they leaned forward to get their legs into the water. He looked over at Frankie and me. "Shoes off!" he commanded again. I hesitated, for fear they would notice the darns in my stockings, but Frankie was next to my children in a flash and I stuffed my poor footwear out of sight. The poem I stuck in my shoe.

Frankie held my children as Carr took off all the clothes he could with decency. The boat was the only place in which they felt free from the spies paid for by her family and probably by others too. Even so, Frankie, Carr and I all donned large sunhats to protect ourselves from the heat and from gossip—the river was always busy and the barge carried Frankie's arms.

Through the hot months that summer we often took refuge on the river. When Carr could not accompany us, we stayed in the houses of her family on the shores of the Thames, all the way to Oxford. She disliked being in Westminster in the heat, but wanted to be near Carr when business brought him back to Whitehall from the King's summer progress. We spent many days lying under the shade and privacy of the barge's canopy, the flitting of blue-green dragonflies exaggerating the torpor of the world around us. Elsewhere there was drought, hunger and plague; but on Frankie's gilded craft, on the glass-green stillness of the river, we were at peace.

"You look like toadstools," said Henry, giggling at our huge hats. Carr grabbed him and dunked him to the waist, my boy crying he laughed so hard.

"Ladies are not foul fungi," Carr said, and I smiled to think how Frankie once dressed in the colors of one and how long ago that seemed.

"What's this?" said Katherine, pulling the scroll from its hiding place. Frankie grabbed it and began to recite in her most pompous voice, imitating Sir Thomas Overbury. "'The Wife,'" she began. The first verses were to be expected; the usual things about woman being the daughter of Eve, made of man to obey him. She lifted her eyebrows at: "One, thus made two, marriage doth reunite, And makes them both but one *hermaphrodite*." By the eighteenth verse she was flagging, irritated by the poet's insistence that love can only in *one* person be found and, once married, no weak and worthless lust should rupture that bond. Carr clapped her performance, which pleased Frankie at first, but after a while it annoyed her that he did not see what we both did.

> "'*Rather in her alive one virtue see,*
> *Than all the rest dead in her pedigree.*
> *Gentry is but a relic of time past:*
> *And love doth only but the present see . . .*'"

Frankie looked at Carr. She could say little in front of my children but it was clear that the poem was a pointed and public criticism of her. She read on, reciting aloud the most offending phrases.

> "'*Domestic charge doth best that sex befit,*
> *Continuous business; so to fix the mind,*
> *That leisure space for fancies not admit:*
> *Their leisure 'tis what corrupteth womankind.*'"

Carr pretended to point out fish to my children, but his attention was fixed upon Frankie's anger.

She handed me the scroll and I read the forty-seven stanzas, most of them dealing with women's moral weakness. Overbury insisted upon the worthlessness of beauty, especially if its owner bestowed it on more than one man, and its lack of value when compared to goodness and obedience.

"Your friend advises you very publicly," I said finally, my outrage too great to smother.

"I do not dictate his scribbles," said Carr, not arguing with the fact that the poem was a denunciation of Frankie.

"He attacks my honor," she said. It was both statement and warning.

"He knows nothing of love. Let us not waste this beautiful day fuming at his poetry."

Frankie took the scroll and, staring at Carr, tore it into little pieces and threw them into the river. They floated, like ash or petals, but fish soon came and swallowed them.

"I heard that you challenged Sir Thomas Overbury to a duel," I shouted to Sir David as we struggled through a mob pressed together like eels in a barrel. It was the end of June. We pushed forward until we reached the stage on which stood the gallows.

As I had entered Palace Yard, just after dawn, it was clear that here was none of the carnival atmosphere typical of a public hanging. The usual crowd of flap-eared newsmongers, lawyers, drabs, thieves, beggars, and innocents up from the country to pursue a claim in the courts was swollen by tidings of witches in Pendle and Northamptonshire that had brought the fearful out with the sightseers. I was dressed soberly and masked, but it was no protection. Within a few minutes of arriving, a hand grabbed my privities.

"Lift your skirts, Molly. I'll have you for sixpence!"

All the fury I had quashed, at Arthur's irresolution and the myriad indignities of widowhood, burst from me. I elbowed my attacker so hard that he let out a great belch.

"Widow Turner?"

I whipped round, appalled that someone had witnessed the skirmish. Sir David Wood, a Scottish courtier, was grinning at me.

"Ah'll nae take my chances with ye in a fight!" he said, bowing as best he could in the mob.

"Sir David." I dipped a knee.

"Let me be of service," he said, putting a hand in the small of my back and pushing us toward the gibbet. The man about to die was a Scot, and Robert Carr had asked me to move among the crowd to hear what was said of the "beggarly bluebonnets," as those who had ridden into England with King James were known. I would tell him the truth. In the short time since he had become Frankie's lover, we had come to feel sympathy for each other. Despite his finery, he was a foreigner in London, despised by people afraid that he and his kind were taking what was theirs.

"Overbury refused tae come into the field," Sir David answered. "That malicious dog bites the heads off others tae stand taller himself. There's a man who could hang without a tear shed." I was prevented from asking what offense Overbury had offered Sir David by a great roar from the crowd announcing the arrival of the condemned man. Baron Sanquhar, a Scottish noble, had murdered the man who put out his eye in a fencing lesson several years before. Taking a life for an eye was more than the Bible advised, but the life had been a common one while the eye belonged to a Baron of three hundred years' pedigree. No one expected him to hang.

"He was avenging his honor, the bloody fool," shouted Sir David into my ear. "He only ever held his son in his left arm, so the boy would nae be scared by seeing his blinded eye." I did not know that the Baron had a son; the boy was not born of Lady Sanquhar. On the few occasions I had met his estranged wife, she had struck me as profoundly aggrieved to have been married to a Scottish lout and proven kidnapper. I could picture her expression later that day if he was not granted a gallows pardon, a wounded resignation that would not disguise her relief at being set free.

"That's Sir Edward Coke. They say he'll be made up tae Lord Chief Justice. He'd be glad tae see a Catholic hang," Sir David said, nudging me to follow his gaze. Coke sat in his coach, his gaze pitiless. I guessed him to be in his early sixties but with none of the softness of some old men. He was very lean, his face all sharp angles and points. "His delight has always been tae trample on the unfortunate. I'll be looking at his face when the pardon arrives!" Sweat tingled in my armpits to see hatred of my faith so openly displayed.

"Let it be known," bellowed Sanquhar, "today I die a true Catholic!" The answering scream of rage from the crowd hurt my ears and my heart. Sir David and I moved closer together. The rest of the speech was swallowed up by insults hurled at the condemned nobleman. Silence fell only when the noose was placed over Sanquhar's head. He craned his head toward the stairs, searching for the messenger who would convey the King's forgiveness, but none appeared. Only as he was maneuvered over the trap door did his face lose all color. Only then did he believe he was to die. I pitied him to have so little preparation, then thought perhaps it was better that way.

I looked away as he dropped. However miscreant, this was still a life created from his mother's body, brought into the world at great risk, nurtured for year upon year, fed, taught, loved but ended in ignominy with no legitimate issue. I hoped his mother no longer lived to know the shame of it, and that someone would care for the son who knew only one side of his father's face.

I was not sure what to report to Robert Carr: that I was afraid the crowd would beat me to death if they knew I too was Catholic? That Sir David had stopped shouting once he saw the murderous looks his accent provoked? That it seemed justice, life and death were dispensed at the whim of the King?

"I thought he would be forgiven," said Sir David, his eyes bright with tears. "He must have given offense once too often. It's a lesson for us all." Whether he was shaken by the loss of a fellow Scot or the arbitrariness of the King's justice, I could not tell.

14

O nly in November did storms and fierce winds break the summer's hold. I was busy with new commissions for the Princess's wedding to the Elector of Palatine; so many guests were expected that the King had banned the wearing of farthingales and women were anxious about how to display their family's wealth on so reduced a canvas. I was tired after a night disturbed by drinkers, celebrating the King's deliverance from the Powder Plot. Barbara and John were nearly always in the household of Baron Ellesmere and I missed them and their help with the younger ones. The drafty house made the candles burn down fast and the latest batch of syrup I had made for Mary's cough was too thin. The summer seemed to belong to another life.

I had just persuaded Mary to take a nap when Arthur walked in. I was so startled that I cried out, but he paid no heed at all. He took me in his arms but all the while stared about as if looking for a lost and most beloved child. We had not spoken since our quarrel. He sent notes with our monthly stipend, explaining why I should apologize, but I had not.

"Arthur? What is it? Have you a fever?"

"It was the swim at Richmond," he said, holding me at arm's length but not looking at me. "The doctors say he ate too many oysters beforehand. They put pigeons on his feet." I led him to a stool onto which he dropped, head in hands. Our children came to the door and he beckoned them in, hugging each of them fiercely. "He had beaten us all at tennis, he was hot and spent an hour in the river." He shook his head back and forth, like a horse bothered by flies, and I gently shooed the children out of the room. "They shaved off his hair." I stroked his back as he talked, raved almost. It was a good while before he calmed and leaned his weight against me. He put his arms around my waist and his head against my belly, as he had done when I carried his babies. Then he was still for so long I wondered if he had fallen asleep, as children often do after a storm of weeping.

"Arthur?" I whispered. "What has happened? Is it your father?"

He looked up at me then, confused. "My father?"

"Someone has died?"

Arthur let go of me and looked down at his hands as he clasped and unclasped them.

"My father's death would be sad indeed but not against Nature," he said. I sat on a stool and put my hands on his, suddenly afraid. Of what grief was I to learn?

"Arthur?"

"It is the Prince. Prince Henry has died."

I could only stare as if he had told me that one of my siblings was killed. The heir to the throne was not my son, but every woman I knew wished that he were son, husband or brother to them, in such high esteem was he held. That God could take His great hope from us augured ill, though I did not know why I felt quite so profound a dread.

"Forgive me," Arthur said quietly. "I have cared too much what others think." We looked at each other a long time. The light from the flames changed his countenance continuously, from young man to old husk, as if I saw before me all the ages of man. He must have seen and thought the same, for he stared at me with care and longing and fear all whipped up together in his expression. He took my hands in his. I knew before he spoke what he would ask and so loud a buzzing filled my whole body, even out through my skin, that I could not hear his words. He waited for my response, his eyebrows raised a little.

"I could not hear you, there was such a . . ."

"Will you marry me?" he repeated, pulling me close. Our long pent-up desire was poured into the kiss he gave me. At first it was tentative; I was the one who pressed my lips harder to his, to bring heat into his love. Very quickly he was kissing me as if I were air, sun and rain in one and our tears mingled, each of us wiping them from the other's cheeks. Of course, I said yes.

Arthur had to leave soon after to guard the Prince's body. The following day he returned, deprived of sleep, and every day thereafter for the four weeks that the Prince lay in state. As Master of Arms, Arthur and the grooms of the bedchamber attended the corpse in shifts. He described how the body had been embalmed and lay on view in a coffin under a black velvet canopy. The chamber, and the three that led to it, were draped in black from floor to ceiling and lit only by candles. Every mirror in the palace was turned to the wall. Only churches and the gates of St. James's Palace were crowded. Food markets were allowed brief and hushed trading hours, while all other business and entertainment was suspended. I remained at home with the children. The death of our Prince, the calamity to our nation of his passing, made petty the rupture between my lover and myself. Arthur and I wanted to marry quickly, but death was all that was being commemorated.

Not until the day of the funeral did I venture beyond my parish, and only then because Frankie requested it. The streets were empty of wheeled traffic, the city hard with frost. I walked in the black stream of mourners that surged through Ludgate onto the Strand, joining others until an ebony river flowed around Westminster Abbey, where the body of our beloved Prince was to be buried.

In the bitter air, the grieving were wreathed in white by their sighs. The windows of every house along the funeral route were draped in black and the sky boiled with yellow and gray clouds laden with snow. Death had snatched color away with the Prince's life. He was to have been the redeemer, the clean-living, fervent young man who would deliver the country from the strange times of King James. His death was a terrible blow to us all.

Frankie was sitting red-eyed in her chamber, Brutus in her arms. She did not look up as I entered but stared into the fire. "There is a rumor that the King poisoned Henry, from jealousy," she said.

I tutted and removed my outer clothing. "He fell ill after swimming in the river. He went in hot and there was a bad odor," I said, bending to kiss Frankie's cheeks. She looked at me sharply, for only Arthur could have told me that, and I hoped she would broach the subject so that I did not have to bring it up myself. She did not. "If anyone left off their mourning weeds they would be set upon," I said.

"It is the same here. The Queen has lost her wits with grief, the doctors fear for her life. The King is in bed with vomiting and spasms in his limbs. The Princess cannot eat for crying. Her wedding will be postponed. Prince Charles walks around clutching the little bronze horse he brought to his brother's bedside as Henry lay dying. All entertainments for Christmas are canceled. His death has brought back all our losses."

"You are thinking of Margaret?"

Frankie nodded and fat tears fell on Brutus. "For her, always, and my own children who will never be born. I long to hold a baby of my own so much that I fear my grief will turn to madness," she said, lighting forbidden tobacco in a silver pipe. "Robin is never let out of the King's sight." She stared into the glowing strands in the bowl as a trickle of white smoke escaped her lips, making her look like a beautiful dragon.

"The Prince's death will bring change to us all. We cannot foresee how, but the King will not keep Robin so close forever," I said. "Something good has come of it at least. Arthur has proposed."

There was no joy in Frankie's expression and she quickly looked away from me. She did this when she was struggling against harsh words.

"Then you too will leave me," she said finally, but I knew that she was also unconvinced of Arthur's merit. A manservant entered and Brutus jumped from Frankie's arms and skittered to the door.

"It is time, my lady," he said, closing the door to trap the dog. Frankie stood to pin the veil on my hat where it had come loose.

Muffled against the gelid December day, we walked through the palace to the King's Way, where scaffolding had been erected for noble ladies of the Court to watch the passing bier. There was no sound but the distant thump of great drums that made manifest the absence of the Prince's heartbeat.

I brooded, as did we all that day, upon death. I had survived childbed six times but would I outlive the younger Arthur? Would my children, and perhaps grandchildren, gather around my bed as they had for George? When I was a child and my first little tooth wobbled out of my gums, I was upset that my body had a will beyond my control. The same feeling assailed me again when my menses came and each time I became pregnant. How would I be, I wondered, when illness, not the short illnesses of life but the chronic and final diseases of death, began to overtake me? How strange I found it, not to know when and how a moment of such import would occur.

As the drummers turned the corner, I could feel vibrations in the cavities of my body; there was profundity in bearing witness to a moment that would change the course of all our lives and the lives of those to come. The first mourners of the procession passed before us, at least five hundred in front of the catafalque and the same number behind. Arthur was among the Prince's household servants, carrying the white stave of office that he would break and throw into Henry's grave. The coffin, under a black pall and canopy, on which were embroidered the Prince's many coats of arms, rolled silently over the straw-covered cobbles. On top of it, dressed in the Garter robes of the Prince of Wales, was a wooden effigy with wax face and hands so like the dead Henry that it provoked gasps and crying in its wake. The King, the Queen and Princess Elizabeth were too heartbroken to attend, and so it fell to Prince Charles to lead the mourners, walking behind the bier like a little ghost, still clutching the precious bronze horse. He was accompanied by Frankie's father, her great-uncle, and Robert Carr. Her husband was several rows behind.

Frankie leaned over and whispered to me, her eyes flicking between Essex and Robin. "I will not lie beside Essex for all eternity whatever happens." Slowly, she turned her eyes to me, as if her words were lamps approaching through a dark mist. "Prince Henry despised my family and loathed Robin. Now that he is dead, something might be done about my marriage." Perhaps it showed a cold heart to think of her own advantage when the heir to the throne was passing in his coffin below her nose. I think the opposite. Unlike most of us that day, she knew him. They had grown up at the same time, often in the same palaces. She remembered the feel of her hand in his when they danced. His death, and with it that of his heirs, made finding her own happiness more urgent.

"My great-uncle Northampton is running the country now, with Robin," said Frankie, looking toward him. "I shall request an audience. Perhaps you are right to be hopeful of change."

I had not said that I was hopeful of change. Only that it would come. And if her great-uncle were involved, I would be more afraid than hopeful.

A summons from Lord Northampton, requiring me to attend Frankie at Salisbury House, arrived two days before Christmas, but with no hint as to the reason. As Weston and I walked to the Strand, I prayed with unusual fervor that Frankie was not ill, discovered in adultery, badly beaten by her husband or suffering any other calamity.

Salisbury House reared up like forbidding cliffs, three stories high with taller corner towers. The new palace had been built by Robert Cecil, Earl of Salisbury, and was now occupied by his son, William Cecil, Frankie's brother-in-law. It was so recently finished that the wall brackets lacked torches and the coats of arms were not yet gilded. Many of the windows in the inner court were shuttered but I could see that the rooms behind glowed brightly. The sound of music filled the air, growing loud at one point as a footman opened the main doors to let out a dog. The Howards and Salisburys were marking Christmas away from a court in mourning. I walked toward the sound of laughter, but Weston took my arm and steered me instead to a door in an unlit corner.

"These are Lord Northampton's instructions," he said. I wondered how it was that Weston knew this house and this entrance.

We climbed a winding stair to a cramped and bare passage on the second floor. I had heard that concealed ways for servants were fashionable in new houses, but never expected to use one. I could well imagine old Maggie's indignity at being hidden from us, as if she were something shameful; this was one new fashion of which I did not approve.

Weston found a door that emerged near the head of the principal staircase. The sound of voices and music was loud from the floor below. A maid, clearly waiting for us, led the way to a richly furnished bedchamber but immediately retreated, indicating that Weston should follow her. To distract myself from worry, I tried out the chairs set against the walls. I had only George's chair in my house; we sat on stools or cushions on the rare occasions there was time for sitting. There was as much furniture in this one bedchamber as I had owned in my lifetime. As I rose to look at the plaster coat of arms over the fireplace, I heard a burst of loud cheering in the distance, then a door closing on the sound. The same maid rushed in, followed by Frankie. She stopped dead on seeing me.

"Anne! You here?" she said.

"Your great-uncle sent for me," I said, alarmed by Frankie's high color. "Did you not know?"

"No. But how glad I am to see you," she said, embracing me briefly. "There is no time. He is coming soon. Bring me a sharp and clean knife," she said to the maid, who dashed out. "My great-uncle has ordered Essex into my bed. You heard the cheering?"

My hand flew to my mouth. "Why? Has Essex accused you of loving Carr?"

Frankie looked suddenly exhausted. "No. He hinted that I was bedswerving but he has always done that."

"I will not let you kill yourself, Frankie."

She looked puzzled, then laughed rather loudly; she had been drinking heavily judging by the flush on her cheeks. "I would sooner kill Essex than myself. If he enters me, there must be blood." I could sense the wheels in her mind frantically spinning. "That must be why my great-uncle sent for you. You can let blood."

The maid returned with a small knife for scraping hard skin from feet. Frankie and I looked at it askance. "Have you wiped it?" I asked.

The poor girl nodded. I took the knife and held it close to a candle; it was encrusted in places with dead skin, which I pared off with my fingernail.

"Essex will see the cut," I said, suddenly realizing the problem. "It must be my blood."

"No," said Frankie immediately. "Lady Cheke let blood to cure an itch last month and was dead in two days. I cannot ask it of you."

"No, you cannot, but I offer myself freely. How can it serve your great-uncle to prove you an adulteress?"

"I thought he would agree that the marriage is of no value if I cannot have heirs. Now, it seems he means to force them on me."

The maid began unlacing Frankie's clothes. I poured her more wine and examined the cleanliness of her undershirt. "It doesn't matter if I stink," she said.

"For a man who loves horses more than women, a clean shirt will be less enticing," I said and commanded Frankie to wash. Clean and perfumed, I arranged her against the tester with care; chaste yet ardent would be most dampening to Essex.

"Do not cut yourself," she said, as I drew the curtains around the bed.

"If he manages to enter you, pretend great pain and I will . . ." I could say no more for Lord Essex arrived, trailed by his manservant. He scowled at me and I feared he would send me away, but he did not.

He yanked open a bed-hanging and I saw Frankie inside, pulling the sheet up to her neck. I frowned, worried that too much timidity would excite him. Indeed, he threw off his gown and quickly entered the bed in his nightshirt. Essex's man closed the curtains and went to sit in the window.

"Snuff them," I heard Essex order. Frankie, as she described to me afterward and I could hear for myself, knelt up and blew out the candles on her side of the headboard. To get to the other sconce, she had to lean over Essex. As she did, Essex pulled her down to sit on his member, already hard.

She yelped. His thrust missed and so he rolled her onto her back, pushing up her shirt so forcefully it bunched over her face. As he prized her legs apart with his knee, Frankie clawed the shirt down so that she could breathe. Essex had taken off his shirt and Frankie told me later that she snorted in surprise at seeing her husband naked for the first time.

"His member went limp," she said.

"It will not happen if you discourage me," I heard Essex snap.

"Why would I help a beast like you?"

I dipped my head to my sewing and the gentleman turned to look out of the window. There was no pleasure in eavesdropping on this pair.

"So be it," said Essex in a hard voice that did not quite disguise his mortification. He sighed, as one who considered himself much maligned, and got out of bed.

"A light," said the Earl, leaving his gentleman to close the door. Frankie sat with her knees drawn up, her head buried in her arms. When I embraced her, she was shaking. It was a long while before she stopped repeating, over and over: "How could they order him into my bed? How could they?"

That Christmas, for many, there was only grief.

PART TWO
February 1613

15

After St. Valentine's Day, I was again summoned to Salisbury House, this time by Frankie. The place looked blind, with every window shuttered and snow unswept in the courtyard. I knocked on the main doors and an ancient custodian eventually opened them and led me to the same bed chamber I had been in before Christmas. Here at least the shutters were open and the furniture uncovered, but no fire or candles burned and the room was cold and untidy.

"In here," came Frankie's voice from an adjacent cabinet that I had not noticed previously, the walls of which were covered in huge chevrons of garish color. She sprawled in a chair beside a fire, at her elbow a nearly empty decanter, a glass, a cone of gilded sweetmeats and a heap of scrolls tied with ribbons of pale blue silk. More were scattered on the floor, untied and variously curling like wood shavings. Brutus was chewing on one.

"At last," she said, although I was early. "It's better if you sit," she said, observing me flinch at the sight of the walls.

"I have never seen the like."

"Dornix. My sister claims it is the latest fashion in wall-coverings. It is giving me a headache." Frankie wore an unlaced house gown and her hair was tangled and dirty. She was a little drunk although it was early in the afternoon.

"You are alone?"

"There is no amusement to be had at Court since Prince Henry died so my family left after the wedding."

"Did it pass off well?" Frankie's great-uncle had led Princess Elizabeth down the aisle past her brother's effigy to marry the Elector Palatine.

"Nothing was more magnificent," said Frankie in a singsong voice. This sarcasm was new and I did not like it. Her mood was capricious and destructive.

"Have you received more poems?" I asked, nodding toward the scrolls.

"No, which is why I look at old ones. The King still keeps Robin by his side, day and night. I haven't seen him for a fortnight with all the buttering up he has to do of foreign princes." Frankie tossed the scroll she was reading onto the floor.

"My separation from Essex has led to nothing."

"It has only been six weeks!" I said. Having been unable to penetrate Frankie when ordered into her bed at Christmas, Essex had finally admitted his sexual insufficiency to her family; this had, it seemed, been Lord Northampton's plan. They had been allowed to separate; Essex moved to his grandmother's palace on the Strand and Frankie continued in her grace-and-favor apartments.

"Six weeks is an eternity at Court," said Frankie, kicking at the litter around her. "Other countesses, younger ones, are paraded before Robin while my family do nothing. My great-uncle will not even inquire whether an unconsummated marriage can be dissolved; Essex must ask him to do so first! My family say I will show myself disobedient and lustful if I do anything at all." With the care of someone who knows they are drunk, she placed her empty glass on the table. "While they fret over my honor, I grow old. I must do something for myself, Anne. I have asked someone to come who can help."

"Help how?" I asked, a momentary vision of sham apothecaries in their stinking shops forcing its way into my mind.

"In the same manner as Simon Forman."

"No one is as trustworthy."

"Trustworthy?" she said, rather loudly. "It is not even safe to keep these." She picked up what scrolls she could and tossed them into the fire. It was a few moments before brown patches bloomed across the words of love. The skin did not blaze but darkened and fell apart.

We both started at a knock on the door. I left the stifling cabinet and saw a barrel-like woman standing in the doorway to the bed chamber, the custodian just visible behind her bulk.

"Am I to come in or not?" she said, resting her weight on one leg.

"Yes, do," said Frankie, who had followed me. The woman turned and shut the door in the retainer's face. I looked pointedly at Frankie but was ignored.

"You must be Mary Woods? Would you care for anything?" asked Frankie.

"Ale and cakes, if you please," said Mary, plonking herself on the only chair without invitation. Frankie's look of astonishment made me smile. She would as much know how to procure ale and cakes as to raise a corpse.

"Forgive me," said Frankie, waving her arm about vaguely, "but we are alone. Next time I shall ensure that there is plentiful ale and cakes. I have wine?"

"I don't touch spirits," grunted Mary Woods. Frankie turned her back and made a face at me that said "What a character!" but I did not smile back. The woman was ignorant.

"What are your talents?" I asked.

The washerwoman looked at Frankie as she answered. "Finding lost valuables, damping or increasing men's ardor, untying marriage vows, predicting the sex of babies, the time of going to childbed and death." She folded strong arms under the shelf of her chest.

"Your methods?" I asked. The malapert ignored me. "How do you 'untie marriage vows'?" I insisted.

The woman turned from Frankie to me, running her eyes over my plain attire with utmost insolence.

"Prayers to small devils and, if a woman can give it to him, a potion. The prayers work without, but it's slower."

Forman had always conversed with angels. To conjure devils was a hanging offense. It was only a matter of months since the country had been set on edge by the discovery of covens in Yorkshire; hanging the witches had not quelled fear of their evil. It was deemed possible that they could still work magic from the grave.

"We want it to happen quickly," said Frankie, sitting on a stool opposite Mary Woods, who did not uncross her arms. "How long might it take?"

"How long could what take?" asked Mary Woods, looking at Frankie and pursing her fat lips so they oozed out from her face like raw sausages. The room grew dark as snow began to fall outside. Frankie hesitated and I cleared my throat, willing her to keep quiet.

"To release me from my marriage?" she whispered. I began to suspect that Frankie was ill as well as drunk. The separation from Essex appeared to have removed all discretion.

The visitor made a mummery of looking around her. "Got ghosts, have you? Who's going to hear us?" Frankie shook her head and looked at her hands. I had not seen her cowed before. Desperation had weakened her.

"Once you pay me, I can start work straightaway," said Mary Woods, her voice loud. "My clients are satisfied within a few weeks."

"How?" I repeated.

A smile spread across the wide jaw of Mary Woods. "My husband keeps from my bed and does not complain who takes his place. He bored two holes in my chamber door to watch me with another man but said nothing and never will. He is in my power and so is any man I choose."

Frankie's eyes flicked over this grubby laundress to see what made her so tempting to men. I was convinced of nothing but the woman's impertinence.

"Yet he remains your husband. What proof have you of putting marriages asunder?" I asked again. Essex would never welcome Robin into Frankie's bed; though separated, they were still married.

"You doubt me?" said Mary Woods, looking out of the windows at the swirling gray sky.

"To break the holy bond of matrimony is beyond the powers of most . . . healers," I said.

"I don't break it. My devils do. They do as I say, just as men do."

"What do they do?" I said. It was growing so dark in the room that the woman's moon face was all I could clearly see. Frankie put a hand on my arm.

"Speaking of my work lessens its effect."

"You don't wish harm on the husbands?" I insisted.

The washerwoman lumbered to her feet and nodded at Frankie. "Your friend is too suspicious, m'lady. I'll go before I'm trapped by the snow. They say it's going to be bad."

Frankie stood and blocked Mary Woods's path to the door. "Whatever you do . . . your work . . . please start it on my behalf." The woman turned her head to me in triumph before replying to Frankie.

"Grand ladies promise much and perform little. I need payment before I start."

"And if it has no effect, do you return the payment?" I asked. I could not credit what was happening.

"It does work," snapped the woman, "and if the husband is protected by angels, or by devils more powerful than mine, then it is better the marriage is left intact." At that she simply held out her hand. Frankie did everything on account, she never had coin. She tugged a large diamond from her finger and handed it over.

"My lady!" I protested.

"This is very precious. It is a token of my good faith but must be returned when I pay you the proper fee. Do you wish for coin or a gift?" said Frankie.

"Three shillings," said Mary Woods, poking the ring down the fleshy fissure between her breasts, whose vastness defied attempts to cram them under lacings.

"Come to me in ten days to tell me how you do," said Frankie.

"And for payment," Mary reminded her. Frankie opened the door herself. The washerwoman bobbed a meager curtsy to her and ignored me.

As soon as the door was shut, I rounded on Frankie. "That woman is a charlatan or a witch! How could you allow her here, let alone tell her you want rid of Lord Essex. The penalty for witchcraft is hanging!"

"She is not some poor hag from Pendle."

"The difference may not be obvious to a jury. You gave her jewelry that can be identified as yours!"

"I had no coins," said Frankie. "Essex gave me the ring, I never liked it."

"Your impatience will undo you."

"Too much patience and Robin will be married to someone else. I do what I have to."

"You must retrieve that ring and never see Mary Woods again," I said, almost shouting. Frankie narrowed her eyes at me.

"You'd better be gone before the snow is impassable," she said. She marched into the cabinet and slammed the door but it was thin and without a latch and rebounded with little noise.

I should have done more to stop Frankie paying Mary Woods that day. I already suspected that her yearning for Robert Carr would lead her to foolish acts that even her love for me would not restrain. I wish with my whole heart that I had fished that ring from between that laundress's monstrous breasts and chased her out with a poker.

16

After a few days of snow it began to rain and continued interminably for a fortnight. I hoped that Frankie had retrieved the ring and sent Mary Woods away with a flea in her purse, but I kept my distance. I taught the younger children to cook biscuits and listened to Arthur's grief for Prince Henry and his hopes for a position in Prince Charles's new Court. He increased our stipend and I used the extra money to prepare for our wedding. Prince Henry's death, the rain and high winds, put fashion from people's minds; had Arthur not proposed, God knows what would have happened to us. It was a thought that made me sensible and grateful. I did not trouble him with where we would live after we were married, how the children would be educated, whether I would have my own carriage and other such matters, and I made all the arrangements with the church.

In early March, Arthur arrived at my front door just as a messenger was handing me a note. I could tell from the seal that it was from Frankie. An apology, perhaps? I wished that I was already married and could hide away on my husband's estate.

"My father has come to visit," said Arthur, not dismounting.

"Will you come in? When will I meet him?"

Arthur was looking at the note in my hand. "I hear she is in trouble," he said. I felt so powerful a dread at his words that the noise around me seemed to hush, as if the world itself flinched from me. "There is talk that a cunning woman has been arrested who claims she was working to rid the Countess of her husband. You had better go to her." I could not tell whether his grim expression was from care for me, or displeasure that I was friend to a woman caught up in scandal. He did not ask if the rumors were true, which I took to be a good sign. He either trusted me to know nothing, or to be discreet if I did. If it was now discovered that Frankie had seen a cunning woman, how soon might Arthur discover that we had also used Forman's skills to encourage him to marry me?

"I can meet your father and go to Frankie afterward?" I said, but Arthur was already turning his horse. He nodded goodbye.

I ran back inside for my cloak, deciding to catch him up. He would take the route through Ludgate barrier to Fleet Street, but the lanes and courts between my house and the gate out of the City were choked with mud and deep puddles, traffic on wheel and foot struggling in both. Arthur's horse must have picked an elegant course through the obstructions for I did not see him ahead. I fell to worrying about Mary Woods and whether Frankie could be questioned or was too high placed.

Northampton House, at Charing Cross, was newly finished. Many humbler dwellings had been razed to accommodate its grandeur, which was significantly greater and more proximate to Whitehall Palace than that of the Cecil mansion, Salisbury House, situated further east along the Strand. For all that Northampton and Salisbury had been allies, they were also the greatest of rivals. As Northampton had no wife or children, he could spend all his money, and more, on himself.

I called into the porter's lodge and was taken by a servant across the huge courtyard, surrounded on each side by wings of the house. The main façade had an open loggia along its length, as if this country had good enough weather to require shade. Instead of passing through the grand doorway at its center, more magnificent than anything I had seen at the Palace of Whitehall, we turned right under the loggia to the corner tower. We climbed two flights of tightly twisting stairs and emerged into an impressive gallery that occupied the entire length of the wing. Northampton's clients, and others seeking favor, stood about, talking quietly and looking at the views. Large windows faced Westminster, and others on the south looked over formal gardens to the river and beyond, to

Lambeth Marshes. It unsettled me that Lord Northampton's outlook included the house of Simon Forman. Outlined against the view was Frankie. I noted at once that she was dressed very finely, in the boldest of my designs, with a tall hat made taller with long plumes; but as she turned, I saw that deep shadows lined the sockets of her eyes.

"Mary Woods has made a scandal and been arrested," she said, steering me to the end of the room where there were fewer people. I could smell Frankie's sweat. "She cozened me of my ring and then left for Norfolk, so I sent a man after her but she had already sold it for a pittance in London. He called the Justice of the Peace there and she defended herself by saying the ring was payment from me, claiming I asked her to murder my husband."

"She has accused you before a justice?"

"It is her word against mine."

"She had your ring."

"I could have said she stole it but my man told the Justice that I gave Mary the jewel for safekeeping before a masque when she was working as a laundress at Salisbury House. But now they know Mary never worked there, so they have clept him up too."

"Why did he say such a thing? There have been no masques since the Prince's death."

Frankie looked uncomfortable. "I didn't think they'd know that so far from London."

I fought down my rage at her idiocy.

"My parents are here, with my great-uncle."

"They will kill you and throw your body in the Thames," I said.

"Or worse, they will force me to return to Essex, to disprove the rumors that I want him dead."

Wretchedness and impatience had driven her to ignore my counsel and resort to foolish measures. I wanted to save her from rashness as she had saved me from destitution, but still I thanked my angel guardian that Arthur was to relieve me of dependence on her. Frankie would always be in my soul, but I would soon be free from the scandal and gossip that followed her like begging children.

A high servant, probably Lord Northampton's steward, entered the chamber. "The Lord Northampton calls the Countess of Essex," he bellowed. Even those too polite to do so before now turned to stare at us.

"Your hat is brazen," I said. "You will annoy them with such a display."

Frankie began unpinning it with clumsy fingers. I swapped it for my own more modest confection.

"Shall I wait for you?" I asked.

Frankie mumbled something.

"What?"

"You are summoned also but I will tell them you had nothing to do with it," she said, setting off behind the steward. My heart began beating fit to jump out of my chest as I followed her the length of the gallery to a set of ornate double doors. At our feet lay the pelt of the leopard from the Tower.

"She didn't last long," muttered Frankie. She stepped high over the dead creature so that even her hems did not brush it. I followed, hoping to be sent away once Frankie had described my attempts to stop her calling for Mary Woods.

Lord Northampton sat in a large chair at the head of a long table. His dark eyes, watery with age, were watchful and his hands, strangers to plow and sword, stood out against his black robes. To his left sat Frankie's father, a fat, profligate but largely genial man, known as overly indulgent of the women in his family, especially Frankie. Behind him, beside the fireplace, stood her mother.

Lord Northampton shifted, wincing slightly as if every movement caused him pain. I wondered if he wore a hair shirt or spiked belt under his robes. He frowned at the hat on my head but otherwise ignored me. I felt very sick.

"Tell us you have never set eyes on Mary Woods," he said to Frankie.

Her father twisted to glare at his wife, whose alchemical experiments were well known. He clearly felt she was to blame for Frankie's predicament, but she ignored him.

"I asked her to attend upon me once," said Frankie.

"And after this short acquaintance you gave her your diamond ring and a commission to poison your husband?"

"I never asked her to poison him!" cried Frankie. "I gave her my ring as surety that I would pay her three shillings, as Mistress Turner is my witness."

Lord Northampton stared at me and I nodded.

"A diamond ring is too great a surety for services any fraud on the Southbank could purvey. What did she promise you?"

Frankie hesitated a long while. I hoped she was remembering my warnings not to talk to Mary Woods.

"To help me be free from Essex." There was silence in the room, disturbed only when Frankie's mother slumped into a chair beside the fire.

"She has accused you of asking for a poison that would lie in a man's belly three days before killing him."

"She is lying! She said she would talk to devils."

"And yet you have lived separate from Essex since Christmas. There would be no need for some spell to keep him from your bed," said the Earl in a restrained voice. "What else can the word 'free' imply other than to seek his death? In what other manner can one be free from a spouse?"

"The woman is a liar. She predicted that I would be free from my husband and, without asking any more of her, I requested that she do what she could to hurry this situation into being. There was no talk of poison or murder. How could she, a low woman, poison my lord in his great house in Chartley? It is a ridiculous claim."

Northampton's face resembled that on a funerary monument.

"You understand that Mary Woods is known throughout Norfolk as a cunning woman? By paying her you were meddling in witchcraft. Witches meet a most unpleasant death, a fact well known to you due to recent events in Pendle. Your own King has written at length against such practices. You have read 'The Hammer of Witches'?"

Frankie shook her head and Lord Northampton looked at me; I shook mine as well.

"'The Hammer.' Does that imply forgiveness for those who give suck to the Devil and his minions? Yet you meet with a witch, pay her princely sums and allow her to tell all manner of ludicrous tales of husband murder. Whether Mary Woods speaks the truth or not, henceforth your own name will be forever linked with witchcraft and wickedness. Are you wishing to follow your illustrious forbears to the block?"

Lord Northampton rose from his chair and walked around the table, causing our eyes to water in the crisp light that pierced the windows behind him.

"To be separated from bed and board does not give you license to behave as you please. I need hardly point out that you owe obedience to your father, as previously you did to your husband, until such time as your marital situation finds resolution. Your first obligation is not to your own desires but to the perpetuation and advancement of your family and to providing a worthy example to those beneath you. Your father and I enjoy the closest possible trust from His Majesty. This cannot be put at risk because of your discontent. However," he said, pausing to ensure he had our full attention, "I know there would be no woman on this earth more obedient to her husband than you, if that husband had the means within him to perpetuate your noble family. Is that not the case?"

"Yes, my lord," said Frankie, uncertainly.

"Self-interest is, of course, misplaced in a woman," continued Northampton, "but this foolish action of yours with Mary Woods provides ample evidence of your determination to be free from the man you accuse of making you unhappy. Be warned, Frances, that no man can make a discontented woman happy. You do, however, have some cause for complaint. The Lord of Essex is a gelding, not suited to be a husband."

"You are a perverse and unbiddable girl!" burst out Frankie's mother. "I am ashamed to hear such things. You have been married in the eyes of God and should make the best of it as is within your power. You have turned Essex from you with your unkindness and unwillingness. He is not able to know you because you make it impossible for him. The Queen herself is displeased."

Her distress was sufficiently profound that she forgot her usual "hmm."

"Wife," said Suffolk, "let us hear what our uncle has to say."

"There is nothing to say and indeed nothing to be done," his wife insisted. "Frances must cease her complaining. There is such gossiping about her that the Court will not contain it and base persons at large will be free to tittle-tattle about us in every tavern in the land. The Howard name will be an object of derision."

"The people are ignorant," said Suffolk.

"Broadsheets and libels are as popular as daily bread and the King himself takes note of them, for he desires his courtiers to preserve the glory of the Crown, not tarnish it." She turned to Lord Northampton. "Frankie was fifteen when she married and not a child. She should be grateful for the honor of bringing together two families that were previously asunder. You are a Howard, Frances."

"My dear," Suffolk began.

"She needs an annulment," said Lord Northampton, as casually as if she needed a new horse. His audience fell silent, transfixed by shock. Even I, who had kept my eyes lowered throughout the conversation, stared at the Earl. A hint of a smile came into his eyes, like a boy who has shown himself cleverer than his older brother.

"That is impossible," said the Earl of Suffolk.

"It is against God," whispered his wife.

"Is it possible?" asked Frankie.

"It is difficult, of course," said Northampton. "We are the only Protestant nation with Catholic divorce laws stricter than are now observed in many Popish lands. I would estimate that at least one in three of our peers live apart from their spouses, yet none are legally divorced. We cannot expect this to be a simple matter."

"Annulment by a woman?" asked Frankie's father. "Can the law accommodate such perversion?"

"Is it not evident that you have raised a daughter who thinks it is right to take matters into her own hands, whatever the consequences?" said Lord Northampton, and I wondered if he knew just how far we had taken matters into our own hands. Frankie hunched her shoulders; she was thinking the same thing. "The qualities of obedience, silence and forbearance are lacking in her and these faults will affect us all," her great-uncle continued. "If she has risked her neck to associate with persons such as Mary Woods, what else might she do? It is far better to help her be rid of Essex and see her remarried as swiftly as possible, to someone suitable to us and more acceptable to Frances. The Earl has insufficiencies not to be borne in marriage."

"Who would marry a willful and credulous fool with no reputation? If she brings a case for annulment, she announces to the world her own lust and disobedience," said the Countess of Suffolk. "'Can she not contain herself?' That is what people will say. And what if others seek to follow her example? Do you really wish the Howards to be known as the murderers of marriage? How then will we stand in God's eyes?"

"Our house is no stranger to drama and yet we have weathered it and sit high in the King's regard. Frankie has beauty and wealth on her side, if not obedience. There will be suitors. We have a fine precedent in the eighth King Henry," said Lord Northampton, seemingly confident enough of his high standing in the eyes of God to ignore the Countess's fears.

"He was a man and a king," said the Earl of Suffolk.

"Frances is a Howard and the King is fond of her, although he does not yet know of Mary Woods. He will not be hard to convince. It is quite wrong that Frances be imprisoned in a marriage with no hope of being made a mother. Essex has been heard talking openly of his father's execution and of Lord Salisbury's part in it, especially now Salisbury is not here to defend himself. His hatred encompasses us all. Our hopes of reconciliation through Frances's marriage have not been realized and I am sure it is not through any lack on her part." He smiled at his niece and I thought of the leopard's pelt.

"There is no love in the marriage," she said.

"You sound like a fool," snapped her mother. "Love comes with time and sacrifice. Essex is among the greatest earls in the country. Is that not enough for you? You are become greedy, and that is a very great fault. All this talk of love matches . . . Twaddle!

Think of your own aunt Penelope. She was branded an adulteress, concubine and whore for her love of a man not her husband. Do you remember her face during those months, Frances? The scandal killed them both. Do you think it will be different for you?"

I confess I had sympathy for the Countess's fear on this point. How vicious is the spite of those who suspect another of having greater pleasure than are they. Arthur and I were always careful not to appear too happy in public.

"There is no way to be rid of a husband and have one more to your liking unless you wish to follow Penelope down the path to oblivion. Will love sustain you through disgrace when your family name means nothing? Will your children be grateful for their poverty and loss of rank? Only husbands can prompt desire in their wives. Do you wish to be called a whore? My lord, I think you cannot have her best interests at heart when you talk of divorce. If she is free from Essex she will nag us to marry that primped Scotch puppy of the King's."

Lord Suffolk, who had looked rather sleepy during his wife's tirade, suddenly awoke. "What!" he exploded, gaping first at his wife and then his daughter. "What!" The Earl's fury was so great he could not reach the words to voice it. Lord Northampton looked warningly at the Countess.

"By God, husband, can you be so blind? The entire Court knows of it. The Lord Rochester has been making advances to Frances for years." I did not look at Frankie nor she at me, but we stiffened, like boys about to be whipped.

"But he is the King's man," said Lord Suffolk.

"Indeed so," interrupted Lord Northampton. "With the passing of our cousin Salisbury and Prince Henry, God rest their souls, Robert Carr is now the *primum mobile* by whose motion all the other spheres must move or else stand still." Which was why Northampton was prepared to help Frankie rid herself of Essex; no other marriage could be as advantageous to the Howards as an alliance to the King's favorite.

"That mincing Scot in our family?" shouted Lord Suffolk, standing up. Frankie stepped closer to me. "Are your wits all eaten by fever? A page whose every penny is spent on the adornment of his body and the frizzing of his hair? I cannot understand a word that passes his lips. I wouldn't have him muck out my horses. How dare he address my daughter!"

"Quite, husband, quite. He's been given Raleigh's home, Westmorland's land, he uses Sir Thomas Overbury's wit and now he would take another man's wife; nothing his own but ambition. I will have no further part in this business. Whatever plot you are hatching, my Lord Northampton, I do not give it my blessing, and for you—you who have given more succor to good Catholic families in this realm than any other man—to seek the divorce of your own great-niece, I would not have thought it possible. I wonder if you are quite well."

"We must indeed consider the matter of Sir Thomas Overbury," said Lord Northampton, entirely unmoved by her speech.

"That vicious weasel? Why?" asked Frankie's father, growing increasingly distressed.

"He has overstepped himself," said Lord Northampton. "Since returning to Court he brags that, were it not for him, Carr would have neither fortune, wit nor reputation."

"Probably true," acceded Frankie's father.

"'Carr leads the King but Overbury leads Carr' is a pretty saying that has come to the King's ears." Although his expression changed not a jot, it was clear that Lord Northampton himself was the conduit. "The King dislikes Overbury for too conceited a carriage of his recent good fortune. His best friends speak indifferently of him. He is an insolent, thrasonical man, possessed by ambition and vainglory. He is naught and corrupt. He caused a rift between myself and Sir Richard Morrison for which I soundly rebuked him."

"He uses Carr for his own advancement," agreed Frankie.

Her father began to splutter again. "Do you meddle now in politics, Frankie? Will you be carrying a sword next?"

"Overbury befriended Carr when the young Scot was an insignificant page with no expectations," said Lord Northampton, ignoring his nephew. "He is your greatest rival, Frances, for his success depends entirely on Carr's love."

Lord Suffolk sank onto his chair and rubbed his eyes, as if to scrub away the thought of Carr loving Overbury. "How is it possible?" he said, to no one in particular.

"Divorce is not possible for the English, with the rarest exceptions," said Lord Northampton. "However, if one studies the decretals relating to matrimony advanced by Pope Gregory the Ninth in the thirteenth century . . ." here Frankie's father cleared his throat ". . . by which term, 'decretals,' I mean a papal decree concerning a point of canon law. It is stated that if a husband testifies under oath that he is impotent, and his wife confirms his admission, then their marriage can be annulled. Of course, should Essex later put a child on another woman, then he will have committed perjury and will be forced to take Frances back."

"I can testify that Essex is impotent," she said.

"Only a man's testimony is taken into account. A woman can only confirm," replied Lord Northampton.

"Why would any man admit impotency if he is thereby barred from taking another wife for fear he prove virile with her?" she asked.

"Indeed, that is the difficulty," nodded Lord Northampton. "However, in his commentary, Thomas Aquinas provides us with a path through the maze. He states that if a man and wife have lived together three years without consummating their marriage, this could be taken as proof that the husband is victim to witchcraft. A man, being a rational being, has control of his body unless otherwise tampered with by some external force, such as a witch. The Church would then be able to dissolve the marriage and both husband and wife would be free to remarry, on the supposition that the witchcraft concerned only the relations between the man and his wife, not with another woman he might marry subsequently. Both you and Essex could agree to that, I suppose?"

Frankie appeared unsure.

"Might people not assume that it was I who encouraged a witch to subject my husband to evil influences?"

"It would be a brave man who accused a Howard of *maleficum*," snorted Lord Suffolk, seeming to forget that even as he spoke a woman lay in prison for theft of a diamond ring used by Frankie to secure services of a magical nature. I wondered anew that this man, with wits so few, had charge of the country. The Earl of Northampton, on the other hand, had the memory of a wronged fishwife. He stared at Frankie.

"Your question is a sensible one, Frances, but I fear only you know the answer to it. If people did, as you fear, assume it was you who subjected Lord Essex to *maleficum*, would they have reason? Or, perhaps more important, would they have evidence beyond the ring you gave to Mary Woods?"

"How can this end well?" said the Countess, surprising me with the note of care in her voice. She approached and took Frankie's hand, a gesture that seemed to embarrass her daughter. "Forget the plays and poems that lead you to romantic notions. Romance is as mist, fragile and disappearing with the slightest wind, the slightest heat. You will stir up our enemies if you seek to divorce Essex. The Queen will be among their ranks, Essex and all his allies, the Bishops, all haters of Catholics and of the Cecils, and countless others we cannot imagine. It has never been done that I remember, and most especially not by a woman. Even if you achieve your wish, you will pay too high a price for it. Your reputation will be forfeit and without that you will be an exile, as if dead. Learn to love Essex. He will give you a child if you win him over. That is the way, Frankie, that is the way." She waited for her daughter to look her in the eye, to squeeze her hand, to give some acknowledgment of her words, but Frankie stared at the floor without moving.

The Countess dropped her daughter's hand and looked to me to open the door. I am not a servant, so I did not move. She opened it herself, and with that moment of pride I lost many commissions to dress Court ladies.

As the door closed, Frankie turned to her great-uncle.

"Other than the words of the washerwoman, and my ring, there is no proof that I have attempted to be rid of my husband."

Lord Northampton gave her a hard look and turned to her father.

"Then we shall petition the King to establish a Commission to discuss the annulment of Frankie's marriage. It seems to be for the best," concluded Lord Northampton. I had thought him fond of his niece; now I suspected that the notice he paid to Frankie was solely because she was of use to him.

Her father looked at Frankie with love and doubt; he was close to crying.

"I would speak to your father alone," said Northampton, and we quit the room.

"Would that I had kept you away from Mary Woods," I said as we made our way downstairs. I was to be married the next day but did not remind Frankie of it for fear it would upset her; there were still so many obstacles to her own happiness.

"She has prompted my family to action. The scandal will be forgotten." I knew that would not be so, because it shook the ladder on which we all perched; her mutiny against those who ruled her and the God who decreed it should be so would find few sympathizers.

Her coach was in the courtyard and we proceeded immediately to Whitehall, where Robin Carr's steward awaited us.

"My lady," he said quietly, "Viscount Rochester awaits you. I can take you to him."

Robert Carr had been in Royston with the King for several weeks, hunting. It was the first time they had met since the Mary Woods scandal broke and I wondered how he would greet her.

"Frankie, I will return home," I said, keen to finish preparations for the morrow and relieve old Maggie of the care of the children.

"Please stay, I need your company."

By which she meant I was to act as a chaperone in this palace of gossip. The steward led us to an apartment that was under renovation and empty. By the time I entered the chamber, Robin and Frankie were kissing. The steward withdrew and I sat in the window and pretended not to be there. In between kisses, Frankie said: "I have wondrous news."

I admired his agility, for it was merely a momentary pause in his smile, but I saw fear cross Carr's features. Did he think she was carrying his child?

"My Lord Northampton will seek an annulment for me."

He tucked a curl behind his ear several times as he gazed at her. His face showed not fear anymore, but bewilderment. It was a strange tableau. A perfumed creature of the King adored by a woman whose strength of purpose exceeded his own.

"Can it be done? By a wife?"

"No. My Lord Northampton and my father must pursue it," she said, an edge to her voice that I knew to be disappointment. She had expected her lover to cheer, not to ask procedural questions.

"Your great-uncle is the last man I would expect to consider an annulment for anyone, especially his own kin," he said.

"Are you happy at the news?" prompted Frankie.

He could have smiled and kissed her, whatever his doubts, as a real courtier would have done. But Robert Carr was more honest than that.

"Frank, my love, be careful. Essex is the son of a hero, however deep his faults. Your union will be picked over like a barrel of apples. It is you who will be found rotten, not because that is the truth but because it is always so. More will condemn a wife who disobeys her lord than a husband who misuses his wife."

Frankie began to twist the lace on one cuff. She turned from him and sat in the window. "The King does everything he can to promote marriages between his Scotch and English subjects."

"I'm the King's man, Frank. I'm with him under sun and moon now the Prince is gone. Everything I have comes from him and can be taken away by him."

I felt for Carr as he stood looking sadly at Frankie's back, wanting so much to please, pulled in all directions. Since finding favor with the King, he turned everything to gold for others, but was unable to gratify himself.

"I want us to be together in God's sight," she said, very quietly.

Carr went to her then and stroked her hair. "I am afraid for you, is all. You . . . we must tread very carefully. The Court is alive with vipers, many with a grudge toward your family." She turned and rested against him like a hawk on the wind.

For several hours they talked quietly and I lay, dozing, on a folded dust sheet, thinking of all the things I had to do for the morrow. Each time I suggested we leave, one or other of them begged me to stay a little longer. They had been apart for weeks and had much to discuss, including the possible annulment, which held much danger but perhaps also a chance for their happiness.

It was nearly midnight when Carr finally put on his cloak and we accompanied Frankie to her apartment. After that, he offered me his coach to take me home, by way of thanks for my patience, but I refused, not wanting the inhabitants of my street woken by the sound of a carriage. What tittle-tattle would follow the sight of me arriving home after curfew in a nobleman's conveyance?

As we walked together through the dark courtyards of the palace, slippery with the moss and slime of winter months, I pictured myself at the door to Arthur's manor, looking at the children running through his fields to the wide, sunlit horizons beyond. He had described to me the air of the place, perfumed by Persian roses he had planted all along the front of the house, and the avenue of beech that separated his home from the rest of the world.

"You!"

I was wrenched from dreaming by Sir Thomas Overbury, who stood not ten paces away. As his eyes moved from Carr to me, his choler appeared to double. He shouted, for the whole palace to hear: "That is her procuress! You've been with that base woman!"

A knot of servants standing a few paces behind Overbury fell silent. Great heat flared up inside me. Overbury's insult to me was grave, but that offered Frankie was unpardonable, as was clear from the servants' shocked faces.

Carr walked up to Overbury, waving at the servants to leave as he did so. Overbury held a large scroll in one hand but with the other he gripped Carr's arm, shouting all the while.

"I've been working all night on this . . ." He shook the parchment under Carr's nose. "I search in vain for you to sign it, worry what has befallen you, and all the while you've been lying with that notorious baggage . . . Do you not know that the value of property is diminished if shared?"

"I hope you have no plans for the morrow," Carr said loudly, turning to me, "you'll be fair beat."

"I am getting married," I said, fury provoking a reply when normally I would have stayed silent.

"In truth?" said Carr, surprised enough to forget Overbury for a moment, even though the man was still jerking his arm. "Then I insist you take my coach," he said, pleased for me even in the midst of Overbury's tirade.

"You give suck to the gadabed's bawd?" Overbury shouted, dropping Carr's arm. His pale face flickered in the torchlight like a malevolent devil, his black clothes disappearing into the shadows. The injury he did me pricked like a spur, perhaps because there was truth in it, but I replied to Carr as if I had heard nothing. Frankie had taught me the power of being inscrutable.

"Thank you, my lord, I will take it gladly."

A strange noise escaped Overbury, something between a snort and a squeal. He snatched up his gloves, leather with stiff cuffs, and slapped Carr hard across the face with them. Carr was so astonished it took him a while to speak.

"You hit me now?" he said, incredulous.

"Behave as a child, be chastised as one." Overbury's arrogance had swollen fit to burst since his being readmitted to Court, even though it was only Carr's intervention with the King that had brought it about. "If you'd rather demean yourself with that doxy than work on the King's business, agree to what you owe me and I'll leave you to truck with the whore's servant," he spat.

"You'd not have a penny were it not for me!" shouted Carr, finally riled. He snatched the gloves from Overbury's hand and threw them as far as he could across the courtyard.

"You won't manage without me. You'll crawl back."

"I have legs of my own to stand on," retorted Carr.

"Did you think you could keep it secret from me? You are bewitched, there can be no other cause for your madness. Be rid of her."

"You think you're the King now? He's the only one can tell me what to do!"

As they insulted each other, the watchful servants memorized every word. In the morning, the whole Court would know that Sir Thomas Overbury had accused the Countess of Essex of being a base whore. Had Overbury stabbed Frankie, he would not have inflicted greater damage. The only return from such defamation was to be offered a full and public apology or else for her to kill herself. Even without evidence, and in full knowledge of the accuser's spite and jealousy, he could ruin Frankie with those two words.

"Mama, you are beautiful," said Mary, staring up at me. It was not yet nine o'clock but I was dressed, with Barbara's help, and satisfied with what I had achieved. It was over twenty years since I had last been a bride and I hoped that what I lacked in youth, I made up for in charm and competence.

Henry came toward me, his hands behind his back. The little conjuror brought forth a small bouquet of red anemones.

"We saved our pennies," he said, blushing. I thanked him and his sisters, their gift a blessing on the marriage.

"John, go to the church. As soon as you see Arthur, run home and escort me there."

He left and Barbara offered me a cup of ale, but I was too full of nerves to eat or drink, and could only walk about the parlor, laughing at the children's chitchat and their wonder at my glamour. Before marrying George, I had felt mainly dread. Arthur was everything George was not, and nothing that George was. At last, our union was to be blessed by God.

The minutes passed and John did not come.

"Where is John, Mama?" asked Mary. She was now nine years old and astute.

"Is Sir Arthur poorly?" asked Katherine.

"Why doesn't he send a note?" asked Henry, remembering Arthur's previous messages. I was more alert to the passing of time than ever before; each person who walked beneath the window, every word spoken, every breath, brought with it a growing dread, so that when the quarter bell rang I thought I would go mad with waiting and sent Barbara after John. At the half-hour, they returned together. They looked confused and upset. By the noonday peal, old Maggie called the children to dinner as if to a wake. As the bells struck one, Barbara helped me out of the dress for which I had paid more than I could afford and returned it to the pawn merchant. I did not cry. I felt nothing. I was numb, as if drugged, so heavy a weight pressing on my heart that it could not move me. John went to seek Arthur, but he was not at home.

It was a little after the four o'clock bell when Arthur arrived. He looked not at me but all about, as if in a stranger's house. Even so, the sight of his handsome face revived me sufficient to stand as he walked into the room, but from under its boulder of care and sadness my heart began to beat so fast I was distracted, as if this were death itself advancing. Parts of my body that were usually dry, such as my cheeks, forearms and the backs of my knees, gave up a sweat; I could feel it pricking up through my skin, and I was so cold my chest trembled.

"Madam," he said, as if reading from a letter. I sat but he did not. "As Prince Henry's body servant, my position at his Court ceased the moment he died. I had hoped," he looked increasingly uncomfortable, "to join the Court of Prince Charles, now installed at St. James's Palace, but I have not." He cleared his throat. "It seems that Prince Charles is aware of my . . ." Arthur struggled ". . . our long association." My body reacted strangely to the news that the heir to the throne knew our sin. The muscles down my back convulsed. Arthur stared at me and I fought to appear calm.

"I do not know how he has heard," Arthur continued, more his normal self. "Charles and his brother were not close and now that Henry is gone perhaps Charles wants things to be different. He is only thirteen. But neither he nor my father will own me while I am entangled with you. I must renounce you," he finished in a rush.

Finally, I was sufficiently goaded to speak. "Your father? But you invited him."

"I did not invite him. He heard rumors that I was to marry and rode down. It is the news of the Countess of Essex's involvement with Mary Woods that has persuaded him you are of bad character," said Arthur with unusual bluntness.

I almost laughed. My connection with Frankie, which had once appealed to Arthur, was now the reason to abandon me?

"And you?" I said. "Do you also think that I, the mother of your three children, am 'of bad character'? You know full well that the Countess did not meet Mary Woods through me." There was a long silence, filled by the muted sounds of the outside world. Arthur winced at every noise the children made upstairs.

"It does not matter what I think," he said eventually, "but what others think."

"Make me your legitimate wife, which I am in all but name, and then there will be no scandal attached to us. Your father will come to accept the situation. He will love his grandchildren."

Arthur looked vexed.

"It is not seemly to marry a woman who can no longer bear children and those . . ."

"I can bear children! I still bleed."

". . . And those already born cannot be mine legitimately unless I own them, which I cannot do without great damage to my reputation and prospects. My father has made that clear."

"It is acceptable to fornicate with a woman for ten years, to have three beautiful children by her, to allow her to buy you clothes and care for you. But to marry her invites scandal?" I moved closer to Arthur; he stepped back.

"I am sorry you hoped we would be married," he said, increasingly calm in the face of my agitation.

"Hoped?! It was to be today!"

"The date was discussed some time ago. We have not spoken of it since."

"Indeed, you have not spoken to call it off! And now you intend to forget about me and all that is yours in this house?"

"I cannot give you an allowance, if that is what you mean, for I have debts."

"Debts greater than those you owe our children? Not to mention the promises you gave to a dying man?" I asked. Arthur did not reply but twisted his cap in his hand, letting the long plume on it flow through his fingers with every revolution. He spoke without raising his eyes.

"If we meet in public it will be as if I do not know you. I will not write or see you again." He hesitated as if to say more, perhaps of how he regretted his treatment of me, how sorry he was that he could not behave with honor, that he would miss watching his children grow, but in the end he just left. He talked with kindness to the urchin holding his horse, but not to me.

I ran out and grabbed his arm, not caring who saw or heard me.

"Who will teach your son to ride, to handle a sword, to become a gentleman? Your girls adore you! They squeal with delight when you appear and beg to be in your arms. Mary needs medicine and doctors for her cough. You would ride away from all the love that is yours in this house because there is a moment of gossip about the Countess of Essex? There is always prattle about her; it has nothing to do with me. We are your family."

My words hit the soft point behind his newly donned armor. He held my shoulders and looked directly into my eyes, a tear falling each time he blinked. He leaned forward and I lifted my mouth but he kissed my cheek, quickly turned away and swung up into the saddle.

I ran along, clutching at his foot, but he treated me as any beggar and steered a careful route along the narrow row. I knew that this would be the last time I saw him there.

I watched as he disappeared and then for a long time afterward, jostled by all who passed. Finally, I turned and tried for home as if struggling against the weight of the gray Thames rushing me out to sea. I think Mistress Bowdlery found me. She pulled me from my knees and dragged me home. I curled before the fireplace, a tiny warm patch in the cold room, half in the ashes, half on hard boards. Dust to dust. Would tears, mixed with wood ash, form lye to burn my skin and make soap of me? Then I would serve a purpose. Soap with which to wash my children even if I could not feed them.

A door opened. Arthur with moth-shadowed face? No, mud on worn hem, it was old Maggie who helped me to bed. My mind wandered, further and further into the dark wood. How long does it take a small child to starve?

I lay that way for two days. Even the embraces of my children gave no comfort, for I had failed them. My sister's voice could not penetrate my madness and my younger brother's kindness made me shrink deeper into my shame.

Frightened, old Maggie sent for Weston, who was sufficiently perturbed to ask Frankie for help. It took him two days to find her; she was hiding in her apartments in Greenwich Palace, away from the gossip that was washing around Whitehall about the nature of her friendship with Robert Carr. She came without hesitation, her face obscured by a deep hood, bringing rum and tincture of opium. I wished she would leave; I did not want her to witness my degradation, but she lay beside me on the bed, stroking my hair and chafing my hands. As I did not speak, she talked, mainly of the scandal Overbury had incited with his insult to her.

"I need you, Anne. Overbury will scupper my annulment. He is hand-in-glove with Archbishop Abbot, both support my husband; without your wits I have no hope of getting the better of him." There was never a mention of Arthur. "I can appoint my own household when I marry Robin, and you and the children shall live with me. You will be happily married yourself soon; Mr. Palmer has intentions toward you, it is quite plain." But I did not believe that Frankie or I would marry again; the angels had turned on us.

After a further day and night of my torpor, Weston reappeared.

"Sir Thomas Overbury is arrested and in the Tower, held close prisoner," he announced, out of breath. This news at last cut through the wool in my skull. For the first time in days, I felt that my head and my body were no longer two divorced entities. Frankie, who had barely left my side, stood; the place where she had lain quickly cooled.

"How do you know?" she demanded.

"The Earl of Northampton commissioned me to take a letter to Viscount Rochester who is ill in bed . . ."

"Robin? What ails him?"

"A griping in the guts but it is not serious. The Viscount told me its contents. Sir Thomas was arrested today, during the meeting of the Privy Council."

"On what charge?"

"For refusing the Embassy in Russia."

Frankie let out a great laugh. "Of course he refused it! How could he interfere in everyone's business from Moscow? Was Robin surprised? Distressed?"

"I could not tell."

"To be held close, forbidden letters and visitors—Robin must have asked that of the King," Frankie said, turning to me. I heard, but to my increasing distress, I could not respond; I was locked inside my body. Frankie let out a sharp sigh, impatient with my self-absorption, but I swear I could do no other. She began to pace, muttering, enacting in her mind's eye all the possible consequences of Overbury's incarceration. Suddenly she stopped.

"Weston, I need a new service of you. If my great-uncle can get you the position, would you act as Overbury's jailer? Someone we trust absolutely must guard him, to be sure he steals out no letters."

I could see wisdom in the idea; a written accusation from him would immediately halt the annulment. Frankie would pay Weston, which I could not, but I felt his reluctance and I did not like the proposal either. He was old and should have easier employment. I often needed him at home, not merely for his service but for his unfailing loyalty and steady company. This would be another sacrifice I made for Frankie's happiness.

Weston was silent a long while, waiting, I think for me to find a pretext to excuse him from this task. But I could not rouse myself. How to shield Weston when I could not protect my own children from want and harm? He glanced at me, but I failed him.

I failed him.

He did not look at Frankie but at his hands as he nodded. I am sure he agreed only to protect me from Overbury's spite, which would damage me as much as Frankie.

After Weston left, I turned my face to the wall and drifted off. I did not seek death; rather I sensed that life was drowning me. I do not remember how long I lay that way as there was nothing to which memory could cling, but at some point I became aware of pain. It disturbed my stupor at the bottom of the deepest, blackest, coldest sea. A spiteful imp tormented me with pins and sharp pinches that made me wriggle and squirm until I was forced to surface. I flailed at the devil who tortured me but by the light of a single candle, opening my eyes, I saw Frankie standing over me brandishing a needle.

"She wakes!" shouted Frankie, flushed from her attack. She hauled me up, propping me on a cushion, and washed my face with a wet cloth. Old Maggie hovered beside her with a hot posset that she put to my lips before I could sink again. Her face was a breath away from mine and I saw tears streaming along her wrinkles. I stroked the glistening drops that fell on her hands, spotted with age, and the gratitude I felt warmed me a little.

Frankie took the cup and raised it.

"A toast to Anne and Frankie." She drank and then pressed the cup into my hand. The warmth and weight of it shocked me. I had become a ghost.

"Say it," said Frankie, squeezing my fingers on to the cup. She wanted to pull me back from hopelessness, as I had her, but I was tired of struggle. She put her hands either side of my face and blew into my mouth as midwives do to silent babies. The love of one who shares the tribulations of your sex can be as consoling as any marriage. Frankie was showing me that I was not worthless because I had been thrown away.

"To Frankie and Anne," I mumbled and took a large swallow.

"Louder. Remember, things always change."

"To Frankie and Anne," I said, not believing it.

"Christ alive, Anne, shout!"

"To Frankie and Anne," I said, clearing my throat for it was a long time since I had spoken. Frankie grabbed the cup, drained it, and threw it as hard as she could into the fireplace. We both shrieked as it smashed against the backplate. Rum spat blue in the flames. I spun out of bed to stamp on the embers that erupted from the fire and flew over the hearth onto the wooden floor.

"Now you are dancing!" said Frankie, laughing.

18

A month later I was greatly recovered and waiting anxiously with Frankie in her parlor.

"You are sure of the veil?" I asked, perhaps for the third or fourth time, never more nervous than at that moment. Many people had parts to play, I alone aware of them all. If I had forgotten or overlooked a single thing, if anybody was late, or early, if anybody veered from the agreements they had made or was loose with protocol, both Frankie and I would be entirely undone. It was a strange and unpleasant sensation, to be in a position of the utmost strategic importance, with peril not power my only reward.

"Lord Northampton has reassured me on that point," said Frankie. "I feel like a tennis ball frayed with overplay," she said, fidgeting ceaselessly. She took my hand. "In truth, you risk much. I will never forget my debt to you, Anne, never."

I was about to wave away her thanks, as I tended to do, but her gratitude brought me such fear that I could not. If there had been a middle way, a safer path, I would have taken it; but without Arthur, I had only the choice of living boldly or barely surviving. He had stopped our stipend and requested of Baron Ellesmere that John and Barbara leave the household so as not to see them more; that was a fearful day. I kept hold of my mind, but my skin broke out again in itchy red patches. Frankie found John a position at her parents' palace at Audley End, but Oxford was out of his reach. Barbara was home until I could find her another position. Thomas came to tell me that he could not lend me money. I did not doubt his lack of cash; he spent all he had chasing around town, buying clothes and girls beyond his means, much as George and I knew he would.

Prices were rising, and for the first time I was truly afeared of how I was to feed and keep us warm. Everything that could be sold had been, except for George's chair; we ate the cheapest food, lit no fires even on wet days and no longer took wherries, as resoling my boots was slightly cheaper. I had to search the muddy grass and sparse bushes of Lincoln's Inn and Moorfields for ingredients for Mary's syrup. George's cat had to catch her own food and every other day I did not eat. Eustace, my younger brother, paid some of my rent, which staved off eviction. Even marrying Weston would not help us for long; he was an old man with a son of his own to leave his property to when he died. As the widow of a doctor I had some slight respectability that might allow me to find clients among the middling sort, those who knew nothing of Arthur. Loyal and caring though Weston was toward us, he was a rough man, paid to collect debts because others feared or owed him. As his wife, I would lose the little respect I still commanded and Frankie would be forbidden friendship with so low a person as I would then be. My worries sometimes gave me pains in the head that made my words come out backward. My life as a widow careened on turbulent waters; I felt very keenly how rocky was the bottom, how flimsy the boat, and how very nimbly and hard I must row. I kept a firm grip on Frankie's hand, as much for my own comfort as hers.

I was glad of the distraction when her steward announced a woman of middle age and a nervous girl, at least five years younger than Frankie.

"Lady Monson, good day, and this must be your daughter," said Frankie, hiding extreme nerves under a warm smile. The Monson women curtsied low. Lady Monson was wife to Sir Thomas, Master of the Armory at the Tower and Master Falconer to the King. Reputedly the best falconer in Europe, he was also a client of the Howard family, Lord Northampton in particular, and friend to George and Simon Forman. It was Sir Thomas who appointed my brother Eustace to the royal mews and I had always enjoyed his company and was fond of his wife. She was a stout matron with nine living children and a necessarily practical bent of mind.

"Your ladyship, may I introduce my daughter Janet," said Lady

Monson. Frankie smiled at the girl and presented her with a small box. The girl opened it mutely. Inside was a ring of garnets and small diamonds.

"A token of gratitude," said Frankie. Lady Monson smiled on behalf of her shy child.

"Perhaps we should begin," said Frankie. I led Janet to the bed chamber. Laid on the bed were copies of the clothes Frankie was wearing, in the same pale green silk, made by a tailor living as far from Frankie's as possible.

"Your waist is smaller," I said as I helped Janet to change. I set about the white-faced girl with a box of pins. The shoes were slightly large, so I stuffed rags in the toes, then arranged her hair and powdered her skin until she looked as identical to Frankie as possible.

Once dressed, I took Janet into the closet off the bedchamber and helped her lie down in a large linen press. I smoothed the dress around the girl, closed the lid and, out of habit, said a prayer. A virgin at Court is rarer than a diamond in the Fleet ditch and it had taken much effort to discover one. The closet door was well disguised when shut so I hoped it would remain unnoticed. Lady Monson was taking her leave as I joined Frankie, promising to return when we sent her word.

"If this fails I am finished," said Frankie. I resisted reminding her that we would both be finished, but I did stop her pouring herself a drink.

"You must smell the same as well," I said. "Let us pray that this is the final hurdle."

If it was the last, it was also the worst. To have to prove her virginity, even though it was Essex's insufficiency under examination for the annulment, had brought a cold fury into her soul I had not witnessed before, not even at the worst of her husband's cruelties. While admitting impotence in his marriage to the Annulment Commission, Essex had implied that Frankie was not chaste. The head of the Commission, Archbishop Abbott, a sincere but narrow-minded Calvinist who virulently hated Catholics, Howards and divorce, ordered her searched even though her virtue was irrelevant to the case.

"Lord Northampton is pressing Overbury to make cause with us," said Frankie, making a small snorting sound.

"Is that not good?" I said.

"The damage has been done. Everywhere I go I feel a new disrespect. No matter how many times he apologizes, people will never forget that he called me base."

I could not argue. At Court, in the Exchanges, even in the back streets, there was frenzied talk about women's disobedience to men, the breakdown of law and order, the canker of corruption and effeminacy that tainted the King himself. Frankie was the perfect scapegoat, representing everything most hated: a pretty, pampered woman with independent ideas, a Catholic, a courtier. The libels and broadsheets boosted their sales by illustrating their broadsides against her with stock woodblock prints of half-naked harlots. I must have frowned, for Frankie asked, "It touches you too?"

"The few clients I still have invite me in the hope that I will give them gossip about you. No one pays me."

"Once Robin and I are married, we will bore people with our respectability."

"And if it is brought up in Parliament?"

Frankie laughed and patted my arm. "Why would Parliament be interested in whether the Earl of Essex can stiffen his member?"

"If your annulment is granted and you marry Carr, Parliament will not want a powerful Catholic family allied to the most important man at Court after the King. When they pause in their hateful speeches against Catholics, they fill the time with railing against the King's favorite and the Scottish."

Frankie looked hard at me for a long while, before shaking her head. "The King does not listen to Parliament; Parliament listens to the King, and he wants the annulment. You worry too much."

"That is true," I said, looking away from her. I rehearsed each step in my mind while Frankie fiddled with the gold chain around her neck. The knock came.

Into the parlor processed the six inspectors appointed by the Annulment Commission; two midwives of fair repute and four noblewomen of mature years who were all mothers, Lady Mary Tyrwhitt, Lady Alice Carew, Lady Elizabeth Dallison and Lady

Anne Waller. All looked discomfited to be there and Frankie did nothing to lessen their unease. With an admirable display of mortification, she curtsied to the noblewomen and offered them refreshment. All refused, as anxious as Frankie to be released from the ordeal.

"Lady Carew, it has been some time since we have had the pleasure of each other's company," said Frankie, quietly. "May I offer you my hearty good wishes on the birth of your first grandchild. Is that a picture of him?" she asked, indicating the locket that hung from a long chain around the neck of Lady Carew.

"It is he," said the lady, flushing with pride and opening the jewel to hold out the miniature within for Frankie's inspection. She praised the child and the fine workmanship of the limner and jeweler. In return, Lady Carew praised Frankie's own valuable chain. Frankie made to go but Lady Carew stopped her, blushing furiously.

"My lady, we have been told to inspect your chamber before we begin, I am sorry."

"Do not be sorry, Lady Carew, I am happy to oblige. Mistress Turner, would you be kind enough to show Lady Carew into the bedchamber? Does any other lady need to accompany you?" asked Frankie. In the end, I showed Lady Carew and a midwife into Frankie's chamber. Lady Carew gave it no more than a cursory glance but the midwife took her time. She moved the arras to check that no one hid behind and spotted the door into the closet. My stomach clenched but the midwife stopped short of opening the presses in there. She finally nodded to me and we returned to the parlor.

"To save us all from great distress, the noble lady may be veiled," said Lady Carew, cringing with embarrassment. "And no questions shall be put to the Countess during her ordeal, but she shall return to this room afterward if there be any matters to discuss. These are the orders of the Commission," she said, and I was sure that the Earl of Northampton had exerted his influence to ensure them.

Frankie and I withdrew to the closet off the bedchamber where I retrieved Janet from the linen press and helped Frankie into it, removing her necklace, which I gave to the girl to put on. After closing the closet door, I helped Janet to lie on the bed and pulled a veil over her head, making sure that it entirely hid her face and neck and that only the gold chain fell below it.

I opened the door to the inspectors. The midwives gathered at the foot of the bed but the noble mothers hovered by the door. I stood at the head, ready to calm the girl, or even put a hand over her mouth should she cry out.

"If it please you, m'lady," said the midwife who appeared to be in charge. The noble ladies turned their backs as one while Janet Monson slid further down the bed and raised her knees. I was careful to keep the veil in place and patted the girl's shoulder as the midwife pulled up her skirts to reveal two white legs. She held her candle close, with care not to burn the skin, and the midwife carefully pushed two fingers through the bush of dark hair and into the private place. The legs on the bed twitched in surprise and stiffened, but no noise came from the veiled figure. The midwife moved her fingers around briefly and then withdrew them, wiping them carefully on a damp cloth.

"Ladies, if you would come and inspect?" invited the midwife to the noblewomen huddled by the door. Janet gave out a little scream and struggled to sit up. The ladies in the corner turned and my heart thumped in horror. If Janet revealed herself in her panic we would be entirely undone.

"My lady, your modesty will be preserved," I said, leaning over to hide her face from the onlookers, digging my fingers into her shoulders as hard as I dared without making her scream louder. "It is nearly over," I said kindly, glaring at her in warning through the thick veil. Janet slowly sank back and I breathed again.

Hesitantly, none of them wanting to reveal even a suspicion of eagerness, the noble ladies shuffled to the end of the bed. The candle was held close again and the midwife held the lips open. Janet groaned.

"If you feel about a finger's length within, you will notice a closing, which shows that no man has ever entered this passage. Lady Carew, would you care to confirm what I have felt?"

"Oh no!" said the good lady, horrified at the thought. She would not be known as the lady with a finger in the Countess of Essex. The midwife looked at the other ladies but all three shook their heads.

"Very well, I will do my best to show you." The midwife pressed her finger down on the entrance, causing the legs to stiffen again. "I am sorry, my lady, forgive me." The noble ladies made the briefest and most feeble attempt to peer into the passage, the midwife announced herself satisfied, and the group withdrew.

I helped Janet off the bed, raising her veil to find the girl's face flushed and sodden with tears.

"Hush, child, hush. You did well and the Countess and your family will be proud of you. A little prodding like that is good practice for when you will be married. Indeed, you'll be lucky if you get it so gently then." The girl cringed and I left her to compose herself while I helped Frankie out of the linen press. The necklace was swapped back and Janet sat on a stool in a corner. Frankie did not look at the crying girl.

I hurried into the parlor.

"I am sorry to have kept you. The Countess is distressed," I told them. The ladies looked drained themselves and even the midwives seemed nervous.

"I shall be able to report back to the Commission that the Countess of Essex is fit for carnal copulation and still a virgin," proclaimed Lady Carew. "On this we are all agreed." Within a few moments the women had retrieved their cloaks and were gone.

19

We became like two sparrows, Frankie and I. Lord Essex refused to return her dowry until the Annulment Commission had made its decision, and her family were prodigiously in debt from building the largest private house in the country, bigger than any royal palace. "Spend and God will send," was the motto of most courtiers, although Frankie's parents got most of their money from bribes and from siphoning off monies meant for the navy and soldiers' wages in Ireland. It was barely a secret; Frankie had told me this with no embarrassment because it was normal at Court and the King himself survived in like manner. Everyone was tremendously in debt; there, liberality was next to godliness.

As her parents had no longer any need to buy her obedience, Frankie had little money and I none. I became her fripperer, taking objects to pawn merchants, the money from which she spent on theater tickets and a few spangles to avert suspicion that she was short, while I spent my portion on food, medicine and coal. She was generous, as always, and lived in expectation of great riches if the Commission granted her release from Essex. Although her own family, especially her parents, were famously profligate, Carr was their equal. Marriage to him would cure our financial ills; tables so heavily laden drop more than crumbs for those who wait patiently.

In her apartment, emptied of her husband's possessions and his sulking, there was a feeling of abeyance. The news that an annulment was to be considered provoked so great a storm of rebuke, from pulpit to market stall, that Frankie went out rarely and always heavily cloaked. This imprisonment, aggravated by her impatience to be married and to start a family, made her short-tempered and anxious. Girls eight or even ten years her junior were paraded daily before Carr as prospective wives.

It was a strange time. I was not under the governance and protection of a father, husband or lover. Arthur's desertion of me caused gentlewomen to cease requesting my help. Frankie's parents offered me small payments in return for acting as their daughter's chaperone; I could not refuse the money, and so I slept many nights that winter on a narrow truckle in her chamber. I hated to be away from my children, but old Maggie looked after them in order that I could earn at least something.

One of those nights started like many others. Frankie and Carr were talking past one in the morning, and I could not sleep.

"Do you like it?" he asked. "The King ordered it. It's wee but it's not a bad likeness." The bed-hangings were closed but I could see their bodies in silhouette. I guessed Carr had given Frankie a miniature of himself but, unbidden, the image of Judith severing Holofernes's head came to my mind, the blood hot and strong-smelling, the maid wincing as the still twitching head dropped into her sack. I sat up, revolted by my own thoughts.

Frankie opened the bed curtain but I continued to watch; it was too dark for her to know whether I slept or not. She walked naked to the mantel, picked up a candlestick and returned to bed without closing the curtains. The sanctum brightened as if angels slept there. She held the pendant close to the flames and I wondered how it was for Frankie to hold in her palm a tiny painted image of the man, gorgeous in jeweled silk, who now lay damply naked beside her.

"It is perfect," she said.

Robin knelt up and put the chain, on which the miniature was threaded, over her head. I should have looked away from their nakedness, but I did not. "Now my head is always between your breasts. Did you know that miniatures are stuck to playing cards? Guess which suit I chose."

"Hearts," said Frankie, putting the candlestick on a table.

"I didn't think of that," said Robin, sounding surprised. "It's diamonds!" he laughed, keeling onto his side and pulling her down with him. "I have a lot to learn about love. But do you see how thin I am? My life is all work."

Frankie stroked his chest and I was moved by the simple gesture. Many times she had listed to me the features in Carr that she most loved: his eyes with their dancing lights, so unlike the dark, ever-narrowed gaze of her suspicious husband; his golden beauty and love of adornment equal to hers; his neat, white teeth. She was astonished by the way he loved to kiss and stroke her; his smell, with no hint of horse; his hands, keen to discover every inch of her; his loud and eager laugh; a mind that struggled with politics and law but reveled in her.

There was only one thing about Carr that disquieted her: his need to be loved by everyone, the English and the Scots, the Queen and the King, Essex, Overbury and her family, a craving for acceptance that could never be fulfilled in a riven Court.

"I had to visit the worms with the King today," Robin said. "You know he's appointed a groom of the chamber to take some with us whenever we travel?"

"Would I were a worm, I might see you more. Are they thriving?"

"Not really but it gives the King such pleasure to get silk from ugly worms for the cost of a handful of leaves that the keepers pretend there's more silk made than there is. He wishes he could spin it himself, what with the Treasury as it is." Robin laughed, then corrected himself, as if the King could hear him. "That's not unreasonable of course, but the place stinks."

The palace clock struck two, the chimes rolling across the black, cold night and into their luminous bed.

"I must go, the King will not be pleased I wasn't with him this night. I'm like his wee greyhound, always called to heel. But, Frank, I have to tell you, Essex and his crew plot against me. Here's the one place I'm safe from being moaned at or stabbed."

"Here you are safe," she confirmed, impressing me as ever with her seeming confidence when I knew she was terribly afraid that the annulment would not be granted or that Robin would waver.

"Blasted Overbury has put everyone against me with his meddling and his high carriage of himself," said Carr, deep anger in his voice. "It's hard to find someone to take his place; the work's too much for one man."

"Does he write to you?" asked Frankie, all innocence.

"He can't, but I send letters in. I tell him I'm working to get him a pardon, just to keep him quiet 'til he apologizes to you, but he's as stubborn as a bull to the butcher." Fear tightened Carr's voice as he spoke of the overwhelming nature of his duties; he may not have missed Overbury's friendship, but he yearned for his help and his ability to shield the favorite from the constant pestering of those seeking favor.

With much kissing and promises of another visit soon, Robin left. Frankie called softly, to see if I was awake. She invited me into the comfort and warmth of her bed, and we fell asleep instantly.

A little while later I was woken. Someone was in the room. It was still dark and freezing air crept under the covers as Frankie moved, already awake.

"Weston was waiting in the Privy Corridor for me with a letter from Overbury." It was Carr back again.

"Take light from the fire, my love, I cannot see you." Carr lit a candle and I climbed down from the bed to wrap Frankie in her shawl.

"Weston says Overbury's brother-in-law visited him yesterday. Lidcote's his name."

"How was he allowed?" said Frankie.

"I don't know, he must have paid the right man. Weston swears he searched this Lidcote, on going in and coming out of the cell, and found naught on him. But Overbury claims he's written a full account of our relations and that Lidcote will circulate it widely."

Frankie stared at him in horror. "Oh, God in heaven."

I stared too, but also I was confused. Was Overbury threatening to reveal Frankie's infidelity, in which case he must have evidence we knew not of; or his own secretest love of Carr, which was shared by the King? The first would destroy Frankie, the second would destroy the Court; it would be suicide, but then Overbury was the sort of person who would enjoy dragging as many people as possible into hell with him.

"This same Lidcote told Overbury that I am not working to

secure his release. Overbury writes that I am 'the most odious man alive.'" Carr waved the letter at Frankie. He kicked the metal fire grate with the toe of his boot. The fire was banked and the few sparks that escaped burned out at the peak of their glowing arcs. His face was closed in a way that Frankie could not have missed. It was clear that he was terrified to have an enemy who knew so much about him. Perhaps he also felt regret at deceiving his best friend, or at least for having been found out in it?

"I'll call on your great-uncle Northampton."

"How can he help?" said Frankie. She had told me that Robin had recently gone against Northampton's wishes in choosing a new Under-Secretary of State and that her great-uncle would pretend to forgive him but would exact revenge at some future point.

"He has more spies than anyone. You and I must stay apart. Overbury'll need to apologize to me now, as well as to you."

Frankie made a gesture to stop him, kiss him, but he only patted her shoulder and left. In the enveloping night, we heard the logs shift in the fireplace, slowly consumed by a gentle burn. Outside, despite the late hour, footsteps echoed in the courtyard below, torchlight reflecting like thousands of distant fires in the diamonds of the window. We returned to bed but neither of us slept.

Two days later, Weston visited me with dread news. The moment he took his leave, I left the house and stumbled about the streets, looking for the painter Larkin's building. It was but fifteen minutes from my door, but the way was clogged with goods' carts from the wharves and people in such numbers that we were pressed to a standstill every few paces. I ducked through courts and branching passages but there was no escaping the crush; I felt I was being smothered in oilcloth, my ears deafened not by the swearing and vexation that surrounded me but by Weston's urgent whispers.

Although I am blessed with a sanguine temper, able to appear calm when ruffled, this was different. The morning was punctuated by Mary's worsening cough that strained my heart until I thought it would crumble like moth-eaten fabric. Barbara and old Maggie went about with red eyes. Every night I woke at two or three of the clock, if I slept at all, full of worry.

When I was close to shouting at the people blocking my way, I spied a servant of Frankie's in a courtyard to my right. A boy with fingers stained red led me to a studio on the top floor.

I tried to calm myself as I looked for Frankie. Large windows in the north wall cast a glow over the real and the artificed. The boy returned to his task of grinding pigment on a stone, another was cleaning brushes, and two apprentices painted curtains and carpets into the backgrounds of portraits. Frankie's sisters and mother were depicted there in such colorful array that Frankie was for once obscured. I finally spotted her, beyond the artist at his easel, standing motionless beside a huge chair. I nodded briefly at Larkin as I passed.

"Forgive us," called Frankie to the painter as she abandoned her pose to kiss me. "I have finally been persuaded to sit for a portrait, to mark Tommy's wedding to Elizabeth Cecil. She is eighteen." Frankie was fishing. She was older than Elizabeth but still twice as beautiful, as she well knew. "Are you ill?" Frankie asked me, suddenly serious, seeing my eyes half-closed from the pain in my head and heart.

"Robert Carr has asked for Overbury's release," I told her.

Frankie's face, so filled with love and concern a moment before, stiffened like a death mask.

"How do you know?"

"The Lieutenant of the Tower was drunk and talkative last night. Weston came to see me this morning as soon as his watch was over."

"Robin will not sacrifice me for Overbury," she said.

"An intimate friendship of many years cannot be easily surrendered and Carr is suffering remorse at his friend's long imprisonment," I said. Tiny pearls of sweat broke through the ceruse on Frankie's skin. Her self-assurance was worn paper-thin, the slightest stress tore it.

"They will abandon the annulment," she whispered, to herself.

I glanced at Larkin, to be sure he could not overhear. "Visit Robin."

"I have tried. He says we are too closely watched. The outcry about the annulment has shocked him and the King has refused him a London house and wants him close at all times." I could picture it all: the King forever pawing at Carr, like an old woman strokes a cat, the old crone's love answered by a purr, which gives her purpose. Carr had to wind himself around the King's ankles, ever agreeable and wanting of favor. He who was called the most powerful man at Court was nothing but a pet. His whole life, since birth, had depended on the King for its shape and direction. Even then, although the King was agreeable to Frankie being rid of a bad marriage, Carr had not asked it of him, the Earl of Northampton had. It suited the King to agree, and so it must suit Carr too. Purr, purr, around the King's bony, bent ankles. I had sympathy for him; sometimes I felt the same.

"If Overbury is released, he will run straight to Essex. They will bribe some servant for evidence of my love for Robin and use it to bring down my family. If that happens, Robin will have to fall with me or restore Overbury to his side. Simon Forman was right. Overbury is my greatest enemy because he still loves Robin."

"Or hates him with the same passion. Can he be bribed?"

"No. He seeks only to destroy us."

"Could the Lieutenant of the Tower threaten him?"

"The Lieutenant has used every form of intimidation, short of violence, to persuade Overbury to apologize to me; he says he has never met a more stubborn man."

"What of the letter of denunciation Overbury says he smuggled out?"

"My great-uncle is sure he would have heard already of any such a letter. He thinks Overbury is bluffing to get Robin to act . . . it seems to have worked."

A voice carried up the stairs, chastising the young apprentice for his sluggardly pace. "My lady mother," said Frankie, stepping back into her pose as if the ground where she stood was red-hot. "Shall we continue?" she called to Larkin, who was equally enthusiastic to look busy.

The Countess of Suffolk marched into the room, her gaze upon everything. With admiration, I noted that Frankie's face was already impassive. Only her hands were restless.

Lady Suffolk greeted neither of us, but stood behind Larkin and watched critically as he painted, looking from easel to daughter until, with a slight tut, she moved to a full-length portrait leaning against the south wall. It was of herself. She spent some time appraising it before walking slowly past others of similar size and composition, all painted to commemorate the marriage of her second son, Thomas. She paused by some covered paintings in the corner. "Who is under here?" she called the length of the studio. Larkin pretended not to hear. The Countess flicked at the coverings before the painter could stop her.

"Herberts, Russells and Seymours, hmm? What is the happy event?" she said, with so sharp an edge to her voice that I worried she had intelligence about these members of Essex's crew. Since Frankie's separation from the Earl, they had formed a close-knit party.

"If he be not Master Rubens, a painter cannot refuse commissions," said Larkin.

The Countess stared at Larkin but he said no more. "I will stay a while, hmm?" she announced, pleasing no one, and a chair was brought. "Mistress Turner, I am surprised to discover you here. I have seen you little of late."

"I have been at home, my lady," I said. "I have a daughter in poor health."

"I'm sorry to hear it," said she, brightly, "that must leave you little time to follow fashion. Hmm?" She looked me up and down with exaggerated amazement at the modesty of my attire and I grew hot at the insult but said nothing. There was no money for me to make or repair clothes. Soon there would be none left for bread and broth. Frankie was also studying my worn hems and the thinning silk at my elbows.

She waved me closer as her mother told Larkin how to improve the likeness.

"Weston says Overbury is very ill and Dr. Mayerne has been in attendance, which will soon put an end to him," I told her, expecting a smile, but Frankie remained serious.

"Are you quite well?" her mother called out.

"Doctors kill people all the time with their physick," murmured

Frankie. I knew what she was hinting at, but I would not take the bait.

"But Robert Carr might be too distraught at the death of his best friend to marry the woman he hated."

She nodded, but without appearing to consider what I had said. "If Overbury is released, we will not survive it." She returned to her pose, looking straight at Larkin, but her attention was on me.

"This portrait will be of an old woman if you two do not stop gossiping," called out the Countess.

"What are you saying, Frankie?" I said, very softly.

"Is it not plain? If Overbury is released, he will stop at nothing to prove my adultery and halt the annulment. You and I will be forced apart and cast out. I will be sent to Chartley, the whipping boy of my husband, dead while living. And you? How will your children eat? If Overbury is freed he will kill us as surely as if he ran us through."

Larkin lowered his brush in frustration.

Frankie was right. A pawn, once swept from the board, is not mourned.

Talking to herself, she continued, "If I were a man, I could end this with a duel. There would be only honor in it. But it will have to be done with a woman's weapons."

She kept her pose, and I mine, and her mother nodded and sat back in her chair, but I did not draw breath for a long time.

"No," I said finally. "Even if he dies and we are not caught, we will face God's judgment." I had seen plays in which women go mad when their desires are thwarted; they reach for the dagger or the vial of poison, and everyone dies. I wanted no such conclusion. "You would draw us onto the rocks, doing wrong in the name of good. You would lead us to a dog's death." But the news of Overbury's imminent release had made her heart burn; had she been a man, what a soldier she would have made.

"You would put Overbury's hook in your own cheek?" she asked.

"You are brave beyond caution," I warned. Was it my own ignoble passions that drew me to her—pride in my talents, greed for higher place, and safety from want? There were times I feared I used her as ill as everyone else. I did not want to risk my life for Frankie, but she was right that to do nothing was to be ruined by Overbury and give up on living.

"Think of Icarus. Better to fall from the sky than die in prison."

As I looked at Frankie by the steady north light of Larkin's studio, I saw Judith surrounded by her enemies. She was fighting to escape the man who hated her, the laws and customs that imprisoned us, to marry the man she loved. Despite all that she demanded of me, I admired that.

"I will speak to Weston," I said finally, amazed at the boldness of my voice, "but if we are discovered . . ."

We did not kiss or embrace. I curtsied to Frankie's mother as I left, but she gave barely a nod in acknowledgment. She had no idea what risks I took to save her child and her family from disgrace.

Outside, the brightness of late summer took me by surprise: I had expected darkness. I leaned against the warm brick, closed my eyes, and saw a network of tiny lines, a delicate tracery of life. I thought of Sir Thomas Overbury and wondered whether he too saw blood-red lace when he closed his eyes. I prayed fervently that he would die from the illnesses that assailed him and spare us the need to quicken his end.

I recognized James Franklin at once as the feculent character I had encountered in the backstreet apothecary shop who had behaved with too great familiarity toward me. In one hand he held a long, thin branch, wielding it like a staff of office. He lurched into a bow, revealing the single lock of reddish-gray hair that lay down his back. I stood quickly, the better to move away, for his was the rankest compound of villainous smells ever to reach my nostrils.

I led Weston into a corner. "How can you bring him to my house? He is . . . unsteady," I said.

Weston clicked his tongue in irritation. "How much choice do you think I had?"

"There must be a person of better character."

"You cannot choose a poisoner like you can a maid. Have you no stomach for this?" He appeared relieved and ready to leave.

I studied Franklin. He was on one knee, stroking George's cat. The two youngest children huddled around him, asking questions I could not hear. Mary was sitting by the fire, feverish and bored, humming tunelessly. We were gathered in the kitchen because the day was cold, although it was early September.

"I never thought you should take this path, you know that," said Weston, eyeing Franklin among the children. "But now you are so far along, it is better to keep going. He's a strange man, but who of sound mind will do what you request?"

"Mary, please stop humming," I said. Weston looked askance at my sharp tone but since agreeing to help Frankie murder a man, I found myself always with an ear half-cocked for the constable at the door and snapping more often at my children.

The apothecary gave the cat a final stroke and rose unsteadily with the help of his stick, which he then poked into corners around the range as if afeared mice might be hiding there.

"Tell him to get something that will lie in the belly a few days before it . . . is effective," I said.

Weston nodded and immediately summoned Franklin to follow him.

"I hope Mistress will be pleased with my work," he leered, bowing to me. There were liver spots on his balding scalp.

"What's your stick for?" asked Mary, wide-eyed at his strange behavior.

"It's cut from a hazel tree at midnight on Good Friday and charmed in the name of the Holy Trinity to find silver and gold."

"Do you find silver and gold?"

"Often."

"Mama, can we get a stick like that?"

The visitor bent down and stroked her cheek with a filthy finger. "I'll cut you one next Easter time."

"Franklin," said Weston, and the man juddered upright. I could only stare after him as he shuffled out. The cat, freed from his attention, jumped onto Mary's lap. My little girl had taken care of the creature since George's death, for she believed something of her father survived in it. I felt the same, although I knew it to be exactly the sort of superstitious belief for which Catholics are despised.

Two nights later, I was pulled from the deepest sleep by Mary tugging on my hand.

"What is it?"

"The cat is mewling," she said.

"Does she want to go out?"

"She is walking in circles," said the little girl through tears. I hauled myself out of bed. The room was cold. "Come lie in my warm patch," I said, helping Mary climb into the bed. Her body was hot as an iron and my heart sickened to feel it. I left the cover untucked to cool her fever. "Daddy will be cross if we don't make her better," Mary insisted. I cringed as I too heard the dreadful noise the animal was making, almost screaming.

I ran downstairs into the kitchen. Moonlight through the windows made a shadow lattice on the cat's white fur as it paced. Mary was right; she was curling around herself in circles. Sitting briefly, then standing again. The noise was terrible and I shut the kitchen door behind me so that the other children did not wake. The tortured animal began retching and sinking, then dragging itself up again. I bent to pick her up but she hissed. Close to, I could see a brown seepage from her ear.

"Do you have Mary's sickness?" I murmured. "Is your ear painful? Now it is burst it might feel better?" Unconvinced, I poured a little milk into a bowl, and placed it on the floor near the cat. She began to screech again. The noise was terrible. I felt so helpless that I pressed my hands over my ears as hard as I could. The door opened slowly and all the children stood there, staring in horror. Mary crept in and knelt beside me.

"That is blood, Mother," she said.

"Sometimes you children have that," I said, trying to compose myself. "It is very painful but then something bursts and with this brown emission comes relief."

"But she is still screeching," said Mary. She reached for the cat but it hissed at her too. With tears streaming down her face, Mary went to sit in the chair by the empty grate. As she did so, a picture came into my mind of Franklin crouching over the cat. Cold bile rushed up my throat and I ran to the back door to be sick.

"I cannot bear it!" Mary cried out, putting her hands over her ears as the cat howled again. I wanted to comfort my child but could not for disgust at myself. I shooed them all out, carrying Mary upstairs, then returned to the stink of my vomit and the screams of the cat.

I cried for the animal and for George and Arthur and Mary and dreams now impossible.

Before dawn, when the watch lamps were out and cooking fires not yet lit, I let myself out of the back door into the clear air of St. Paul's yard, carrying a small parcel. Around the preaching cross the cobbles had been lifted for the construction of a new wall. I began to dig in the exposed earth with a large spoon. My eyes were stinging. Putting the cat out of its misery, as it clawed at my arms, had felt like drowning one of my own children. I sobbed as I harrowed the earth with the blunt wooden tool. I was lost. My soul was damned. I stabbed the earth harder and harder, ripping into it as if ripping into my own body to let out the evil.

The spoon snapped and I fell on my hands into the shallow pit that I had gouged. The shattered wood scraped my wrist and blood welled up. I did not stem it but pushed myself up to kneeling and gently laid the shrouded body of George's cat in the grave. Blood dripped onto the white napkin and spread like mold across the damp linen. I left the spoon where it lay and pushed the earth over the small corpse with my hands. This sin would need repaying. Pray God it was on me that vengeance was wrought for I could face my own death better than that of any of my children. May God spare Mary, I begged. May it never be my child that I bury. May this creature find a place with George and carry to him this message: I am sorry.

From Cheapside to Charing Cross, the poisoner trailed me. Drops of warm rain exploded on my hood with the soft noise of threshing flails. I was sweating yet cold as if I had taken too much tobacco. The skin inside my elbows and behind my knees itched mercilessly and bled, and as I walked I prayed that the same would not happen to my hands and face, as it had when George died; just when it was imperative to conceal my agitation, my body risked trumpeting it.

Franklin spoke only once, as we passed a tavern open late. "I'm hungry," he whined. I was hungry myself but could not watch this man stuff his belly, with the knowledge I had of him.

Inside the palace precinct I moved quickly. The soft night rain would be insufficient to sweeten the place. A bleary-eyed servant bowed as I entered. He took our damp outer clothes, led us to Frankie's bedchamber, and quickly withdrew.

I entered first and told Franklin to wait. The room was well lit, although candles in the many stands were almost burned down.

Frankie sat with her little dog on her lap, Prospero perched on the back of her chair, picking at his feet. The monkey, Caesar, had been given to Harry, for it had made life miserable for Brutus.

"Put on your mask," I said, "he's here."

Frankie looked up at me, affronted despite the worry in her face. "Servants," she swept the air with her hand as if indicating a large crowd, which I suppose it was, "may not feel much loyalty, but they cannot move against such as us. It is not those we need fear."

Being more friendly with servants than Frankie, I doubted her assessment; they could not publicly condemn their masters, but gossip caused its own harm. There was no persuading Frankie, however, and so I showed Franklin into the room and moved away from the high-smelling man, indicating that he should stay put.

"This is Mr. James Franklin of the Parish of Paul's Undercroft," I announced.

Frankie stared, fascinated and horrified, as if he were a great toad discovered in her piss-pot. He crouched over in a bow and shuffled forward. From Frankie's lap came a low snarl as Brutus bared his tiny teeth but, to my astonishment, Frankie placed her hand in the apothecary's stained fingers and allowed him to kiss it.

"My lady, you are even more beauteous than is said on the streets of London, where you are known as the most beauteous of all the beauteous ladies at Court."

"I don't know how you can tell, all crouched over like that. Do stand up," said Frankie.

"I humbly lay my credentials before you," he continued as he rose upright, "for I can treat all manner of maladies of the body and mind and . . ." As James Franklin rattled off his fields of expertise, which I knew to be exaggerated, I whispered in Frankie's ear.

"He poisoned his first wife . . . and has killed George's cat."

Frankie's eyes grew wide as she looked up at me. "Innocents?"

I pictured my poor cat, with Overbury's face, turning in circles, mewling in pain. What had been an idea, a possibility of freedom, had taken ugly form. In Larkin's studio, where all was heroic and nothing real, the thought of murder had been as in a play or a painting. But when George's cat bled from the ears and suffered agonies, the plan had become as hideous to me as the man who would abet us in it. Having spent many hours trying and failing to think of an alternative, I sat abruptly on a stool at Frankie's feet.

The corrupt apothecary's voice faltered and he looked uncertainly between us.

"I can raise spirits and converse with angels," he finished.

"I do not doubt it," said Frankie, taking one hand off the dog and rubbing my shoulders, "but what we need is a poison that works in a manner that is delayed yet effective with one dose."

Franklin rubbed the side of his nose and smirked as if he were suddenly a co-conspirator.

"There is only money in this for you," snapped Frankie, handing me her glass, "not friendship nor obligation."

He dropped his grin. "There is cantharides or mercury sublimate. Both will act as you require."

"What of powder of diamonds?" asked Frankie. If I was surprised by her knowledge, the poisoner's eyebrows shot up as if to fly off his face.

"It will do the same but is more expensive," he replied. He lifted the flap of his waistcoat and dug about underneath to retrieve a leather pouch. From it he pulled a glass vial, the size of his thumb, and held it up.

"This is water of white arsenic. It can be put in drink or food without risk of being tasted. Husband murder is become common," he added. I noticed that Frankie did not correct his assumption. She was learning discretion, at long last. "There's a play about it, full every day, after the true story of a Bedfordshire goodwife what poisoned her husband. But they could have choosed from any number of such stories. The newsmongers say it is the fault of men for not disciplining wives in their gossiping about the marriage bed. If a husband cannot give pleasure, it leads to discontent sufficient to commit murder," sniggered Franklin, looking boldly at the Countess, but the giggle caught in his throat and turned to coughing. He wiped his mouth on a putrid rag, then used it to dab the sweat from his brow. I looked away. As neither of us took the vial, Franklin placed it on a table. "What of payment?" he asked.

"You will be paid when we know the bottle holds more than ditch water," said Frankie. "You may show yourself out."

Franklin looked ready to argue but I got to my feet and stood between them. He stuck out his chin but did not persist. Grumbling quietly, he shuffled on weak legs to the door. Brutus leaped from Frankie's lap but she pulled the leash and scooped him up, rubbing her cheek against his downy head.

"I shall go behind to be sure he steals nothing," I said.

"He hopes to make more out of us than that," said Frankie. She picked up the vial in two fingers, examining it before a candle. "What company we keep these days," she said.

"We will join that company for all eternity."

I thought she would argue with me but she looked up and nodded. "I have searched for a different way. I visited my great-uncle to hear his response to Overbury's letter, to be rebuked ferociously and at great length for allowing such gossip to arise. He thinks it is more important than ever to bring Robin into our family, to constrain my ever-more-belligerent husband, but is at a loss about Overbury. Robin saw me briefly; he is overwhelmed by the King's business. He wants Overbury released to keep him close. I told him it was too late for that, but Robin would not listen. I was sure it was right to take matters into our own hands, but now that I have met Franklin and see you so pale and unsure . . ."

The candles had burned down and we were in darkness but for the embers of the fire.

"I am no Judith," Frankie said, very quietly. "I am not saving my people. I save only myself and those who depend on me."

"Can you persuade one of your brothers to fight him?"

"Overbury is too ill and too low in rank for my brothers to fight. If we wait any longer, the King may release him. We must decide tonight."

In the early hours, in an apartment that was silent save for a parrot's chatter and a tiny dog sniffing the air that blew in under the door, she held the vial toward me. I could have refused it, and for a long moment thought to do so. If used, we could both die.

With the greatest reluctance, I took the vial and wrapped it carefully in my handkerchief before putting it in my pocket. Neither of us smiled. It was not an occasion for smiling.

"I will send word when it is done," I said. "We will need to pay Richard Weston to administer it."

"With what?"

"Give him a position in your household. Pursuivant? How much is that worth a year?"

"Two hundred pounds; it is a good post. Is he not too old?"

"Frankie, we want him to risk his neck for us. That is surely worth your accommodating a pursuivant who is not so nimble on his legs."

"Of course," she said. "Offer him the position and another two hundred besides. I will find it somehow. And take these for the children," she said, handing me a cone of sugared almonds. I stuffed them into my pocket, then, remembering what else was in there, quickly removed them. Frankie dropped the gold chain from her neck into my free hand. It was the one Robert Carr had given her and that she had worn every day since.

"We can never tell Robin about this."

That was evident, but she said it for her own reassurance; if Carr discovered that we had poisoned his closest friend, we would have risked everything for nothing.

I left without a candle—I could find my way from Frankie's rooms blindfolded—and closed the door on the dog's whines.

At dawn, I trod the narrow streets. Every time someone opened a window or a child yelled for its morning slops, my skin prickled as if a ghost stood by my bed. I had barely slept, could not eat and was exhausted. When I reached the haberdasher's where Weston's son William worked, my throat was so dry that my voice came out as a croak.

"This is physick. Take it directly to your father at the Tower."

"Is he sick?" William's face creased with worry.

"He is the fittest of us all. The physick is for someone else." I watched as he was swallowed by the dark interior of the shop. The vial was on its way.

Poison is a blunt instrument compared to a skillfully wielded blade. Where a head rolls or a body drops, with poison results are hard to predict. A person can die of another illness in the time it takes poison to work. Then a person can be accused of murder who has not, in fact, been the instrument of death. And what if someone else takes the poison by mistake? Or the cup in which it is administered is not properly washed? Or the empty vial is retrieved from some midden by a dust-picker, a little child Henry's age, who puts it to his lips not knowing the danger . . . I scrabbled in my pocket for another flask from which I took a large sip of juice of dried lettuce mixed with chamomile, to calm my nerves and my bleeding, scabbed skin.

As I stoppered the flask, I talked quietly to myself, as if to a child awoken by nightmares. *There is nothing to fear, no one is out there, no one is watching, no one wants to steal me away.*

I tied a mask carefully around my face and left the City through Ludgate as the sun rose and the air turned to gold. I looked intently at the world around me, to chase away the images that cluttered my mind. Soon all would be muffled in morning smoke but for that brief, clear moment the city was beautiful. Perhaps all would be well? Frankie would marry the man she loved and enjoy a long and happy life with many children, and I would live under their protection until, perhaps, I could consider marriage myself. Mr. Palmer was not indifferent to me. In fact, it was clear that he admired me by the way he looked in my direction even when far greater persons were present. I smiled and the muscles behind my ears ached from underuse. As I passed my old home on Fetter Lane, I decided to visit Thomas on my return. A mother can forgive anything in her child and too many people in my life were fleeing from me.

The watch at Temple Bar let me into the Strand. Here the stone and brick mansions of Frankie's relatives were jostled by wooden slums. As I walked by the Love's Nest a girl, no more than ten years old, glared at me from under her red wig. I pulled up my hood, the brief moment of hope erased by the sight of that pitted face, the still-unformed body eaten from within by disease and misuse until no thickness of paint could disguise the corruption of her young flesh. She would be dead before she was fifteen. Mistress Bowdlery's daughter was somewhere walking these streets. The speed with which the family had sunk made me feel nauseous. I quickened my pace. I would do anything to protect my girls from whoring.

"Would the Countess of Essex accept six gold sovereigns and a redemption price of fourteen in twelve months?" said Sir Richard Ingram, minutely examining the chain I had brought to him. He had plans to give it to his wife or mistress, I could tell, given the interest he was showing in it.

"The chain is worth far more than the first price and far less than the second," I replied. Sir Richard's hanging eyebrows drew together and half obscured his small eyes.

"It is the need of the customer that sets the value," he said, leaning forward and smiling. I leaned back.

"The Countess of Essex would be greatly surprised to hear that you thought her desperate and had offered such a low price because of it."

I did not flatter myself that I could better Sir Richard in argument, only that I could remind him of where his interests lay.

"The Countess is lucky in you, at least," he finally replied. "Eight sovereigns and a redemption price of ten in a twelvemonth. You will not take issue with that?"

"I take issue only on behalf of my friend and also accept your offer on her behalf," I said, inclining my head.

I watched Sir Richard count out eight gold sovereigns from a heavy bag. My heart ached as he returned the bag and locked the strongbox. I would have many uses for those coins shut up in darkness, doing nothing but gathering more to themselves. He stood, walked around the end of the table and held out the bag to me like a morsel to summon a dog. My neck stiffened and the hairs on my arms prickled a warning. He was not tall, perhaps a head taller than me, but he was strong. With extreme wariness, I stood and took a few paces toward the door before extending my arm. As my fingers closed around the purse he pulled it back into his chest and his other hand shot out and grabbed my breast. I cried out and tried to jump back but his grip was too tight. He yanked at my skirt and spoke low and fast into my neck.

"You can have more. Show me kindness and I will help you. You are in want. We can help each other." He was pressing his groin against me, pushing me to the wall, his fingers digging excruciatingly into my bosom.

My mind slowed. Hands, pain, breath.

"I am spoken for!" I shouted suddenly. Sir Richard hesitated at the thought that there might be a man to answer to. In that brief respite, I ripped free and fell toward the door, scrabbling at the latch and stumbling downstairs, shouting for my cloak.

I staggered from the house, shouldering aside any person who came too close, not stopping to visit Thomas, buy what I needed or tarry in any way until I turned into the familiar bustle of Paternoster Row. Here I leaned against the wall of our house and wiped sweat from my face. I could hear the children's voices inside but not what they said. I was not quite recovered by the time I opened the door, but people were beginning to notice me standing motionless in the street.

Henry cannoned into my skirts.

I swung him up, although at seven he did not always allow it, and buried my nose in his hair to rid me of the memory of Sir Ingram's meaty breath. The boy squirmed his way down to the floor, his body taking less time to fill with love than did mine. He held a wooden spoon in his hand, on the shallow bowl of which someone had drawn a face in charcoal, the features smeared. Around the stem of the spoon was a knitted frill.

"It's you!" said Henry, waving the spoon in my face. I leaned heavily against the wall, seeing in my mind's eye the shattered spoon lying beside George's dead cat.

"We had almonds with sugar. I ate mine," he said. Katherine ran up and tried to push a sticky sugared almond between my lips.

"I saved it for you," she said.

"I saved one too!" shouted Henry.

"You ate it," said Katherine.

"I saved it first!" said Henry. Barbara arrived with worried eyes that I found hard to look at.

"Have they been good?" I asked.

"They are all good children," she said. "Mary has drunk something but not eaten."

I fished in my purse for a golden sovereign. Barbara stared at it suspiciously and I was grateful that the money was not compensation for Ingram's satisfaction.

"This is from the Countess," I said, looking my daughter squarely in the face. "You are to go straight to the Blue Feather and talk only to Mr. Price, not any other serving there. Tell him of Mary's fever, the smell of her water, the loss of flesh . . . anything he wants to know. After this payment he may extend us credit again, so say nothing to make him doubt our worth. Be sure to question him about each simple and how it is to be administered. No purges. Be sure no false coin is mixed in the change." I handed Barbara our shared cloak, wondering how long it would be before I could buy my daughter her own. "If you are hungry, buy a pie while Mr. Price makes up the physick. Do not pay a vendor with that coin, change it with the apothecary first."

Barbara curtsied and as she slipped through the door I wondered if I had, after all, made a fearful mistake. Had I missed a chance? Should I have let Ingram do what he wanted? With the money he offered I could have kept my household afloat, bought Barbara a cloak, paid old Maggie who had worked for nothing the past six months because she had nowhere else to go. Had I sent a vial of poison on its way when I could have lifted my skirts instead? I stood staring at the door, feeling Ingram's fingers digging into my breast. Was it not worse to kill Overbury than to become a pawn merchant's whore?

"Take the children out with you to buy provisions," I said to old Maggie, pulling another of Ingram's coins from my purse. "I need not warn you of the dangers of such a coin. Bring back the change from which I shall pay you what you are due. There may be no more for many weeks so have a care what you buy."

I helped old Maggie get the children out, then sat on the stairs, letting my head drop into my hands as thoughts of Ingram's veined nose forced themselves into my mind. I would have caught the pox from him; his cheeks were scarred, there was no doubt he carried it. He might not have been generous after he had fornicated with me, valuing me as low as he had tried to value Frankie's necklace. As low as did Arthur. The little flame of anger always within me since he had left suddenly leaped into a great torch of indignation. What power would I have had over Ingram once he had taken me? None at all.

I stomped upstairs. What man would marry me if I caught the pox? Not a one. I reached the top of the stairs and for the first time in weeks relief warmed my stomach. Fighting off Ingram had been the right choice. If only all my unthinking actions were worthy.

Mary's eyes opened as I peered around the door to the bed chamber.

"You were not long in bed last night, Mother, or did I dream that?" she whispered as I sat beside her and lit a candle.

"Open wide," I said. I held the candle as close as I dared. Mary's throat was deep crimson, pustulated and swollen.

"You did not dream it, sweetling," I said quietly, blowing out the candle, for the light hurt Mary's eyes. I placed a hand on my daughter's burning forehead. "I was with our Countess."

As Mary smiled a little split opened in her bottom lip. I wrung out the cloth that sat in a bowl beside the bed and wiped her hot face and the blood from her lip. I gently patted a balsam on to it. Since Mary had fallen ill, I would wake up every morning beside her and straightaway feel her forehead. Every day, my heart sank along with any hope that the fever had broken. I would encourage Mary to drink, despite the pain, and kiss her all over her face. Sometimes it was an hour before I could leave the room.

My daughter slipped into a restless doze and I sat stroking her small hand. I was proud of the little girl's fighting spirit and, in that moment, proud of my own too.

PART THREE
Christmas, 1613

21

The tremendous chatter in the bedchamber flew up like star-lings as quiet washed in from the doorway. The crowd yielded, their bodies bent low; even Frankie and Robin seated in bed did their best to bow. As the sighing of silken skirts subsided, I could hear a light tapping. It was the King's Italian greyhound, picking its way between the obeisant rows, stopping frequently to look back at its master. Brutus trotted up to sniff the King's dog, but the little creature cowered away, its skin shivering.

When the King finally appeared on the arm of a gentleman of the bedchamber, he opened his arms wide and cried, "My dear lad!"

Stiffly, he climbed the wooden steps to the marital bed and set-tled against the barrow of his favorite's legs. These he patted and rubbed, making the groom shift about like a schoolboy. For all his carping about the King's demands, I could see that Carr sought the love of this man who was, at the least, both sovereign and father to him. Two weeks previously, he had been made Earl of Somerset so that Frankie would suffer no loss of rank when they married. From page to earl in six years; I did not wonder that he appeared dazed on occasion, and sometimes afraid.

That this moment had arrived was a miracle, dearly bought. At the back of my mind I could still hear Weston reciting a ditty sung in every ale shop, tavern and marketplace between here and Dover, since news of Frankie's annulment became known.

> There was at Court a lady of late,
> That none could enter she was so straight,
> But now with use she is grown so wide,
> There is a passage for Carr to ride.

When I was young, there was no news. Gossip perhaps, about neighbors, but nothing of high persons. Since then, a great hunger has arisen in the bellies of ordinary people to know everything that happens beyond their own parish. The streets are littered with the ballads and broadsides ripped from the doors of churches and walls of taverns to make way for the next. No person is safe from the libelers and intelligencers, not even the King, and especially not the Howards. It was printed that Frances had depraved habits, suffered from the French pox, could not contain her lust and so on, all for the scandal of her escaping a cruel husband not of her own choosing. The only good thing was that Sir Thomas Overbury's death was never mentioned in the broadsheets.

The King reached out and took the silk of Robin's nightshirt in his fingertips. "How fine worm-spit can look on a man," he said. "Eh, lassie?" he addressed Frankie. "Are ye content? Rid of yer gelding and riding a stallion now, eh? Is he going to make a mother of ye? Did ye do yer duty, Rabbie? Got over yer cold feet?" The King's eyes were damp at their red corners.

"Aye, Sire," said Robin, looking down at the King's hand on his leg. Frankie made to take out the bloodied cloth that I had put there the night before, but the King waved this away with an expression of distaste. "No need, no need," he said. "Ah feared it was an omen when the mechanics of yer masque failed last night."

"My own machine works fine, Sire," said Robin, grinning.

"A've more than a thousand pounds for ye and a wee present for the Countess," said the King, waving forward a page. The boy carried a cushion to which was pinned a golden cross, set with precious stones and suspended from a thick chain. James pulled it off, ignoring the pins cascading to the floor, and leaned across Robin to drop it over Frankie's head.

"The jewel cost three thousand pounds," he announced to thespian gasps from the crowd. Frankie and Carr smiled their gratitude, but I kept watch on the onlookers from my position behind the bed on Frankie's side. I knew that the King's public show of generosity would unite a good number of the Court against the new Earl and Countess of Somerset. Those who had hoped that the scandals surrounding Mary Woods and the annulment would reduce the couple in the King's eyes were being told by this gesture that they had not.

The King leaned forward and kissed Robin full on the lips. Then he climbed from the bed and left the room, trailed by his flimsy dog. The moment the doors closed behind him, the starlings fell to earth. Wave after wave of them pressed close to see the jewel on Frankie's chest.

"I can bear no more kissing," she said to Robin. He laughed, the first I had heard from him in weeks, although he was not looking at Frankie but greeting and embracing the well-wishers come to pay court. Frankie had concluded that it was grief and remorse for Overbury's death that had caused Robin's reluctance to marry her once it was possible. He had assured her of his love, but I sensed that something between them had been lost; they had not made love on their wedding night, exhausted by the ceremonies and a tedious masque that had dragged on until the early hours, but perhaps also because the memory of Overbury stalked them both.

"He might as well have lain between us," said Frankie. "I think I see him sometimes and so does Robin." We rarely mentioned him by name.

I too thought I saw him. His death had been protracted and terrible. From April to September he had languished in the Tower, isolated from every contact except with his jailer, Weston, and the Lieutenant of the Tower, Elwes, who was charged by Northampton with persuading him to apologize to Frankie. Our first attempt to poison him had little effect on his already sick body. Dr. Mayerne's remedies further complicated the picture, for it was unclear whether Overbury's condition later worsened through our efforts or those of the royal physician. We resorted to sending in tainted tarts and jellies, but still Overbury struggled on.

We had given up with poison and were considering a different approach when Weston informed me of Overbury's death. Frankie and I were as surprised as we were shocked. Weston had been out first thing in the morning buying beer for Overbury when the end came and he was unforthcoming when I asked about the circumstances. I did not wish to question him further; he looked as distressed as were we. And now I saw Overbury across courtyards and through windows, and it was even less pleasant an experience than when he was alive.

Murder and marriage is not a happy mix, and I wished for Frankie and her husband's sake that Overbury's death would not forever stain their union. "Try to appear enraptured, it will help him believe he made the right choice," was all I said.

Frankie had sought a modest wedding at Audley End, something to heal wounds and cause no strain. Her parents had readily agreed, not wanting more odium heaped upon her head for marrying so soon after the annulment of her previous union, but Queen Anna had chosen to demonstrate her disapproval by deciding at the eleventh hour to attend the wedding and insisting it be held at Whitehall, where festivities could only be lavish. It had become the centerpiece of the Christmas celebrations and would continue for days.

"I need a drink," said Frankie.

"The Archbishop of Canterbury is leaving the room without wishing you well," I informed her. The Archbishop had led the Nullity Commission and spoken out strongly against it. Frankie nudged her husband and nodded toward the door.

"My Lord Archbishop," Carr called out, sitting up higher. The Archbishop halted as if there were a crossbow at his back. He turned and bowed slowly, looking only at Robin, whom he could not afford to snub. Robin frowned, whether at the Archbishop's ignoring of Frankie or at her nudging, I could not tell.

Around the Archbishop were his allies, including the Earls of Hertford, Bedford, Montgomery and Southampton, the Herberts, the Russells and the Earl of Pembroke, who had expected to be made Lord Chancellor on the death of Salisbury, though the King gave the post to Robin. Lord Northampton called them "the vicious crew" and they had pointedly refused the couple's invitation to join the ceremonial tilt to mark their wedding. For them to shun the wedding breakfast as well was impossible due to the King's presence. Frankie's first husband was under house arrest for seeking a duel with her brother Harry. The two of them had got as far as France but the Ambassador had found them there and escorted them home.

The Archbishop said nothing and made no move forward to congratulate the newlyweds.

"Show him your displeasure," Frankie whispered, but Robin only nodded, at which the Archbishop bowed briefly and walked out.

"He has insulted us," Frankie said.

"He has insulted you," Robin replied.

I watched Frankie fight back a response. All eyes in the room flickered from her to the group of Essex supporters, who looked ready to follow the Archbishop's example. Frankie dropped any pretense of smiling. Nearly every important position at Court was still held by a Howard, by blood or marriage, or else a Howard client. Her face invited her enemies to show themselves. The silence was becoming uncomfortable as the Earl of Northampton arrived by their bedside.

"My lords and ladies!" he cried, in a loud voice for an old man. He swiveled to address all gathered there, including the malcontents. "United by God and King, I offer to the couple before us my heartiest good wishes." His herald stepped forward to present wedding gifts, distracting many from the Archbishop's slight. The bed's coverlet soon disappeared under largesse of a value greater than had been seen at any wedding before this.

"A sword and gold to the value of one thousand and five hundred pounds," the herald announced as a page stumbled forward with an elaborate sword for Robin and a chest of gold coins for Frankie. Northampton's generosity was met with nods and murmurs. I wondered what he would expect from Frankie in return.

"From Her Majesty Queen Anna, silver dishes curiously enameled."

"They must be from Denmark," whispered Frankie. Carr did not reply.

". . . From Sir Ralph Winwood, a new town coach." This provoked clapping, for it was a fine wedding present. Encouraged, Sir Ralph stepped forward and Robin indicated that he might speak.

"My most noble and honored Earl and Countess," he bowed, obsequious as ever, "allow me to offer the use of my best horses to pull your coach to the Lord Mayor's entertainments in honor of your marriage?" Robin inclined his head.

"We shall not give them back," Frankie whispered to him with a giggle. She looked tipsy on the gold, jewels and envy heaped upon her. "He wants you to get the Secretary of State position for him. That's worth a few ponies." Again, Robin did not respond, and I could see that Frankie would poke him until he did.

"From Sir Edward Coke, a basin and cover of silver gilt." Frankie did not acknowledge the present, for she did not care for the Lord Chief Justice. To his wife, whom we had spied with Simon Forman and whom he openly called the "the thorn in his side," she gave a gracious welcome.

Frankie's father approached and chatted amiably to Robin, whom he had come to like. They were united over several matters, including the grievances they bore against Lord Northampton who, Frankie said, was becoming cantankerous in his old age and overly fussy. They both displayed coldness to him, and I wondered at this division in their ranks when the malicious crew were hunting for any weakness.

Lord Northampton moved away and walked to the head of the bed. I thought he had not seen me there, but he began talking so quietly that I alone could be his intended audience.

"The King has made clear his continued love for the Earl of Somerset, but his opponents muster forces." I did not know whether an answer was expected of me, so I remained silent. "A meeting is to be held soon at Barnard's Castle between the Lords Pembroke, Herbert, Russell, Seymour and Essex, to discuss how best to oust the King's favorite and the House of Howard." I thought of the covered portraits in Larkin's studio. Were these out-of-favor nobles having themselves painted to immortalize this meeting? "Frankie's father and the Earl of Somerset are unwilling to recognize the dangers, and my niece runs headlong into them. I strongly suggest that she take heed and advise her husband to do likewise."

I looked directly at the Earl for the first time. His eyes were brown like Frankie's but full of calculation. I felt not seen but assessed.

Frankie was climbing down from the bed and I moved to shield her from the prying eyes of those searching out smears of virgin blood. We went to the garderobe and I bolted the door as Frankie sat and leaned her head against the cold bricks of the outside wall.

"They hate me, all of them, for escaping tyranny. I will have satisfaction against the Archbishop and Essex and all their faction," she said, looking tired.

"If you like, you can," I agreed.

"Yet I feel afraid. I think Robin preferred me as a mistress."

"That is not unusual. He needs time to adjust."

"I pray I fall pregnant at once, so I can leave this place," said Frankie, and I thought how much she had changed.

"Maybe you should stay. Your great-uncle just warned me that Essex plans to unseat Robin," I said, relaying Northampton's warning.

"That man would see danger in an infant's crib," said Frankie, standing once more.

"But now that Robin is married, there will be times when he is not by the King's side."

"Let us hope so," she said.

I unlocked the door and Frankie walked through the crowd, dignified, but twisting her lace cuffs between thumb and forefinger. I had tried and failed to cure her of this habit, for it revealed all that her face disguised.

I thought of the only person who did not care that Frankie was a despoiler of lace, Mistress Bowdlery. A vivid picture came to mind of the lace-maker sitting on her doorstep earlier that week, watching me remove from Paternoster Row to Frankie's household.

"You'll forget us once you're with your countess."

"No indeed," I said, although I would happily consign Paternoster Row to the Devil. It had been the backdrop to a disreputable and poverty-stricken period, which was now over. My life, and that of my children, was to be transformed by honor and wealth; not my own, but close enough to rub off.

"I have something for you," Mistress Bowdlery had said, retrieving from the deep pocket of her apron a square of fine linen. I recognized at once the labor that had gone into the decorative embroidery of my initials and the needle-lace border.

"It is beautiful," I replied, tears burning. "When the Countess sees it she will order a hundred." We had smiled at each other then, united by widowhood and motherhood, both knowing we were unlikely to meet again.

"Someone sit on your grave?" said Mr. Palmer, joining me. I was both surprised and delighted to see him there and had not time to hide either from him. He kissed my hand and stood firmly beside me in the line forming to tour the new Earl and Countess of Somerset's apartments. I tried not to look too often at him, but was aware of everything, from the little coughs that indicated a slight sore throat, to the wear on the outside edges of his shoes.

There was plenty to discuss as we began our jaunt around the forty-one-room apartment, stuffed with precious objects from ports unimaginably distant. The King had given them the rooms previously occupied by his daughter, the Princess Elizabeth. These were situated away from the river, facing St. James's Park. Mr. Palmer made fewer and fewer comments, for what was the point of this visit but to remind the Court of the dominion of the Earl and Countess of Somerset? He looked out of the windows at the trees; he loved beauty, not power.

The most startling thing to me was not that every manner of modern and exotic furniture was displayed, but that the Earl had no bed. Despite being married to Frankie, it seemed the King still expected him to spend every night at Court in the royal bedchamber. I knew this would be a mark of great favor to the couple that neither of them wanted, but as Mr. Palmer made no comment about it, I too held my tongue.

The finale of the tour was a long room with walls covered in large paintings. Only then did Mr. Palmer return to his usual animated self.

"My Lord Somerset has created this gallery from a bowling alley. It says much about the man, does it not?" He bent closer to whisper, "It is unsurpassed even by the Prince's collections. The Earl has bought twenty-nine cases of statuary, at a cost of over two thousand ducats, only fifteen of them here displayed. He is the first in these isles to collect such statues."

I doubted that Robert Carr had yet paid for them. Some poor dealer in Venice would be waiting a long time, perhaps until the King granted Carr more land or another pension, for meager installments to reach him. Since moving in with them, I saw that he maintained position by spending money he did not have; the King kept his nobles in check this way. Displays of extravagance won his attention but threw his courtiers into such grave debt that only he could relieve it; they all owed or depended on him for money. Frankie had so little cash that she could not pay Weston what she owed him. Nor could she pawn her clothes or jewelry because almost everything in the apartment was yet to be paid for except the wedding presents, and they could not be pawned until the benefactor had been invited to see the gift in use. Carr also borrowed from a City moneylender, as did every courtier of rank, in return for contact with the monarch. If that courtier fell from grace, then the money dried up and great insistence, unto harassment, was placed upon the repayment of debts. I had pressed Frankie to find Weston the money she had agreed to pay, for he had had no employment since his role as jailer was concluded.

"I will pawn my green silk when the portrait of me is finished," she promised, and I told her that I would keep her to her word for Weston was not a man to disappoint.

"Does the collection please you?" asked Mr. Palmer, bringing me back to the present. I saw that this was no empty civility. I hesitated before speaking. Since Overbury's death, I had developed an intense dislike of Italian painting.

"It disturbs me," I ventured finally, "that the human appetite for violence and lust is so much on display. It is perhaps a result of the hot climate in Italy."

Mr. Palmer looked steadily into my eyes. I saw no scorn for my parochialism. "I have never viewed it in that way," he said at last, "but I fancy you are correct."

"It is generous of you to say so," I replied, warmed by his gentle manner.

"Are you and the children happily settled in the Countess's household?"

"We are, I thank you."

"Now that we are close neighbors, I hope we will meet again, soon and often," he said, holding out his hand. He meant what he said and, without hesitation, I gave mine to him and he kissed it. Three times.

22

While young, we strive for everything we want. Later, we clutch at what we have and hope to lose nothing. By my age, you realize that contentment is found within the heart only.

After Frankie's marriage, there followed eight months of exquisite happiness. Robin recovered from his guilt and grief at Overbury's death and his love for Frankie returned. He seemed relieved to have one less master. Frankie established her household at Chesterford in Suffolk, and we avoided the Court. Although I remembered Lord Northampton's warnings, it suited me also to be away from the City and Whitehall. My three younger children ran through fields and gardens, growing strong and clever on fine food and tutoring. I no longer had to work and could be with them always. Servants oversaw our basic needs so that I could spend my time teaching the youngest fine manners and helping them with their lessons. Mary recovered from her illness, a blessing for which I thanked God and Frankie. Old Maggie had been brought into Frankie's household and had the opportunity to rest for the first time in her life.

Chesterford is near Audley End, where my dear son John was learning the skills of a gentleman, from wielding a sword to carving a goose. Visits from him were a delight, as were those of Mr. Palmer, who came to discuss new purchases more than was strictly necessary. Each time, he requested that I walk with him in the gardens and sit by his side at mealtimes. He was contemptuous of the empty flattery typical at Court; we spoke of ideas and experiences, neither of us attempting to impress the other.

Frankie and I lived like a happily married couple: the one energetic, the other quietly content. Like old Maggie, we were also in need of rest. I was restoring myself, growing smooth and glossy, thinking perhaps Mr. Palmer might soon ask for my hand, as he did not appear to consider me too old and burdened. At the end of five months, he brought me a small painting of flowers and fruit, by his own hand. My initials were wrought in the foliage; that he had been thinking of me all the while he painted it made me blush with pleasure.

Frankie's father became Carr's close companion as they sought to free themselves from the control of Lord Northampton, who demanded great efforts from them to maintain networks of clients and patronage. The younger Howards were convinced that, following Frankie's marriage to the favorite, they were unassailable; "The Dominican" became an embarrassment, whose suspicious nature was dismissed as a failing of great age. He was a relic of the old Queen's time, too sensitive to the tides of power, having swum long against them. He pestered Frankie and Carr with matters they found dull and was increasingly unhappy that his influence on the Privy Council was eclipsed by his nephew's alliance with Robert Carr.

On the fifteenth day of June, six months after the wedding, I returned to London to help Frankie fulfill her promises to Weston. I tramped up the stairs to Larkin's studio trailed by two of Frankie's maids, half-buried beneath bulky linen sacks containing the clothes she had worn to her brother Thomas's wedding. Larkin had need of them to complete Frankie's portrait, for only the head and hands were finished. The bright June sun made it hard to find my footing: now blinded, now in darkness.

The painter greeted me quietly and led me to a life-sized wooden figure in the corner where once had stood the covered portraits so disturbing to Frankie's mother, now hanging in the long galleries of Howard enemies. Accustomed to the comfort and peace of the countryside, I thoroughly disliked coming back to London and gave my whole attention to the task at hand, the sooner to be finished with it.

I paid no heed to the small knot of people in the studio and waved the servants forward as Larkin undid the buckles holding the mannequin together. He proffered a wooden arm for me to thread through the armholes of the bodice I had pulled from its protective sack. A waft of Frankie's perfume, Aqua Mellis, provoked in me the most curious and powerful sensation that the mannequin would transform into my friend once it was fully dressed. I could almost hear her laugh.

As I dressed the dummy, I remembered how beautiful Frankie had looked at her brother's wedding, dancing with Robin. She had stolen attention away from the bride, who after all was only a child. My fears about the depth of Carr's love had faded. They appeared so happy together that even Queen Anna had been moved to smile upon them, though the King's love of his favorite showed no sign of abating.

As for my fears that our crimes would be discovered, they too were receding. In the nine months since Overbury's death, few had mentioned Carr's erstwhile closest companion, not even Carr himself.

"How soon will the portrait be finished?" I asked Larkin.

"I had hoped it would be delivered by the end of next month, but I have another to do in a hurry," he said, nodding at the group fussing around the huge chair that he used as a prop and that Frankie herself had leaned upon. As I looked over, I noticed, with a little shock of surprise and pleasure, that Mr. Palmer was among them. He saw me at the same moment and at once came over.

"Mistress Turner, delighted," he said, bending to kiss my cheeks several times. Larkin was called away to the group and I indicated to the maids that they should finish dressing the mannequin without me. "The country continues to suit you," Mr. Palmer said, with a wide smile. "How are the children? Is Mary's cough quite gone?" No other man asked after my children. It irked me that the unavoidable consequence of my increase in sentiment toward Mr. Palmer was that I felt more nervous each time we met.

"It has, thank you, Mr. Palmer, and Barbara is now with the Countess of Salisbury." After the death in earliest infancy of four boys, Frankie's younger sister had finally produced a girl who looked likely to live. Catherine had, however, been assailed by an incapacitating dread that this child too would die, so Barbara had been sent to distract the Countess from her terror and to help care for the child. Once she had recovered, it was my hope that the Countess would be sufficiently grateful to find Barbara a husband.

Mr. Palmer's face suddenly fell. "I have been remiss in not offering my condolences."

I looked up at him, uncomprehending.

"Forgive me, you did not know?" he said.

"What do I not know?"

"The Earl of Northampton was called to God this morning."

I was astonished; not so much by the Earl's death, for he had been battling a gangrenous sore on his leg for a week, but that Mr. Palmer had heard of it before I had. No one had told me or asked me to send word to Frankie even though I was staying in her apartment. I felt suddenly exposed. Lord Northampton's fixation had been the pursuit and preservation of power for himself and his family. The younger generations were lax in their safeguarding of the family fortunes.

"I feel as I did when Queen Elizabeth died. The Earl has been with us for so long that his death seems to usher in a new age," observed Mr. Palmer.

"Indeed," I agreed. With Lord Northampton gone, there would be greater freedom but less safety. I did not like the unease Mr. Palmer's announcement stirred in me and changed the subject. "I am surprised to find you here. Larkin's paintings are not very Italian."

Mr. Palmer chuckled. "His portraits are beautiful in their own manner, and the subjects appear to their best advantage."

"Are you sitting for him?"

"Bless you, no! Even Larkin would be hard pushed to make a silk purse out of me. I have arranged a sitting for a person who needs no adornment whatsoever, but who is receiving a great deal of it right now." I noticed that Mr. Palmer did not offer to introduce me and that he seemed ill at ease.

"I have brought Lady Frances's clothes so that Larkin might finish her likeness," I said, seeing her portrait displayed on an easel near the group. "Won't you come and look?"

He pronounced it "very good," which I thought untrue. Larkin had captured the intensity of Frankie's gaze perhaps, but not her playfulness, nor the fierceness with which she pursued her desires.

A burst of laughter caused me to look at the young man being painted. I tried not to stare but could not help myself.

"He is like Tiziano's Adonis, is he not?" Mr. Palmer said, quietly.

"Only more alluring," I said, such was the perfect, smooth beauty of the long-limbed youth. "Who is he?"

Mr. Palmer sighed and looked down at his hands, rubbing them together as if paint clung to them. "His name is George Villiers," he said quietly.

"George Villiers?" I repeated. "I have not heard of him."

"I believe you will," said Mr. Palmer, who was about to say more when Larkin called over: "To whom is the portrait to be sent when completed?"

Mr. Palmer grew as mute and stiff as one of Larkin's figures. In the end, it was George Villiers who spoke, in a voice so high that I could not help smiling. He was just a boy. A very beautiful boy. But his reply wiped the smile from my face.

"My Lord of Essex."

All pleasure drained from me at those words. Essex had found his instrument of revenge. I pictured Robert Carr beside the exquisite George Villiers and saw that this young man stood a very strong chance of ousting Carr from his place at the King's side.

"Mr. Palmer, forgive me, I am late for a meeting with an old friend." His strange behavior suddenly made sense to me. I saw by his expression that he regretted as much as I the circumstances of this meeting. He took my hand to stop me hurrying away.

"I arranged for the portrait before I knew of whom, and for whom, it was. I hope you believe me."

"I do, sir," I said. He did not release my hand but looked into my face with concern.

"May I call on you again?"

"I hope you will, Mr. Palmer," I said with a curtsy, and meant it.

I chivvied the maids to finish their lacing and sent them in the coach back to Whitehall while I made my way to Charing Cross, my mind churning with thoughts of George Villiers and

255

the consequences I could foresee if the King were lured to the bait. They were not all catastrophic; played well, Carr might enjoy greater freedom from the King to spend more time at home. Babies would arrive more quickly, they could become a proper family and Carr might at last have his own bed.

I heard the tolling bell, aware now that it was for Henry Howard, Lord Northampton, ringing out every year of his life. The peals reverberated across the Parish, throughout Whitehall, along the lines of patronage, duty and debt to his estates, the Cinque Ports over which he ruled and down through the younger generations of Howards to whom he had been patriarch. I wished he still lived, to steer us safely away from the siren power of this beautiful boy.

I came to a halt across the street from Northampton House and watched the dead Earl's servants, in full mourning, cover the gateway and windows with black cloth. It was clear that his death had been anticipated, if not by us. Frankie was being kept away from the center of the spider's web by her father and her husband.

Weston arrived at the final bell and with uncharacteristic reverence pulled off his cap.

"Seventy-four," he said. "My sister lives in one of his almshouses and receives a gown a year and a hat in every seven. He was a generous man."

I did not agree that to relieve a few paupers when you have created a thousand was so great a deed. The misery of Mistress Bowdlery and countless others like her was increased by high taxes on raw materials that made Northampton wealthier than they could ever imagine, but I said nothing.

"You'll need to tread warily now," said Weston. I was both embarrassed and touched by his instinct to protect me that had not abated despite all I had asked of him. "The Earl took care of the business the Countess and . . ." he could not say "her husband"; as a Catholic of the last century he did not believe that Robin was Frankie's husband, it was beyond his faith and his experience ". . . don't bother with. He kept people in their places by scaring or rewarding them. If your friends are so much in love with themselves they forget their clients and their enemies, they'll suffer for it—and you with them."

I heard more than Weston's resentment at not being rewarded as he had been promised by Frankie; the smell of turpentine and pigment filled my nose. He turned and began walking on his bandy legs across the busy street toward St. Martin's Lane. I kept pace with him.

"I suppose the Earl of Northampton's honors will be divided between the Countess's father and Robert Carr . . . How does she do?" he asked, without enthusiasm.

"The King has visited them in their new home at Chesterford and the country air does her good. She had the merest sniffle in March and you would have thought she was sick unto death, the way the King and Carr doted on her." I pictured not Frankie as I spoke, but the way my own body had slowly unclenched the further I was from Court; a single glimpse of George Villiers in Larkin's studio had coiled me up again.

"This city's too crowded with traffic and foreigners," Weston grumbled, looking more ancient than his sixty-five years. "It's all gone mad."

We reached The Swan and Weston found us a table and bought two cups of ale.

"Move back home," I said, taking a sip and grimacing. I was habituated to the good French wine and well-spiced ale of Frankie's household.

"My William and his child are here. Does she not want children?" Weston said, steering the conversation back to Frankie. He seemed to think a divorced woman would not have natural urges.

"Of course," I said, not mentioning how much effort was spent in trying to make them.

"She has all but what she most desires, eh? 'Tis a common complaint at Court, it seems. It's a strange thing to leave your husband for another one. When she meets them both in heaven, by whose side will she stand?"

"Carr's, I would think, for his company was ever the more agreeable." Weston's smile dropped quickly.

"How much did they get?"

"I have no idea," I lied. The wedding celebrations had cost ten thousand pounds and the gifts had been valued at more than twice that. Yet the Earl's expenses that year had amounted to ninety thousand pounds; a maid lives on a pound a month and could no more imagine the Earl's way of life at Court than she could if he lived on the moon. I unbuckled the purse at my waist and gave it to Weston. "One hundred guineas. You will need to have patience for the rest and a position."

"Overbury died," he whispered. "Why do I not receive all that was promised for my part in it?"

"It took so long, it could have been from natural causes."

I noticed that Weston did not defend himself against this suggestion.

"Did Northampton pay you for services beyond delivering letters?" The directness of my question surprised me. This was a misgiving I barely knew I had. Had our attempts failed and Weston then been paid by Northampton to finish off Overbury? The Earl could be confident of hiding his crime under ours.

"I was working for you," Weston said, but I could tell from his expression that he had become Northampton's man more than mine. I wondered whether it was before or after Overbury's death. A new knot of fear tightened in my stomach, to find that even someone who loved me was not entirely on my side.

"How exactly did Overbury die?"

"I've already told you, I was out buying him beer when he passed. He was very sick from all those emetics and purges he took. He came into prison with griping in the guts and a sore on his back that grew great and stinking while he was there. I bathed him daily under a blanket, so ashamed was he of the canker. Even the softer bed I found him made no difference." Weston had a caring streak running close to his rough surface. He pulled up his sleeve suddenly and stroked the paler flesh on the inside of his forearm. "He had a golden pellet lodged here, by Dr. Mayerne, to make it easier to open a vein to let blood. The skin was red and hot around it. To my thinking, the King's physician killed him faster than anything you and the Countess planned."

"'Planned?' You did not use our poisons?"

"A man at death's door cannot eat much of tarts or jellies, be they wholesome or not."

Had Weston thrown away our poisons, convinced Overbury would die of natural causes and Dr. Mayerne's treatments? To admit it would be to risk losing the money and the position we had promised him. He had been ready to poison Overbury for us, whatever had actually occurred, and for that he felt he deserved full payment. I contemplated challenging him again for the full truth, but knew his stubbornness was greater than my own, and that I would get nowhere. There were many good reasons not to make an enemy of him.

"They have huge debts," I said, turning my thoughts away from Overbury to the cases of statuary and paintings on their way across the Mediterranean Sea to join those already in Carr's collection. "They are favorites at Court and have honor and position to maintain but insufficient estates to pay the expenses."

"The pursuivant's position was worth two hundred a year and she still owes me a hundred," he said. That sum, equivalent to what Carr spent every month on gloves alone, would keep Weston comfortable for the rest of his life. I wanted him comfortable.

"As soon as Larkin is finished, Frankie will pawn the clothes he is painting and pay you from the proceeds," I said, although she had made many such promises that she did not fulfill. Sir Thomas Lake, a privy councillor, had paid her two thousand pounds to be made the Secretary of State, but her husband advanced his own client, Sir Ralph Winwood, he who had given them a coach for a wedding present. Frankie had kept Winwood's best horses and had not returned Lake's money. Now even someone as lowly as Weston was disappointed in her.

Carr also promised more than he delivered. He had asked a pleasing man called John Donne to turn down holy orders for a good position in his administration yet kept him waiting for months before finally turning him away, without compensation. This was not the way to keep followers happy. Weston was right: Lord Northampton had taken much greater care to foster loyalty.

"And the position?" Weston asked, but it was not within my power to grant anything.

"To have you in her household would be a daily reminder of what has occurred," I said gently. "She will look for something else that is suitable."

Very quietly, he placed his mug on the table. "So I am good enough to sin for her but not to be in the same building? And yet I hear that the loathsome Franklin is admitted to her bedchamber whenever he wants."

I pursed my lips, as much at Frankie's behavior as at Weston's complaint. "Franklin is helping her conceive a child."

Weston's eyebrows shot up.

"Not that way," I said. "He brings medicines and says prayers to angels and, for reasons I will never understand, he amuses her. I tell her plain not to let that truckling cat's paw visit at all, let alone be given the privilege of the bedchamber, for he is untrustworthy to his core." I hoped that our mutual abhorrence of Franklin would unite us, but Weston did not even nod as he drained his cup and got to his feet.

"You might have thought that the scandal with Mary Woods was lesson enough to keep away from certain folk. What I did for the Lady Frances has led to great reward for her and nothing but idleness and poverty for me. If she doesn't look to those who helped her when she was down, she won't spend long on the up."

Weston escorted me out of the tavern but did not offer to accompany me to Whitehall; he knew without doubt now that I would never marry him. It pained me to see him walk away with shoulders hunched.

"Richard!" I ran after him and kissed his cheeks three times. "Thank you. Thank you for all you have done for us. I promise you will receive your full reward." He blushed and gave me a bow before leaving.

As I passed Northampton House, an appalling sense of foreboding hit me, such that I hid in a doorway, struggling to breathe. Cold stone at my back, I saw the little things—a boy being painted, a debt unpaid, an old man dead—that would lead everything to slip away from me.

23

It was as green and fresh in Suffolk as London was filthy with coal smoke and effluent. When I returned to Frankie, I said nothing of Weston's disgruntlement, nor of George Villiers. Her menses had ceased to flow and I was anxious not to alarm her. She had been married only since Christmas and her husband was already away on progress with the King.

At the end of July she bled heavily and the child was lost. To ease her sadness, we decided to join Robin. Under the red August sun, veiled with dust from a burning mountain across the seas, I traveled with her. We met with the King's party at Apethorpe Hall in Northamptonshire, Sir Anthony Mildmay's house.

Mildmay was a blustering, old-fashioned man, at least sixty years old or more, who hated foreigners, especially the Scots, French, and all Catholics. So he was no friend to Robert Carr or the Howards, and suffered the King's visit purely out of duty to the Crown. He put on a hunt, inviting the local gentry and a young man of low degree but great beauty. The King's eyes were out on stalks when this youth rode by and he was invited to dine that day, although his low birth should have barred him. Carr was occupied with state business and I was not invited, but Frankie could not stop talking about the unexpected guest while she undressed that night; how he danced with supreme elegance, how he made everyone laugh, how he was more beautiful than any woman she had ever seen.

"'George!' they cried. 'George!'" she told me. "'Villain,' was it? Not a very English name."

"Villiers," I said. "George Villiers."

"How do you know?"

"I saw him at Larkin's studio."

"In London? But he is just a local boy. Whose page is he?"

"He is not a page. His portrait was commissioned by the Earl of Essex."

Frankie stopped wiping the makeup from her face and stared at me.

A few days later, the King's delight in George Villiers became known to Robert Carr. The King suggested Carr meet with Villiers, befriend him, guide and rule over him, but Carr flew into a rage such as I had never seen in him. He refused to summon Villiers, no matter our efforts to persuade him of the benefits of this course. I was in the chamber with Frankie when Villiers, with impeccable manners and sensible of his lower rank, called on Carr instead.

"My lord, I offer myself with utmost humility and love to be at your service in 'soever which ways you command of me." He bowed so low and gracefully that he looked more swan than human. The King's retinue was awash with gossip about this young god; the rumor that he had learned dancing and etiquette at the French Court was clearly true.

Frankie and I smiled warmly at the young beauty and at each other, delighted that Carr should be honored in this way. With George Villiers on the King's arm, Carr would have more time for Frankie, for the burdens of state and for his own leisure.

"I will have none of your service and you shall have none of my favor! If I can, I will break your neck. Of that, be confident!" Carr shouted, so loudly that a hush fell over the anteroom. George Villiers was brave enough not to recoil, but Frankie and I did, afraid a fight would ensue. Carr began waving his arms as if shooing away a herd of inquisitive heifers. Utterly astounded, Villiers backed toward the door, offering Frankie and me a quick bow before fleeing.

"My lord, what ails you?" asked his wife. "Villiers offers you his loyalty."

"I do not want it," he spat, "nor any advice from you. Leave me."

* * *

For the rest of that year and into the next, the Court was more vile than ever Frankie or I had known it. One moment the King would favor Villiers, the next Carr. With Lord Salisbury and Lord Northampton dead, it seemed the King was trying to rebalance his Court, curbing the power of the Howard family by playing them off against the Essex crew. No business could be transacted; clients did not know whom to follow. Howards held every major post, yet the Essex camp looked confident that this was about to change. And with Overbury dead, Carr had only Frankie's father, whose understanding of politics was deficient, to lean on. The Earl of Essex and his allies sought to topple the Howards completely, and truly they had discovered a magnificent weapon.

For long hours Frankie and I worried over Robin's surprising and undignified behavior toward Villiers and increasingly toward the King himself. After the progress we returned to Suffolk, but by spring, Carr's distress at the rapid rise of George Villiers truly alarmed us. Frankie decided to move to her elder sister's house at Rotherfield Greys, near the busy Thames port of Henley, so that she could travel to Court more easily to shore up her husband. For me, the move had a more pleasing aspect, for Mr. Palmer had family in Oxfordshire. He paid us visits when Carr was at Greys, ostensibly to discuss artworks, but always he and I walked together. The children begged to be allowed to join us on these walks, for Mr. Palmer was a brilliant mimic, in particular of animals and birds and, sometimes, of myself, and we would laugh ourselves hoarse. I did not attempt to rush him into a proposal, I had learned that lesson, but allowed our friendship to grow at a pace that was natural to it. He had asked that I sit for him, that he might take my likeness—surely the act of a man in love?

Toward the end of April, after a week's silence from Robin, we traveled by barge to Whitehall. The outer chamber in their apartment was crowded with people seeking his intercession with the King, but I noticed that they were less well-heeled than when Frankie and I were last there, lacking the connections to know that Carr had a rival who was winning the greater part of the King's favor. The inner hall and receiving chamber were likewise busy, but Frankie acknowledged no one until we entered the privy chamber where her husband was seated at his table. Head resting in his hands, he was reading a letter, while behind him a group of advisers stood talking together.

"If you please," said Frankie, standing at the door. The men rarely saw the Earl's wife and it was with some reluctance that they left. I shut the door behind them and sat in the farthest window.

"My dearest," said Frankie, crouching beside her husband's chair to look up into his face, taking his hands in hers.

"You here?" he said, not moving to embrace her or even to smile.

"I could not leave you to face these trials alone," said Frankie. "But be reassured, my darling, that Villiers cannot rival the long and deep affection that exists between you and your King, by whom you have been favored above all others for ten years and who has looked to your care since you were born; you are of the same nation, you speak his tongue. Go to him. Apologize for your anger and swear it was born of love. His feelings for you will increase tenfold."

Carr stood abruptly and glared down at his crouching wife.

"You'd have me grovel?" he said. "The King promised me his love until death."

I saw, as clearly as if Carr had cut open his chest, the furious child within, elevated, isolated and stunted by the King's attention.

He snatched up the letter he had been studying from the table's littered surface, shoved it into Frankie's hand and returned to his chair with his back toward her. She came over to where I sat. From the great red seal, I could see that the missive came from the King. The writing was in an educated hand but frequently blotted and sometimes crossed out—a message from the heart.

A piece of ground cannot be so fertile that, either by nature or rank manure, it becomes fertile also for strong and noisome weeds. It then proves useless: those worthy and rare parts and merits of yours have been for a long time, but especially since this strange frenzy took you, so mixed with strange streams of unquietness, passion, fury and insolent pride, and (which is worst of all) with a settled kind of induced obstinacy, as it chokes and obscures all these excellent and good parts that God has bestowed upon you. The trust and privacy between us allows you a great liberty of speech with me, yet this new art of railing against me with the tongue of the Devil, this cannot be liberty or friendship.

I have borne these passions of yours with grief, in the hope that time and experience would allay them. But you have woken me in my sleep to rail at me, it seems deliberately to vex and weary me; your outbursts were coupled with dogged and sullen behavior toward me; your utter distrust of my honesty and friendship toward you; and fourthly, and worst of all, you have in many of your mad fits done what you could to persuade me that you hold me not by love but by fear, that I am so far in awe of you that I dare not offend you or resist your appetites. I leave out of this reckoning your creeping away from lying in my chamber, notwithstanding my many times earnestly soliciting you to the contrary.

This letter proceeds from the infinite grief of a heart deeply wounded, a grief such as I have not known since my birth. Neither can I bear it longer without committing an unpardonable sin against God. Be not the occasion of the hastening of my death, through grief, I who have prayed for you, which I never did for any other subject alive but you.

What King would commit to paper such words of love and despair? How could he allow anyone, even his favorite, to know feelings so intimate? Looking at Frankie, it was clear that she was similarly appalled. I held her hand as we read on.

Your furious assaults at unseasonable hours, my sadness and want of rest, have now made it known to many that we are in cross discourse. There must be amendment in your behavior toward me. The best remedy for this I shall tell you with my tongue. But to ease my grief, tell me that you never think to hold me but by love. I told you two or three times that you may lead me by the heart, not the nose. Let me not apprehend that you disdain me or that any of your former affection is cooled. Hold me by the heart and you may build upon me as a rock. I shall constantly show you affection and allow no other to rise in degree to even a twentieth of the favor I show you. Your good and heartily humble behavior will wash out of my heart all past grievances, yet never shall I pardon myself for raising a man so high as pierces my ears with such speeches as you have given me.

Do not you and your father-in-law hedge in the whole Court such that it depends upon you? I have set down my position, make of me what you please, either the best master and truest friend, or, if you cause me to call you ingrate, no earthly plague shall be worse than my wrath.

Frankie looked up and pointed out the last line, to be sure I had read it. Her face was flushed and I saw in it pain as well as fear. She left the letter on the window seat and walked over to her husband. Despite the anger he had shown, she curled her arms around him.

"My love," she said, "you are part of my family now."

I could not see what comfort lay in having a mother-in-law who despised him and a guileless father-in-law, but Carr rested his head against Frankie's and I understood that he did not love the King most as a man and bedfellow, but as the father who had protected him since birth, when his own father had died fighting for James's mother. The King's admiration for Villiers was to Carr the agony of being cast aside for another son judged worthier.

I felt more afraid than ever, for I know that grief cannot be tamed or turned, but is a mighty rushing river that will engulf any bank built to contain it until it has run its course. Carr's suffering was splitting him open. The father whose embrace he had never known, the best friend whom he had betrayed, the wise old counselor from whom he had turned, all were dead; and now the King was replacing him with a younger, more beautiful man, and he was expected to make room without complaint. I wondered whether anybody's love could rescue Carr from that torment, and I worried that Frankie's passionate, forceful, provocative love would not provide the foundation he needed.

"Soon, we will be our own little family." Robin looked up. He searched for confirmation of her meaning. "He is not yet quick but I am sure," said Frankie, putting a hand over her belly, not with the soft pride of most expectant mothers, but the severity of an avenging angel. "For our son, my love, you must be calm and play a clever game. Promise me, my darling, that you will not be the card that makes all the others tumble? Villiers is pretty, but we are powerful."

"I'm to be a father?"

"You are, my love." This was a huge gamble; she had missed but one bleed. "You will be the best of fathers to our son, of that I have no doubt." I was watching Robin and saw that, far from knowing how to be a father, he was still in need of one himself. The gift Frankie hoped would bring him strength might prove the greatest challenge of all.

"Frank, I'm pleased as a cat with its nose in butter, but I must go now," he said, rising and pulling her up with him. "The King's to visit the Queen in her bedchamber today. That vile lad'll be in attendance, so I must be too."

"The King did not invite you?"

"He knows I'm like a shepherd at lambing with state business. I've to find a wife for Prince Charles who will please everyone, and money to fill empty coffers, and other miracles that would tax the Lord Jesu himself."

"Then look to them, my lord, for the King gives you charge of great matters. His confidence lies all in you. Let Villiers concern himself with the petty ones."

Robin looked at his wife for a good while, weighing up her words, then nodded and walked back to his table. "You talk a good deal of sense, wife," he said, with a smile that would have warmed the heart of the bitterest shrew.

"God's blessing in all your heavy work, my love. I will walk now and leave you in peace," said Frankie, blowing him a kiss.

"Send my men back in," said Carr, looking down at his papers and missing the kiss.

I followed her from the room and out of their apartments.

"Where are we going?" I said, as we passed the guard, Frankie's clacking heels betraying urgency.

"To the Queen's apartments."

"In truth? Are we invited?"

"As the daughter of the Queen's Keeper of the Jewels, I am always invited."

"You did not mention before that we were to go there."

"Because I did not know before that my husband was *not* invited. If matters are so serious that he is excluded when Villiers is present, I must help him back into the King's favor."

I had a hundred questions, but we were already entering the Queen's gallery, where it was dark, hot and heavily perfumed. Frankie suddenly stopped.

"I feel sick," she said.

"The perfume, it's heady," I said, delighted at this further indication of pregnancy. "Come back outside."

"Too late," said Frankie, straightening up.

I turned to see the King swaying slowly along the gallery, arm in arm with his newly appointed cupbearer, George Villiers. Behind them came at least sixty members of the Court including Frankie's father, who looked uncomfortable beside the Lords Southampton, Pembroke and his erstwhile son-in-law, Essex. Frankie kept her head lowered, perhaps to avoid Essex or because it was a shock to see George Villiers and not her husband on the King's arm.

The new favorite was two heads taller than his monarch and, I guessed, at least three decades younger. His perfectly turned legs were encased in white silk and contrasted most favorably with the bandy limbs and crumpled stockings of the King. His dark brown curls were lusciously frizzed and looked to be the work of the finest wigmaker but were, on closer inspection, native to the wearer. The King, his own appearance far less regal than that of Villiers, was patting and pinching the youth's unbearded cheeks every few steps.

Frankie pushed to the front of the crowd lining the gallery, pulling me with her.

"It takes three thousand of these," the King was saying to Villiers, holding up a scruffy cocoon, "to make a pound of silk. There's that much in your shoe-roses," he said, popping the cocoon into Villiers's hand. I thought back to how the King had also wooed Robin with talk of silk. "My courtiers would wear it even if it came from wee bairns boiled alive."

In the laughter that followed, it was Villiers and not the King who noticed Frankie. He bowed deeply and I had a sudden and ridiculous urge to giggle. Handsome men have ever unseated me. Frankie did not curtsy, Villiers's rank being lower than her own. The King looked suddenly exhausted.

"Your Majesty," she said, only then sinking low.

"Rise, Lady Somerset," he said, showing less warmth than he had a few weeks before. Frankie wobbled slightly as she stood and smiled shyly. I saw this for the masquerade it was, but the King was instantly alert.

"My Lady Somerset, are you ailing?"

"Sire, I am with child," she said.

"Christ alive and all hail Him!" swore the King, who sought the happiness of those close to him as long as it did not impinge on his own. "That's a good business. Rabbie must be cock-a-hoop?"

"My lord is very pleased." Frankie smiled. The King looked her up and down, as if to assess whether she was likely to behave as embarrassingly as her husband, then said, "Lady Somerset, this is George Villiers."

Frankie dipped her head in a friendly manner. She, at least, behaved with grace toward the King's new dog.

"I am your servant, madam," said Villiers. The King clapped his hands in appreciation of his new favorite showing such courtesy to the pregnant wife of the rival incumbent.

Although he was but twenty at most, Villiers's manners were more refined than those of Carr. His voice, as I had noticed at Larkin's studio, was high and, for the English at least, easy to understand. He moved with grace and his beauty was unadorned but for the sumptuous yet sober materials of his clothes and six strings of fat pearls bubbling across his chest like spume crusting a black sea. Nothing about him was gaudy yet there was boldness. In his hat was a profusion of red ostrich plumes at which I stared a fraction longer than was entirely polite.

The King moved away on Villiers's arm, leaving Frankie to face the earls of his entourage, even the one by whom she had been violated. She looked at the floor until those of her rank had passed and then whispered to me.

"They have mortgaged their estates to dress him. The outlay has borne fruit." Her voice was as sharp as her mother's.

We moved toward the open doors of the Queen's bedchamber but made no attempt to enter. The King and Villiers were standing near the foot of the great bed, in which Queen Anna had spent most of her time since her eldest son's death. The two monarchs spoke formally to each other, as if from a script.

"The King has not looked this happy for months," said Frankie.

"You will hurt the child if you worry too much before it is moving," I said. There was laughter from within and we craned forward.

"My lord," said the Queen, whom we could not see, "as George Villiers is so great in your esteem, should he not be ever close by you as a gentleman of the bedchamber?" There was clapping and cheering, and it was clear that this delightful surprise had been anticipated by a good number of those present.

At that moment a shout from the gallery made us turn, as did other courtiers in the doorway, to be met by the extraordinary sight of Robert Carr marching as if to fight a fire. He was flushed, his silk hose splashed with mud and his cape hanging askew from his shoulder. Frankie walked quickly toward him.

"My love, what are you about?" she said, forcing him to a halt. Carr stared through her.

"I've no time to talk," he said, "there's rumors that the King's new cur is to be knighted. I've to stop it."

"Stop it?" said Frankie, rearranging his cloak and poking his frizzed hair into place. "No, Robin, you must not. The whole Court is gathered. He is only to be made a gentleman of the bedchamber, it's nothing to . . ."

"Him in the bedchamber? I'll not have it!"

"Think of the child, do not go in!" whispered Frankie with furious urgency, trying to hold on to her husband, but he barged past her, dislodging his cloak again from his shoulder. The Queen's guard barred the door to him, which was as shocking to see as Carr's panic, but he forced his way through and plunged into the crowd.

The King scowled at this dramatic arrival and no one bowed, perhaps unwilling to disturb the proceedings, perhaps because they could see which way the King's favor was streaming.

"Sire," said Carr, "any gentleman of the bedchamber must be a knight. This one's too lowborn to be by your side." Frankie and I were not alone in staring at him in horror. His wits appeared to have been entirely overridden by fury. Robin Carr would surely be arrested for challenging his monarch in so public and insolent a manner, but the King's voice was calm when he spoke.

"Tha's a good notion, my dear Somerset, a good notion indeed."

Carr blanched. The King did not look at him but at his wife.

"It is St. George's Day," announced Queen Anna, loudly, "the best of days to knight our George."

"Have we a sword?" asked the King, looking about theatrically, as if a sword might appear from behind a courtier's ear. Carr turned his head from one monarch to the other, stupid with rage.

"God help us," whispered Frankie. We were pressed close by the crowd and I could feel her hands fidgeting. "The King will not suffer this much longer. Robin will ruin us."

"Here, my lord," said the Queen, her voice clear and bright in the embarrassed silence within the chamber. I could see only her hand as she drew a large ceremonial sword from its hiding place on her bed, struggling with its weight. The knighthood had been planned all along and Carr looked even more the fool for not knowing of it.

"This cannot be," he said. "I'm head of the bedchamber and I do not approve it . . ."

"You'll nae tell me what to approve! Be silent or I'll send you out in chains," the King snapped, shaking with anger. He glared until Carr lowered his eyes, cheeks aflame, then took the sword from the Queen and patted the back of her hand, clearly relieved that she approved this new favorite despite her glee at the embarrassment of the old.

Turning to Villiers, the King said gently, "Kneel, George." Villiers stepped forward, eyes fixed upon his monarch.

The King touched the great sword to Villiers's shoulders, while Robin Carr shifted on his feet like a spooked horse, then passed the sword to the Earl of Pembroke and held out his hand for the new knight to kiss. Villiers did so with touching humility, a blush on his pale cheek as he rose.

The King acted then as if Carr were not in the room. He wished his wife good health and, having waited for George to offer her the deepest of bows, processed out with him. Carr barged his way to the front of the line that followed, at the heels of his monarch and Villiers.

24

"Sit," I commanded.

Frankie sat.

"Weston has been arrested," I told her.

Frankie jumped up. Her eyes were huge and full of questions. She flapped a hand at me, unable to speak. I helped her back onto the stool.

"I do not know the charge. He was taken at dawn and is held close prisoner at Sir Thomas Parry's house. I cannot see him."

Frankie's fright helped me calm the terror that had been building within me since William Weston had come to the apartments, too early for it to be good news.

"Parry?" repeated Frankie, her wits reviving. "He is a privy councillor. Robin helped him to the position. I shall ask for news," she said, standing and moving to the door. I grabbed her arm.

"Do not go out there until you are calm."

Frankie looked blankly at me until the implication of my words struck home. Weston was arrested. She must appear to be above suspicion.

"He will not talk, I am sure of it," I said.

William's face was before my eyes. He had delivered his news a word or two at a time, gasping after his sprint to Whitehall. I had heard it with lowered head, then hurried back through familiar rooms, now filled with threat. In Frankie's privy chamber a maid had been lighting candles to banish the darkness of the morning and her mistress, nearly seven months with child, was sitting with other noble ladies. We spent more time at Court since Villiers was made a knight, to entertain and charm the wives of men whose loyalty the Howards needed. My three younger children grumbled at the loss of their country playgrounds, but frequent visits from Mr. Palmer compensated them somewhat. He was teaching them to play tennis and he and I had reached the stage of kissing. It was so pleasant that I was in no rush to hurry matters along.

In May, Frankie's brother-in-law had been made a Garter knight at the same time as Lord Fenton, a noble from the Essex camp. The Court had split down the middle in choosing which retinue to favor. The King had forbidden George Villiers to join either, keeping him close on the steps of Denmark House, the Court of his Queen. Carr had ridden with Baron Knollys, the seventy-year-old husband of Frankie's sister Elizabeth. This lord was judged to have slightly more knights in his train, over three hundred of them, all dressed in black and white with matching feathers in their hats, but those of Fenton were better dressed, in yellow and gold, on finer horses, and he was thought to have carried the day. The King smiled with obvious pleasure on the effort expended to gain his favor. By the end of the month, it was clear that Villiers would supplant Carr.

"We stand too high for justice to reach us," said Frankie, her usual poise returning.

"To reach you."

"I will protect you."

"I know you will try. If I am arrested, please look to my children."

"It will not come to that," said Frankie. "Robin and my family will have Weston released. Someone must warn Franklin."

"He talks such copious rot it will be hard to stop up his mouth."

"Then we must give him sufficient cause. Robin will convince him that . . ." Her voice trailed off as she saw the difficulty of enlisting her husband to silence the corrupt apothecary who had provided the poison to kill his closest friend. "Robin will never forgive me," said Frankie, so quietly I could barely hear. "We cannot tell him."

"How not? If I am arrested, he will be told why. Will you deny all knowledge?" I said, frightened as never before that Frankie might turn from me.

"He will not abandon us," she said with such conviction I was slightly cheered. "I will get his help without telling him the problem."

By evening, Franklin had been summoned; Carr was listening

to his wife's breathless and confused attempts to explain why Weston had been arrested. Love, fear and pregnancy were working magic; she looked more beautiful than I had ever seen her. A clock on the mantelpiece interrupted, and for all ten chimes she gazed at her husband, who appeared soothed by the beauty of her face. The final note faded as gently as twilight, but I was full of foreboding.

"Why would anyone accuse Weston of hurting Overbury? He could not cause injury as a close prisoner, it was all bluff to get my attention," said Carr. "Frank, you are making no sense." He looked at me. "What do you know?"

I shook my head, my thoughts too confused to risk speaking.

"There is a chance," said Frankie, "that Mistress Turner and I will be questioned because Weston is known to us."

Carr drank the wine Frankie handed to him and held up the glass, watching firelight jump off its cut surfaces. A man angling to replace Overbury as Carr's secretary had given it to them. Carr put the glass on the floor and rested his foot on its rim.

"My love," said Frankie. Carr pressed and pressed his foot, but the glass did not break. "Let me take that," she said, crouching down. Carr stamped, making no more noise than if he'd been crushing a beetle. Splinters exploded outward, batting against Frankie's skirt, one lodging in the silk like a large diamond. She rose quickly.

"I've concerns enough of my own! Speak plain. Why is it that Weston's arrest alarms you so?" Since Villiers's arrival, an anger we had never suspected in Carr surfaced at the slightest provocation.

We had arrived at the moment I had anticipated since being drawn into Frankie's world; the moment when she would either show that our friendship was unbreakable or prove George's fears correct, that ultimately I would be sacrificed as payment for riding high on her shoulders. Previously, Frankie had always had something to gain from our friendship; now the opposite was true. Protecting me would not serve her. Overbury's death could so easily be portrayed as my doing; Weston, Forman and Franklin were all my connections. Frankie could play the innocent, unhappy girl, manipulated by an older, greedy, jealous confidante . . . she could throw me to the dogs and save herself. I saw blood soaking into the sand of the lion pit and knew that the sacrifice would not be mine alone, but also that of my children.

"The coroner testified that your friend died of a consumption. But now your enemies seek any excuse to unseat you. They are whispering that Overbury did not die naturally but was murdered."

"What?" Carr interrupted. "Why? By whom?"

"My love, it is pure invention! They say that Weston could have killed Overbury with poisons from an apothecary called Franklin. It seems this Franklin is mad with the French pox and will say anything to anybody. You must tell him to keep his mouth shut."

Carr stared at his wife as if she were made of wax and was melting before his eyes. She stepped toward him, but he flinched.

"Be calm, my love," she said.

Before he could reply there was a knock at the door.

"It will be Franklin," Frankie said. "Talk sternly to him, husband."

"Here?" said Carr. "A man accused of abetting murder, in the chambers of the King's closest adviser? Do you want me hanged for treason?"

"Impress upon him the importance of silence," Frankie said, touching his arm tenderly. Carr jerked away. I felt truly sorry for him, drawn into something of which he had no notion, that would bring him no good. I felt yet sorrier as I opened the door.

Carr stared, appalled by what manner of man was Franklin. His stench went before him and he was drunk. Carr gave his wife one long look, brimming with hurt and mystification, then excused himself to his privy chamber, shutting the door on her pleas.

Franklin spoke without invitation. "What's amiss?" he asked, nodding at Frankie's belly. I could not look upon him without picturing George's cat, turning and mewling, as if the poor animal were still at my feet.

"Weston has been arrested," said Frankie.

"Back to his old tricks, is he?" said Franklin, laughing.

I could contain myself no longer.

"You had better hope he says nothing to send you to the rope!" Franklin looked confused.

"It's not for me to worry about. Never my idea."

"Lord save us," I said, desperation worming its way in.

"My husband will save us," said Frankie. "He will save us as long as we say nothing, admit to nothing. There is no evidence. Keep quiet, do you understand?"

Franklin shrugged his shoulders.

"Are you mad!" I shouted.

"You must deny everything," Frankie repeated very slowly. "If you speak, you will be hanged."

The wretch pretended to strangle himself and made his eyes bulge.

I stared at the strange performance, suddenly cold. I was back on my knees at Paul's cross in the gray light of dawn.

"No, Frankie," I said, very quietly, lifting my eyes to hers. "It is I shall hang for you both."

Three days passed in a strange lull, as if we were becalmed; I stayed in the apartment and kept the children close, allowing nothing to distract my attention from them, and yet the speed of my heartbeat and lack of appetite were constant reminders that, elsewhere, Richard Weston was answering questions about his time as Overbury's jailer. Killing Overbury could bring us down, but not in the way we had expected. Had he been alive when George Villiers was first brought to Court, he might have counseled Carr to befriend this young rival and keep the King's favor, then no one would have dared move against him.

Barbara, not yet betrothed, had left Lady Catherine's household, or perhaps was sent away because of the scandal. She refused to say that was the case, but she would not have added to my troubles for the world. I was glad that John, at least, would not know for a day or two what was unfolding. My brother Eustace visited, to know how I did, but other than him, Frankie and I received no visitors at all, not even from our families, although Frankie was summoned briefly to her father.

"My father has told Weston that his son will be hurt if he confesses," Frankie informed me. I was horrified, but she was impatient. "Neither of us wants that, but it is the only way that we can all escape justice. If Weston does not confess, then there is no principal to charge with the crime, and the case cannot be tried. There is no one on this earth who can frighten me into confessing guilt, not even the Lord Chief Justice."

I did not ask what she had told her father to enlist his help. The knowledge might damage us further if I were tortured. Although I was terrified of being questioned, it seemed that Weston and

Frankie would deny everything and it was now up to me to keep quiet. Yet I wondered, again and again, would Weston or Frankie sacrifice me if great pressure were put upon them? Only when it was all over would I know if they had held fast or failed me.

Frankie's father had been informed of the events that led to Weston's arrest, which meant that Carr had been too, although he said nothing to us. The Lieutenant of the Tower, Sir Gervase Elwes, had lost his job and was seeking another from Baron Ellesmere, that same for whom Arthur was steward and in whose household John and Barbara had served. Elwes, in an attempt to disprove his reputation for drunkenness and corruption, informed Lord Ellesmere that he had thrown away poison intended for a prisoner, even though he would have stood to gain had the prisoner died. Lord Ellesmere saw immediately how magnificently he could profit from this information, given that the prisoner was Sir Thomas Overbury.

Frankie was beside herself with fury at Elwes, but I saw it as inevitable. Just as Weston had never been paid what he was promised, Frankie and Carr had been neglectful of Elwes. Had he been cosseted by them, he would have had no cause to make so horrendous a blunder. Elwes's confession had been sent to the King some months before. It was he who had ordered the investigation, behind Carr's back, which had led to Weston's arrest. The last line of his letter burned across my mind's eye: *if you cause me to call you ingrate, no earthly plague shall be worse than my wrath.* He had given up on Carr, and now the King himself was our enemy.

At night I sat beside the children as they slept, Henry sprawled among the warm, soft-breathing bodies of his sisters. I lit a new candle each time the previous one burned down. It was inevitable that I would be questioned. How could I ever explain my arrest to them?

Frankie stayed by my side, even for much of the night, as neither of us could sleep. We talked quietly through our story, agreeing on the smallest details. We would deny everything; Frankie had learned this during the scandal over Mary Woods: the most important thing was to insist on our innocence and not yield.

The wolves could not wait to tear us apart. Frankie's steward brought us the broadsheets, reluctantly, in which we read that "for a whore's sake, Carr murdered his dearest friend," and that he was capable of heinous crimes because he was a foreigner, low-born, lenient to Catholics, too fond of fashion and extravagance and, most important, already guilty of that darkling sin of too great a love for the King. It was not difficult to know who had fed this effluent to the newsmongers.

"They're saying that Lord Northampton is not dead but in Rome with the Jesuits and that he, together with Robin, poisoned Prince Henry as well as Sir Thomas," she read out. Suddenly she dropped to her knees and scrabbled together the printed pages that littered the chamber floor, snatching one from my fingers and flinging the whole lot on the fire. "We should leave for Greys."

"What point is there? Weston is known to be my helpmeet. It will not be long before they come for me."

Frankie and Carr argued constantly, both of them in tears. She insisted on the coroner's verdict, overseen by fourteen witnesses, that Overbury had died by God's hand, and dismissed everything else as a malicious attempt to bring them down. Elwes had been bribed by their enemies, she insisted, and there was no truth in his confession.

When the maid came for me at ten in the morning on the fourth day, my children were at their lessons. I kissed them and pressed all the love in my heart into the skin of their cheeks.

"Why are you sad?" Henry asked.

"I'm not sad, sweetling, I wear black when I want people to treat me nicely." Henry seemed to find this sensible and went back to his slate.

"I may be late," I said to Barbara, hugging her close.

"What is it?" she asked, sensing a difference in this departure.

"I do not like to leave you so long."

"Do not worry, we will be merry," said Katherine, drawing when she was meant to be learning her psalms.

Carr had ordered Frankie to stay in her parlor, not because he disliked me but so they might distance themselves from legal processes used for the lower orders. I longed for an encouraging embrace and a few words to shore up my courage.

Two parish officers awaited me in the entrance hall, one old, one young, perhaps father and son. They were looking about at the splendor of their surroundings and did not immediately notice my arrival.

"I am Mistress Turner. How can I help you, sirs?" I asked serenely, although I felt sick and light-headed.

"We have orders to accompany you to the house of Alderman Smith, to answer questions pertaining to the death of Sir Thomas Overbury," said the elder. There was little respect in their manner.

I feigned surprise. "I will come willingly, sirs." The maid brought me my warmest shawl and cloak.

"No bag?"

"Bag?" I said, genuinely surprised.

"If you're detained."

"Detained?" I said, my wits blunted by fear. "Why would I be detained?"

The older one shrugged and gripped my arm painfully. At that moment Frankie arrived, in defiance of her husband's command. Her belly preceded her like a bowsprit; she was dressed in her most luxurious house gown, wearing far more jewelry than she would usually at that time of day, her highest heels, hair arranged on the tallest pads. Her face was white and heavily made up and she looked unearthly, frightening, like a vengeful Goddess of the Ancients. She came to a stop close to the beadles, towering over them by two heads, and the cold haughtiness of her expression worked instant magic, as it did on everyone who met Frankie in this mood.

The officers bowed very low until she permitted them to rise.

"Who are you?" she demanded.

"My lady, I am Officer Cartwright of the Parish of St. Mary's Undercroft, and this is my son Jimmy."

"Your being sent here is a mistake," said Frankie, her expression so severe that the younger beadle repeatedly blinked. "The Earl of Somerset is to speak to the King later today."

Both men nodded and the elder released my arm, but they did not retreat.

"With apologies, my lady, we have orders to bring her in," said Officer Cartwright.

"From whom?" Frankie demanded.

"Lord Coke, my lady."

She was careful not to look at me, but we both knew that Lord Coke would not be intimidated by her. She would need to mobilize the most senior members of her family.

"Then I would have you take the utmost care of my greatest friend," Frankie said. She embraced me and I felt like a child before her, she was so tall. "You will be home before nightfall," she said, squeezing my cold hands. She had not abandoned me, although disobeying her husband would not endear either of us to him.

The beadles behaved like a guard of honor throughout our journey into the City. At the alderman's house I was shown into a parlor, a comfortable room that reminded me of my home with George, and I all but expected the alderman to greet me with apologies and put me in his own carriage back to Whitehall.

Within a few minutes Lord Chief Justice Coke strode into the room, which I had not expected, and settled himself behind a trestle, his eyes slit thin in his rodent face. Beside him sat a man with writing materials and behind him stood an older man whom I took to be Alderman Smith. No introductions were made. There was no Frankie beside me compelling these men to show respect, and all three of them looked angry and fierce. I knew this was intended to frighten me and it did.

"You are Mistress Anne Turner, widow, previously of Paternoster Row and now residing in the household of the Countess of Somerset?" said the man with the quill. Before I could nod, Lord Coke addressed me in a thin voice.

"Widow Turner, why did you give Richard Weston poisons with which to murder Sir Thomas Overbury?"

My head was dizzy with terror but I did not falter.

"I have no idea of what you speak."

"Come, Weston has confessed," said the Chief Justice.

I said nothing, from fear that I might give myself away by accident. I did not believe him.

"Weston's story that Sir Thomas Overbury died of a chill did not hold for long," said Lord Coke, with a tiny smile. "On the second day of questioning he admitted to showing the Lieutenant of the Tower a vial of clear liquid with which you supplied him. On day three he admitted that you had told him to give it to the prisoner but not to partake of it himself." Coke raised his eyebrows, as if that gesture might prompt me to confess all.

"I am entirely at a loss," I said, my faith in Weston cracking along with my own façade of self-assurance. I had not known what to expect, but certainly not this immediate attack from Lord Coke. "Richard Weston told me that Sir Thomas Overbury sent him out for beer at about six o'clock on the morning he died. Weston was not half an hour gone, but Overbury was dead when he returned," I said with conviction, for this was indeed how my former servant had described it to me. "Weston believed that Sir Thomas had succumbed to illness, emetics, physick, or a combination of the three."

"This matter is of the greatest urgency because it involves those close to the King."

"It does? I have told you all I know," I said.

Coke stared at me without blinking and water gathered in my mouth and down my throat, a prelude to vomiting. I would not swallow; he would know my guilt if I did. I calmly held his gaze, willing my eyes to speak of honesty. Not until my mouth near overflowed did he look away to nod at the alderman, who led me from the room to a small, wintry cell that smelt strongly of rust and wet stone. There was nothing in it but a truckle with a thin straw mattress, the barest of blankets and a bucket. The narrow window was unglazed and rain puddled on the floor below it.

"What are you doing? I cannot be here, what of my children? They have lost their father and will be mighty afraid, not knowing where I am. The Countess of Somerset awaits me . . ." The alderman ignored my mounting hysteria and left me, without candle or fire, closing the door behind him. When I heard the key turn in the lock, I sat for fear I would collapse.

I have been kept close prisoner ever since, over six weeks, seeing no one but the Lord Chief Justice and Alderman Smith. Enforced isolation can turn you somewhat mad; loneliness folds me in upon myself. The voices in my head grow so vile that I welcome even the company of my accusers.

That first day, I moved the hard truckle away from the rain that blew in with each gust. Outside there is a drop of thirty feet to the river and the echo of boatmen's calls and shimmering reflections on bright days are the only life in the cell.

After a few days, desperation to see my children overtook me. I did not eat, wash or sleep, but lay down and remembered every detail of their lives from before they were born to kissing them goodbye as they sat at their lessons. I pulled threads of memory from my mind, carefully separated each one and laid it with utmost tenderness, like clean clothes, on that child's pile, until I was satisfied I had missed nothing. After that, I did the same with George, until the lid of his coffin closed and darkness came upon me. I dared not think of Frankie beyond praying that she was trying to free me; I had only to keep to my denials.

Each dawn my hopes returned that I would be freed; each afternoon they faded with the light. I imagined Frankie summoning important persons, writing letters, cajoling her father and Robin. I did this to stem the ocean of regret that would otherwise have drowned me. At night I slept little, but once I dreamed of George Villiers walking in the Privy Garden, his chest swathed in pearls, leaving a trail of silk which the King gathered lovingly as he scurried along behind.

The many notes I received from my children, my brother Eustace, Frankie and Mr. Palmer, cheered me a little. Frankie told me that Robin was working for my release and sent me sea coal for the fire. I hoped he was working harder for me than he had for Overbury.

One day, after about a week, the notes and letters stopped. Why did my children no longer write, nor Mr. Palmer? Had they been persuaded of my guilt? Had Frankie lost the baby? Was she ill? Dead? Had she abandoned me? If she, or my children, threw away my love, then all that was left would be my pride, my vanity and my stupidity.

When I again stood before Lord Chief Justice Coke, I felt very much smaller than the first time. Even so, my hopes were not gone that I would be freed.

"Richard Weston claims that you instructed him to give a clear liquid to Sir Thomas Overbury and that the Countess of Somerset would reward him well if he did," said Lord Coke, leaning forward.

"I cannot think what pressure you have put upon the poor man to make him fabricate such tales." Coke's response was a slight narrowing of his eyes.

"Weston has had a visitor in the person of Sir Gervase Elwes," said Coke. "The former Lieutenant of the Tower has made a full, written confession of his part in this plot. He managed to persuade Weston of the futility, indeed harmfulness, of continuing to lie." I looked away from Sir Edward, out of the window. Gulls screamed through the air, hurled about by the gusting wind. The chimney moaned but I did not speak. Coke shifted in his chair and blew sharply through his nose.

"Mr. James Franklin . . . You deny knowing him?" Reluctantly I pulled my gaze back to my inquisitor.

"Franklin is among my acquaintance," I said. "I sent him on occasion to see how Weston did."

"Why had you concern for him? Was it not rather news of Sir Thomas Overbury's health you sought?"

"I had very slight acquaintance with Sir Thomas Overbury and would not seek knowledge of him; Weston I have known for many years."

"Are you familiar with the law as it concerns murder? Only by admission of guilt before trial can the King grant clemency."

"Poor widows are rarely the beneficiaries of clemency, from any source."

"You speak boldly for a woman."

"I speak only the truth, my lord."

"Come, Mistress Turner, your guilt is clear, but that of much greater personages even more so. If you were led into crime by them, clemency is possible."

I have never liked people who do not take me seriously; there is no clemency for widows who abet murder. Coke let out a long sigh worthy of the stage, and from the corner of my eye I saw him nod to the alderman who banged on the door. After a few moments, it was opened from without. Into the room, shoved by an unseen hand, stumbled Weston, his face bruised and swollen. He regained his balance with difficulty since his hands were tied.

"Weston!" I cried, moving toward him.

"Be still and silent," said Coke, extending an imperious finger. I stopped. Weston was bowed, beaten, his clothes, hair and beard filthy. No one offered him a stool and he did not look up.

"Speak," ordered Coke.

Weston slumped further.

"Mistress Turner paid me monies to give a clear liquid to Sir Thomas Overbury." His voice was a dry recital. "She was following orders from the Countess of Somerset. This liquid was poison."

I could not stop myself. I rounded on Lord Coke. "You have beaten him about the head! You have tortured an old man. Look at him! What evil is this?"

"Mistress Turner, your feigned concern for an ancient retainer does not convince me. You are held here as an accessory to murder. I believe that you acquired and gave poison to Richard Weston with the express purpose of murdering Sir Thomas Overbury, foe to your friend the Countess of Somerset. The sentence for those found guilty but who plead innocence is always death. In this case, Mistress Turner, given the import of these matters and the seeming complicity of personages close to the royal presence, tell us the part played by the Earl and Countess of Somerset and your willing repentance will be noted when punishment is decided."

Without thinking, I put a hand to the small hat on my head, perhaps because I could not believe that anything would stay put in this gale of accusation.

"Those afflicted with pride and vanity," said Lord Coke, observing me closely, "easily fall prey to the greater sins of which you stand accused."

"It is a crime to wear a hat now?" I snapped, my composure gone. "What poor Weston has been forced to say is no concern of mine. I will not confess to crimes I know not of."

Weston lifted his eyes to mine for a moment. I saw in them not defeat, or fear, nor even resentment, but admiration for my steadfastness in the face of a bully.

At a nod from Coke, the guard wrested Weston to the door. I

ran forward, ignoring Coke's shouts, and raised Weston's hands to my lips. I kissed them gently as he looked into my eyes with such deep sadness that my guilt felt too vast for my body to carry. I knew that even after this torture, Howard heavies would visit Weston and "press" him to remain silent at his trial, by threatening his beloved son, William. It was my fault. I had thrust him, unwilling, into Frankie's world, and for most of the time he had tried to drag me out. The guard wrenched him from me and the door was closed.

How had this happened? Why had Frankie and Carr not secured my release, and Weston's too? I looked around for somewhere I could sit; there was nowhere. Was Frankie also being questioned? I felt almost mad with knowing nothing.

"What have you to say?" Coke asked me.

"I must beg you grant bail for the sake of my children."

Coke looked up to the ceiling as if there lay patience.

"Very well, Mistress Turner. Petition me for bail. I shall refuse it. Let us see if your friends are in a position to overrule me. Alderman Smith? Has Mistress Turner received any messages?"

"This gentleman is spy as well as jailer?"

"Several notes from her children whose distress at her absence is genuine," he said with a note of kindness that undid me worse than Coke's aggression. "They are in the apartments of the Countess of Somerset and—"

"Mistress Turner's children are not my concern," interrupted Coke. "Other messages?"

"Several from the Countess of Somerset." Coke nodded at him. The man pulled a letter from a leather satchel and unrolled it. "This latest says, 'My dearest soul, be of good cheer, you shall want for nothing . . .'"

"That is addressed to me," I said.

"Continue," ordered Coke. A cold serpent of terror rose within me, swelling, making my heart race as it constricted my organs and pushed up into my skull, bringing with it a senseless hiss which made it hard to hear the men's voices. "With this note came a diamond ring and a chain and cross of gold, for Mistress Turner's financial comfort, which I have in safekeeping. The Countess writes, 'My lord will go to Court within three or four days to pro-cure your delivery, my truest friend.'"

Frankie had not abandoned me. She was writing, sending me the jewels on her body to keep me alive, but they were being kept from me.

"When was that sent?" said Lord Coke.

"A week ago."

Coke leered at me. "And yet here you are."

Why was I not allowed bail? It could only be that Robert Carr had lost the power to grant it; that Villiers and the Essex faction had the upper hand. Coke stood. "When you decide to stop clinging to faithless friends, I will take your confession myself."

26

W hen Alderman Smith came to tell me that there would be a trial, I was too numb to respond. Weston had not withstood Coke and the forces behind him. At the sight of the coach in which I was to travel to the King's Bench, completely draped in black cloth, all courage deserted me.

"It is a hearse."

The coachman attempted to herd me inside but I refused. I would be unable to see out. If my children were waiting on the route, I would miss them. He sneered openly and I felt all the terror of recent weeks press upon me. My attire spoke of trustworthiness and honesty: a smart black dress with simple yellow collar and a black hat pinned onto carefully arranged hair. What had been said and written about me as I sat alone and undefended in the cell, that even a coachman treated me with contempt?

"If you do not mount, you will be constrained and carried in," he said.

I could not will myself into it.

"The drapes allow you safe and anonymous passage," said Alderman Smith, gently clasping my elbow. He helped me up, staying the coachman's hand as he went to slam the door, closing it softly himself. The black cloth was pulled down and I was in darkness.

Although I could not see, the sounds told me where I was. On King Street, the rumble of the wheels was dampened by straw. I was yards from Frankie's apartment. Did the children know I was passing? Did she? I strained to hear their shouts. I longed to see them; I pictured Frankie, statuesque and remote, my children gathered around her, remonstrating with the driver and pulling me from the blackness; all I could hear were the sounds of daily life and it amazed me that beyond the darkness, life continued.

The coachman yelled and flicked his whip to force our passage through Westminster Palace Yard. A bleeding bear, salivating dogs, a half-blind baron: their deaths entertainment for the crowd. That was the moment I fully understood that I might be next.

The horses whinnied in fear as the coach was rocked by the mob. I shrank into the dark interior but the drapes were thrown up and the door opened. I was pulled out, the press of people shouting, grabbing, ripping at my dress. Was I to die here at the hands of a vengeful mob? Officers of the court arrived to push back the crowd. Briefly, I felt the light of the cold October morning pressing on my face before I was bundled forward.

Westminster Hall was dark and quiet after the crowds, but there was no time to stop and calm myself, to put my clothes and hair back in order before I was marched through the huge, soaring space, blinded at intervals by shafts of light from windows set high in the walls. As my eyes adjusted, I saw that hundreds, even thousands, of people were staring at me from tiered benches set on scaffolding, six rows high. I had become a player, a lone woman denied the script.

Whispering began as I passed so that by the time I neared the boards of the King's Bench there was a storm of chatter and calling out. I kept my eyes lowered in modesty and terror, looking briefly to right and left for my oldest children, Frankie or Robert Carr, even Arthur or my brother Eustace and sister Mary, or Mr. Palmer. I saw no one I knew.

I was ushered to the Bench. I heard Lord Chief Justice Coke announced, followed by a jury not of my peers but of nobles. With lowered eyes, all I could see were clerks with their writing desks round their necks; it frightened me to know that these proceedings would be read for evermore. Before my arrest I had read libels and pamphlets every day that besmirched men's honor, even that of the King, by twisting events to make any point the writer wished. Would someone look back at this time and think those broadsheets and these notes from the trial were truthful because they had survived when a lone voice can only fade?

A clerk called for silence and began to recite the date, the seventh day of November, sixteen hundred and fifteen, my full name and that of my dead husband, and then the arraignment, in a flat voice that slightly lulled me into a state of hopeful confidence, for it sounded so unlikely.

". . . that she did comfort, aid and assist Mr. Richard Weston in the poisoning of Sir Thomas Overbury while that latter was held close prisoner in the Tower of London resulting in the death of Sir Thomas on the fifteenth day of September in the year of Our Lord sixteen hundred and thirteen."

"Mistress Turner," said Lord Chief Justice Coke very loudly. "Do you not know that to wear a hat in this place is an insult to the members of the jury whose greatness far exceeds your own? Remove it at once!"

I fumbled to remove the hat, placed so precisely to denote myself a gentlewoman, as Lord Coke feigned mounting irritation to a rising gale of laughter from the audience. Cheeks scalding, I had no choice but to pull it off. Hair straggled around my face and I pictured the first time I had met Frankie in her chamber, with her lunatic tresses. I felt entirely naked, my messy head uncovered in public. I tried to pin the stray hairs back to recreate an impression of calm control and honesty. As there was nowhere else, I placed the hat on the floor by my feet and pulled from my purse a black silk square, which I tied over my head. But the armature of my appearance had been shattered. Lord Coke appeared satisfied with his opening salvo.

"Mistress Turner," he boomed, not looking at me but to the crowd and jury, a well-rehearsed performer. "You are here on trial for your life"—he paused to allow the audience to react—"as accessory to the poisoning unto death of Sir Thomas Overbury. You are accused of the willful destruction of a creature made in God's image, the worst of crimes, employing the worst of weapons, to inflict the worst of deaths. How do you plead?"

I lifted my face.

"Not guilty, my lord."

Lord Coke looked down at the bench before him and appeared to puzzle a small point of order, waiting for silence to fall again.

He knew how to caress his audience. This man judging me had also collected the statements and evidence for this trial and was able to dismiss anything that disproved his accusations and retain everything that supported them. I was guilty until I could prove my innocence but I had no means to make a case for myself and who would dare speak up for me?

"If you persist in your claim of innocence, I have no choice but to put to you the evidence we have gathered to the contrary, to the detriment of your honor and that of other persons known to you. Will you not change your plea?" This harrying made Coke appear eager for my welfare and the restitution of my good name. It made him seem beneficent while I knew him to be seeking only his own glory through my downfall, whether I be guilty or not. I shook my head in so small a manner that I was taken by surprise when Coke bellowed in response, as if rallying troops to march.

"So be it! I say these crimes are the result of implacable malice, being the malice of a woman. Let us establish what manner of creature is this that stands before us. You who pretend to be good-wife, friend and mother but are truly a whore, a sorcerer, a witch, a bawd, a Papist, a felon and a murderer!"

The crowd erupted. What manner of man would address a gentlewoman in this fashion? I had no idea what he meant and could neither speak nor shake my head.

"Let us begin with 'whore.' Is it true that you were married to George Turner, medical doctor and member of the Royal College of Physicians, an honorable man by all accounts?" I nodded, relieved to have some good said of me. "Is it also true that you conducted an adulterous relationship with one Sir Arthur Waring during the last years of your marriage, without discretion, such that it was known to your husband, who was inveigled in his Will into leaving the sum of ten pounds to Sir Arthur, to buy a ring inscribed 'Let Fate Unite the Lovers'?"

The crowd jeered and abused me; I heard it over the rushing of blood in my head. The Lord Chief Justice could not prove me a murderess, for there was no proof, but he could destroy my reputation and thereby damage Frankie and Robert Carr by their closeness to me. "Speak up, Mistress Turner. A goodwife or an adulteress? Did you have carnal relations with Sir Arthur Waring, over a period of several years, while married to your husband?"

I remained mute. There was no defense, except that many others, of every rank of society, did the same. To the crowd gathered here it was of no matter that I had loved my husband and that I had begun an adulterous liaison only with his blessing after George himself was incapacitated. They would think it all a very Catholic carry-on, and nothing could save me from that brand, "adulteress."

The edifice of respectability that I carefully maintained, that was necessary and normal in the world, crumbled in the face of his next statement. "The Court has been informed that your three youngest children are the bastards of Sir Arthur Waring. Do you deny it?"

"My children are good and obedient. Why do you drag them into these proceedings?" I said, my voice shrill even to my own ears. The audience gasped so loudly that I felt sucked back, as if into a whale's mouth. What sort of woman argued back to a judge? I pictured the faces of my youngest three. They knew only that Arthur came to see them from time to time, not that he was their father. Now the shame of illegitimacy would blight their lives. In that moment my hatred for him was even greater than my terror. If he had accepted responsibility for his own children, I would not now be on trial for my life.

"It is well known that the devil Adultery opens the door to the devil Murder. Adultery is not a private sin but a crime against the common weal," declared Coke. "Obedience, subjection and propriety are the attributes of a godly woman." He raised his eyebrows at the jury, as if they were his partners at tennis. "And now to your role as sorcerer." The crowd quietened, anxious to miss nothing.

"I put it to you, Mistress Turner, that you conspired with one 'Dr.' Forman, a notorious necromancer, conjuror of devils and caster of false horoscopes, to bewitch Sir Arthur Waring into acting in accordance with your own cupidity and lust. When Sir Arthur failed to marry you after your husband's death, you asked Dr. Forman to conjure devils to torment your lover until he submitted to your will. What say you?"

Coke was telling the jury that I was a witch, no different from those hanged in Pendle. My body felt too heavy for me to keep upright. I needed a chair, a hand to hold, a friend or a lawyer to put my case so I need not speak. Here were only hostile or curious onlookers at a show better than anything playing at the Globe.

I shook my head. All I could do now for myself, for Frankie and for my children, was to maintain my silence.

"Again, denials! If we believed every depraved person who denied their crime, our gallows would be dismantled and our state with it. Crimes of the nature you have committed are grievous not only unto their innocent victims but also unto the very fabric of England; they strike at the heart of all we hold dear and would bring us to barbarity and lawlessness were we to let them go unpunished, such that virtue and prosperity would leave these shores and render us no better than animals. You, who would deceive your husband, who would have another man's children without shame, who would conjure devils to torment your lover—you are a whore, a sorcerer, and I put it to you that you are also a witch!"

Lord Coke punctuated his accusations with violent shakes of his outstretched arm, as if ridding himself of some foul creature gripping onto his hand. It was clear to all assembled that this case had inspired him to greater wrath than any he had dealt with before, greater even than that of Guy Fawkes and the Powder Plotters, for here was evil hidden among the petticoats of a woman.

The crowd was alive with excitement. They hushed only when Lord Coke indicated that a witness was to be brought in. From behind a wooden screen entered Simon Forman's widow who, with great hesitation, approached the Bench when invited.

"State your name," said Coke gently.

"Mistress Anne Forman."

"What have you to relate of the Widow Turner?"

Anne Forman spoke with great show of humility and timidity.

"Mistress Turner came to see my husband many times and oft went to his study, being there closeted with him several hours at a time." The audience hissed its disapproval.

"Was the Widow Turner always alone in her visits to your husband?"

"On one occasion she came with the Countess of Somerset, the Countess of Essex as was."

"Let us be clear," Coke said. "You saw with your own eyes the Countess of Somerset, Lady Frances Howard, previously the Countess of Essex before the annulment of her first marriage, daughter of the present Lord Treasurer of England, at your house by Lambeth Marshes, there to consult with your husband?"

"Yes, sir . . . My lord." To declare Anne Forman a liar, because she only saw Frankie masked, would be to prove I had been there.

"To what purpose?"

"She hated her husband—her last one, I mean, not this one— and wanted rid of him." The noise from the onlookers was too great for her to continue. Lord Coke did not stifle the crowd's disapproval. Eventually, Mistress Forman was able to continue. "I have a letter here from her to my husband." The clerk stepped forward to read it but Coke beckoned him over and took the letter himself. It was clear from the ease with which he read Frankie's hand, and the exaggerated outrage of his expression, that he had seen this before. He read it aloud.

"'Sweet Father, I crave your love although I hope I have it and shall always deserve it. Please send me what you promised, for it remains as ever here. My lord is merry and drinks with his men; he abuses me as doggedly as before and I begin to think I shall never be happy in this world. Please, keep the Sweet Lord unto me and, if you can, send me some good fortune, for truly I have need of it and be careful you name me not to any body, for we have so many spies, that you must use all your wits, for the world is against me, and the heavens favor me not. If I be ungrateful, let all mischief come unto me. Give Mistress Turner warning of all things but no one else for fear others may tell my father and mother, and fill their ears full of tales.

'Your affectionate, loving daughter, Frances Essex.'

"Who is 'the Sweet Lord' that Lady Frances would have Forman keep faithful to her? Of course, the man to whom she is now married, Robert Carr, Earl of Somerset. And who the gentleman she claims 'abuses' her? Her then husband, Robert Devereux, Earl of Essex. See how she signs herself? Daughter!" thundered Coke. "She calls Forman 'Sweet Father,' she who is daughter to the King's own Lord Treasurer, and all because the woman standing here introduced Lady Frances to a user of black magic and sorcery. I say to you, this woman is a witch!"

Again, the audience brayed and yelled, crude as groundlings in the theater yard. Coke motioned to the clerk, who went to a small trestle and pulled a black cloth from it. Underneath lay several objects. He showed one to the jury, some of whom stared while others looked away in distaste. The clerk then gave it to Coke, who held it up for all to see. It was a statue of two figures, cast from black lead, a man and a woman, naked and lying belly to belly.

"These copulating figures were used by Dr. Forman and Mistress Turner for their spells. Here is the brass mold from which it, and others, one must assume, were made. Were hairs, or nail clippings, or some such given into the lead to make the figures more potent?" asked Coke, not waiting for an answer but seeking to plant the thought into the minds of the jury.

Next, the clerk brought around a black scarf, covered in white crosses, then a parchment with the names of the Trinity written upon it, and another on which was stretched a piece of what appeared to be skin, bearing the word "corpus," along with names of the devils Lord Coke accused Forman of conjuring to torment Robin Carr and Arthur Waring if they proved unfaithful toward Frankie or me.

A doll was held aloft, sumptuously appareled in a silk dress held together with pins, the French Baby I had made with a garment design for Forman's wife.

"A puppet, into which pins are stuck to cause pain to whatever unfortunate the witch Turner wishes to torment!" shouted Coke. The crowd strained forward for a better view and a mighty crack issued from the scaffold. The spectators screamed and began pushing and yelling to get off the precarious structure before it collapsed on them.

"The Devil is here!" they cried.

"He is angered by the exposure of his works!"

Those on the lowest tier of benches began running to the doors, pushing off the spectators trying to scramble down from the benches above. A couple of people fell and made a great clatter as they tumbled.

I jumped at the sound of a mighty hammering. It was Lord Justice Coke, banging his gavel with all his strength. The clerks of court, several of whom looked shaken and afraid, called for order. The boards on the scaffolding were checked and, with much fussing and testing, the crowd reassembled. Lord Coke contained his irritation, wanting the crowd on his side to add weight to his lurid accusations in the absence of any proof.

"What say you of these tools of witchcraft?" he asked me.

"I know them not. The doll is but a—"

"You had *nothing* from Forman?" interrupted Coke.

"Only simples."

"Simples? Simples for your own health?" Here I stumbled, realizing too late that I had better say nothing. "For whom were they intended? For Sir Arthur Waring?"

I made no sound or movement; anything I said or did would be interpreted in an evil light.

"So when a man fails to do as you want," Coke continued, "you avail yourself of a sorcerer to make potions, knowing not what substances be in them, and give them to your victims?" Coke turned to the jury with a look of weary triumph, as if he hated the world of women.

Mistress Forman spoke then, without invitation. "Your lordship, after your visit I searched the house one more time." I wished that I truly were a witch, for then I could strike this woman dumb. Mistress Forman was a fool, destroying her dead husband's reputation along with mine. His bravery and success in treating victims of plague would be quite forgotten and she would forever be known as the wife of a sorcerer and necromancer. What honor was there in that? "I found this." From a pocket at her belt Mistress Forman pulled a small notebook covered in worn green linen, bound with a lace. I had read this notebook on nearly every visit to Forman; it was a list he kept of adulterous courtiers and the names of their lovers. She handed it to a clerk who unwound the lace, opened the page and read.

"'Herein is a list of which Ladies Love which Men at Court.'" Coke leaned forward, eager for evidence of Frankie's affair with Carr, as did the crowd, again with much creaking. The clerk hesitated, reading silently what he had been requested to broadcast. Looking deeply anxious, he handed the book back to the Lord Chief Justice. The judge read the first few lines then snapped the book shut and slammed it down on his desk. The name at the top of the list was that of his own estranged wife. He stared at me with such loathing that I knew he considered hell the only fit place for me.

"Do you deny that you used witchcraft and the summoning of devils in your attempts to force Sir Arthur Waring into matrimony with yourself, and Sir Robert Carr, afterward Earl of Somerset, into matrimony with Frances Howard, then Countess of Essex?"

"I do," I said, but Lord Coke turned away, wincing, as if it hurt to listen to my denial.

"Should these sins not be enough for any woman? Adultery, sorcery and witchcraft? To this let me add another. You are a bawd—as much of a bawd as any common brothel keeper, acting the pander between your great friend, the Lady Frances, and Robert Carr. We have depositions from the trial of your manservant Richard Weston, describing how you arranged for Robert Carr to meet the Countess of Essex at your house in Paternoster Row, in private, at night. At other times, you arranged for a farmhouse to be made available beyond the village of Hammersmith, where the Countess went to meet, for two hours at a time, the aforementioned Robert Carr. Weston has confessed to carrying letters between them, given to him by you. And for all this time the Countess was the wife of the Earl of Essex, and you did facilitate that terrible sin of fornication between her and her lover. What say you to this charge?"

The crowd could not restrain themselves in light of such revelations. I felt faint but there was no rail to hold, nor chair or stool on which to sit. To defend myself would, in the same breath, be to damn myself.

"Speak, madam, or we must take your silence for confession of guilt."

"I am innocent of the crime of which I stand accused. I murdered no one." To confess anything at all would be to condemn Frankie.

"Woman is born guilty of the sins of Eve and only in perfect purity and good conduct can she redeem herself. Once she has committed any sin, even that of vanity, her weak virtue is prey to all the evils natural to her sex. She who steps away from the path of duty, who puts herself beyond the guidance of husband, father or brother, is lost to wickedness. You have acted of and for yourself, which is itself against the proper bounds of womanhood. But how shameless is your conduct! An adulteress, a witch, a sorceress and a bawd, reveals herself capable of any crime, including that of murder."

I shook my head.

"Do you deny also that you are a poisoner?" cried Lord Coke, leaning out over his bench to emphasize the words as they struck at me. "Poison. The most devious weapon, for it takes a man away when he expects it least and cannot defend himself. It gives him no time to repent before death, is easily concealed and used, as hard to prevent as to discover. There is no manner in which evidence of poisoning can be attained, thus we dispense with such proofs in trials of poisoners. If testimony were required in cases of poisoning, the King might as well proclaim impunity. It is an Italian device, fit for the Court of Rome, a crime of cowardice, of women, and of Papists. Is it true that you are a Catholic, Mistress Turner? And the Countess too, and Richard Weston, and the Lieutenant of the Tower, and all those involved in this plot to kill an innocent, Protestant man?"

The crowd felt themselves on safe ground with this accusation. They shouted and would have thrown their shoes at me had they been assured of retrieving them.

"The principal in this crime, Richard Weston, confessed to receiving a vial of clear liquid from you, with instructions to give the same to Sir Thomas but to taste not of it himself." Coke paused. "If this vial were but an innocent tincture, why should you warn him of it? James Franklin has confessed to acquiring poisons, many of them—aqua fortis, mercury water, great spiders, white arsenic, and more. Sir Gervase Elwes at the Tower has confessed to knowing that you and the Countess sent such a vial to Weston, and also jellies and tarts tainted with the same.

"You, lacking title or wealth, made yourself indispensable by slipping between Court and the villainous apothecaries and necromancers who are your friends. You are a canker one knows not of, silently lying within a body until it kills. Corruption at Court poisons the whole land. Like beauty, it secretly works its way into men's hearts and is hard to defend against. Was it you or the Countess of Somerset who planned the murder of Overbury? When Richard Weston was tried, he said, 'This be a net for small fishes, that the great ones swim away!' He was speaking of the Earl and Countess of Somerset, was he not, Mistress Turner? And of the late Earl of Northampton, whose letters to the Tower also condemn him." Coke nodded at the clerk, who lifted a letter from the high table beside him.

"'*God is Gracious in cutting off ill instruments before the time wherein their mischiefs are to be wrought. Bury him this very day, between three and four in the afternoon, with all haste and without ceremony, for the putrefaction is in an advanced state. Allow not his brother-in-law Lidcote to remove the body.*'"

Coke waited for the crowd to quieten.

"Why is it that Lord Northampton wanted none to see the body save the coroner? And not even the correct coroner for the Tower jurisdiction, but the coroner for Middlesex. Was the Middlesex coroner Lord Northampton's man? Is it not the case that those 'great ones' sought Overbury's death, such that the Catholic faith might be restored in this land?"

At this the crowd erupted. "Treason! Catholic traitors!" Lord Coke let them rant.

"Weston did not keep your secrets during his trial, Mistress Turner, as you must have prayed that he would," he finally said, holding up his hand for silence. "He confessed to participating in this, the most heinous and hateful offense of our times. He is dead, hanged two weeks ago at Tyburn for murder. What say you now?"

Weston was dead.

Hanged while I sat alone in the alderman's cell. Was his beloved son William witness to it?

Stupefaction kept me upright as Lord Coke pointed at me and shouted, "The crowd of witnesses to your crimes envelops you. I say again, you possess the seven deadly sins. You are whore, bawd, witch, sorcerer, Papist, felon and murderer. Confess it!"

27

Someone felt their way down the three steps into the cell; I heard a hand sliding along the stone wall. Was it Mr. Palmer? Frankie? The executioner come to ask my forgiveness for what he had to do? All they would see was my hair, the only point of light in this narrow prison.

"Something to warm you?" I heard Alderman Smith ask of the visitor. I lay on my truckle, face to the wall.

"I do not drink, sir." A man's voice I did not recognize. "Just a table and chair if you please. I am anxious to start directly, as the Lord Chief Justice must have her confession."

"Ah, then we must jump to it if Sir Edward has our salvation to hand," said Alderman Smith. A bristling pause.

"I am against the commodious accommodation of criminals; she wants for nothing, I see," said the newcomer.

"Save her freedom, her children, her friends and all hope," the alderman replied. "Since the trial she has not washed, spoken, risen from her bed or eaten. She is hardly in her wits."

"If her abjection is real, she can be brought to the Lord."

"You seek her salvation, Dr. Whiting? I thought you were here for a confession? Tell her of God's forgiveness, sir, and do not dishearten her further or she will be dead before they can hang her."

"There are no candles," said this Dr. Whiting, irritated to have been told his business.

"Who pays for them? She's been here six weeks and I've had nothing for her keep." Scrabbling in a coin belt. "I'll send someone along."

"Bring fire too, if you please, it's cold as death in here."

The door banged closed and was locked.

"No vermin, no lousy cellmates urinating on your silk and defecating where they stand. Comfort will not speed your redemption," was his opening address. "I am Dr. Whiting, a minister of the Church, sent by the King's Bench to hear your confession, that God might forgive and return you to His flock." Was I to have no peace, even after receiving sentence of death? I did not move. The bells rang eight. It was morning, I think. Would I know that hour again?

I heard him moving about as if my body was in the cell but my mind was elsewhere.

"It is within the human heart that Satan builds his nest. God never had fewer servants than in our days; where God has least, the Devil has most. He has forced his way into your mind and filled you with loathsome ambition. You have sought a higher state than that God ordained you and committed sins without number when all that God asks of us is to know our station. We must cheerfully and virtuously fulfill the duties appropriate to our lot, making ourselves useful to others as did Jesus; to do so is the only preparation for the life everlasting. Was it also you who poisoned Prince Henry?"

His accusations and questions I could not differentiate from the clatter of boatmen below, the screams of the gulls and the gusts of wind that made him pace faster about the freezing cell; all and none reached me. I cannot say how much later it was when he shook my shoulder. "Widow Turner, if you confess, your children will be brought to you."

I rolled over to look at him. He turned his back to me and moved to look out of the narrow window, perhaps thinking I would speak more freely that way, as children chatter when traveling behind their parents in a cart. His hair was gray and close-cut to his skull; on it he wore the black cap of his calling, and over his thin, straight body a black robe. The crowds were gathering at Tyburn Tree, I could feel them pressing around me, but Frankie could still save me from that end. For that hope, and for love of her, I would say nothing of import to this man for why was he bribing me with the hope of a visit from my children? Even so, to see them again, to hold them, was my greatest wish. I heard myself whisper over and over, "Thank you."

"Richard Weston poured away the poisons you gave to him," he said. I thought I had misheard but he turned to me. His face was deeply lined and severe but perhaps there was also kindness there, well hidden. "The Lieutenant of the Tower also attested that he and Weston threw away the poisons you brought."

"Then I am free?" I said, confused. I sat up slowly and my head spun.

"Whether by poison or smothering or other means, Sir Thomas Overbury died at the hand of Richard Weston with your complicity. Perhaps the Countess encouraged her great-uncle, Lord Northampton, to rid her of him? What are the late Earl's dealings in this? There is no little suspicion cast upon him."

"As God knows everything, Dr. Whiting, it cannot be He who seeks information."

He looked at me, clearly appraising how to approach so brave-mouthed a woman. Finally, he sat, perhaps hoping to appear more friendly.

"When I took Richard Weston's confession, he said the King's justice is 'a net for small fishes.' Do you feel the same?"

Tears pricked and fell but I paid them no heed. "You saw Weston? Did he speak harshly of me? Was his son present at . . . Did he make a good end?" How baffling it felt for this stranger to have seen my near-constant companion more recently than had I. But Dr. Whiting would not be drawn to tell me more, and perhaps that was wise on his part.

"Please answer my question," he said.

"Justice is dispensed at the whim of the King: he dislikes women and knows none of the poorer sort, so certainly it must pain him less to punish them."

"And what of Lord Northampton in this business?" It was irritating Dr. Whiting that I spoke in general terms when he wanted specific moments to take back to Lord Coke, to prove the guilt of the King's closest advisers.

"There was never anybody had a window into Lord Northampton's mind, nor his heart either," I said, but I thought he was more to blame for Overbury's death than Frankie and I had realized at the time. Since hearing his letters read out at my trial, I believed he used Frankie to cover his own killing of Overbury, so that Carr could be brought into the Howard sphere. Even so, I had intended to murder Overbury. I made great efforts to that effect and, in so doing, had caused Weston's death. I deserved to die, in that there was no injustice, although I prayed Frankie could still save me.

"Perhaps so, but was it he who had Overbury killed?"

"I have told Lord Coke all I know." Even talking about a dead man might somehow condemn Frankie.

"Would it ease your tongue to confess to a Papist priest? I have authority to release one from prison, although I consider it not in your best interests." I shook my head. "You have been proven guilty and condemned to hang. What will you confess?"

"I have been declared guilty. There was no proof." I took Mistress Bowdlery's handkerchief from my sleeve and twisted it between my fingers. "I confess only the truth I have learned: that there can be no freedom when you love. One prevents the other."

"You attempt philosophy with me?"

"Frankie," I said, barely stung by the confessor's words. Compared to the insults of Lord Coke, his manner was mild.

"What?"

"If I called her Frances, or my lady, or Countess of Somerset, she would wonder what was wrong between us. Have you news of her?" The man blinked at my directness and lack of humility. I wanted to rage, to scratch at my face; that would tell the story well enough. For Frankie, my blood. But I have a horror of violent reactions. It was always Frankie who cried out her pain and her love, and for a long time I thought she must feel more than I and that was why she commanded every person and event into her own story, including me. But the loss of my children kills me more surely than will the rope, so now I think I feel as much as she.

"Your friend has been arrested, as has her husband. The Lady Frances attempted to take her own life and that of her unborn child, by laying wet cloths on her belly. By chance a maid discovered her before fatal illness took hold. Do not let pity for your friend tie up your tongue, for she is not thinking of you but only of her own selfish desires."

That news left me numb and I could feel nothing but the cold . . .

cold like the earth into which my body would soon be lowered for all Eternity. I pressed my trembling fingers against my lips, picturing the moment my last and only connection to this life would be a cord, as was my first. I do not know how long I stared at him, thinking only of my abandoned children, of Frankie and Robin clept up, of what misery drove her to attempt to take her own life and that of the child for which she had longed for so many years. We are all caught, from the highest to the lowest, in webs of custom and propriety; those that cut themselves free do not swim away but are destroyed.

"You will see your children if you confess," said Dr. Whiting.

"Your false promise is barbaric," I said, and saw in his eyes that, indeed, he was lying. "If I fail to repent because you insist I sacrifice my friend in order to do so, then your soul will be stained by the desire for advancement as much as is mine. Lord Chief Justices come and go, but God does not. Be careful whom you choose to serve if serving both becomes impossible."

A servant brought in candles and laid a small fire, and for all that time we said nothing, but the confessor broke his gaze from mine and contemplated his folded hands as if he still held the high ground, which we both knew he had lost. When the servant left, the confessor said: "You wear collar and cuffs dyed the saffron yellow you made fashionable at Court; is that not a conceited display inappropriate to a widow condemned to death?"

"I have not changed clothes since my trial, Dr. Whiting." It clearly discomforted him to find no other sign of evil upon me: my lips not mean, my brow not heavy, no warts in sight. Perhaps in a murderess of good birth they are not to be expected? He was unsure; I suspect I was his first. He stood and put his rump before the flames.

"Perhaps she hates you, who once loved you?"

"I am not allowed to see my children, but I have not a second's doubt of their love for me. With Frankie it is the same. Your attempt to make me distrust my friend will not make me betray her." As I said it, I knew it was equally true that Frankie would not betray me.

"I attempt to convince you only that God is a better receptacle of your faith than Frances Howard. How often was the Countess with you when you visited the apothecary?"

"Never."

"Never?"

"She shops at the New Exchange."

"The skin displayed at your trial on which were written Forman's prayers, did it come from a child?"

"It was the skin of a pig. I could tell you of fifty others who write prayers on pigskin."

He only shrugged at this for he probably knew several himself, so widespread is the practice. "And the doll? Did you prick it to make Sir Thomas die?"

"It is a female doll! A French Baby wearing designs for Simon Forman's wife. I have a hundred more at home. Do you think that because I paint my face and wear yellow ruffs, I would torture a hundred women too?" For the first time, I saw unease in his expression. He believed me. "My trial? Fabulous drama! Did you attend it, sir? Mr. Shakespeare and Mr. Jonson together would be hard pressed to bring together in one play scenes of adultery, bastardy, witchcraft, poison, Popery, conspiracy and treason, but Lord Justice Coke managed it with consummate skill. To witness my distress at first hearing of the hanging of my friend, Richard Weston, must have been worth the price of admission, even at ten pounds for two seats."

For the rest of the day Dr. Whiting harangued or sermonized me, baiting me with snippets of worrying tidings about Frankie and her husband. I knew that the chance of Frankie's relatives ensuring my release, or hers, was small. Still I believed that this was not my time to die; I would see her and my children again.

On the second day of my confession, Dr. Whiting began in his usual censorious manner, but I was distraught and lay on my truckle, looking at him only because there was nothing else at which to look. He moved to the window, staring out to the most distant point for so long I wondered if he was one of those who could fall asleep standing. It was so cold, I was sure he would freeze if he did not move. When he finally spoke, his voice was softer, perhaps more his own.

"It is not a simple matter, to separate good from evil," he said, as if making a confession of his own. "God knows the difference, of course, but His voice is sometimes very quiet. When I look at the multitude of souls afloat on the river, some straining against the tide, some speeding with it, it strikes me how hard it is to follow the hand that guides. And truth? When I was young, I thought it was much the same as experience; now I know we take different truths from the same experience." He seemed to have waged some internal battle with himself and come out with the word of God in his ear, not that of Lord Coke; his voice remained gentle, even skeptical, as he continued his questioning, although he did not shy from searching inquiries or blunt assertions. He still looked for a slip from me with which to convict Frankie or Robert Carr or Lord Northampton, but with less enthusiasm.

"How did you hear of Sir Thomas Overbury's death?"

"Richard Weston sent his son William with the news. Frankie was as shocked as I." We had, by then, decided that he was immune to poison.

"The Countess of Essex must have been thankful that Sir Thomas could no longer disrupt the annulment process?"

"You still think of me as the witch Lord Coke conjured? Two painted Papist whores, bored with our lapdogs, murdering a man out of spite and lust? The relief Frankie felt at release from her violent and impotent husband was much lessened by Robert Carr's grief."

"His grief was not so great that he refused the earldom the King offered him six weeks after his best friend's death. Not so great as to make him reject the woman Sir Thomas hated above all others. Did Robert Carr help you to kill Sir Thomas?"

Frankie had been more afraid of Robin finding out than of anything else.

"Between ourselves, Mistress Turner, I see little justice in haranguing a woman denied a lawyer, who has not even a feather to record the accusations against her nor a stool on which to sit. To speak in public was case enough against you at the trial. But the Lord Northampton? The Lord Carr? Why do you suffer in their place now?"

I do not think Dr. Whiting understood that the friendship between Frankie and me was powerful enough to determine the course of our actions; perhaps he had no friend like that or, I suspect, thought women too doltish to experience profound sentiment for any creatures other than their own children. But over the three days of confession, so intimate in their sadness, he came to know me and, I think, to like me. He brought me a Bible, in English, the first that I had read. We had one at home but it was in Latin and only George could read it. When I still attended secret mass the priest read to us, but again in Latin.

"As bestower of life, it is a mother's responsibility to guide her children and lead them to God," said Dr. Whiting, "and how can she acquit herself of this task without the aid of His word? I have marked out certain passages for you. Spiritual comfort is greater than that bought with money and power."

Alderman Smith visited the cell often, to be sure that Dr. Whiting did not pressure me unduly; he brought coals or warm caudles for which he did not ask payment. Twice he brought me notes from Mr. Palmer, in defiance of Lord Coke's orders. The short letters offered me encouragement, detailed his efforts to procure my release as he was convinced of my innocence, and expressed his love. He told me that he wanted me for his wife, if I would have him. If I would have him! He must have heard Lord Coke's denunciation of me as everything most evil in this world, and still he would marry me. His words did much to calm me but I remembered Baron Sanquhar, looking in vain to the steps of the scaffold, waiting for a pardon from the King. I tried not to hope, but of course it was impossible, for there was so much love still in me for my children, for Frankie and her child to come, for the good Mr. Palmer, for the grandchildren I might hold, for every little detail of the world that had become so precious in the short time left to me.

On the fourth day Dr. Whiting arrived looking very tired. "Mistress Turner, it is my heavy duty to inform you that your execution is set for the morning." My body jerked in violent spasms, as if shoved from all sides by unseen hands. It lasted only a few moments, an involuntary expression of my shame and terror at so humiliating and painful an end.

I was both overwhelmed by the sure knowledge of my death

and relieved to know when it would be. I thought of the only other hanging I had witnessed. The speed of Baron Sanquhar's drop, his weight straining the silk noose, the twitching of his body. Hanging for the wealthy is quick and almost painless, for the long drop breaks the neck immediately and ends all sensation. Even the burning of the rope is lessened by its being silk. At Tyburn there is no drop, only a slow strangulation as the cart on which stands the condemned moves away. I would need a friend to pull my legs and break my neck, and the rough hemp rope would burn my skin before the bones popped apart. I wondered who would take on this dread burden and whether it was among the confessor's tasks to arrange.

"Will my children be forced to witness it?" I asked, my voice a whisper.

"No."

Dr. Whiting knocked on the door and asked for a caudle to be brought. When it arrived, he put the steaming cup in my hands but I could not drink. My eyes were inward-looking and unaware of my surroundings.

"Where does your brother lodge?" he asked, several times.

"My brother Eustace?" I eventually replied. "He is not in London but Westminster, in service to Prince Charles. He lodges in a small court off Scotland Yard, at the sign of the Brown Bear." Dr. Whiting addressed a note and knocked on the door. A servant entered and after some negotiation as to price, agreed not to return until he had delivered the note into the hand of Eustace Norton himself.

"I thank God, sir, that Lord Coke is not my confessor. You are kinder," I said. "If I ask the alderman to give you the cross and chain Frankie sent me, would you pass them to Eustace? They will affray, in small part, the cost of caring for my children."

"Will he take on their care?"

"No, but I trust him to make a wise decision as to who should raise them and to keep an eye over them until they are grown. Perhaps my sister Mary will. She will need money as her husband is not charitable. Barbara loves them, she will help."

"Shall I also give your brother the ring?"

I was unable to say more so the confessor waved me forward to sit close to the fire and took away my tepid drink. I did not hold my cold hands to the flames but looked at them, resting in my lap. It was too late to seek comfort.

"If you come into His fold and repent of your sins, then you will know the joy of His love and salvation. God loves all His flock, even those who stray." Just as I loved Thomas, even though he had been an undutiful child. "To know God's forgiveness will give you courage to face tomorrow," said Dr. Whiting. "If you appear reformed and chastened, the crowd will wish you well and ensure the good treatment of your children hereafter."

"Since the trial I have become the greatest exemplar of evil from one end of the world to the other."

"You can alter that," he said. He wanted me to convert as much for his own reputation as my salvation, but I saw his reasoning.

"Dr. Whiting, would you do me the honor of calling me Anne? I am tired of this formality between us." He was surprised but agreed without asking the same of me.

"Did the Countess of Somerset press you to silence?" he said into the growing darkness. "She has failed in her promise to protect you, yet still you do not condemn her."

"Of what can I condemn her? She brought me joy, she loved my children and saved us from starvation. When those with obligations toward me faltered, she remained loyal. Her spirit and high ideals inspired me, and she allowed me to display the fruits of that inspiration upon her body; in her company, I was seen and heard."

"She asked much of you in return."

"Frankie and I are different faces and ages of the same spirit. That is why I was drawn to her . . . but I should have counseled her better. I am the elder, I should have led her more faithfully and been a truer friend. After George's death I stumbled toward what I thought was a future, but it has proved to be an illusion with no substance. I thought there would be time to become virtuous, once I had reached a place of safety."

Dr. Whiting was looking at me, mystified, but the bells rang six o'clock and he moved to the window, looking down at the wharves.

"Will you join me?" he said. The slats of the truckle creaked as I pushed myself up. I looked through the narrow opening that punctured the thick wall. Down on the nearest wharf a man was carrying a torch. I recognized his familiar outline. My brother Eustace was bringing my children to me! John, my fledgling gentleman, lit the way for Barbara, the two younger girls and Henry. Only Thomas had not come. I cried out and crammed myself as far through the window slit as I could.

Among the group there was much pointing, turning and cupping of hands over eyes.

"They cannot see me!" I began to shout but Dr. Whiting begged me to stop for fear of discovery. Instead, he took up the candle and gave it to me. I held it close to my face and heard him light two more and hold them aloft, so that our window was the brightest in the building. He passed me my handkerchief with which to wipe my eyes but instead I waved it about.

The wind was brisk and the candles burned down quickly. Dr. Whiting brought more but after they too sputtered and died, I dared not request more for fear of getting him into trouble.

After that I stood in darkness, knowing that we were as close as possible even if they could not see me. Dr. Whiting left me alone at the window, only moving to put the blanket around my shoulders and then his coat on top of it, for I was shaking violently.

The seven o'clock bells made me jump. On the wharf I could make out the children being steered away by Eustace. The three youngest dragged their feet and ran back. I heard them crying, "Mama! Mama!" I did not flinch or turn away. Although I had no hope of being seen, I held out my arms to them. They were pulled away by their siblings and within minutes a torch appeared, carried by a guard. I looked at Dr. Whiting, frightened.

"Have they been arrested?"

"No, no, they are safe. The alderman told me he would keep the guards until after seven. He intercepted my note to your brother."

"Was he angry with you?"

"I think it was the first time he was pleased with me in all the years we have known each other."

I was clutching his arm very tightly. He led me to the truckle and I sank onto it. I was speaking, but my words came out as a curious monotone, as if talking in my sleep, and I could not bring life to them.

"Mary did not cough, even in this cold and wind. She is still well. . . . They are not thin, someone is feeding them. . . . Eustace is kind. . . . Barbara will help him. . . . She can be mother to them and . . . John will give whatever money he has. . . . Henry, who could not love him? He will win hearts despite his mother's infamy."

He let me prate, sensing perhaps that not to do so might cause my heart to burst. After I know not how long, I took a long, shuddering breath. "That was an act of true kindness and I thank you," I said.

He took from his jerkin a small packet. "This arrived some time ago, at least two weeks, I think. The alderman gave it to me this afternoon."

I could not untie the ribbon with my trembling fingers so the confessor cut it with his knife. The linen fell open to reveal a nest of fine pearls.

Gently, I pushed a finger into the pearls and saw that they formed a long strand. I wound them round my hand and rubbed them against my cheek. There was a note.

My dearest Anne,
Every day since your arrest I have written, sometimes many times a day, I have sent money and jewels, and even a boy in a wherry to shout up to your window. Now I am arrested and kept close prisoner. No one will give me news of you; this note I have got out with one who cares for you, at great risk to himself.

I thought that must be Weston before remembering, with a sharp pain, that he was dead. Perhaps Mr. Palmer? It would not be Arthur, and Frankie would not let my son take such risks.

The baby remains quick within me. I wonder how he survives the anguish and torment I feel, not only for myself but for you, the most loving and loyal friend I will ever have. I never meant for matters to take this course. I know you believe me.

I long to hear from you. You are more to me than any friend has ever been. I send with this note my most precious possessions. They hold my love within them. Keep cheerful, for my family and Lord Carr work tirelessly for our release. All will be well and we shall soon be reunited.

Until that day,

Your loving sister

Frankie

P.S. Mr. Palmer came today to ask what should be done with the paintings yet to be paid for.

By that final line I knew that it was he who cared enough to risk bringing me the parcel. I would have liked to know him better and longer; we could have been happy.

"Lady Somerset is held at the house of Lord d'Aubigny, half a mile from here. She begs daily to see you."

"Does she know of my sentence?"

"She does. It was after she was told that she attempted to take her own life. She is watched day and night as she remains in grievous low spirits."

"I know how to comfort her in those moods. No one else relieves them like me, not even her husband. Who helps her?"

"It is to *your* comfort we should look."

That she had not abandoned me meant that my death was not wasted. I prayed that her babe be safely delivered and that she would discover the love and happiness in him that I enjoyed in mine.

"I have told you all I can," I said.

"You have related nothing to help Lord Coke build his case," the confessor said.

"Then I ask pardon, Dr. Whiting, for Lord Coke will not smile about it as you do."

"I am not sure Lord Coke has ever been seen to smile."

"Please tell me how I should make a good death," I said then, very quietly.

28

Today is the fourteenth day of November, 1615.

I have known Frankie for nearly seven years.

She is twenty-five years old and eight months pregnant.

I am thirty-nine years old and about to die or be pardoned.

Before dawn a young woman is shown into my bitterly cold cell. By the light of two candles I note that she is not much older than Barbara.

"What is your name?" I ask, as if the day is ordinary, which it is not. The girl remains mute, a reminder to me that I have no authority, even over a low servant. I try to smile so as not to frighten the girl. I could not bear to frighten her. She is life.

She pours water into a bowl and it steams in the icy air. I dip a cloth into it, enjoying the warmth on my cold hands. Every sense in me is greedy for what little there is left to experience. I stare into the small mirror the girl has brought and am shocked by how sad and tired I look. My hair, dirty gray strands among the gold, is pulled back from a face hollowed out by fear and regret.

I put the mirror down.

"Do you know how to dress me?"

"Yes, mistress."

The girl unpins the black silk I have been wearing since the trial. The feel and smell of it is sickening and reminds me of the stench of the silk farm. Layers are peeled off until I am naked. The maid casts furtive and anxious glances at my shivering body, perhaps looking for signs of witchcraft: a birthmark shaped like a goat, a wart that bleeds, freckles in the shape of the Pope's mitre, as had the confessor. There are mainly goosebumps. For the last time, I also look at my body, shaped by life. My breasts are sinewy from the suckling of six infants; my belly and hips scarred by the reversals of fortune that led them one year to be round, the next flat; my toes are slightly crossed from the long wearing of pointed shoes with heels. Yet my body has more good years left in it; years in which I could have cradled children and grandchildren. It grieves me that this good, strong body will go to waste.

The maid has brought a pile of clothes that I recognize as my own, and I take up a white undershirt. From the care with which it has been pressed, I can tell that Barbara has prepared it. That my daughter has had to perform such an onerous task is so dreadful I bury my face in the scented linen and weep. It is these unexpected moments of unbearable pain that bring death closer than all Dr. Whiting's talk of the hereafter.

The maid indicates that we must continue and I let myself be dressed. I repeat to myself the confessor's words of encouragement. In the end, it was no great wrench to leave the Church of Rome and join that of England. God is above rivalry; He sees into my heart and knows that I am truly repentant. I was glad to do something in return for Dr. Whiting's kindness.

Barbara has sensibly chosen one of my cheapest outfits, of thin black baize, with loose sleeves; if I see my children, I will be able to hold them. I have always known how to dress for any occasion, a hanging included, and my daughter has learned well from me. The yellow collar and cuffs, in which I have taken such pride, I leave off.

The girl brushes and ties back my hair, pinning a black veil to it which she folds back, like a young groom about to kiss his bride. How far from that am I. I pick up the handkerchief embroidered by Mistress Bowdlery, now filthy and misshapen. I feared having her life above everything, but at this moment I would give my last farthing to be sitting on the doorstep in Paternoster Row with my children around me.

A knock at the door startles me. The alderman enters and a gush of bile rushes into my throat to see him dressed entirely in black: for my death.

"Will I be cut down with dignity? Do not let my body tumble, my children could not bear that! Who will lay me in my coffin? Do I have a coffin? Who has bought the coffin? Is there money for it?"

The questions mist the air between us in the freezing cell. He puts his arm around my shoulders and holds me firmly within the dark folds of his cloak, perfumed by the sprig of rosemary pinned to it. The pressure calms me. I pray oblivion will be as comforting.

I give him the letter I have written for my children and, as he takes it, I see a fresh yellow collar and bands in his hand, of greater ostentation than I ever wore.

"Lord Coke orders you to wear these," he says. I could picture Coke's narrow lips spitting the words, knowing what a good spectacle I would make, tricked out in the yellow I introduced to the Court, too busy following fashion to follow the Ten Commandments.

"Can he?"

"I have never heard of it," my jailer replies with the faintest shrug. I take the cuffs from him, automatically rubbing my thumb across the weave to feel its quality, and throw them from the window. The wind snatches and tosses them high before they skitter down to float on the dark face of the Thames. I look at the stiff, waxy lace and wonder why I once cared for it so much.

I turn to Alderman Smith, who is looking at me in surprise.

"What can he do, hang me?" I say.

He laughs shortly, not at my feeble quip, but to honor my courage. Handing me a large sprig of rosemary, he helps me on with my thin cloak and gently steers me from the cell and through the great hall.

The sight of the tumbril is as fearful as expected and I climb up quickly, before my legs fail me. There are no seats, so I stand as we trundle from the City through St. Giles and along Oxford Street to Tyburn village. People stare, they hiss and jeer, but I keep my head low and concentrate on my hands gripping the rail as I sway and jolt. The rosemary is crushed against my palms and I am grateful for the scent that distracts me a little from my terror. I whisper the prayers Dr. Whiting has taught me. God is waiting for me.

After an hour or more the tumbril slows, a huge crowd blocking the way. For a wild moment I think some incident has occurred and the hanging will be postponed; in that time, could Frankie find a way to have me pardoned? Even under arrest, I expect miracles of her. I raise my eyes and with a great jolt see the monstrous

Tyburn Tree rearing up ahead; the shock of it floods me, my ears ring and my vision grows dark at the edges. The crowd will not stop my execution; they are here to see it.

It takes time for the tumbril to force a way through the spectators and the many carriages carrying courtiers, wealthy merchants and, for sure, the Lord Chief Justice. I do not look to see if Arthur is among them. The tumbril finally halts beside a cart carrying my coffin. It is very cheap.

The tumbril is unlocked and the back lowered. Dr. Whiting climbs up beside me.

"Someone wishes you Godspeed," he whispers, nodding toward a meager figure at the front of the crowd. It is Mistress Bowdlery with Eustace beside her. When the lace maker spots me looking at her, she cries out: "God sees your kind acts. He will have mercy!"

Those around Mistress Bowdlery stare at her in surprise. The words start a new possibility in the crowd; the potential for good will toward this sinner. In my simple black dress and veil, with my thin white face and praying hands, I do not look like the malicious, spiteful, greedy whore they expect. I lift the hand in which I grip her handkerchief. Mistress Bowdlery vigorously nods encouragement and keeps calling out, "God bless you, God bless you!"

Mr. Palmer is not in the crowd. Horror of public hangings was another sentiment we shared, and I am glad he will not see me die. To my brother I give just one look, long and final, in which I try to make my love for him clear. I dare not do more, for I must not cry. I do not look for my children. Dr. Whiting has written to Eustace with my final wish that they not witness my end but remember me as their loving mother, all of them forever in my heart. My other request was that I not be hanged alongside Franklin.

A noise makes me look up. Above me, three men are straddling one great beam of the triangular gallows, adjusting the rope that will hang me. Twenty-four felons can be hanged at a time here; I thank God I have it all to myself. The crowd falls silent and I stare out at the faces staring back; it is like seeing the sea for the first time.

"Are you ready to give your speech?" says Dr. Whiting.

For a moment panic empties my head and I can remember

nothing. Dr. Whiting takes my hand briefly and reminds me of the start. I clear my throat and speak, slowly and calmly, as he has taught me. I am contrite and modest, announcing with gratitude that I have taken Protestant communion. The mood of the crowd, already softened by Mistress Bowdlery's cries, warms; some nod, others smile encouragement. I speak of my conviction of the good judgment of my King, I repent sincerely of my sins, especially those of vanity and pride, and ask all gathered to pray for my soul. Some in the crowd shout back, "God rest your soul, sister!," "God be with you!," others bow their heads and pray silently for me. Although I am terrified of the rope swinging above me, I am also euphoric. I think of the pity of those around me, and of those I love who are already dead and waiting for me. I think of my guarding angel, who is nearby, waiting.

My voice catches only once, when I ask the Lord to show mercy upon my six children. I hear sobbing in the crowd and can see what I will become; in these few minutes of beseeching remorse and re-pentance, dressed with the simplicity and modesty of a Protestant martyr, I am become a paragon of reform, the lamb returned by the Good Shepherd to God. My death will remind the crowd of their compassion and mercy. It will make them good, for a few hours at least. I will be spoken of with kindness and my children will not need to hang their heads at my memory.

What I do not say, but feel, is loyalty to the greatest friend of my life. She will be pardoned for the King is fond of her and her actions have allowed him release from Carr's bitterness. The great love she holds for Robin will bear fruit. The risks we took will lead others to want what she has: freedom from cruel husbands and a say in whom they marry. Beneath the dread I feel a core of heat: it is joy at the actions we took, the chaos we created, the possibilities we saw, the lives we led; it is love.

A man on the beam shouts down, telling me to put the noose around my neck. I turn and take the rope in my shaking hands. It is rough and heavy. From the crowd come shouts of "God bless you," as I put it over my head. It weighs down my shoulders. Dr. Whiting pulls the black veil over my face and I feel someone attempt to take my arms and tie my hands behind my back. Dr. Whiting wishes me

Godspeed and promises to carry out my instructions, but I barely hear him. I wrench my hand free and press my handkerchief into his hand. He tucks it into his sleeve.

"May you stand forever in God's love," he says softly. Suddenly I grip on to him. When he leaves, I will die. How can he leave?

He pries my icy hand from his chest and holds it to his mouth, blowing warmth on to it. I cannot let him go, cannot die without fighting to live.

"It is not for yourself but for your children you must be brave," he reminds me.

An image of Barbara comes to me, choosing the clothes in which I will die. I thank my eldest daughter for her courage, and for sending sleeves wide enough for me to bend my arms and feel my own heartbeat. It is fluttering as if winged but, while I still have life, I will do what I can for my children.

I am so cold.

Dr. Whiting climbs down from the tumbril and leaves me to face my last moments alone. Again, someone takes my arms and this time I allow them to tie my hands behind me. The rope is heavy, there are so many faces. I am greedy for the light in my eyes. A shout, and the horse slowly pulls forward. I tiptoe along the carriage floor as it moves.

I must not fall.

Summer 1650

Ricocheting along the hard-rutted lanes, Barbara repeated and reworked the words, over and over, until meaning fled and only fear remained.

"My mother's final request was . . . My mother asked that I . . . My mother humbly requested . . ."

It had been a long journey but still she had not perfected her opening address. In the broiling and crowded coach from London to St. Albans she had thought to start by introducing herself. As the horses were changed and she had eaten, she had decided to begin by presenting the gift she had in her pocket. As the coach continued to Luton, she wondered if it were safer to say nothing and wait to be asked questions. In Luton, it took so long to find someone to carry her to Woburn that she was forced to stay at an inn, sharing a bed with fleas, lice and a much younger but fatter woman, who snored and shifted all night.

In the morning she set off alone in a hired coach, more of a roofed cart, its driver seemingly delighted to be released from his normal duties of conveying straw for the making of hats.

The journey to Woburn Abbey was not long and within an hour they turned in at a gatehouse, where the ground became smoother. The driver ceased whistling as the weight of grandeur fell upon them. The drive, a mile long at least, passed through woods, hay meadows, kitchen gardens and around large ponds to another gate that led into a paved courtyard. Standing at the foot of what appeared to be a recently added façade, Barbara wondered if she should have used the tradesmen's entrance. She yanked on the iron bellpull before she could change her mind. Although only a few years off sixty, she looked a decade younger and was well enough dressed not to be taken for a servant. She was shown into a large parlor and asked to wait.

She had only time to look through the windows when the rustle of silk announced Lady Anne, Countess of Bedford. She was perhaps more beautiful than her mother had been, with the same dark eyes, but a more reserved air. Her pale hair was her father's, but the red-brown of her mother's lay just beneath. Thirty-four years of age, she was born days after Barbara's mother died. Recently Lady Anne's husband had been fighting in the wars between King and Parliament, switching sides more than once, and the strain of it showed in her face. Judging by the size of her belly, she was also pregnant and soon to give birth. Barbara curtsied but before either woman could speak, a loud screech made her jump.

A green parrot sat on a perch in one corner of the room. Barbara stared at it for some moments.

"Prospero? Can it be?" she said.

"He thinks I am my mother," said Lady Anne, picking up the bird, "so he is friendly to me; but he chases the dogs and savages strangers." Gingerly, she placed the parrot on Barbara's forearm. Prospero placidly sidestepped upward until he came to rest on her shoulder, whereat he tweaked her ear gently with his beak.

"He remembers you," said the Countess.

"We spent a lot of time with him." Emotion threatened to overcome Barbara then. Noticing this, Lady Anne replaced the bird on his perch and sat, inviting her visitor to do likewise.

Barbara had written to request an audience; it had been granted by return. Now she was surprised to see that the Countess appeared as anxious about their meeting as she was herself. Anne Russell, Countess of Bedford, born Anne Carr, had a famously happy marriage, five children, a sixth on the way and time for more to come, high titles and many houses; and yet she was unsettled by Barbara's presence.

"I am very pleased you have come," she said, a glimmer of her mother's warmth behind her guarded expression.

Anne Turner's final wish had been to tell Frankie that she never betrayed her, nor stopped loving her; but Barbara had blamed Frankie for her mother's death. The anguish and grief that lingered long after the hanging had made it impossible to visit her. So, she had come to see her child.

"More than three decades have passed since events drew our mothers together," said Lady Anne.

"This visit is prompted by the knowledge that I will soon meet my mother again," Barbara said. As trained to secrecy and discretion as any courtier, Lady Anne gazed impassively at her guest, but Barbara knew she would be working hard to understand the full meaning of these words: that Barbara was ill and saw death ahead of her; that she believed her mother had been admitted to heaven but that she would not see Frankie there. The Countess got to her feet and Barbara regretted her choice of words, but Lady Anne did not quit the chamber. Instead, she sat beside her visitor and opened the locket that hung on a long chain around her neck, so that Barbara might see the miniatures it held.

"Taken from a portrait of my mother by Larkin. The original is lost."

Lost? thought Barbara. Frankie had been decried as "the rotten branch that must be lopped from the noble tree" at her trial after Anne's death. Events occurred soon afterward that brought down her family. Hers was not a portrait to hang in the long gallery but to throw on a bonfire. How could it have been for Anne, growing up in the shadow of so infamous a mother?

"It is a good likeness," said Barbara, politely. Facing it was a miniature of Robert Carr, Lady Anne's father, who had died a few years previously. Anne closed the locket and pulled from her sleeve a letter, much crumpled. "This, from my mother, says all I find it hard to."

16th of August, 1632, Chiswick

Dearest beloved Anne,

This letter I leave in the safekeeping of my legal secretary to give to you after my death. Although it is not my hand that writes—I can no longer hold a pen—these are my words, the last you will receive from me.

You will have been told that you were given your name to please the late Queen, Anna of Denmark, but this is a falsehood. I had always thought to call my first daughter Margaret, after my little sister who was taken to God at a tender age. But I named you Anne in memory of my dearest friend. You have not heard of her, except perhaps some false slander that came to your ears while unprotected by me. She was my truest friend, accused of many things, and hanged. The three youngest of her orphaned children were taken in by her sister and the eldest three managed as best they could. What little money I have, I send to them, but none will visit me.

Anne was bold, her wits were quick and leaned toward originality; she was courageous and loyal to the end. Although it is true that we attempted to kill a man who tried to destroy my honor and keep me from your father, we failed. Her manservant, Richard Weston, and the Lieutenant of the Tower threw away our poisons. They both confessed this, before they were hanged, but only that which suited Lord Coke came out at the trials. He relied on the prattling of James Franklin, apothecary, who said anything to spin out his own life a little longer. Franklin was executed on the day you were born. What bitter pleasure I felt when Lord Coke fell from the King's grace soon after Anne's trial, for his cruel and inflexible methods and the arrogance of his self-belief.

I kept silent when I was arrested, in the hope that Anne could be saved. After she was hanged, I confessed to take blame away from your father, for at the time I did not care whether I lived or died. The King sought your father's downfall and through me he achieved it.

My only joy since Anne's death has been in you, and I wish you to hold to your heart what I now write, for this lesson I learned the hardest way.

Refuse to marry until you are old enough to know your own mind and heart. I advise you to wait until you are at least twenty or more, for which you will be condemned as an old maid but heed not the jibes. Learn your likes and dislikes. I have always encouraged this in you and your father has allowed you an education. Never gamble with your life or those of others.

Cast your net wisely. Know that I love you and will do so beyond death.

Your ever-loving mama,
Frances Carr

* * *

"The poisons were thrown away?" asked Barbara, very quietly. Her eyes had suddenly filled with tears although she had not cried for her mother in a decade.

"It seems so, although my mother wanted to die nonetheless; she felt responsible for the deaths of four people, including your mother. She often said she was dead while living. She loved me but was sometimes so melancholy she could not show it."

"She married the man she chose," said Barbara, but the Countess turned away and stared through the window. After a long silence she looked again at Barbara.

"My father refused to speak to her after their trials. The King pardoned her quickly for her apparent contrition, but she stayed with my father in the Tower for six years, until he was also released. He blamed his fall on her and they were never reconciled. The only thing in her life of which she was proud was me, and of the fact that her annulment did a little to change the opinions of some on the matter of arranged marriages, despite the outrage it caused then and still does." The Countess laughed despite her tears, and her visitor saw in her the same defiance that had been evident in her mother.

Barbara hesitated to mention the Earl of Essex, in case Lady Anne found the subject distasteful, but she was intrigued to hear how Frankie had received the news of his second marriage. It had taken seventeen years for him to consider it; so great and vociferous was his prejudice against women.

"My mother tried to warn Elizabeth Pawlett against marrying him, but my father forbade her. I am not happy that Essex's second marriage ended as disastrously as his first, but my mother had some satisfaction in their separation after only one year, for it proved his inability to make a wife happy."

The newsmongers had made the whole country aware that Elizabeth Pawlett had conceived a child six years after her wedding and that her husband accused her of infidelity and said he would disown the baby unless it was born by a certain date. It was, and he grudgingly acknowledged his only child, a son and heir. The boy died a month later, along with the last vestiges of the marriage. After Essex's death, his widow remarried and bore two healthy daughters.

"You, at least, have married a man you love?"

"When William and I fell in love, his father would point at me in a room full of people and cry out, 'This one was born in the Tower!' He was a harsh Puritan and friend to Essex; he opposed my mother's annulment and sat in judgment during her trial. Even so, she encouraged me to wait for William when his father sent him to Madrid to forget me. Only the huge dowry my father scraped together changed his mind and even after we were married, my father-in-law never lost an opportunity to speak badly of my mother. She has been blamed for bringing about these strange times of Regicide and brother fighting brother, all order turned on its head; yet I believe your mother, and mine, were women of courage," said Lady Anne.

There had been a stone at Barbara's core, which her body had accommodated these long years. It had weighed down her hopes, stopped her marrying and often blocked off laughter. As Lady Anne spoke, she felt it shifting. She had expected to find someone brittle, ready to defend her mother and deny her past. Instead, here was a woman of deep understanding, who recognized and shared in Barbara's long-held grief.

Barbara took from her pocket a worn handkerchief, embroidered with the initials A.T. She did not dab at her streaming eyes but opened it. Nestled within were a diamond ring and a string of pearls; the times she had wanted to pawn them were without number, but her mother's wishes stopped her. She thought it might upset Lady Anne to know that the ring had been sent to the fifteen-year-old Frankie by the fourteen-year-old Earl of Essex, with a terse note as to its value but no word of love; that Frankie had given it to a cunning woman who had pawned it; that it had been retrieved and later sent to Anne Turner during her detention, along with the pearls; that Anne had passed them to her confessor, hidden in this handkerchief, while she stood on the tumbril seconds before death.

Barbara put the ring and pearls into Lady Anne's hand and said only, "Your mother gave these pearls and this ring to mine. Their friendship was the most important of my mother's life." Lady Anne took them both and held them in her hands as if she could feel the two women through them. She slipped the ring onto the index finger of her right hand. It was a little big but looked well against her white skin. The pearls she rubbed against her cheek, closing her eyes.

"Are these Margaret's?" she asked.

Barbara nodded.

"My mother told me about her sister and these pearls. She hoped the jailer had not stolen them and that they had been placed in your mother's coffin."

"They were, but a Mr. Palmer arrived just before the lid was shut. He knew my mother well and thought she would not like the waste. When Dr. Whiting came to bury her, he gave me the note with her final wishes. Mr. Palmer was right. I have kept them safe ever since, waiting for the right time to give them back."

"I thank you for your kindness in coming here," said Lady Anne, still rubbing the pearls with her thumb. "You have eased my heart and I hope that, for whatever time God grants us, we can be good friends." She leaned forward and put the pearls over Barbara's head. "My mother would want you to have these." Then, quite unexpectedly, she embraced Barbara for a long time. Barbara could feel the movement of the child inside her belly.

The sounds of footsteps and laughter came to them and Prospero squawked, "Hail Mary!" The chamber door was thrown open and the Countess's children burst in; two ran, one toddled, one crawled at speed and the smallest was carried by his nurse. Without suspicion or fear of Barbara, they clambered onto the laps of the two women seated side by side, seeking affection and asking questions.

AUTHOR'S NOTE

At the time of the "Overbury Scandal," as the events detailed in this book are usually known, English women already had a reputation on the continent of being too independent of their husbands, drinking in taverns and frequenting theaters with no male chaperone. That two of them could have poisoned a courtier out of lust and venality fits the various tropes of female behavior widely held at the time and, seemingly, since. Mine is not an attempt to whitewash their actions but to give Anne and Frankie greater complexity of motive: to reclaim them from the limbo of misogynist stereotype where wraiths lament at how they are reduced. The furor provoked by Anne and Frankie was so great that they lost all individuality and became icons co-opted by various parties to prove the villainy of such women, the rottenness of the English Court, the immorality of the courtier and so on. My research has been more than an exercise in bringing to light, but of sifting through centuries of prejudice and assumption (interesting in its own way) to find something that feels truthful to the known facts and to human behavior. Of course, my job really begins where the facts end. This is a work of imagination within the bounds of possibility. Mistress Bowdlery and the beadles are fictional, but all other named characters are mentioned in letters, Wills and records of court cases. Anne's lover was called Sir Arthur Mainwaring, not Waring, but for obvious reasons (if you watch *Dad's Army*) I changed this slightly. I could not have Arthur Mainwaring appearing alongside Frankie Howard.

ACKNOWLEDGMENTS

I would like to thank my agent, Eugenie Furniss, whose advice and encouragement over the years of writing this book have been invaluable. My United Kingdom publishers, Bloomsbury, have improved and beautified it: a special thank-you to Alexandra Pringle and Allegra Le Fanu, and to Sarah Murphy at Flatiron Books in the US, who asked perceptive questions. David Lindley's open-minded approach in his excellent book *The Trials of Frances Howard* (Routledge, 1996), set me off in search of Anne and Frankie and was a scholarly and entertaining foil to the vitriol and assumption slung at my protagonists in many other books on the subject. Steve Cook at The Royal Literary Fund gave me work, confidence and a writing community exactly when I needed it, and huge thanks also to Greg Klerx for telling me about the RLF and sharing the writing journey. Research has taken me to many archives, libraries, museums and old houses and to all those who keep these alive, available and polished, I offer thanks, but especially to the staff at the London Library, my second home for many years; to Nick Humphrey, Curator in the Furniture Department of the Victoria and Albert Museum; and Elaine Uttley at the Fashion Museum in Bath.

I have plundered too many books and articles, of and on the period, to list them all, but I found particularly helpful and interesting the work of historians Linda Levy Peck (*Court Patronage and Corruption in Early Stuart London*, Routledge, 2003; *The Mental World of the Jacobean Court*, Cambridge University Press, 1991; *Northampton: Patronage and Policy at the Court of James I*, Allen & Unwin, 1982; and *Consuming Splendor*, Cambridge University Press, 2005); Ann Rosalind Jones and Peter Stallybrass ("'Rugges of London and the Diuell's Band': Irish Mantles and Yellow Starch as Hybrid English Fashion" in *Material London ca. 1600*, edited by Lena Cowen Orlin,

University of Pennsylvania Press, 2000); Alastair Bellany (*The Politics of Court Scandal in Early Modern England: News Culture and the Overbury Affair, 1603–1660*, Cambridge University Press, 2002); Neil Cuddy ("The Revival of the Entourage: The Bedchamber of James I, 1603–1625" in *The English Court*, edited by David Starkey, Longman, 1987), David Bergeron (*King James and Letters of Homoerotic Desire*, University of Iowa Press, 1999); and Keith Thomas (*The Ends of Life: Roads to Fulfillment in Early Modern England*, Oxford University Press, 2010), and warmly recommend anyone interested in the period to seek out these publications.

Several writers of far greater skill and experience than my own have been generous enough to read the manuscript (or part thereof) and given very helpful feedback: Helen Cross, Andrew Miller, Catherine Temma Davidson, Lucy Ellmann, Gillian Slovo, Sarah Dunant and Susan Elderkin, and also Diana Carr, Gillian Stern, Edwina Bowen, Allen Samuels and special thanks to Shireen Jilla and Francesca Brill, whose wisdom and kindness lit every step of the way.

For the love and support of my parents, Anna and Robert, my sister Camilla, and my favorite un-parents, Alan and Sheila, I feel deep gratitude. I offer love and thanks to my husband, Paul, and to my three daughters, Lily, Jasmine and Cecily, who inspire and amaze me every day.